Dark Loch

Charles P. Sharkey

Ringwood Publishing
Glasgow

First published in Great Britain in 2014 by
Ringwood Publishing
7 Kirklee Quadrant, Glasgow G12 0TS
www.ringwoodpublishing.com
e-mail   mail@ringwoodpublishing.com

ISBN 978-1-901514-14-8

British Library Cataloguing-in Publication Data
A catalogue record for this book is available from the British
Library

Typeset in Times New Roman 10
Printed and bound in the UK
by Lonsdale Direct Solutions

Acknowledgements

In writing this novel I am grateful for the support and encouragement I have received from family and friends, in particular my partner, Lesley Walker. Her enthusiasm for the story and constructive criticism has been invaluable.

Further thanks also go to Kevin Gallagher and Jim Blake for their helpful view of early drafts.

My gratitude extends to everyone at Ringwood Publishing, in particular Sandy Jamieson and Isobel Freeman for giving me this opportunity to become a published author.

Finally, I am grateful to my editor, Mira Yankova, for her candid advice and diligence in bringing the book through the final stages before publication.

About the Author

Charles P. Sharkey

Charles Sharkey has spent the last twenty five years working as a criminal lawyer in Glasgow. He lives in the south side of the city.

In the last few years he has been working on his ambition to become a published writer and Dark Loch is his first novel.

He is already hard at work on his second novel "Sticks and Stones" which Ringwood should publish in 2015.

He also writes songs under the name Charles Sharkey.

Prologue

France 1916

The darkness was so black it felt like there was no end to it, an infinite void of nothingness. Sometimes he was unsure if he was alive or floating somewhere between heaven and hell waiting for his earthly sins to be tallied and his eternal fate to be decided. At times he thought he could smell the burning flesh of hell below, other times the sweet scent of heaven above. His body, where was it? He could not feel his arms or legs to move, his mouth or tongue to speak, his eyes to see. Was he dead? The scent of heaven came to him again, a heady fragrance bringing a calm trance to his mind as memories filled the blackness with opaque colours from the life he was not sure he still had to live. Fields of red poppies, blowing in a gentle breeze, stretched for miles into the distant hills, shrouded in the shadows of white clouds floating slowly in the solid blue sky. Voices...? He could hear voices ... *Mother ... Mother is that you... it's me... I've come home.* Darkness again, the sweet scent had gone. Silence... Now his mind was swirling in a different direction, the odious smell of hell permeating the mystery of his being. The sound of thunder, far off, but coming closer ... louder. Was he only to be given a glimpse of heaven, to make the depths of hell more hideous, and torment him as to what could have been? Had his sins been so great? He could feel the reins in his hands and the soil beneath his feet. Was he walking? The thunder grew louder, the rain was coming and the field had to be ploughed. Onwards, he could see the earth open up before him, rich and black ... enduring. The thunder turned the sky dark; the rain fell as the great blade sliced through the soft soil, now turning to mud. A crack of lightning streaked across the sky; the rain was now lashing against his face to torment his thirst. Still the plough cut through the field. He then turned to see the furrowed land behind him, and let out a cry of anguish. The ruptured ground had exhumed the interned bodies of nameless men, grotesque in their putrid decay. The lightning opened the sky to a crimson furnace. Horror! *Dear God, this is hell!*

1

His broken body was lifted onto a blood-soaked operating table. The smell of chloroform began to overwhelm him as confused dreams rambled through his mind. In the distance the bombardment continued to rumble while a young doctor gouged at the wound to remove the twisted shrapnel. The scalpel sliced through the leg muscle, eking out the metal fragments. He groaned. The nurse applied more chloroform and wiped the sweat and mud from his face. He became still again, and drifted back into dreams so real that he could almost feel the wind and the rain on his face.

Chapter 1

Scotland 1895

There was only one road to Glenfay. It meandered through the twisting glen for nearly eight miles before it reached the village. The high, rugged mountains gave shelter from the fierce winds in winter, casting long shadows on the glen in the warm summer evenings. Loch Fay was a deep sea-loch which stretched out through treacherous channels to the Atlantic. The fields around Glenfay were a patchwork of green and yellow hues. The surrounding moorland kept its dark winter shades throughout the year, with only the purple heather daring to bring summer scent and colour to the wind-swept hillside. The Macnairs' cottage stood on the edge of a hill on the outskirts of the village, overlooking a burn, which flowed down the hillside and into the loch. The Macnairs were a much-respected, God-fearing family, who had lived in the glen for many generations, so it was not surprising that the news of Callum's birth was celebrated across Glenfay. Even the Laird, whose own wife was expecting her second child, sent down a bottle of whisky to the cottage with his best wishes to the family. When the bottle arrived at the door, Jamie Macnair raised the first glass to the health of his son; the second to the Laird's unborn child. Two children destined to be born into the world so close in time and space, but so far apart in reality. Jamie Macnair did not have these thoughts in his mind as the whisky warmed his throat and his mood. His wife was happy. She kissed her baby's head and smiled at her proud husband. The long pains of childbirth were now a suppressed memory. The hours of agony turned to unbridled joy.

Callum was six years old when the old Queen finally died, but life went on much as before and in early spring, when the winter frost was out of the ground, Callum helped his father harness two plough horses to start the enduring cycle of life again. Bruce was a three-year-old black colt and Glenda was a sedate old grey mare, who kept the plough straight when her less experienced partner's mind wandered. The great coulter and ploughshare drilled uneven at first before the horses found their stride and Jamie Macnair his touch with the long reins. To keep the plough true was hard work, and Jamie cajoled the two horses with shouts and whistles. Before long, his hands were burning and blistered with the coarse reins. Eager to help, Callum followed behind his father in the furrowed black earth, lifting stones and throwing them in the ditch at the side of the field. He could see the sweat saturated on his father's shirt and waistcoat even though there was still a cold chill in the air and no sun in the grey, dour sky. Jamie only stopped when his wife, Betty, hollered from the bottom of the field that he was no use to her dead, and that his dinner was on the table.

Before long the grey daylight turned to darkness. Callum carried a lamp to guide his father and the horses over the last bit of unturned ground in the lower field. Then the sky suddenly clapped with thunder as the last drill was finally turned by the over-worked horses and plough-blade.

Exhausted, Jamie sat for a minute on the stone dyke at the bottom of the field and lit his pipe. "Ye done fine today, son. I wouldnae have been able tae do it without yer help," he said, as the rain began to fall. Callum smiled, while his father looked thankfully up at the sky, before tapping the hot tobacco out of his pipe. "Let's get these horses down before we're drenched."

The long summer months promised a good harvest that year and it was not long before the hay was waist high and in need of the scythe. Callum sat in the barn as his father sharpened the scythe blade, and told him about the ancient times when the Macnairs fought alongside the likes of William Wallace and Robert the Bruce, and how they picked the wrong side at the battle of Culloden and ended up losing their great swathes of land and fine houses to the traitors who would rather have a German king ruling Scotland than one of their own. He spoke with even more bitterness of how the greedy landlords had turned many a Macnair and his neighbour off the land to breed coarse looking English sheep, making even more money that they didn't need. Callum did not understand much of what his father was saying, but he liked to listen anyway. It was much better than mucking out the byre.

Betty had another twinge of pain as she cut the scones into farls, leaving them by the window. After a few minutes it eased and she carried on as normal, knowing fine well that the bairn was not ready for the world just yet, not when she still had this year's preserves to make. She sorted through the baskets of blackberries, raspberries and redcurrants that she and Callum had collected over the past few days, and put them in a large pot. The smell of the scones cooling at the window sill eventually reached the barn. Jamie Macnair was not one to turn up his nose at a warm bannock. "Let's get a bite tae eat, son. Yer mother's tempting us wi her scones again," he said, hanging up a scythe with the other tools he had sharpened that morning.

In a few weeks, with all her preserves sealed in an array of jars in the cupboard, the twinges became acute and Betty knew it was time to send Callum for Mrs Ramsay as her husband helped her into bed. Jamie then stood by the window and anxiously waited for the midwife to arrive; the groans from the box-bed were hard for him to abide.

Mrs Ramsay rushed up through the glen like a gust of wind, with Callum running to keep up with her. Jamie was grateful to see the stout, resourceful woman at the door and nodded towards the box-bed. Callum began to feel a little frightened when he heard his mother screaming, while the midwife ordered his father about like she owned the place. Once Jamie had set a large pot of water to boil, Betty's sister Morag arrived and ordered him and Callum out of the house to let her sister have some peace to suffer her ordeal without useless menfolk hanging about the house. Jamie, relieved, headed back up the field to pick up the scythe he had dropped in the hay that morning.

With her body saturated in sweat, Betty screamed obscenities that made her sister blush. With Mrs Ramsay soothing words of comfort, the expectant mother heaved and cursed with every agonising contraction. Then, finally with one great effort, the baby emerged into the world. "I never knew ye knew so many colourful words, Betty Macnair," said the midwife as she held the newborn by the feet and gave it a skelp that set its lungs roaring.

"I didn't think I knew them meself," said Betty, taking the baby to her breast.

"The devil is in all of us," lamented Morag.

In the upper field, Callum was tying bales of hay with his father and a few neighbours, who were helping to bring in the harvest. The unusually warm weather inspired some of the women to sing as they gathered the freshly cut barley that fell in the wake of the men's sweeping scythes. They sang in Gaelic and, although still a little confused, Callum sensed from his father's smile that everything was going to be fine. He began to hum along to the familiar tunes that his mother often sang around the house.

After a while, Callum noticed his father's face reddened when the womenfolk teased him about something that Callum could not quite understand. The teasing stopped when his Aunt Morag came running out of the house, waving a tea towel over her head shouting frantically. "Jamie! It's a boy. It's a bonnie wee boy." Jamie got to his feet, his face bright with joy and ran down the freshly-cut field towards the house with a trail of neighbours scuffling along behind him. Callum stood perplexed in the empty field with a solitary magpie picking away at the abandoned food. That was Ewan born.

Chapter 2

After his morning chores, Callum attended school for four hours each day and soon established himself as one of Miss Bothwell's brightest pupils. She did not have the same high opinion of her most recent charge, a sullen boy by the name of Angus Campbell, who would rather be working in the fields than be cooped up in school.

The Campbells were not by nature crofters, but cottars, seasonal workers who travelled the countryside in a horse-drawn cart, with all their worldly worth in two big wooden boxes, following the work and the changing seasons. That all stopped when Angus' mother became seriously ill with pleurisy, which forced the family to settle in Glenfay.

Norman Campbell was a severe man who had the years of thankless toil etched on his furrowed brow, and was the unhappy owner of a tormented whisky-stained mind. Dour when sober, he showed little interest in his neighbours, who he felt looked down on his kind as nothing more than tinkers with no roots in any land, let alone their own. Bitter with his poverty, he had long given up the Kirk and what he saw as its pampering to the rich who fed its coffers to save their damned souls from what they deserved. He would not even acknowledge the minister if he passed him on the brae. Whisky was now the only spirit he believed in.

Campbell saw no need for his son to have any education other than what he needed to learn to work in the fields. When the minister called one day to insist that Angus attend the village school, Campbell sent him packing with a litany of obscenities. It took a few well chosen words from Charles Dunbar to convince Campbell that he had no choice in the matter and that it was part and parcel of his employment that his son should benefit from the free schooling, which was sponsored by Dunbar's own patronage.

"The boy will thank you when he grows old enough to appreciate the value of an education," said Dunbar as Campbell grudgingly doffed his cap and gave way to the Laird's unyielding will.

Angus was by then thirteen years old and as tough as any cottar twice his age. He had learned to endure the hardship of their travelling life with a stoic indifference and knew nothing else but the open roads and the changing seasons. Restless to move on, he found it hard to settle in the glen and the thought of having to go to school filled him with dread.

On his first morning, Angus, kept himself to himself, but it did not take long before some of the other children began to whisper and point in his direction. His big labouring boots and shabby clothes made him stand out from the others in the small village school. Glad to have someone his own age in the class, Callum Macnair moved from where he was sitting to take up a seat next to Angus.

"Hello tae ye, my name's Callum."

"And what's that tae me," grunted Angus, before turning to look back out the window towards the heather covered hills and the mountains beyond.

As the hours passed, his lack of participation began to irritate some of the other children in the class as much as it infuriated Miss Bothwell. Callum was more curious than irritated and once the bell finally rang to end the day's lesson, he followed his belligerent classmate from school. "Why don't ye like school?" he asked, when he caught up with Angus on the back road home.

"Whit's it tae dae wi' ye?"

"Nothing," Callum replied, slightly startled as he looked back into Angus's angry eyes. "I was only asking..."

"Well don't be asking," sneered Angus, turning his back on Callum, and continuing with his aggressive walk home.

During the next few weeks, the only time that Callum noticed Angus showing any interest in class, was the day Miss Bothwell brought in an old newspaper cutting about the Wright brothers' first powered flight, which took place only four years earlier. Callum could see he was hanging on her every word, but when the lesson was over, and the Kitty Hawk back on solid ground, Angus resumed his solitude.

One morning Angus' attendance at class came to an abrupt end. The days went by without him. During the second week of his absence, Callum decided to wait after class. "Miss, is Angus Campbell coming back to school?"

"Not for a while, I wouldn't think. His mother has been unwell again. They need him to tend to things at home. Were you two friends?" she asked, leaving Callum somewhat embarrassed and stuttering, "No…yes…sort of."

"Why don't you go and see how he is getting on?" she suggested, taking a couple of easy reading books from her cluttered desktop. "Give him these. Who knows, he might even read them."

Callum walked the half mile or so beyond his own house, before stopping for a moment when he saw the funnels of smoke blowing in the breeze above a cluster of trees. His hands felt sweaty. He gripped the thin books tightly and walked up the overgrown path. He began to have his doubts and could hear his mother's voice in his head when he opened the broken gate. *"A queer lot, tinkers that don't stay in one place long enough to see the grass grow. That cottage they're living in is no better than a byre."* He shut the gate back over and looked at the front of the house for a moment. To Callum, it didn't much look like a byre even though the plaster around the door was disintegrating with neglect, exposing the raw stones to the elements. There was rubbish lying all around; old broken cartwheels, rusty tools and small piles of ashes from the peat fire, but he had seen worse. He knocked the door gently and waited anxiously for a few minutes. He was about to walk away when it suddenly opened.

"What do ye want?" Angus's father demanded; his face gaunt and weather-beaten.

"Is Angus at home?"

"He's out tending tae the sheep!" The door closed as quickly as it had opened.

Still a little apprehensive, Callum went around the back of the cottage and out into the fields. He climbed over a stone dyke, and could see a flock of sheep moving down the hillside, kept in check by two dogs, and the constant whistles and shouts of the shepherd.

"Angus!"

"Aye, whit dae ye want?" came the hostile reply as the first of the sheep in the flock passed Callum on the hillside.

"Miss Bothwell asked me tae give ye these," shouted Callum, waving the books in the air to show that he was there on school business and not out of his own curiosity. Angus walked straight up to him, stopping only a few feet away. He stuffed his hands in his pockets and showed no intention of taking the books. There was a deadly silence as they stared at each other. "She said that she'd be over to see ye next week, tae see how yer getting on."

"Tell her no' tae bother herself and ye can take those bloody books back."

"I was asked tae give ye them. So here, take them," insisted Callum. He thrust the books towards Angus, who in turn grabbed them and threw them over a dyke into a mesh of bracken and nettles.

"Ye better get them!" shouted Callum, staring into Angus's defiant eyes. "Ye better get them or…" he stuttered, clenching his fists.

"Or ye'll what?" Angus taunted, secure in his obvious physical advantage.

"I don't know why she bothered tae send ye books. It's obvious yer too damned daft to read even yer name, never mind…"

Before he knew it, Callum was lying on his back with his nose bleeding. The blow had stunned him and blood trickled into the corner of his mouth. He wiped it away with the sleeve of his jumper and tried to get up.

"Who are ye calling daft?" shouted Angus, standing over Callum with his fists at the ready. Callum's head began to clear. He got up on one knee. Still dazed, he raised a submissive hand above his head. "Well, get up," Angus demanded as he relaxed his guard. Seeing his opportunity, Callum suddenly dived at his opponent's waist, knocking Angus off balance. They both fell into the thick bracken around the dyke. In a panicked attack, Callum punched and struggled to gain superiority over Angus's greater bulk. He soon became aware of the lack of fight from his adversary. Pushing the damp fringe of hair from his eyes, he could see that Angus was out cold.

Still breathing heavily, Callum rose from the motionless body and stood over it in a quiet moment of triumph. He was relieved, but a little apprehensive. "Get up!" he shouted, in a nervous shrill, but Angus continued to lie still, except for the breeze that ruffled his dark hair. Callum began to fear he had killed Angus. While these thoughts were rushing through his mind, Angus slowly moved his head and opened his eyes. He looked confused and too weak to get to his feet. "Get up, ye fat bastard!" Callum shouted, relieved that he would not face the gallows.

Angus sat up and groaned. "Ye can put yer fists in yer pockets. I'm no' coming out for another round," he said, touching the back of his head that he had hit on a stone hidden under the heather.

Callum lowered his fists when he saw the bright red blood on Angus's fingers. "Are ye all right?"

"Aye, I'll be fine."

"I'm sorry, I ..."

"The sheep!" Angus shouted. They both looked down the hillside and saw the flock escaping through a breach in the dyke and heading towards the village. Angus tried to get to his feet, but fell back onto the crushed bracken. The dogs followed the flock onto the brae, barking frantically, causing the nervous sheep to quicken their pace.

Callum ran down the field, calling the dogs to lie down, and to his surprise they responded to his voice. With the dogs out of the way, the excited flock slowed to a grazing pace and Callum began to urge them back along the brae. Recovered from his mild concussion, Angus staggered down towards the sheep whistling and shouting his commands to the dogs as he went. The two dogs soon had the sheep clambering back into the field. The crisis over, Callum watched for a while as Angus gradually coaxed the hesitant animals into their pens. Forgetting about the books, Callum began to make his way back towards the village.

He was almost halfway home when he heard the heavy crunch of boots coming up behind him on the loose pebbled path. He turned to see Angus.

"Wait! Will ye," shouted Angus, waving the schoolbooks. Callum stopped; reassured in the tone of his voice that Angus was not intent on starting another fight. However, he was sufficiently apprehensive to take his hands out of his pockets just in case. "Wait, will ye!" Angus called again. "Ye can take these and tell the teacher that I'll be back next week."

"Why don't ye hang on tae them?"

Angus looked awkward for a moment and then handed Callum the books. "There's nae point. Yer right, ah cannae read."

"Oh," was all Callum could think to say in response. He took the books and watched Angus make his way back over the brae.

Angus returned to school the following week, but not in the manner he had planned. That morning Miss Bothwell was late for class and her absence led to an outbreak of what can only be described as riotous bedlam. Some of the younger boys were chasing each other around the desks, while a handful of girls were arguing over the disputed ownership of a one-eyed doll. "Here she comes with the Reverend!" shouted one boy, who preferred to stand on a table like a nervous meerkat, keeping watch at these times of uproar. The mention of the Reverend caused an instant response and those not already in their seats scurried towards them. A hush came over the class. Books were opened at strange and uncharted pages, arms were folded and mouths were closed tight. Only the most audacious continued with rather subdued exchanges right up to the moment the brass door handle turned.

Miss Bothwell entered the classroom, followed by the serious, stony-etched face of Reverend Knox, holding Angus by the scruff of the neck and dragging him into the room. The Reverend placed a wet hessian sack on Miss Bothwell's desk. She stood, pale faced by the window, while her uncle addressed the frightened children.

"Good morning, boys and girls!" he said in his gruff, dictatorial manner.

"Good morning, Reverend," came the collective response.

"I assume that you have not yet said your morning prayers?"

"No, Reverend."

With an impish grin on his face, Angus stood behind the minister, who was now leading the class in a vigorous rendition of the Lord's Prayer, his eyes casting their stern gaze at anyone not fully engrossed in the 'spiritual' experience. The class was gripped with anticipation when the prayer neared its 'Amen'. Callum looked at the shabby figure of Angus standing in the corner barefoot, his trousers dirty and wet. There were splatters of mud on his legs and blood trickled from a small cut at the side of his left knee. The hessian sack was dripping water onto the floor. Callum noticed the distinctive tip of a salmon's tail fin sticking out the bottom. While he pondered Angus's fate, he was startled by a sudden slap to the back of his head. "Ah!"

"Amen. Have you forgotten the Lord's Prayer, boy?" the Reverend growled, still considering whether or not to give Callum another slap.

"No, Reverend."

Satisfied with his execution of summary justice, the Reverend turned his attention to the main culprit of the morning. With his usual religious zeal, he began to tell the other children how 'this evil boy' was caught by the Laird's gamekeeper near the River Lea with a salmon he had no right to. "He has brought shame and disgrace on his family and this school, and you will now see how I deal with thieving poachers! Let this be a warning to the rest of you, and never, ever, think of doing such a thing or you'll get the same treatment. Always remember that God knows what you're thinking and doing at all times, and he tells me everything. Get your hand up, boy!"

Angus hesitated for a moment, watching the thick willow cane being raised over the Reverend's dandruff-covered shoulder. "Come now! Get your hand out, boy." Taking a deep breath, Angus tentatively raised his left hand. When it reached a satisfactory level, the cane came down on it with a violent blow that caused half the children to recoil with fear. "Again!" demanded the Reverend, with anger flaring in his self-righteous eyes. Mumbling curses to himself, Angus squeezed his throbbing hand between his right arm and his side and mentally prepared the other hand for the same treatment. The Reverend impatiently slammed the cane down on Miss Bothwell's desk, causing her to jump with the fright of it. "Hurry, boy! Get your hand up. God's work must be done with haste! The devil is in ye, boy. Now get that hand up." The cane thrashed both hands a total of three times each; six of the best! The other children watched in quiet admiration as not a single tear came to Angus's defiant eyes. No one had ever got more than three of the cane before, and no caning was as zealously administered as the six that Angus Campbell had suffered. "Get to your seat, boy, and if you're ever found anywhere near that river again you'll get the next six on your bare backside."

Embarrassed, Miss Bothwell blushed at her uncle's unexpected crudeness. She hated his violent use of the cane on any of the children, but she never dared interfere. She was relieved when he finally bid her farewell and left for the Kirk. With a curse on his lips,

Angus sat on both his throbbing hands and laid his face against the coolness of the desktop.

"Are ye all right?"Callum whispered.

Angus turned his head and smiled. "Ye fancy a bit of fishing tomorrow?"

It was a fine spring morning and the sun was already high over the summit of Ben Cruchan, its warm yellow glow glistening on the calm waters of Loch Fay. The sheep grazed in the lower fields, still burdened with their heavy winter coats, which would soon be feeding the hungry looms at the Laird's mill. A playful family of otters splashed around the shallower waters of the loch, catching the occasional fish, which they tore apart with their sharp teeth, while floating nonchalantly on their backs. A nervous-looking grey heron waded near the banks, with one eye on the otters, while searching for small fish and molluscs in the shallows. The lilac flowers of the huge rhododendron bushes at the foot of Leaburn Castle were in full bloom.

With the sun on their backs, Callum and Angus climbed up the hillside overlooking the castle. They found a breach in a dyke, which gave them plenty of large stones to sit on in the warm sunshine.

It did not take long before Angus got bored sitting about doing nothing.

"What's it ye want tae do anyway?"

"We could try down at the shallows. There's some good fishing down there."

"Are ye mad? If they catch you again, they'll put you in prison."

Angus did not answer; he had spotted a rabbit on a knoll on the other side of the stone dyke where Callum was sitting. With a not too careful aim, he threw a stone at the nervous-looking animal. The stone flew only inches past Callum's head, landing a few feet away from the surprised rabbit, which immediately disappeared down a nearby burrow. Callum was so startled at the stone coming towards him that he lost his balance, causing some of the loose stones on the top of the dyke to give way. He fell backwards, screaming as he disappeared, head first into a ditch of bracken and nettles.

"Ye stupid idiot!" screamed Callum as he fought to free himself from the stinging nettles. "Help me, I cannae get up!"

"Giv' me yer hand," said Angus, hanging over the dyke, with both his legs dangling in the air. He stretched and stretched until he finally grabbed Callum's frantically searching hand. "Don't pull. Don't pull!" shouted Angus as he and part of the dyke collapsed down on Callum. As they twisted and turned to free themselves, they suddenly became aware of giggles of laughter.

"Who's that?" asked Angus, stopping for a moment to listen.

"How should I know? Get off!" moaned Callum, pushing Angus away.

"You both should be in a circus," giggled a strange voice from a little further up the hill. "That was very funny."

Callum stopped struggling and got to his feet first to see the owner of the voice standing with a slightly older looking girl behind him, still trying to control her fit of giggles. The boy had laughed enough and looked sternly at Callum. "You will have to rebuild the dyke or I will tell my father," he said - his voice so strangely different from any that Callum had ever heard before. The boy was of a similar age to Callum and Angus, but spoke with the authority and manner of an adult. He was wearing a tweed suit of grey and blue, and with his matching tweed cap and walking cane tucked under his arm, he looked like a miniature country gentleman.

"Who the hell are ye?" demanded Angus, getting to his feet and scratching the nettle bumps that were spreading all over his bare arms.

"I am Duncan Dunbar, and this is my sister Caitriona," he

replied, raising his hand to indicate the girl standing behind him. "Our father owns this land."

The girl had stopped giggling as soon as her brother had started speaking. Now, she seemed shy, turning to look across Loch Fay, avoiding the stare of the two curious boys. Her pretty face was framed with long dark hair, which caught the bright sunlight. Caitriona's clothes were less formal than her brother's. She wore a simple summer dress and a pair of sandals. Callum could not help but notice how brown her skin was in comparison to her brother's pale, freckled face. She was carrying a wicker basket under her arm, which was overflowing with wild flowers she had picked on her morning walk.

"What's that?" asked Callum, pointing to the basket.

"It's none of your business!" replied the boy aggressively. "That's what it is, none of your business," he added in his voice of practised supremacy.

"It's none of your business. That's what it is, none of your business," mimicked Angus in a fit of exaggerated laughter.

"Don't be beastly," said the girl. "They're flowers if you must know."

"Flowers!" They both laughed even louder.

"What are you laughing at, you stupid boys?" demanded her brother. "Never mind them, Caitriona. They're only common rogues. If the stones are not placed back on the wall when I return tomorrow, then I will tell our father. We will see how funny you think you are then. Let's go, Caitriona."

Callum and Angus watched the boy and his sister descend the path towards the foot of the hill. Every so often the girl would break away from her brother and rush into the heather to pick some pretty flower not already in her crowded basket. Angus nudged Callum in the ribs as he caught Callum's eyes following the girl.

"Ye like her?"

"Shut up!" snapped Callum, pushing Angus backwards into the flattened bracken.

"Hey!" shouted Angus, trying unsuccessfully to grab Callum's arm to stop from losing his balance.

"Last down is a cow's arse," shouted Callum, climbing back over the dyke and running down the hillside.

The girl stopped for a moment to watch the two boys chase each other. They looked so wild and free. "Hurry, Caitriona! I can understand now why father does not want us speaking to the village children. They're absolutely frightful!"

"I'm coming, Duncan," she said, stealing another curious look at the two strange boys. "They didn't mend the stone wall."

"Well, what did you expect? Come, haven't you enough silly flowers?"

Chapter 3

The church was packed by the time Callum, with Ewan not far behind, shamefully entered. The Reverend cast an angry glare at them. Callum bowed his head and took a pew at the back. It was a few minutes before he braved another look in the direction of the pulpit. The Reverend was reading a passage from Exodus and was soon flushed with spiritual exaltation as though the Jewish flight from Egypt had only happened the other day. Callum moved his attention from the minister's glazed eyes towards the Laird's pew to the left of the pulpit. Even on his tiptoes, he could only see the side of Caitriona's head. She raised her hand for a moment to brush the hair from her eyes. With only a fleeting glimpse of her face, he reluctantly fell back on his heels. Ewan nudged him in the ribs.

"What is it?"

"Nothing," replied Callum, looking back at his bible, which he had been holding upside down.

After the reading, the Reverend turned his attention to the Laird's son and daughter, whom he welcomed back into the parish for the Easter holidays. The congregation were now all seated, and Callum found it impossible to see over the rows of heads and hats, without making himself conspicuous. The welcome formality over, the Reverend began to sing with his usual vigour, while the congregation tried to keep up. "Abide with me …"

Charles Dunbar's lips seemed to move, but no sound could be heard. He was thinking of his late wife, Marie-Claire, whom he always thought of when in church. It was while on holiday in France that he, then a handsome man in his late thirties, met the beautiful young girl who was destined to become his future wife. It was the year of the great Paris Exposition Universelle, and Charles was in Paris with his friend, Edward, Prince of Wales and Princess Alexandra, who were invited by the French Government to open the Exhibition, which ironically celebrated the centenary of the *Storming of the Bastille* and the eventual overthrow of the French monarchy.

Marie-Claire was only eighteen years old, a street artist from Croix-de-Vie, a small fishing port on the west coast of France, just south of Nantes. Dunbar first saw her as he sauntered across the Pont D'iena one sunny morning on his way to meet the Prince of Wales, who was leaving later that day for England. She was finishing a charcoal drawing of the Eiffel Tower when he stopped to admire her sketches. Dunbar was so taken by her vivacious smile and beautiful brown eyes that, before he could stop himself, he bought one of her drawings for five francs. She laughed and giggled at his attempts to be charming in his broken French, with his pronounced Scottish burr making his accent seem quite funny. It took three more days and three more purchases before she succumbed to his desperate pleas to join him for a coffee. His two-week holiday eventually lasted almost two months and they were married in Monaco, seven weeks after they first met.

In the late autumn of 1889, Charles Dunbar returned to Glenfay with his young bride. Even when he showered her with expensive jewellery, she still could not grasp the idea that the man she had married was a Lord, who lived in a four-hundred-year-old castle somewhere in the wilds of Scotland. The reality finally came home to her when she entered the grand oak panelled hall at Leaburn to be greeted by a dozen immaculately dressed servants; the men and boys bowing, while the women and girls performed a well-rehearsed curtsy as she was introduced to them in turn as Lady Dunbar.

Life seemed perfect. There was only one thing missing that would complete the fairytale; the birth of a son and heir at Leaburn. But as time passed, Marie-Clare suffered two miscarriages and Dunbar began to fear for the future of the dynasty. Now plagued with ill-health, Marie-Claire was no longer able to face the society that she had once basked in with so much confidence.

In 1893, Dr Wilson once again confirmed that Lady Dunbar was expecting. This time however it was agreed that she should return to her parents in France for most of the pregnancy to avoid the harshness of another Scottish winter. In the spring of the following year, she returned to Scotland to prepare for the birth and to ensure that the next Laird was born on Scottish soil.

When the birth finally came, it was a long protracted ordeal for Marie-Claire and she suffered twenty-eight painful hours of labour before the baby was finally born in the early hours of the morning. Her weak and exhausted body suffered a greater blow when the doctor and the midwife told her that she had given birth to a lovely girl. Their joyful faces were at odds with the pain their words caused her.

"How are you, darling?" Dunbar asked, sitting on the side of the bed and taking his wife's delicate hand in his own.

"We have a lovely daughter," she said, rather nervously, pulling away the covers from the baby's red, puffy face. "Isn't she beautiful?"

"Yes she is."

"We'll have a boy next time," she said, her eyes filled with tears on seeing the disappointment in his tired face.

"Yes, we will. You must be exhausted. Please get some sleep. I'll send in the nurse to take the baby."

"No! No. I want to keep her with me. Please. I'm not too tired."

"All right, whatever you wish. I'll send in the nurse to sit with you anyway. Try and get some sleep. I'll be in to see you later," he promised as he kissed her on the forehead. Dunbar returned to the library where he spent what was left of the night in a state of drunken melancholy.

It was another two years before Lady Dunbar was confirmed to be pregnant again. Expectations grew as months passed and the fear of a miscarriage subsided. On the second night of the harvest moon, the labour pains started and Dr Wilson rushed to the castle to take charge.

"Why is mummy crying?" asked little Caitriona, running into the library, clutching her favourite doll.

"Go back to bed!" snapped Dunbar, his tone bringing a burst of tears from the confused child. "Oh, I'm sorry, darling. Come and sit on daddy's knee for a while."

The tears immediately disappeared as she climbed on her father's lap. "Why is mummy crying?" Caitriona asked again, rubbing her tired eyes, determined to stay awake until she got an answer.

"Mummy's having a baby. When you wake up tomorrow you'll have a baby brother to play with."

"But why is she crying?"

"She's not crying any more," said Dunbar, suddenly becoming aware of the silence from his wife's room. "Mummy's all right; she's sleeping now."

Caitriona soon lost her fight to stay awake and, after a short while, Dunbar gently returned her to the comfort of her bed. It was now morning and there had been no progress report from Mrs Ramsay for over an hour. Dunbar poured himself another whisky and opened the curtains to look out over the mist-shrouded loch. The breaking dawn was casting its increasing light over its cold, dark waters. The sky was a splash of purple and yellow. In the ancient trees, on the other side of the loch, the deep rasping calls of carrion crows broke the silence of the morning. In time the harbour was alive with small figures climbing into the fishing boats swaying to and fro in the gentle swell. He watched the first of these sturdy boats put to sail, leading the way through the mist and out into the less sheltered waters of the harsh Atlantic.

"Yer Lordship!"

"Aye, what is it, Mrs Ramsay?" he asked, still staring out through the window, lost in his thoughts.

"It's a boy, yer lordship. It's a bonnie wee boy."

22

"A boy! A boy?" he mumbled in disbelief. "Are you sure?"

"Of course I'm sure," she laughed. "He's a fine boy all right."

Dunbar stood frozen to the spot, fumbling his nervous fingers through his thinning hair. His eyes began to fill with tears of joy, tiredness and relief. He gave a thoughtful glance at his father's likeness, which hung over the marble fireplace. Dunbar then straightened his jacket and followed Mrs Ramsay into the hallway, where they met Dr Wilson leaving Lady Dunbar's room. The doctor looked very grey and his eyes were red with lack of sleep. He rolled down his shirt sleeves and stared seriously at Dunbar.

"Her Ladyship is very tired; it's been a very difficult birth," he said with a heavy sigh in his voice.

"Is the baby all right?"

"The child is fine. Mrs Ramsay, you must be exhausted. Why don't you go and lie down for a couple of hours."

"Yes, doctor," she replied, immediately sensing in his tone that there was something wrong. "If you need me, I'll be in my room."

"Dunbar, I have to speak with you," said the doctor, dispensing with formalities, and leading the Laird away from his wife's room and back into the library.

"What's wrong? What's happened, doctor?"

"You have a fine son, Dunbar," said the doctor ominously, as he removed his half rimmed spectacles, which were clinging precariously to his prominent nose, "but I'm afraid her ladyship is extremely weak and will need rest."

"She'll be all right?"

"She's sleeping now, but she'll need constant care and attention over the next few days. I'll have Mrs Ramsay stay over until there is sufficient improvement in her condition. In the meantime if you have any prayers, offer them up for your wife. She almost died giving birth to your son."

Leaburn Castle now had its male heir and the line of Dunbar was saved from extinction, but within weeks the child's mother passed away in her sleep. Lady Dunbar was never strong enough to even hold the child whom she was so proud to have given birth to. The loss of his beautiful wife was to leave the grieving Dunbar haunted with guilt for the rest of his life. A mausoleum for her remains was built in the grounds of the castle overlooking the loch, which became a shrine for Dunbar's grief.

Charles Dunbar raised his head as the Reverend concluded the service with a robust rendition of *'Faith of our Fathers'*. Callum watched the Laird lead his family down the far aisle. He only caught a fleeting glimpse of Caitriona, who walked behind her brother, head bowed and solemn. It was the tradition for the rest of the congregation to stay in their pews until the Laird and his family had left the church. Callum waited impatiently for the minister to leave the pulpit, before rushing to the back door of the church. He watched as the Laird's carriage pulled away from the gate.

"I've never seen anyone so keen to get out of a Kirk," said his Aunt Morag, whom he had not noticed sitting directly behind him. "You ought to be ashamed of yerself," she added with a grin as she took off her hat, which seemed to be annoying her. "She's a beautiful looking girl."

Callum smiled, his face turning a little red. "I'll have tae hurry," he grunted.

"Wait for me!" called Ewan, finally squeezing himself out of the crowded church.

"Hurry up!" shouted Callum, running down the brae with Ewan calling after him to slow down. By the time Callum reached the crossroads, where he could see the castle on the other side of the loch, the carriage was already making its way through the gates and up the gravel path. He watched it disappear out of sight. Ewan, out of breath, finally caught up with him. "Why were you running?"

"Never mind, let's go home before it starts to rain."

"Rain?" said Ewan, more than a little bemused as he looked up at the cloudless sky.

A few days later Caitriona returned to boarding school in Edinburgh and it was the following spring before Callum saw her again. That day, he and Angus had been out cutting peat since the break of dawn. There had been no rain in the glen for weeks and the bog was in perfect condition for cutting and drying the peat logs. Many of the glen's crofters were making the most of the dry spell and numerous stacks of peat lay waiting to be loaded into creels and taken back to the village. Angus had brought along his collection of bird's eggs.

"Why do ye want tae collect these for?" asked Callum, rummaging through the old biscuit tin. Angus did not have an answer and simply shrugged his shoulders.

"Is that a starling's egg?" Callum asked, pointing to a small pale blue egg.

"No! Don't be daft. That's a blackbird's egg. There's a starling's," said Angus, holding up a small white egg. Callum carefully examined the thin shell and the two holes pierced in each end as Angus went through his collection, identifying each species and telling exactly where and when he found them.

"I found a wagtail's nest last year," said Callum.

"Where?" demanded Angus.

"On the other side of the loch near to the castle walls… I was with me feyther snaring rabbits when I found it…"

"The bird might have come back again this year. Why don't we go down and see if the nest is still there?" suggested Angus eagerly.

"Aye, if ye want."

Callum led the way to where he remembered finding the nest the year before, but they only found the shrivelled, skeletal bodies of two pink, skinned chicks lying rotting on the ground under the nest. "A stoat or something must have found it," suggested Angus, pulling away what remained of the nest and throwing it into the loch. "Why don't we look further along? There's bound tae be other nests somewhere about here."

As they fought through the bushes, a flock of quacking mallards fell over one another in their race to get away from the bank and into the safety of the loch.

"I've found one!" shouted Callum.

"Let me see," said Angus, peering over Callum's shoulders into the nest, where five pale blue eggs clustered together in the centre.

"Look!" said Angus, carefully taking one of the eggs and placing it in the palm of his other hand for Callum to see. "Is it a wagtail?"

"Aye, I think so. It's the same size and colour as the ones we found last year. My feyther was sure that they were wagtail eggs."

"Even if it's no' a wagtail, I haven't got any of these," replied Angus, taking the egg from Callum.

"Stop there!" shouted a voice from high above them. "What are you doing down there? I can see you. If you don't come out, I will tell my father and have the Baillie on to you. Do you hear me?"

They emerged to see Duncan Dunbar holding the reins of a small, grey pony. "What were you doing down there?" Duncan demanded.

"None of your bloody business, that's what we were doing," snapped Angus.

"Duncan! Please hurry up," shouted his sister, who was impatiently waiting for him. He waved at her to come over. She

26

mounted her own black and white pony and came slowly towards them.

"I asked you what you were doing?" shouted Duncan, prodding Angus in the ribs with the butt of his riding whip.

In an instant Angus grabbed the whip and pulled it violently from Duncan's grip, before throwing it back at him. Within seconds they were both on the ground shouting and punching each other. Callum tried in vain to separate them. As they rolled around on the freshly cut lawn, shouts of rebuke could be heard from the direction of the castle. Caitriona now galloped across the lawn towards her brother, frantically shouting back at the stable boy to fetch her father.

"Let's get out of here!" shouted Callum, trying to pull Angus free as something suddenly lashed across his face, splitting the skin above his left eye.

"Let him go!" cried Caitriona, threatening to use the whip again. Callum wiped the blood from his face and defiantly stared at her. In the meantime, Angus fought his way to his feet, with Duncan still tightly hanging on to his leg. "Ah! He bit me. The bastard bit me," shouted Angus. Callum turned back towards the castle to see two large black dogs racing along the lawn towards them, their teeth dripping with saliva.

"Come on!" he screamed at Angus.

"Ah cannae get the bastard off me."

"Duncan, let him go," shouted Caitriona, trying to control her frightened pony.

There was a scream before Duncan released his grip on Angus, who then ran frantically after Callum to the end of the lawn. They could hear the growling dogs at their heels and they threw themselves into the thick, stinging undergrowth. Soon, they were rolling, tumbling and scrambling down the steep hill trying to escape the ferocious, snapping jaws. In an instant, one of the dogs jumped into the tangled bracken, catching the back of Angus's leg in its mouth. The dog immediately let go its grip when a sharp branch caught it in the left eye. It howled before retreating back to the castle with its tail between its legs. The other dog followed its injured sibling across the lawn. Two more dogs were released from the kennels to take up the pursuit.

In great pain, Angus fought through the whipping branches to keep up with Callum, but both were soon exhausted. They could hear angry voices above, shouting at them to stop and urging the reluctant dogs to force themselves through the thick clusters of brambles that covered most of the wet, slippery ground around the loch-side.

"Callum, I have tae stop!"

"What? Are ye daft!" shouted Callum, trying to catch his breath. "What's wrong?" he added, on seeing the pain in Angus's face.

"My leg is hurt. I've been bitten by one of those damn dogs."

"God, that looks bad," said Callum, pulling back the tear in Angus's trousers to get a better look.

"I'll be all right, if we can get over tae the other side..."

"What's the point? They all saw us," Callum sighed, sitting down beside Angus and wiping the blood that was still running down his face. "God, we're in trouble this time."

"That wee bastard started it. He attacked me."

"But, Angus, he's the bloody Laird's son. God, I hope I never broke his nose when I punched him."

"To hell wi' him and his feyther. What can they do tae us anyway?"

"Angus. I don't believe ye. They'll probably evict our folks and throw us in jail."

"They've got tae catch us first. C'mon."

They stealthily crossed over the fields and dykes, stopping every so often to look for those that might be on their trail, but no one followed. The two fugitives ran to the back of a neighbour's house looking for shelter. Once in the byre, they quietly examined their wounds. The laceration above Callum's eye was superficial and the blood had already started to congeal. Angus tied a tourniquet with his handkerchief above the gash on his leg and lay down on damp-smelling straw to rest while Callum kept an eye on the road from the castle.

"They're coming," said Callum. Angus got to his feet and limped over to the barn door. They watched in silence. The Laird's long, black carriage proceeded with haste along the winding, undulating loch road. Callum's heart was in his mouth. The carriage neared the Macnair cottage, but his fear turned to a confused sense of relief when it rushed past without the slightest hesitation in the horses' galloping strides. Their eyes followed the speeding carriage. It neared the turn-off to Angus's home. Again, it continued on its way. Angus thought this was a good sign. Callum was not so sure. "Maybe the Laird has sent for the constable."

Their fears of prison and eviction subsided as the days passed and nothing happened. That Sunday, Duncan sat stony-faced beside his father in the family pew with a black eye and swollen nose. Ewan had never seen his brother pray so much, and even Aunt Morag was taken by his new piety. "You would make a fine minister," she said, when Callum hurried past her and out of the Kirk. He did not wait for Ewan to catch up and ran from the churchyard without stopping until he reached the bridge over the River Lea where Angus was waiting for him.

"I told ye," scoffed Angus, dropping a large stone into the fast flowing water, in an unsuccessful attempt to sink a broken branch that he had thrown from the other side of the narrow wooden bridge. "Damn! I missed the bloody thing. They don't know it was us," he added, spitting at the escaping branch as it was swept away. "It's been nearly a week. They must think it was a couple of poachers that gave him that eye."

"I thought the minister was goin' tae condemn us from the pulpit."

"That's what ye get for going tae church."

"It's all right for you. Yer folks don't make ye go."

"Was she there?" asked Angus, turning to urinate into the bushes.

"Who?"

"Ye know who! The sister … the one that cut your eye with her riding whip."

"Why?"

"Och, it's just that I saw her yesterday. Fair pair of udders on her now, ye know. I wouldn't mind giving her this!"

"There's Miss Bothwell," shouted Callum, jumping behind some bushes.

"Where?" Angus panicked before he realised he had been had. "Ye lying bastard look what ye made me dae," he complained, holding his wet trouser leg away from his thigh.

Callum just laughed as he threw a stone into the stream. "Serves ye right."

"Why? Because I was talking dirty about Caitriona," scoffed Angus.

"What are ye talking about?"

"I'm no' daft, ye know. I've seen ye gawking at her," said Angus, sniggering. "Ah don't blame ye but ye've as much chance of getting yer hands on her as I have of becoming the bloody Pope. Where are ye going?"

"Never mind! Just shut up!"

"I was only pulling yer leg…wait for me!"

"Go tae hell," shouted Callum as the skies opened up. That was the end of the longest dry spell in the glen for years.

Chapter 4

A Few Years Later

There was no doubt that Mhairi MacDougall was the finest looking girl in the village and Angus, now seventeen, had courted her for almost a year before building up the courage to ask her cantankerous father for her hand. Mhairi was still only sixteen and Walter MacDougall was not in the least happy to give away his only daughter just when she was becoming useful about the house. However, after three days of tears and tantrums from Mhairi, Walter made a bargain with Angus. "Get a place of yer ain and fifty pounds in the bank and I'll give ye both me blessing."

"It's impossible," cried Mhairi. "I'll no' cook another dinner in this house."

With this threat, Walter thought long and hard, scratching the soft, grey stubble on his pointed chin. *She was no' much use tae me if she wasn't goin' tae cook me dinner*, he pondered. "We'll make it twenty pounds," he declared, "and that's my final word on the matter."

"Twenty pounds! Why no' make it a hundred or a thousand? Who in the village has twenty pounds?"

"No, he's right, Mhairi, we can't get married if we've got tae depend on others tae put a roof over our heads," said Angus, getting to his feet and putting on his coat.

Walter MacDougall never had twenty pounds in his life and he could not see how Angus Campbell, with nothing but holes in his baggy trousers was ever going to overcome such an impediment. Undeterred by the terms of their agreement, Angus shook hands on the bargain with the grinning old man. His thoughts were already on Hector Macleod, who was always telling stories about his years as a merchant seaman and the money he made on long voyages around the world. Angus decided then and there that the only way he was ever going to be able to wed Mhairi was by making his own fortune overseas. He put his hat on and promised his doubtful fiancée that they would marry before the end of the year. His optimistic words did not stop Mhairi's tears as she watched him walk back down the brae with a new sense of purpose in his stride.

When the day of Angus's departure finally arrived, it was a tearful fiancée who embraced him at Marnock Station. They said their goodbyes and waited for the conductor's whistle to blow. With the steam filling the platform, Angus reluctantly let go her hand and promised, in a feigned cheerful voice, "I'll be back before Christmas with more than enough tae get married wi' and buy our ain house … Mind, Callum, look after her fur me," he said, shaking his friend's hand vigorously, before boarding the train.

There was a roar of thunder. The skies opened up as the train slowly chugged into motion. With a heavy heart, Angus waved from the window until the station faded into the distance. That was Angus gone and many in the glen thought it would be for good.

It was a blustery night, with cold winds blowing in over the waters of Lochfay. Few in the glen would be fool enough to venture out in such a hellish night. A fit of laughter shattered the quiet of MacTaggart's bar as Callum and the Murray brothers played a rowdy game of gin rummy.

"All right, lads! Less noise over there," ordered MacTaggart, on seeing the annoyance on the faces of two of his older customers as they tried to concentrate on their game of dominoes.

"Aye, all right, Malcolm," said Callum, taking hold of Hamish's arm. "Try and control yerself!" he urged, while Hamish tried his best to stop laughing.

"Calm down for God's sake, nothing's that funny," said his

brother, shaking his head.

Eventually the laughter subsided. The three friends collected their thoughts and sipped their ale, as a sense of calm befell the bar once again. In the strange silence, the only thing that could be heard was the click-click of dominoes from the other corner of the bar as canny old Hector Macleod continued to make spots disappear before Walter MacDougall's eyes.

"Why don't we tell them tae make less noise," said Hamish, holding his nose to stop another onslaught of giggles.

"Ye miss the big tink, Angus, at times like this," Gavin reminisced, ignoring his older brother's comment.

"Remember the story he told about Mhairi milking her feyther's auld cow," said Hamish, unable to wipe the grin from his face. "And her complaining that one of the tits was useless ..."

"He told her to pull the *udder* one! Very funny," interrupted Gavin sarcastically as he reshuffled the cards.

"Ye both laughed when Angus told the same story!"

"That's the point, Hamish, it's the same bloody story!" said Callum, lighting up his pipe.

"Well at least he's seeing the world," said Gavin in a more sombre tone, as he continued to shuffle the cards.

"Aye, and he might never come back," added Hamish, the first serious comment he had made all night.

"Don't be daft, he'll be back. He only went away tae get enough money tae get married," said Callum, surprised by the anxiety in his own voice.

"Me feyther said that once he's got a taste fur the sea and travelling, it will be hard fur him tae com' back and settle in a wee village like this," said Hamish. "He'll no' have made much money after only four months at sea, anyway."

"That's why he's going away for six months, stupid," said Gavin as he finally dealt out another hand of cards.

"He'll be back!" said Callum, emphatically.

"Ah don't know, Callum. Hamish might be right. Maybe he'll be thinking that there's no' much tae come back tae."

"Yer talking a load of rubbish the pair of ye. He'll be back, like he said, before Christmas. Just ye wait and see. Hurry up and pick a card!"

The brothers looked at each other, but said nothing as the dominoes continued to click in the corner.

The months passed, and the winter eventually lifted from the glen. Fresh spring winds swept away the grey skies, but there was still no sign of Angus returning. In early March, Callum was back out in the fields with his father, getting the ground ready for sowing. The wildlife in the glen was also gradually emerging from their winter hibernation; rabbits were nervously scurrying the fields for early crops to steal; squirrels raced up and down trees in their frantic search for the nuts they had buried in the autumn when food was plenty. The loch was alive again with the long neck grebes and mallards nesting on its banks. Once again, nature's miracle was sweeping over the glen and the naked trees along the loch-side were slowly dressing for summer. For a while life would get easier and before long it would be lambing time on the Macnair croft. For now, at least, Callum had too much work on his hands to be thinking about Angus and his adventures.

Then, in late summer, he received a letter with a large South Africa stamp on it. It was short, but well written, and it was clear that Miss Bothwell's efforts had not been in vain. Angus promised to return home before the summer was over. He was looking forward to a pint in MacTaggart's because the beer in Cape Town was awful.

After reading it a second time, Callum looked at the postmark on the scruffy looking envelope; it had taken over a month to arrive in Glenfay. Angus never mentioned Mhairi or the wedding, so when Callum wrote back, he decided not to tell him that Mhairi had found someone else. What would be the point? He might never return. In spite of the promise in the letter, Angus was away so long now that even Callum had given up hope of seeing him again. How could anyone blame Mhairi for thinking the same?

It was harvest time before Caitriona Dunbar returned to Glenfay, driving through the village in a gleaming new motor car. The villagers, many who had never seen a car before, stood in wonder as it passed them on the way to Leaburn. Over the next few days, the car became a common sight on the narrow roads around the loch as it blasted its horn to signal its sometimes debatable right of way down country lanes and paths, which until recently were only accustomed to the leisurely hoofs of docile cattle and nervous sheep.

One morning, while walking home from the village, Callum stood aside when he heard the car coming up the brae behind him. His heart was thumping as the noise of the engine approached. He stopped on the grass verge to let it pass, quickly looking away when she turned and smiled at him. He felt a sudden panic as the car pulled up, screeching to a slippery stop.

"Hurry up!" she shouted, turning to wave him on. "I'll take you home."

"Och, it's all right!" he nervously shouted back, listening to the coarse sound of his own voice, and instantly hating it. "I'm only up the road, anyway."

"Don't be silly," she shouted, pointing to the grey skies overhead. "It's going to rain in a minute."

The car began to reverse back towards him.

"Jump in," she said, stretching over to open the passenger's door.

"Don't look so frightened. I'm not going to kidnap you or anything," she laughed.

"I don't want tae get yer nice motor car all muddy with me boots," he replied as it started to rain.

"Give them a quick wipe in the grass."

"All right then."

"Have you ever been in a car before?" she asked, watching him clamber awkwardly onto the seat.

"No, there's no' many cars about these parts," he said, stealing a nervous glance at her as she forced the car into gear and pulled out on to the narrow road. The rain was now quite heavy. "Ye don't have a roof?" he asked, trying not to look at her.

"Yes, but it's too much trouble to put it up. Anyway, I like driving in the rain." She smiled at him again, putting her hand through her wet hair, and pulling it away from her eyes.

"Are you living back with your father now?"

"No, I am only here for a few days … I live in Edinburgh with my Aunt. My brother, Duncan, is coming back to help my father run the estate. It's getting too much for him."

"Why do you and your brother live in Edinburgh?"

"My mother died when we were very young and my father thought it would be better if we lived with his sister and went to school in Edinburgh. I love Glenfay, but it's too quiet for me to ever want to live here. I'm too used to the city … You must get awful bored here in the winter?"

"No, there's always work to do."

All too soon the car pulled up.

"How did you know where to stop?" he asked, getting out of the car just as awkwardly as he had got in.

"Oh, I just knew," she said, before driving away, throwing a casual wave over her shoulder. In spite of the rain, Callum stood watching the car race up towards the castle.

That night he lay tossing and turning in the darkness of his bed, his mind tortured by her beauty. He could still see the rain running down her neck, wetting her white blouse against her breasts. He found it hard to leave his dreams when he had to get up that morning.

In September, the glen was bathed in warm sunshine. The last of the harvest was now being gathered in. From the top of the field Callum looked out over the loch as the benign looking clouds drifted slowly above the hills to the east. In spite of himself, he could not stop his gaze drifting to the road leading up to Leaburn Castle.

"Right, son, we had better get some more of this corn lifted while the going is good. I don't like the look of that sky coming in," said Jamie, tapping the ashes out of his pipe on the heel of his boot. "I think there might be some rain on the way."

Callum looked out to where his father was pointing. The western horizon was dark and there was now a cold wind coming in off the sea. It looked like some of the fishermen on the loch had also seen the storm coming and were now heading into port. Callum and Ewan began gathering the cut sheaves and carried them down to the barn as Jamie continued to wield the reaper through the last of the corn.

The winds were not long in bringing the rain to the glen and the sky soon roared with thunder as sheets of lightning flashed over the loch. Callum and Ewan frantically gathered the remaining bales of corn scattered around the field as their father followed them down the hillside. Once in the shelter of the barn, they forked the dry barleycorn into the loft, before spreading the wet bales on the ground to dry out.

"That was a good day's work," said Jamie, looking out at the torrential rain. "We can finish that wee bit at the top tomorrow if the rain lets up."

The next morning the weather was just as bad and very few stirred from their beds before they had to. Betty Macnair was an exception; she braved the foul weather milking the cow and feeding the chickens before the first cock crowed in the glen. Once up, Callum and Ewan helped their father clean out the dung from the byre, scattering fresh straw on the ground before beginning the annual chore of cleaning and sharpening the reapers and scythes in the barn.

"Let's get a bite tae eat, lads. There's plenty of time tae work in this life."

"Stay where ye are," said Betty coming into the barn with a tray laden with food. "I don't want ye all in through the house with those mucky boots."

The two brothers sat on the piles of straw; drinking hot tea and devouring the warm scones, while Jamie puffed on his clay pipe and twisted some corn stalks together in the way his own father had done when he was a boy. "There!" he finally said holding up the woven doll before hooking it onto the outside of the barn door.

"What is it?" asked Ewan.

"It's a corn dolly," said Callum.

"Aye," nodded Jamie. "It will keep the banshees and bogles away when the winter comes."

"Old wives tales," scoffed Callum.

It rained for another six long days and Callum had plenty of time to teach Ewan how to make his own corn doll from the dry stalks of barleycorn in the barn. Each morning was the same; endless grey clouds carried the rain in off the sea and dumped most of it on Glenfay, taking what was left inland towards Stirling and beyond. The sheep looked miserable as they huddled together around the dykes in the lower field.

Then, one morning, the cockerel, which had been too wet and wretched to crow for days, finally welcomed the end of the near biblical deluge, with a hearty cry. A rainbow soon appeared and stretched from one side of the loch to the other, its colours so striking that country-folk, well used to such sights, stopped to stare at its beauty.

By the end of the week, the harvest was finally in and Callum smoked a pipe with his father as they looked at their day's work with a feeling of satisfaction in every puff of tobacco smoke. The barn was fit for bursting with a bumper crop after a rare summer's growth, which would put a smile on the face of even the dourest crofter in the glen. In the lower field, Ewan was still trying to get the knack of using the sickle and practised his technique on a patch of bracken and thistles. Jamie shouted at him to be careful and not to be lashing out or he would be leaving his or someone else's leg in the field. Ewan just laughed and continued to cut the weeds until his arm was sore and the fun had gone out of it. From the top of the field Callum looked out over the loch and the glistening waters as the sun shone across the glen. In spite of the bright sunshine there was an icy chill in the air.

Chapter 5

February 1913

Through the leafless branches Angus could see the dark waters splashing violently against the rocky shore as the castle came into view on the other side of the loch, its ancient walls and turrets defying the elements. He walked briskly along the loch road from Marnock Station, a road he had not walked in nearly two years. In spite of the bitter wind and rain there was a smile on his face as he turned the brae to see Glenfay in the distance. Could it really be two years since he left to seek his fortune, which he now carried in the black rucksack slung over his shoulder? His thoughts were on Mhairi, and his pace quickened with the anxious notion that she may have already found herself a husband, as though a few salvaged minutes would make a difference. Battered by the relentless wind, his pace soon eased off again and he tightened his collar as the rain turned to waves of sleet. On he walked; his battle with the foul weather of little consequence to him when he saw the grey smoke rising from the scattered cottages on the hillside. He would soon be home and have his clothes drying before an open fire, while his mother's broth would quickly banish the chill in his bones.

With every twist and turn on the road he saw old familiar places appear on the horizon that he had often thought about during his long Atlantic voyages, when all that was around him was the endless motion of that vast body of treacherous water. Even now, weeks after coming ashore, he could still feel the swell of the ocean beneath his feet and the salty sea wind in his face. He shifted the rucksack onto his other shoulder as the smell of burning peat blew down the hillside and filled his lungs with a quelled longing that brought back the smile to his lips. There would be no one in the fields on a day like this, he thought, looking across the glen for any sign of life. Apart from the occasional gull looking for scraps of gutted herring along the quayside, the place was strangely quiet. Most of the local fishing boats had already come into the harbour for shelter and those that were still out would be anchored in one of the coast's deep bays, out of the gathering storm that was now taking hold in the glen. He stopped for a moment and wiped the rain from his face when he saw the cottage for the first time. He could almost taste his mother's broth as he quickened his step, only to stop a few minutes later when he heard the sound of laughter coming from MacTaggart's tavern down by the quayside. He stood at the crossroads for a moment as a gust of wind made a last concerted effort to get him home. With a guilty glance at the mist-shrouded cottage, he wiped his lips and turned down towards the harbour as his dire thirst took hold.

The roar of voices soon subsided as he stood at the half-open door and smiled through clouds of smoke at the surprised but familiar faces that turned towards him.

"Well, well, if it's not Angus Campbell. We thought we'd seen the last of you," said MacTaggart, putting down the glass of beer he had just finished pouring.

"Pour me a large whisky, Malcolm, I'm fair buggered ..." said Angus, throwing his bag on the floor and shaking the rain from his cap, "... and there's a drink for anyone wanting tae join me."

Walter MacDougall was first to offer his hand. "Welcome home, lad. It's good tae see ye back. Mhairi will be fair pleased tae see ye safely home. I'll have a whisky, son," he added to a roar of laughter.

"How's she?" asked Angus, encouraged by Walter's tone. "She's no' ran off and got herself married?"

"She'll be up at the house," replied Walter. "You've plenty of time tae see the lass tomorrow. Have a drink and dry yerself at the fire."

Angus took off his heavy reefer jacket and warmed his hands over the flames, as the steam rose from his wet clothes. MacTaggart handed him a glass of whisky and slapped him on the back. "*Slange var,* Angus. Good tae have ye back where ye belong."

"It's good tae be back. Where's Callum?"

"He's through in Marnock," said a voice from the far end of the bar. "He said that he would call in on the way home."

"Hello, Jamie, I didn't see yer there. Ye'll have a drink with us?"

"Aye, sure you know I will."

"Leave the bottle," said Angus turning back to MacTaggart and placing a sovereign on the counter. MacTaggart stared at the gold coin before lifting it and testing its metal between his doubtful teeth.

"Ye think I made it meself," complained Angus, throwing back the glass of whisky and nodding to MacTaggart to fill the empty glasses that clattered on the bar as soon as good manners would allow.

"Sorry, lad, it's not often ye see a gold sovereign in these parts," explained MacTaggart. "The Laird's the only man I've seen with that kind of coin in his pocket and he doesn't part with them very often in here."

"Well, it's as good as any the bloody Laird handed ye and I bet ye didn't put his in yer mouth."

"Sorry, Angus, I didn't mean tae offend … but I don't have enough change …"

"That's all right … just fill these glasses until it's yours to do what ye like wi'. Is there no one working his land today?"

"It's been an awful winter this year," said Jamie, tapping the hot ashes from his pipe onto the floor. The glen's been covered in three feet of snow for near two months. It only started to thaw a few weeks ago and it's been raining ever since. If it doesn't stop soon, we'll all be late this year with the plough."

"I've got a team of horses coming over in a few days, so it had better clear up soon," groaned Hector MacLeod, shaking his head, before consoling himself with another sip of whisky. "I can't afford to have them doing nothing."

"You'll not be able to work that land with a plough for a while yet," said Jamie. "It will need at least a week tae dry out. I did it a few years ago and it nearly killed me. The soil just turned into mud. It has tae dry out … even a few days. That melting snow has left the ground waterlogged. Only a fool would turn their land in this weather."

"All we need is another frost and there'll be no ploughing for weeks," lamented Hector, still shaking his head at the thought of paying for the two horses to stand about idle.

"Ye say the snow was lying for nearly two months … that must have been a hard winter," said Angus, taking his pipe from his pocket and filling it with rich, Virginia tobacco that still had the smell of the plantations about it.

"Harder for some than others," said Jamie, spitting into the fire. "Ye ken the Andersons?"

"Aye, from Dunleer … Hughie …"

"Aye … snowdrifts cut Dunleer off from the rest of the glen for nearly six weeks. When the thaw finally came, a neighbour found the whole family dead. Doctor Wilson said it was a sorry sight for him to endure at his age and still believe in an Almighty. The two bairns were just skin and bones wi' the hunger and it seems that Hughie had taken the shotgun tae his wife and then himself. A terrible sin tae have tae face yer Maker with."

"Why did they not have enough food?"

"Hughie left his crops in the ground too long and it was caught with an early frost. He must have been too proud to let on they were in trouble … When Dunbar heard the news, he sent a letter to each croft in the glen making it clear that we could have a loan of up to ten pounds to help us through the winter and that starvation was not an option in Glenfay. He's not a bad man tae have as Laird."

"Aye, but he wanted interest on the bloody loan," complained Hector, taking the well-thumbed letter from his jacket pocket. "I wouldn't take a penny from him, I'd rather starve."

"He wasn't forcing ye tae take the money, but at least he was giving ye the option," said Jamie.

"That's too bad about the Andersons. It was an isolated place they had, all right," sighed Angus, finishing off his drink, before putting his damp reefer back on and lifting his rucksack. "I better be goin' up the road tae see my folks. There's plenty more drinks left in that sovereign, so order what ye like on me."

"Have another drink, son," said Walter, one eye on Angus while the other followed the bottle in MacTaggart's hand. "You'll have all night tae see yer folks."

Angus smiled at the grunts of encouragement, but it was Jamie's reminder that Callum would be back soon that made him drop his heavy bag back on the flagstone floor. "Aye, all right, for a wee while longer," he agreed, taking the fresh glass of whisky that Walter had thrust into his hand.

"Tell us about yer travels, son!" implored Hector, followed by endorsing nods from the adventure-starved crofters.

After a moment's hesitation, Angus spoke. "When I arrived in Glasgow, it was cold, not unlike today. That night I found a cheap room in a rundown tenement near tae the Clyde. It was a terrible bloody place, with drunks and whores hanging about the close-mouth. After a couple of weeks, the little money I had was gone and there was no work tae be had anywhere. I ended up sleeping rough under a bridge with the rest of the city's down and outs."

"Pour the man another drink," insisted Walter.

"Let him finish his story," said MacTaggart, replenishing the empty glasses, with his mind still on the sovereign that was gradually becoming spent.

"There was no ship to be had, and without a trade no one wanted tae hire me, but I was lucky enough tae get a free meal each day at a Salvation Army soup kitchen down by the docks. I even played the bloody tambourine at their Sunday service with the other hungry beggars, singing hymns we didn't know so they wouldn't stop feeding us."

"That's awful, a bet ye missed yer mother's porridge then," said MacTaggart.

"Aye, but the cold was the worst thing, and I lay each night under that damned bridge shivering to death, listening to the alcoholics talking nonsense to God, wishing I had never left Glenfay."

"Why did ye no' just come home?" interrupted Hector, shaking his head.

"My clothes were like rags by then and I didn't even have the price of a train ticket."

"What happened?" MacTaggart urged. "You're not wearing rags now!"

"Just when I was on the edge of madness, my fortune changed one morning, when I was woken by a sudden splash coming from the Clyde. At first I thought someone had thrown rubbish overboard from a nearby ship and I got up to investigate if there was anything worth fishing out for breakfast. Aye, that's how bad things had got. It was then I saw someone floundering about in the water and heard a commotion coming from the deck of a ship. I quickly realised that a young boy was drowning only ten feet away from me. Without much thought, I threw off my coat and jumped into the river. It was freezing cold and I thought my heart was about to stop, but I still managed to swim out to the boy and grab his collar before his head went under again.I somehow got him back to the riverbank where some sailors hauled us out."

"How did the lad end up in the river?" asked MacTaggart.

"They told me that he had been hanging over the rails when the

46

boat dipped in the water, throwing him overboard. I know I shouldn't be saying it, him being a boy and all, but it was lucky for me that he did fall in. Turns out his father was the owner of the ship and was on board talking with the captain when the boy strayed from his side."

"Was the lad all right?" Walter inquired.

"The boy was fine. The sailors took me on board the ship and gave me a change of clothes and a bowl of hot soup. I stayed there for an hour or so watching the men load the ship's cargo, which was bound for South Africa. I envied them at that moment, like I've never envied anyone in my life."

"Did the boy's father not even thank ye for saving his son?" MacTaggart asked, opening another bottle and generously topping up the glasses along the bar, before finally putting the sovereign in his waistcoat pocket.

"Not at first, no, he was obviously too concerned for his son and left to find a doctor. But the captain thanked me and told me that I could keep the clothes they gave me … but that night, as I lay hungry under that forsaken bridge, the father appeared with two other men from the ship. He told me that the boy was well and handed me a five pound note as a reward. I told him that I did not save the boy for money and refused to take it."

"Why on earth did ye no' take the money, Angus? You hungry in all," asked Gavin Murray, as his brother Hamish nudged him to stop interrupting and spoiling the story.

"I told him I was looking for work that paid a decent wage and not charity. He looked at me rather strangely for a minute and then smiled. Obviously, on hearing my accent, he asked what I was doing in Glasgow. I told him the whole sorry story. He shook my hand again and there were tears in his eyes as he told me that his son would have surely drowned if I had not been there to save him. He then turned to one of the men at his side and exchanged a few words, before turning back and offering me a position on his ship that was bound for South Africa."

"I would have taken the five pounds anyway," interrupted Hamish Murray, before he was hushed to keep quiet by the others.

"Go on, Angus, did ye take the job?" asked Jamie, through a cloud of pipe smoke. Angus took another drink and grimaced in satisfaction as the bracing heat of the whisky rushed across his chest. His glass was filled again as soon as he placed it on the bar. He then lit his pipe again, to moans and groans of displeasure at this unexpected pause in the story. "Where was I?" he finally asked as the tobacco smoke left his lungs to join the cloud hovering among the rafters.

"Did ye take the job?" repeated Jamie.

"Of course, it was the best thing that happened to me since I left Glenfay."

"So ye became a sailor?" asked Gavin.

"No, not quite. I was employed to travel with his agent, Mr Dunlop, a little fat man who always had a cigar in his mouth and at least one thumb in his waistcoat pocket when he was talking to ye. His job was to make sure the owner got the best price for the cargo when it got to Cape Town. He also had instructions to buy up commodities for the return journey."

"What are commodities?" asked Hamish.

"Ivory, animal skins, textiles, anything of value that could be sold back in Britain for a profit," explained Angus, who had asked the same question when he first heard the agent use the word.

"Did it take ye nearly two years to get there and back?" asked MacTaggart.

"No, we sailed on the next tide and it took me a few days to get me sea legs. The ship eventually reached the Canary Islands where we took on some supplies before the long journey down the coast of Africa. For nearly two months we sailed past endless white beaches and thick green jungles under cloudless skies and an unforgiving sun that made some of the men delirious with thirst. The captain knew the coast well enough and we harboured in ports where the natives were friendly, and where we could trade for fresh food and bring on water. My skin soon turned as brown as any native I saw. Once, in Cape Town, the ship was unloaded and we got a fair price for the cargo."

"What was the cargo?" asked Gavin as Angus stopped to take another drink. "It was mainly locomotive parts; boilers, valves, pipes, rods and all sorts of bits and pieces that are in short supply in that part of the world. We spent the next couple of months buying up anything else that Mr Dunlop thought might make a good price back home. Just when things were going well, the agent took ill with malaria. The poor man died after a few days and we had to bury him out there. We still had a half empty cargo hold and with the captain's permission, I used Dunlop's ledger, book of contacts, along with the little that I had picked up from him to buy the last of the things we needed for the long trip home. When we finally got back to Glasgow, I was paid a handsome bonus by the owner and agreed to stay on with the company for another trip as his new agent. This time we went to the Argentine ..."

"The Argentine, where in Africa is the Argentine?" asked Hamish as the others laughed, even though some of them were not all that sure where the Argentine might be.

"It's not in Africa, stupid. It's in South America," interrupted Gavin, shaking his head at his older brother's ignorance.

"Well that story's for another day," said Angus, turning to Jamie and slapping the bar with the palm of his hand. "Let's have some music."

To cheers of encouragement, Jamie Macnair put his fiddle under his chin and began to tune the strings. MacTaggart took a chanter down from the wall behind the bar and passed it to Gavin Murray, who was one of the few in the glen who could keep up with Jamie's twisting reels. "Let's hav' somethin' lively, Jamie, it's not every day we hav' a homecoming!"

That evening had all the ingredients to rival the wake of Dougie Mackenzie, which was now legend in the glen, and even beyond. As with Auld Dougie's wishes, the drink had flowed freely from the bottles of whisky he had hoarded over the years. His wake, as he hoped, was condemned from the pulpit for its drunken merriment and pagan shenanigans. During one boisterous reel, the coffin succumbed to the violent stamping of heavy boots and gradually slipped from the two chairs on which it was precariously perched, throwing the grinning corpse onto the flagstone floor. In horror, the screaming womenfolk ran from the house as their drunken husbands put Dougie back into his box face down. The following morning the undertakers were shocked to find the house littered with snoring mourners. It was reported by many a gossip in the village that the auld man was so disturbed by his kinfolk's antics that he did not wait to be buried before turning in his coffin. Others said that Jamie Macnairs' magic fiddle got him up for one last jig. Now, once again, Jamie's fiddle was laying the foundations to another legend, the homecoming of Angus Campbell, the glen's own Marco Polo.

Angus placed another sovereign on the bar, obliging MacTaggart to go down to the cellar to bring up the good stuff. As the storm took hold, the fishermen from the last boat to reach the safety of the harbour came in to join the party. More instruments appeared to add to the high spirits that only whisky and music could produce on such an awful day. As one whisky followed another, Angus was beginning to feel a bit drunk and was considering going home, while he was still able to, when Callum appeared at the door, soaked to the skin.

"I've no' missed another wake!" he shouted as he entered the noisy, smoke-filled bar, which was now throbbing with music and laughter that had not been heard in the glen for many a year.

"Look what the wind blew in," shouted Angus, getting up to meet his old friend. "How are ye?"

"Angus! When did ye get back? God! Look at ye!"

"A couple of hours ago. What's that you've got there?" asked Angus, pointing to the small black and white head poking out of a wet hessian sack that Callum was carrying under his arm.

"Isn't she a beauty?" grinned Callum, lifting the nervous little pup on to a barstool. "Two shillings I got her for."

"Who sold ye it?" asked MacTaggart, lifting the pup onto the bar.

"Robby Melrose, from over Marnock way, his bitch had a litter of nine, would ye believe?"

"Aye, but if they're anything like that bitch of his, they'll be as good as useless when it comes tae sheep," said Jamie as he lifted the fiddle to his chin again.

The night's mantle fell over the glen and while the music played, the whisky continued to flow into the wee hours. The storm was now over and the skies cleared to let the heavens appear in all their celestial glory. Charles Dunbar was one of the few that night who would even notice the small red dot that was Mars making its way across the cloudless sky.

Chapter 6

Angus's mother was in tears every time she looked at her son's healthy face smiling at her. He had come home that morning, still half drunk, after waking up in MacTaggart's spare bunk with his seafaring boots still on. Molly marvelled at the beautiful silk shawl he wrapped round her thin, bony shoulders, while his father looked at the ivory handled knife for a moment before throwing it on the dresser.

"I prefer me ain tae that fancy piece," he grunted, before walking out of the house without another word.

"The auld bugger," muttered Angus, taking the knife and sticking it back inside his rucksack.

"Och, son, don't mind him. He's missed ye bad these past few years."

"Aye, 'cause he's had nobody tae take his temper oot on. Here, Ma, don't let him get his greedy hands on it," said Angus, handing his mother ten sovereigns.

"No, son, ah cannae tak' yer money. You keep it fur yerself … fur yer future. What dae I need wi' all that money at my age?"

"Here take it," insisted Angus forcing the coins into her trembling hands, which were old before their time from the relentless daily grind. "Everybody needs money. I've got enough of my own."

"Ye'll be up tae see Mhairi now yer back," she said in a cheery voice that pleased him as she put the money in a purse and tucked it under the mattress in the box recess.

"Aye, I was planning tae go and see her this morning."

"She'll be pleased tae see ye. She was over last week with the last letter ye sent. It took two months tae get here, yer very near beat it home."

"How was she?"

"Well, you shouldn't have said ye would be home last Christmas. It was long passed when she got the letter and there was no sign of ye. I worried day and night about ye."

"I had to wait for another boat … it paid twice as much," he said, taking a light from the fire to his pipe. "Like they say, ye have tae make hay when the sun shines. What's another year at my age?"

"Aye," smiled his mother. He speaks like a man now, she thought to herself, as she stirred the pot of piping hot porridge.

His mind still full of memories, Angus tapped the hot ashes from his pipe on the outside wall. He stood for a moment at the back of the house and watched his father with the plough as the furrowed rig appeared in the wet soil at the far end of the field. He recalled Jamie Macnair's words from the night before … "*Only a stubborn fool would take a plough out in this weather.*" In spite of the strong winds, Norman Campbell struggled on in his mud splattered raincoat and ancient Stewarton bonnet, which had covered many a cottar's head before he picked it up during a bothy card game in Marnock. A black cloud of frenzied crows followed in the plough's wake, squawking and cackling like demented wraiths. Angus looked up at the severe looking skies that threatened thunderous rain as the wind blew the ghostly trees and scraggy whin bushes in every direction. Angus's mind drifted back to when he worked alongside his father at this time of year. They would even exchange a few civil words now and again, but he could not forget that once the old man had a few whiskies in the evening, his temper was brutal and unforgiving. Angus blew the last of the tobacco residue from his pipe and went back to eat the breakfast his mother had just put on the table. "Whose horses are those?" he asked as she poured him a bowl of thick porridge.

"He has them on lease. I don't know who he got them from. He tells me nothing."

"This is a fine bowl of porridge. I missed it when I was away …

the city folk don't understand good food."

"Here, there's more in the pot. It will keep the cold out."

"No, enough's enough. I had better be going before that rain that's threatening comes in," he said, scraping the last of the porridge from the bowl.

With the harsh wind in his face and the constant threat of rain, Angus made his way over to the MacDougall croft. At the crossroads, he watched his father on the hillside for a moment, torn between hate and pity, before carrying on down the brae. The hundred and ten sovereigns in his pocket and the encouraging words of Walter from the night before gave him a confident air, and he whistled happily to himself, kicking the occasional stone into the ditch.

Before he reached the cottage, which was just off the brae in the shelter of wind ravished gorse bushes, Mhairi came running down the road to meet him, with her red hair blowing a blazing trail behind her. She jumped into his outstretched arms and he swung her light body through the air. She laughed with delight at her handsome rover's return.

"Ar' ye still wanting tae get married?" he asked, reassured by her welcome.

"Aye, but no' tae ye," she said, pretending to be offended by the suggestion. "It's over two years since ye left so how dae ye know I'm no' already married?"

"Well, if that's the case, I'd better put ye doon," he said, pretending to apologise for his infringement of another man's wife. "I'd better say me farewell...I'm off tae get the train tae Glasgow."

"The train?"

"Aye, I've got another boat waiting in Glasgow. Yer feyther was right, once ye get the taste of the sea it's in yer blood."

"Ye lying swine," she said, catching the grin escaping across his face. "Me feyther said yer were home fur good."

"Only if ye still want tae get married."

"Ye mean ye'll only stay if I marry ye."

"Aye, isn't that why I bothered tae go away in the first place?"

"Aye, fur six months! No' fur two bloody years!"

"Six months, two years, what's the difference? I'm back now."

"I could be married by now wi' a bairn, what would ye have done then?"

"What I'm goin' tae dae now, if ye don't tell me ye still want tae get married."

Mhairi stood for a moment with her hands on her hips, the wind blowing hard against her clothes, pretending to consider the proposal. "When?"

"Today, if ye like."

"Don't be daft, ye haven't got me father's permission yet."

"Don't worry about yer feyther, and I'll buy ye the best dress in the land," he boasted, showing her the purse full of gold coins.

At the kitchen table, a serious-looking Walter MacDougall considered Angus's fresh proposal of marriage to his daughter. Two years before, Walter was not in the least bit happy to give away his only daughter to the son of a cotter. Two years is a long time, and the return of Angus was now such a relief to Walter that he could hardly keep the smile from his prematurely wrinkled face. His change of mind in the matter was on account of Mhairi's short-lived infatuation with Toby Black, one of the biggest rogues in Marnock.

With only a handful of short letters, and Angus gone for over a year, Mhairi became tired of waiting, and began spending more and more time in Marnock, where she met, and fell for Black. Walter was horrified when he heard who his daughter was spending her time with and did everything in his power to stop her travelling through to Marnock at the weekends. But the more he tried to make her see sense, the more she defied him. He was at the end of his tether when fate intervened, and Black ended up in prison after beating a man senseless, over next to nothing. Now contrite, and afraid of Black herself, Mhairi promised her father that she was over the man from Marnock. Even so, Walter was fearful she would change her mind once he was released from prison.

In spite of his eagerness to give Angus his blessing, Walter would need to give the matter the thought and time that custom deemed appropriate. Controlling his own excited curiosity, he asked in a business-like way whether or not Angus was now in a position to support and provide for her. Angus answered by taking his black leather pouch from his coat and boldly scattering its contents of gold coins onto Walter's shaky old table. Walter lost his composure with the glitter of the coins and could not help rushing to catch those that rolled from the table onto the floor. "There!" proclaimed Mhairi proudly. "He's as rich as the Laird himself," she added boastfully, putting a bottle of whisky on the table to lubricate her father's mind.

"Ye have enough money all right … and where will ye live? There're no crofts around here for lease," said Walter, looking at one of the sovereigns with envy, before pouring himself and Angus a generous glass of whisky.

"There's a fine big house lying empty down by the Lea Brig."

"That house has been empty for nearly ten years, since the auld schoolmaster died in it. What good's that tae any man? There's not enough land around it tae keep a chicken alive."

"I don't intend tae work the land. I've got other ideas."

"Not work the land! What else is there tae do with it?"

"I intend tae buy a share in one of the fishing boats. There's more money to be made in fishing herring than keeping a few scrawny sheep and breaking yer back over a plough."

"Aye, that maybe true," said Walter, scratching the grey stubbles on his chin again as Mhairi got up from the corner and poured him another whisky. "Are ye still here? Away and feed the hens 'til we finish this bit of business."

"Business!" she scolded, banging the whisky bottle down on the table. "Yer no' selling me, ye auld goat! I've as much right tae be here as the pair of ye!"

"Ye'll put the poor lad off the idea all together with that temper."

"I'm staying! So put that in yer pipe and smoke it!"

"Nae wonder I'm grey before me time," said Walter, pouring Angus another whisky. "She's been reading too much about those suffragettes that chain themselves to lampposts if they don't get their way."

"Who's trying to put him aff marriage now!" snapped Mhairi.

"Well if ye still want her, she's all yours," said Walter. "But ye better get up early or ye might find her wearing your breeches one morn."

Walter was a happy man when he poured his future son-in-law another glass of whisky to formally give his blessings to the match.

"Get yer coat, Mhairi," said Angus as he finished his whisky and shook hands with Walter. "Let's go see the schoolmaster's house before it gets dark."

The bracing wind blew in their faces as they stood looking at the neglected building that had once been a fine two storey house. The roof had lost most of its slate tiles and the door hung from its rusty hinges. They looked in at the dreich front room, which was smelling of damp and cluttered with old bits of broken furniture. Mhairi held on to Angus's arm as she trod carefully through the rubble and sheep droppings.

"It's horrible," she said.

"Aye, that's why we'll get it for next to nothing. We'll have enough money to gut it out and make it into a fine house again. In a few months ye'll not know the place."

"I don't know, Angus. It's in an awful state. It will take a small fortune to fix it up."

"We'll have enough."

Chapter 7

The spring sunshine gradually took the dew off the fields and lifted the mist from around the loch shores as the wedding party arrived at the village church. Almost defiantly, the last of the winter snow clung to the mountain tops as the River Lea rushed through the glen with peat-coloured melt water frothing against the rocky foreshore. Angus wore the full highland dress of clan Campbell and waited anxiously before the altar as Mhairi entered the Kirk on her father's arm in a plain white dress that once belonged to her late mother. On cue from her husband, the minister's wife began to play Mendelssohn's *Wedding March* on the Kirk's ancient organ. With the curiosity of a child, Angus could not stop himself from turning to catch a glimpse of his beautiful bride as she walked regally towards him. Standing next to Angus was his best man, Callum Macnair, holding the wedding ring tightly in the palm of his hand, afraid he would lose it if he could not feel it digging into the folds of his skin.

As Walter gave over his daughter's hand to Angus, the minister began his sermon on the sanctity of marriage and the odious sins of the flesh that the devil used to tempt the weak into damnation. "Marriage is for the procreation of children and not for the sinful pleasures of the vain," he proclaimed to the uncomfortable-looking congregation. His voice was hoarse by the time he closed his leather bound bible with its usual clap of thunder before leaving the pulpit and confronting the anxious couple with their responsibilities to each other and to God Almighty.

With their vows finally exchanged, the newlyweds and their guests walked down the brae along the loch-side as the church bells echoed across the glen. The wedding feast was to be held in the village hall which was a good country mile from the Kirk. Angus held Mhairi's hand at the head of the procession until they finally reached the door of the hall.

After a main course of stewed beef and potatoes, which Angus barely touched on account of the butterflies in his stomach, the Reverend called on the groom to say a few words. Angus gave an awkward smile and nervously looked around the familiar faces in the smoke-filled hall. His face was flushed with anxiety as beads of perspiration appeared on his forehead. On rising to his feet, he wiped his large sweaty palms on the sides of his kilt, before fumbling open a small piece of paper, which he produced from his waistcoat pocket. The paper unfolded to show as many scores and crosses on it as words. The clatter of cups and spoons subsided and a hushed silence fell on the hall.

He coughed nervously before speaking. "Ladies and gentlemen... friends and relations..." he began with rehearsed vigour, but within seconds the words dried up and as he glanced back down at the piece of crumpled paper, gripped in his shaking hands, its contents now looked like a cryptic puzzle, which his panicked mind could no longer decipher. Telling stories in a bar with a drink in him was second nature to Angus, but this was different and his mind became completely blank. "Ah ... Ah ..." he struggled, unable to look at the faces gawking at him in silent embarrassment.

"Get on with it!" Hamish Murray shouted, enjoying Angus's discomfort.

"Ladies and gentlemen," he began again, this time bracing himself, determined to say what he had to say to get the ordeal over with.

"I would... I mean. We would... I mean Mhairi and me..." Angus soon lost his way and the terrible silence fell on the hall once again. "We'd like tae thank ye fur being here today and fur all the wedding presents we got," Angus rattled nervously. "I would also like tae thank Jenny and Maggie fur being our bridesmaids and of course, I would like tae thank Mhairi fur making me the happiest man in Glenfay ..."

"In Scotland ye mean," interrupted Walter.

"Aye, Scotland," agreed Angus, sitting down quickly.

"You haven't toasted the bridesmaids," whispered Mhairi, tugging at his arm.

"Ah, I nearly forgot," he said, getting back to his feet. "I would like ye tae all raise yer glasses and toast the bridesmaids. Tae the bridesmaids!"

"The bridesmaids."

Angus sat down again, acknowledging the generous applause his angst-ridden speech received. Cheers and whistles started again as Callum rose to his feet.

"Ladies and gentlemen," he began surveying the audience in a nonchalant manner in sharp contrast to Angus's fumbling, "as best man, I've been asked tae say a few words about the happy couple..." He began to tell some anecdotes about Angus and how he seemed to prefer sheep to Mhairi when they were at school together.

"He still does!" shouted Hamish Murray; pushing back his seat to get out of his grandmother's slapping range.

Norman Campbell was stony-faced throughout the meal and speeches. He sat beside Mhairi's Aunt Margaret and hardly said a word to the woman. Once the meal was over it was only the whisky that kept him from leaving altogether and he took full advantage of the bottles that were placed on the top table. The whisky was just as eagerly courted by the Reverend Knox, who had initially refused to marry the couple on account of the Campbell's failure to attend church on the Sabbath. A promise from Angus that he would attend in future was not sufficient to shift the Reverend, but a payment of two pounds from Mhairi's desperate father finally won the minister over.

As the minister got to his feet, a gust of wind and rain blew open the door at the side of the hall, blowing out some of the candles on the nearby tables. The door was quickly closed and the Reverend regained the attention of his flock by tapping the table with the butt end of his teaspoon.

"Thank you, Callum, that was a very good speech," he said, not having listened to a word of it. "Anyway, this is Angus and Mhairi's big day and I am sure you will agree it has been a lovely day so far. I hope this sudden change in the weather …" he paused, raising his eyes to the tin roof, "doesn't interfere with the dancing still to come."

"It's only an April shower," shouted Hamish, hiding behind his brother.

"Thank you, Hamish; your wisdom is always appreciated. Now, as you all know the groom, himself, who I hear has taken to the bagpipes like a duck to water, has agreed to start the fun by playing for us. I'm sure the Murray brothers will keep him right. So if some of you young men can help move these tables then the dancing can begin."

With the speeches over, the minister quietly slipped out the back door with Walter's two pounds tucked away in his leather purse. In a buzz of activity, some of the more able women cleared the tables, which were then rearranged by the menfolk to clear the centre of the floor. The three pipers were still tuning up when they entered the hall to cheers and whistles. Angus was magnificent with his black doublet jacket, his sporran dancing a jig as he marched in a circle around the hall blasting out, 'Bonny Mary o'Argyll'. The guests clapped and stamped their feet in time to the pipes.

Eventually, Angus dropped out and left his pipes, still heaving, on one of the tables by the door. The Murray brothers took up their rehearsed positions at the far side of the hall and Angus held out his hand for Mhairi, who eagerly grasped hold of it. He led her into the centre of the floor and, after making a gallant bow, took his new bride in his arms as they danced to the delight of their enthusiastic guests. After the first dance, the Murray brothers were happy to leave their pipes at rest and get to the bar as Jamie Macnair's fiddle began to play, accompanied by Hector MacLean on the accordion and Hector's son, Hughie, on the tin whistle. The reels and jigs soon followed one another without a pause.

"One of ye go and give Mhairi a dance. I'm fair buggered," said Angus taking a seat beside Callum and the Murray brothers.

"There's Hamish, he'll give her a dance. I feel a right eejit in this bloody kilt," said Callum.

"Don't be getting me involved. You're the best man."

"Please dance wi' her, Callum. She's sick being asked by all these auld goats that can hardly walk never mind dance," pleaded Angus, sweat dripping from his red face.

"Aye, all right," conceded Callum. "I'll ask her in a minute. Let's go and get a drink first."

The clatter of rain on the tin roof was now drowned out by the thuds of boots on the wooden floor, keeping time with the lively music. Mhairi was dancing with her Uncle Ned; her long red hair a flame against her white dress and her tartan sash. The Murray brothers looked on as the dancers criss-crossed the room.

"Do you think Angus has bedded her yet?" whispered Hamish, nudging Gavin in the ribs.

"Shut up, stupid, there he's coming back," snapped Gavin, pushing his brother's irritating elbow away from his side. Angus pulled up a chair beside the two brothers and banged his tumbler on the table after taking a huge drink that left the glass half empty.

"*Strip the Willow*, I hate that bloody dance. Where's Callum?"

"He's away for a pee," said Gavin.

"He's been away for ages," continued Angus, taking a cursory glance around the hall.

"He's probably away fiddling wi' Maggie McPherson again," Hamish sniggered, followed by a short controlled grunt.

"Shut up!" whispered Gavin, nodding over to where Maggie's

grandmother was sitting.

"Och, that auld hag is as deaf as a lump of wood," said Hamish as he waved over to the old woman. Maggie's grandmother smiled back showing a mouth of broken yellow teeth. "Look at the auld witch; you'd think she was eating cow dung all day."

At this, Angus gasped and gulped in a convulsive fit before spraying the table and the two brothers with a mouthful of beer. The brothers looked at each other and burst into fits of laughter.

A cheer went up when Ewan Macnair shyly joined his father on the rostrum, counting in the time for the next jig with his waving bow. Gasps of delight could be heard over the thuds of heavy boots as the young pretender's fingers danced with ease along the bridge of his fiddle.

"He's only twelve ye know and as good as his father already," proclaimed one admirer.

"Aye, sure it's in the blood all right," said another.

As Callum watched his younger brother play, he smiled to himself, recalling the long nights he had watched his father teach Ewan the jigs and reels he was now playing with such ease. With the whisky rising in his mind, Callum was beginning to feel dizzy with the constant thud of dancing feet on the wooden floor. He staggered back to his chair beside Gavin and Hamish, who were now arguing over the shape of their noses.

"Callum, sure his nose is bigger than mine?" slurred Gavin, feeling the size of his own nose for reassurance. "Sure it is?"

Callum looked at Gavin for a moment. "Aye," he said, turning his back on them both.

"Ye see, I told ye."

"Och, shut up stupid. He's only said that, so as no' tae hurt yer feelings. Yer nose is like an elephant's trunk," said Hamish.

"Aye! And your face is like an elephant's arse. I'm going to find me a woman," retorted Gavin, before getting up to wander around the edge of the dance floor, spilling his beer at every bump he received from flailing arms as the jigs and reels became more frantic.

The music suddenly stopped for a while to let Hector Macleod sing an old Scottish lament. The clatter of cutlery and whispering voices hushed as Hector began: *'On a windy moor, such a cold, cold place...'*

When the song ended and the applause faded around the room, the door at the side of the hall suddenly opened and Charles Dunbar, briskly shaking the wet from his umbrella, entered the hall with his daughter at his side.

"There's the Laird himself in wi' that good-looking lass of his," said Hamish, with a burp of satisfaction as he emptied his glass of beer. Callum turned towards the door to look for Caitriona. He said nothing, but eagerly cast his eyes over towards the crowd that had gathered around the Laird and his daughter.

"Anybody wanting something to eat?" asked Hamish, getting to his feet to join the growing queue at the buffet table.

"Get me a salmon sandwich, Hamish," said Angus, staggering back to the table with a fresh tray of drinks, and immediately noticing Callum's distraction.

"Have ye no' had enough?" complained Mhairi taking Angus by the arm. "The Laird's here wi' his daughter. You'll have tae come over and say hello."

"Aye, give me a minute tae down this," he said, lifting his pint of beer to his lips. "There!" he said with a satisfied grin as he put the empty glass back on the tray.

"Yer a bloody glutton!" said Mhairi, dragging him away to meet their important guests.

"She's a good looking woman now," said Angus, nudging Callum on the shoulder. Callum pretended not to hear and turned away to finish his drink. Mhairi pulled Angus away by the arm.

Crestfallen, Gavin eventually came back to the table. "There's no' a decent looking women in this place," he complained, slumping back on to his chair. Hamish was now too drunk to care. Callum said nothing. He was again watching Caitriona, who was laughing at something Angus was saying to her. Gavin was about to say something, but he had forgotten what it was by the time his brain engaged his mouth. "Do ye want another drink?" he eventually asked. But Callum did not answer, and Gavin got up and staggered over to the bar to drown his sorrows. Callum continued to watch from afar as Caitriona followed her father around the room to meet the other guests, his heartbeat quickened as they came near to where he was sitting with Hamish.

In time, the music resumed and the crowd gradually dispersed from the far side of the hall as Caitriona turned and smiled warmly at Callum. He nervously grinned back, before quickly looking away as his face began to redden. He was relieved to see that Gavin was still at the bar, while Hamish was lying face down on the table, his head bouncing on his folded arms in a fit of hiccups, which seemed to have originated in his boots. Callum sipped his beer and, after a few moments, stole another look in Caitriona's direction but she was gone.

When the night came to an end, Angus and Mhairi were ushered into the centre of the dance floor, while their friends and relations encircled them in a continuous chain of criss-crossed arms. The chain moved in and out to the chanting of *Auld Lang Syne*, as Angus and Mhairi clapped and smiled at this constantly moving circle of familiar faces.

"Where's Callum?" slurred Gavin, taking a seat beside Hamish after cheering the bride and groom off to their carefully prepared room at her Aunt Margaret's house.

"Don't know and I don't care," grunted Hamish. "I think I'm going to be sick."

Callum stood at the edge of the loch watching the silver moonlight on the water's surface. The far edges stretched out into the infinite darkness of the night. A cold breeze caused him to brace himself and he buttoned up his jacket before skimming another stone over the water's surface. He watched it bounce three times before disappearing with a plop into the loch. He looked up at the haunted silhouette of Leaburn Castle in the moonlight. There was a yellow glow from one of the rooms and he imagined Caitriona standing at her bedroom window looking down on him. He picked up another pebble from the edge of the loch and skimmed it across the water. The moon was now slowly disappearing behind thick clouds. He looked back up towards the castle, which was now almost impossible to make out in the blackness of the night. He touched the small scar above his eye, recalling the day she left her indelible mark on him.

The excitement of the wedding day behind them, the following week the newlyweds made their way into Marnock to put a deposit down on the house. It took another month before the missives were concluded and the keys handed over. With the long summer days ahead of him, Angus went about restoring the two-storey house to its former glory. Within a few months the roof was repaired and the walls plastered and whitewashed. When the inside was finally finished, he fetched Mhairi's furniture from her father's cottage and they finally moved in just as the summer was coming to an end. They toasted the house with a glass of whisky before going upstairs, where Angus enticed his wife into the newly made bed.

Mhairi was up early the next morning and travelled on her uncle's boat to Marnock where she planned to buy some new curtains. When she was gone, Angus put on his old clothes and began to paint the window frames at the front of the house. After a few hours, he stood back to admire his morning's work, wiping his paint-covered hands with a rag, soaked in turpentine. He lit his pipe and sat for a while to watch the waves rolling in over the rocky foreshore. The smell of turpentine soon made him feel dizzy and he put away his pipe to give his hands a thorough wash. 'I'll get those other two done before Mhairi gets back from Marnock,' he promised as he dried his hands and put on his jacket.

'Life is no' that bad,' he agreed with himself as he walked along the dry dirt path, kicking stones and jingling coins in his pockets. She's a bonny lass all right, he mused, thinking about her naked flesh pressed against his body all night. His happy disposition was heightened with the aromatic smells of late summer that rushed into his lungs with every breath. Two magpies darted overhead, chasing each other in wild sweeping movements across the fields before disappearing into the woods along the loch-side.

By the time Angus reached the Macnair's cottage, Callum was already walking down the hillside with Tess at his heel. They waved to each other. Angus lit his pipe again, and sat on a stone dyke to wait for his friend.

"How's married life?" asked Callum, throwing his cap down on the grass verge and falling down beside it. "Ye look fair pleased wi' yerself."

"I was wondering if ye would join me in a wee dram, my good man."

"Aye, and since ye want tae be playing at the Laird, then you can pay for it."

"It will be my pleasure."

It was after midnight before Angus staggered home and found Mhairi sitting up by the fire with a face that demanded an explanation but was not prepared to listen to any. She thrashed him with a tantrum of slaps as he tried to kiss her.

"Get yer drunken hands off me! Ye'll no' sleep in the same bed as me tonight!" she shouted, running upstairs and slamming the bedroom door behind her.

"Och, it's a terrible auld life," he mumbled to himself as he tried to sleep on the cold slate floor, with only a few blankets and the whisky to keep him warm. That was Angus well and truly married.

Chapter 8

After a bitterly cold winter, the weather turned fine again, and the ploughing soon gave way to the sowing of barley and potato crops. Within a few weeks the heather was blooming on the hills above the loch and the first shoots were appearing in the lower fields. It was around five in the morning, and Betty Macnair was stooping over a large cast iron cooking pot, which hung from the *slabhraidh*, above the open peat fire. Apart from the flickering light from the fire, the cottage was still in darkness. The morning's porridge spluttered to the boil as she stirred it in a trance, her tired mind remembering the long summers of her youth when life seemed so easy. The wall clock above the fireplace chimed loudly and brought her back from her distant thoughts.

"Callum! It's time to get up! Your father's already out and about," she scolded, scooping a couple of ladles of the thick oatmeal into a wooden bowl.

"Aye, I'm coming," he groaned from the comfort of his bed in the far corner of the room, screened off from the rest of the house by an old curtain. He pulled his head back under the warm bedclothes. Another five minutes, he kept promising to himself as he slowly drifted back into his dreams. These were pleasant dreams, which he wanted to experience as long as possible before the realities of daily life destroyed them. With the sound of banging out at the back of the house and the shuffling of his mother around the fire, he could not recapture the elusive thoughts that seemed so real only moments before.

As he lay awake, the daylight began to seep through the wooden shutters and under the door. He finally jumped out of bed and quickly dressed, pulling his woollen socks on first, giving his feet some protection against the cold stone floor. Ewan was still fast asleep and dreaming about whatever young boys dreamt about.

"Where's feyther?" asked Callum, taking a ladle of fresh water from a tin bucket and pouring it into a bowl.

"He's oot the back getting things ready."

"God, it's cold this morning," Callum said and shivered as he briskly dried himself in front of the blazing fire.

"Eat this and you'll soon warm up," said his mother, handing him a bowl of hot porridge. He opened the shutters to see what kind of weather was in store, his gaze drifting towards the castle where its familiar outline was taking shape with the emerging streaks of daylight.

"Your breakfast will get cold if you stand there daydreaming," said his mother as she sat herself down beside the fire. "It looks like it's going to be a fine morning."

"Aye, but there's still a bit of a nip in the air," he replied, closing the shutter with an exaggerated shiver to make his point.

"Have you shouted Ewan?" he asked, nodding his head in the direction of the box bed, which was still silent and in complete darkness.

"Och, let him be for another wee while. It's too early for a bairn to be up."

"Ah, rubbish. I was up and about at this time when I was his age."

"He's no' as strong as you were when ye were his age," said his mother, placing another piece of peat on the fire. "Don't be wakening him up now," she added.

Callum ignored her words and pulled back the drape and let the warm glow of the fire cast some light on his brother's freckled face and fair hair.

"Och, he's lying there wi' a big grin on his face."

"Come away from there, will you."

"Right, Tess, we had better get out and see how the auld yin's getting on wi' the sheep dip."

Callum took a deep breath of the crisp morning air as he pulled up his collar and emerged from the cottage. The hills around the loch were beautifully covered in the early spring flowers of purple and pink heather. It was still a cold morning but the icy winds of the winter were gone and the morning breeze was more fresh than bitter. Tess followed him to the back of the cottage where his father was mixing the chemicals for the sheep dip.

"Another six or seven buckets will fill her," said Jamie, wiping the sweat from his brow and pouring another bucket of water into the medicated tank.

"I'll get them, feyther. You sit down for a minute and have a rest," insisted Callum, taking the empty buckets from his father's grateful hands. As he made his way to the well, his father sat down by the side of the house and filled his clay pipe with the last of his tobacco. The morning mist was now beginning to clear from the cold waters of the loch and the brim of a feeble, yellowish sun rose over the hills. A stream of sunlight suddenly ran across the glen and over the grey surface of the loch.

"Look!" Callum called, with water splashing around his feet as he stumbled to a halt on the slippery path. "There's Hector and Glen coming up the road!"

Jamie Macnair cast his gaze through a mist of tobacco smoke in the direction indicated by Callum's outstretched arm. "Aye, so it is. Hector said he'd give us a hand this morning. There's no' a better team than them two when it comes tae it."

"Tess! Com' back here," shouted Callum as the young collie ran down the brae to meet the older dog. The two men greeted each other with a vigorous handshake. Hector was a man of some sixty years, although he was not sure of his actual age; he had been born in a time of famine when people had more to worry about than how old things were. His chalk white hair was complemented by a long white beard which was now turning a sort of sallow colour around his mouth, due to his habit of smoking his pipe from early morning until the last puff of tobacco smoke was used to blow out his bedside candle.

Now that the law required sheep to be dipped at least twice a year, Hector found his services to be in great demand. Although the Macnairs had only around thirty sheep, it took most of the morning to simply find them as they were not only scattered over the open hillside but mixed in with all the other sheep that grazed freely on the upper slopes. The sheep were mainly cheviots with the odd black head mixed in for good measure, but so were most of the other sheep in the glen. Only the Laird, with his two thousand or so sheep, had sufficient land to graze his flock on rich low-lying fields, where they were kept in top condition. His flock had all kinds of rare breeds, many of which were regular prize winners at the annual Highland Games held near Marnock each summer.

Betty heaped a second helping of porridge into Hector's bowl, smiling uncontrollably at Hector's assertions that it was the finest bowl of porridge he'd tasted in a long time.

"Och, it's a fine way tae start the morning," he added, scraping the wooden bowl clean of its contents for a second time.

"C'mon, let's get some work done," said Jamie.

"Och, man! Hold yer horses," insisted Hector. "Give the dawn a chance tae break; we've got all day tae get the damn sheep dipped. Sit yersel down and have a smoke wi' me."

"Aye, well. Another five minutes won't hurt," said Jamie, accepting Hector's tobacco pouch.

By noon, the weak spring sun had disappeared behind a blanket of slow moving clouds. A short, but heavy, shower of rain left the hillside looking as if it had just been covered with a thin coat of clear varnish. The fine spring morning had been mysteriously replaced by a cold, damp winter's afternoon.

"Did you hear the cuckoo?" asked Hector, sheltering with the others under a solitary silver birch tree."If ever you need a sign that spring has arrived, that's the sign."

"It doesn't look like spring now," said Callum, sticking his hand out to test if the rain had finally stopped. "C'mon, the rain's nearly off," he declared.

"Well the sooner we get moving, the sooner we can head back," said Jamie.

"Och, don't be in such a hurry, man. There's only a handful of sheep still to be brought down," protested Hector as he lit his pipe again.

"It's all the same tae me," replied Callum, his voice sounding detached and uninterested.

"I see that young Angus Campbell made a great job of that old house down by the quay that's been lying empty since the auld schoolmaster passed away," said Hector.

"Aye, so I hear. It's a fine big house," said Jamie.

"Good luck tae them," said Hector. "They make a grand couple and they must be near a year married by now."

"Aye," agreed Jamie. "He's a good lad and he got the best looking girl in the village."

"C'mon or we'll be here all day," interrupted Callum. "Tess, here lass," he shouted at the young collie.

"Ah well, no rest for the wicked," said Hector as he reluctantly smothered the smoke from his pipe, before tucking it into his waistcoat pocket. "Lead on, young man!"

The three men braced themselves against the bitter wind, and battled their way back up the hillside; their legs now tired and heavy in their struggle through the wet ferns and slippery moss. The sky directly above Glenfay was relatively light as the clouds floated over the hills heading in the direction of Marnock. Tess and Glen sprinted playfully on in front, stopping every so often to look back at their masters' slow progress. When the three men reached the next ridge, they stopped to catch their breath and take in the view below. The cottage was too close to the hillside to be seen and the only indication of its whereabouts was a spiral of smoke which spirited upwards before being quickly dispersed in the wind. When they turned to continue their climb, Callum came across unusual-looking animal droppings. Apart from sheep, the only other droppings that Callum ever noticed on the hills were of rabbits.

"Deer?" he asked as his father and Hector came over to investigate.

"Aye," agreed Hector, prodding the find with the bottom of his crook. "It looks like red deer tae me. What dae ye think, Jamie?"

"Well, it's no' sheep anyway. That's for sure."

"Even I knew that," said Callum. "They're too..."

"Look!" said Hector. "Look," he repeated, with a sense of wonder in his hushed voice. They stood in silence and took in the vision of a wild stag and two hinds grazing less than fifty yards away. It was the stag that stood out magnificently with its thick winter coat and fully developed crown of antlers.

"It's a royal stag," whispered Hector.

"What do you mean?" asked Callum.

"Ye must have heard of a royal stag?"

"Aye, but what's the difference?"

"It's antlers. If it's got twelve points, then it's a royal stag. Look, count them yerself."

As Callum counted, the wind suddenly changed direction and the three deer stopped grazing to look nervously around. The stag's clay-coloured eyes turned to stare in their direction and then with a wild and defiant cry, it darted after the two fleeing females and was gone.

"Magnificent animal," Hector sighed. "When I was a boy you'd see deer like that on the hills every day. Now they're all nearly gone. Shot for sport. It's a damned disgrace."

"Aye, those with money don't care what damage they do," said Jamie.

After a final look in the direction where they last saw the deer, they resumed their climb and followed the criss-crossed paths left in the wet heather by the impatient dogs. Glen and Tess had already tracked down two of the strays. The nervous sheep huddled together, pinned down by the strategic positioning of the dogs and a stone dyke which cut off any escape. "Good girl," called Callum. Tess relaxed her guard on hearing his voice, her tail wagging frantically. Glen showed no emotion.

It was agreed that Jamie should take the two strays down the hillside, while Callum and Hector continued the search for the nine ewes that remained at large. While Jamie cajoled the two sheep down through the heather, a shower of hailstones made visibility even worse. Hector suggested calling it a day. "You and Glen head down if ye like," was all Callum said. Hector felt a twinge of guilt but thankfully it was not fatal and he turned and followed the trail back to the Macnair's cottage and the bowl of hot broth that he hoped would be waiting for him.

Callum continued alone and soon Tess came upon another ewe; only this one was lying dead in a ditch. It looked as though it had been dead for only a few hours and there was no obvious hint as to how it had met its end. There was nothing unusual about finding a carcass in this way, especially one as old as this ewe. He covered the animal with some bracken and heather then carried on looking for the remaining strays. It was not long before he found a second dead ewe. The rump of the sheep had been eaten away and what remained was now infested with maggots. He found a clue to the probable culprit; a fox's den lay concealed in the mangled bracken only a few yards from the carcass. There was a strong stench of urine around the den and he found pieces of wool and blood at the entrance. By now he was soaked to the skin and feeling totally miserable. He decided to give up the search for the remaining sheep. He made his way down the hillside, cursing the foul weather.

As he stood at the front door, scraping the mud off his boots, his mind was still on the two dead ewes. He was determined to go back up as soon as the rain stopped.

"Yer drenched, the pair of ye," exclaimed his mother as he and Tess entered the cottage looking like drowned rats.

"Ye should have came doon wi' yer feyther."

"I was soaked then anyway."

"Aye, all the more reason for coming doon. I'm surprised at yer feyther for letting ye bide up there in this foul weather."

"He's his own man now," said Jamie. "Sit here," he added, getting up to give his son a chair near the fire.

"Here, eat this up," insisted his mother as she scooped another ladle of broth into his bowl.

"Great, Ma, where's auld Hector?" he asked as Tess snuggled up beside him by the fire, her thin body shivering against his feet.

"He's away home," said Jamie. "Did ye find the other sheep?"

"Ah found two, but they were dead."

"Dead?"

"Aye. Ah think a fox got one."

"A fox will no' kill a sheep, son."

"Well a tell ye. We found it only a few yards from a fox's den."

"Where was the den?"

"Up near tae the old Henderson cottage."

"Aye, there'll be foxes up there all right. There's an old badger's den up there. The foxes have been using it for years. But I've never known them tae take a grown sheep."

"Well, they have now. Ah saw the carcass eaten away and it was only a couple of yards from the den. It must have killed it."

"It would have tae have been a big fox and a sick sheep."

"Ah bet if it was hungry enough it could take a sheep."

"Ah don't see how it can be that hungry. Those hills are teaming wi' rabbits. I'm sure if the foxes were that hungry they would be down trying tae take a hen or two."

"The sheep are dead and one's lying next tae a fox's den. What else dae ye need tae know?"

The room fell silent for a moment. Callum devoured the thick broth and handed the empty bowl back to his mother, who was quietly stirring what was left in the pot. Without a word being spoken, she emptied the last of the broth into his empty bowl. The steam was now rising from the legs of his wet trousers, adding to the damp, muggy atmosphere that now prevailed in the cottage.

"The rain's off again," said Jamie as he closed the side shutter. "Why don't we take a walk up this afternoon and see what's what?" he added, taking the rarely used shotgun from the wall.

"Can I come?" pleaded Ewan who was excited at the sight of the shotgun. "Are ye goin' tae shoot the fox?"

"No, yer no' goin' up those hills on a day like this," proclaimed his mother.

"But, Ma! It's no' raining. And I've never seen me Da using the shotgun before."

"Ye heard yer mother. It's no' a day for climbing those hills. When ye get tae ma age, ye'll no' be so keen either."

"But, Da!" he sulked, before turning to Callum for support.

Callum just shrugged his shoulders and went into the backroom to change into dry clothes. Ewan took another desperate look at his mother and father then broke into a fit of crying. This was only tolerated for a few minutes before a sudden slap across his face, from his mother, muted his protests to mere snivels and the occasional glare of token defiance.

"Och, don't be such a bairn," teased Callum as he came back into the room.

"Shut up," sobbed Ewan.

"You'll be up there five minutes and be crying tae get home," said his mother, feeling guilty with her own quick temper.

"I'll no'."

"Well, get yer heavy boots. And don't be giving' yer feyther and Callum any bother. Dae ye hear?"

"Aye," replied Ewan, grinning through the tears as he wiped his eyes and cheeks with the sleeve of his pullover.

"Well, hurry up," said Jamie with a smile. Ewan rushed to get his boots.

It was now late afternoon and, although the rain had remained off, the sky was still very dull. The long grass and ferns soaked their trousers as they brushed by them on the way back up to find the dead sheep. Ewan was happy at being allowed on this great adventure with his father and brother but, as expected, by the time they had reached the first ridge, he began falling behind with his tired legs and heavy boots. Callum and his father stopped for a moment at the spot where they had seen the three deer that morning, giving Ewan a chance to catch up. They both looked around in hope of another sighting of the stag, but there was no sign of it or its female companions. Ewan finally appeared beside them moaning and groaning about his wet clothes and tired legs. He quickly stopped his complaining when his father threatened to take him straight back down the hill if there was another whimper out of him. Tess had rushed on as usual and was scratching frantically at the ground beside the mound of heather, ferns and bracken, which Callum had used to cover the first dead sheep.

Callum pulled the dead ewe clear of the ferns and lifted it up by the hind legs for his father to have a good look at it. After a few minutes of prodding the carcass, a final shake of the head signalled the end of the examination and Callum dropped the sheep back into the ditch.

"Strange," said Jamie, still shaking his head. "There's no' a mark on it."

"Well, it's dead, that's for sure," said Callum, rather sarcastically.

"Yer fox never got a bite at it anyway," retaliated his father.

"We're still goin' tae shoot the fox, aren't we?" asked Ewan, hopefully.

"We'll see," replied his father, before putting two cartridges in the shotgun.

By the time they reached the dyke where Callum thought he found the second ewe, the sky was so overcast and dull that he was not too sure if they were at the right place. A couple of sharp barks from Tess pointed them in the right direction. Ewan was first to reach the carcass after the dogs. "Ugh, did the fox do that?" he grimaced as he stared at the partially eaten remains of the ewe. "Oh, it stinks."

"It stinks all right," agreed his father, repelling back as he caught a whiff of the putrid carcass in his nostrils. "It reeks of fox's piss. Don't go near it!" he shouted as Ewan poked the sheep with a broken branch he had found nearby.

"Over here!" called Callum.

"Aye, that's an auld badger's den," said Jamie, squatting down at the mouth of the hole for a better look into its mysterious blackness.

"What dae ye think now?" asked Callum, convinced that there was no other explanation.

"Aye, it looks like ye might be right."

"What dae ye mean, might be right? Ye saw it for yerself."

"Aye, but ..."

"Ye said yerself the sheep was stinking of fox's piss."

"Aye, but that doesn't mean the fox killed the sheep. It ate it all right and marked it ... but ..."

"Are we goin' tae kill the fox?" asked Ewan again.

"It's probably a vixen wi' young cubs. That's the only thing I can think of," conceded Jamie.

"What's a vixen?" asked Ewan.

"It's a female. A mother fox that killed the sheep to feed its cubs," explained Callum as he continued to prod inside the den with his crook.

"There's no point poking it with a stick. If they're in there, they will be well back. The only thing tae do is tae smoke them out."

"Da, we're no' goin' tae kill the mother and her cubs, are we?" pleaded Ewan, now concerned for the family of foxes.

"You just stay out of the way."

"We won't be able tae get anything tae light. The heather's soaking," explained Callum, throwing another spent match away.

"Ye might get something from Henderson's auld cottage that will burn. Take Ewan with ye."

The Henderson's cottage, as it was still known long after anyone by that name lived there, was just slightly further up the hill. It had been abandoned for years and left to ruin. Nature had already destroyed what was once the byre and only one wall remained standing. The rubble from the roof and the other three walls was now completely covered in ferns and nettles. The cottage itself must have been made of stronger stuff, as all four walls remained intact and only part of the thatched roof had caved in. The old wooden door was still tied closed; the way it was left all those years ago. Callum tried to undo the cluster of knots but, after struggling for a few minutes, he gave up and cut the string with his knife. The door sprang open a few inches then seemed to be blocked by something. He put his shoulder to the door and managed to push it in far enough to see into the gloomy shades of darkness. As he pushed for a second time, Ewan also put what weight he had against the door, which opened enough for Callum to squeeze inside. Ewan refused to follow him into this house of shadows and remained outside where escape still remained possible. Callum lit a match on the rough wall. The shadows began to dance frantically as if the flickering yellow flame of the match brought the walls to life. He looked around nervously; a great iron pot still hung from a metal chain over the fireplace. The room was suddenly thrown back into darkness as he burned the tip of his fingers and dropped the match. He fumbled with another match that lit with a furious blue and yellow flame, but the damp head would not take and it went out in seconds. Again, as the blackness swept over him, Callum began to feel afraid of the long black shapes he imagined reaching out towards him from every corner of the room. In a sudden panic, he tried to light another match. Again it went out. "Shit!"

"What's the matter?" shouted Ewan from outside. "It's starting tae rain again. I'm cold."

"It's all right," said Callum, trying to push himself through the tight gap in the jammed door. "There's nothing in here," he gasped, still trying to free himself from the house. The struggle with the door was fuelling his now rampant imagination, making the hairs stand on the back of his neck. He imagined the long, bony fingers of an old hag reaching out to grab him from behind, before dragging him back into the horrible darkness. A cold gust of wet wind slapped him on the face as he finally broke out from the haunted blackness of the cottage. A sudden flash of lightning caused Ewan to instinctively grab hold of his brother's hand. "C'mon. Let's hurry," said Callum as the inevitable rumble of thunder followed them down the hillside. Within seconds the skies opened up and the rain engulfed them. They hurried down the slippery path. Feeling relieved, Callum stole another look at the eerie cottage just when another flash of lightning cracked open the sheets of grey rain. For a split second he thought he saw an old woman standing at the door, immune from the rain and wind, with her black shawl pulled over her grey hair and waving to them. "C'mon. Hurry," he shouted, pulling Ewan by the arm.

Another rumble of thunder went almost unnoticed as the two brothers hurried back to their father. The last of the daylight was now fading under the dark clouds and they heard Tess barking frantically below them.

"Tess!" called Callum. "Tess, over here."

"Good girl," he praised when her wet head forced its way under his outstretched hand.

"Hurry up, boys," called their father. "We'll get the fox another day when it's no' so bloody wet."

Betty stood wrapped in her shawl at the door, hurrying them into the shelter of the cottage. Within seconds she had Ewan plucked naked from his saturated clothes. His thin white body was covered in goose pimples and he shivered violently as its coldness tried to come to terms with the blazing hot fire. He was soon draped in a dry blanket, while his mother dried him frantically.

"Da! Do ye think the fox and her cubs will drown?" he asked, his teeth still chattering uncontrollably.

"Don't you worry about the fox, son. She'll be all right."

The following day was dull but dry and a third missing ewe was found dead further up the hillside. Callum buried the three carcasses in a pit of lime to stop any disease spreading to the other sheep. The sex of the fox was no longer in question; the vision of a desperate vixen and her starving cubs, cowering in the blackness of the den, was now indelibly fixed in their minds. They brought dry straw from the byre and stuffed it in the entrance of the den. When Callum lit the straw, the smoke quickly revealed the existence of another entrance, as it funnelled out from a mass of mangled ferns and bracken some twenty feet further up the hill. Jamie took up position at the root of the escaping smoke and aimed the shotgun at the hole. With each passing second the tension in his arm increased. It was with a sense of relief that he finally broke open the barrel of the shotgun and removed the two cartridges.

"It must have moved on after smelling us at the den yesterday."

"At least we don't have tae lie tae Ewan now," said Callum. "What about the fire?"

"Aye, ye'd be as well tae stamp it oot."

Once the fire was out, Callum hand-rolled a cigarette and sat down beside his father on a boulder, which protruded through the surrounding damp heather and moss. Tess lay at his feet looking up at him as the sun struggled to break through the clouds.

"You were back late, last night. Did ye get a hold of Angus?"

"Aye, he was in MacTaggart's."

"He's a terrible lad for the drink. Ye would think he'd spend less time in the pub now he's a married man."

Callum did not say anything but merely blew circles of smoke in

84

hypnotic repetition into the air, hoping that the lecture would be short.

"Yer mother was worried; ye shouldnae be out drinking all night without anything in yer stomach. Nae wonder ye looked as white as a sheet this morning."

"I'm fine. I didnae drink that much."

"Maybe so, but I bet ye Angus had plenty tae drink."

"Angus can dae what he likes."

"But ye'll get as bad as him if ye drink wi' him all the time."

"He's me friend."

"Ah know, son. But just be careful no' tae let the drinking get oot of hand. Angus's been away at sea and he's become used tae hard drinking."

"Don't be worrying about me. I'm old enough to look after meself. We better get back down before it starts raining again."

Chapter 9

The dining room was resplendent with Leaburn's finest china and silverware on display for the first time in many years. Directly above the heavy oak table hung a magnificent crystal chandelier, its beauty shimmering in its own candlelight. There were another dozen or so candles on the long table. They were set in fine, silver candlesticks, which family legend insisted once belonged to Bonnie Prince Charlie during his ill-fated time in Scotland. The table had been set for four, although there was ample room for another twenty to sit in comfort.

The present Laird's own likeness hung directly over the white marble fireplace, alongside that of his late wife. In the centre of the table, on a large silver salver, lay a magnificent salmon in a sea of clear aspic jelly. The salmon was skinned from its redundant gills to its lifeless tail fin, exposing its succulent pink flesh. Lettuce, tomatoes, cucumber, watercress, radishes and other vegetation surrounded this majestic fish in its artificial seabed.

Charles Dunbar took his place at the top of the table; his balding head shining under the glowing light of the chandelier. To his left sat Caitriona, her hair styled to accommodate a small diamond tiara, which sparkled with each movement of her head. She wore a stunning, silk dress; its low neckline garnished handsomely with a necklace of blue sapphires.

"Thank you, Father, they're absolutely beautiful," she said, touching the necklace to reassure herself that she was actually wearing it.

"They're only coloured stones. It's you that makes them beautiful, just like your mother once did," he said softly, casting a grieving glance towards his late wife's portrait, while gently squeezing his daughter's hand.

"What's keeping him?" snapped Duncan, impatiently tapping his fingers on the table.

"Give him a chance to get changed; he's been working all day," pleaded Caitriona.

"Yes, Duncan, don't be so impatient and stop tapping the table!" ordered his father. "Roberts! Send young William up to see if Dr Munro requires any assistance."

"No, Daddy, please don't. You know Fraser doesn't like any fuss."

"All right, darling ... Roberts, just go and check if everything is ready in the kitchen."

"Yes, sir," replied Roberts, curtly bowing his head to acknowledge the change of orders.

It was another five minutes or so before Fraser finally appeared in one of the Laird's old dinner suits. The young doctor looked around the room nervously for a few seconds and then gently kissed Caitriona on the cheek, wishing her a happy birthday as he did so. "You look beautiful."

"Thank you, darling," she said, smiling at his embarrassment, while attempting to straighten his bow tie.

"I'm sorry for holding everyone up."

"Don't be silly, doctor," said Dunbar, nodding to Roberts to start serving the fish course. "A short delay only helps to improve one's appetite. Don't you agree?" he added with a hearty laugh.

Roberts served the salmon in his usual calm manner, his thin face and grey eyes never showing the slightest sign of emotion. If the conversations at these dinners ever interested him, it was impossible to detect from his stoic expression. A gust of rain battered off the large bay windows, which overlooked the loch. A nod from Roberts ordered a young servant girl to speed across the room and quickly close the heavy, velvet curtains.

"The weather's been very changeable these last few days. One minute sun, the next it's like the middle of bloody winter. It wouldn't surprise me if we got snow tomorrow," said Dunbar, after washing down a mouthful of salmon with a glass of wine.

"It's lambing season and all we need, on top of everything else, is a late spring," groaned Duncan.

"On top of everything else?" asked Fraser.

"Aye, three sheep were found dead on the hillside over behind the Macnair croft. The vet thinks that it's some sort of disease that's killed them. He's sending some blood samples through to Glasgow for analysis. It may be a couple of weeks before he gets the results back. I've told him to let me know as soon as he gets them," explained Duncan in his forceful tone, which belied his youth.

"It has not affected any of ours yet?" asked his father.

"No. But it's only a matter of time according to the vet. I've told the men to shoot any strays that wander..."

"You what!"

"I told ..."

"I heard what you said, but I just can't believe you said it. Shoot any strays? Those sheep belong to our neighbours."

"Neighbours," grunted Duncan. "They're only our bloody tenants."

"Don't use that language at the dinner table. They may be tenants, but they are still our neighbours. Now go and tell MacPherson and the men that they are not to shoot any sheep, unless I say so."

"Unless you say so! It was only last month that you asked me to take over the running of the estate. You said then that you'd not interfere with..."

"I will not stand by and let you shoot sheep belonging to our tenants, so go and tell MacPherson."

"What now?"

"Yes, now!"

Duncan rose abruptly from the table, throwing his crumpled linen napkin at his half-eaten salmon. The Laird was used to his son's dramatics and simply nodded for Roberts to clear the fish course away. He then engaged Fraser in some light conversation about fishing and hunting and insisted that the doctor accompany him on the moors in the morning. Although not keen on the idea of shooting game, Fraser did not want to appear rude and agreed to join Dunbar so long as his presence would not be a hindrance to the Laird. "Not at all, young man. It will be a pleasure to have you along."

Duncan stood in the middle of the cobbled stone courtyard and stared into the darkness of the stables as the unruly wind almost blew his hat off. "Are you in there, Macpherson?" There was no reply. With the authority inherent in his own self-importance, he marched across the courtyard to the gamekeepers' quarters in spite of the strong winds, which seemed determined to keep him back. He did not have his father's feelings for the 'men'. He hated their coarse manner and, even more, he hated the unarticulated grunts and groans which they tried to pass off as the King's English. He could imagine the fervent activity taking place behind the tattered curtains; the half-skinned rabbits being stuffed under a bed, perhaps even a pheasant or two joining them. The sudden thought of a salmon being wrapped up in some coarse blanket and hidden quickened his step and his face flushed with anticipation and speculative rage. To him, the estate's own gamekeepers did more poaching than anyone in the glen, but he could never catch them in the act. He was sure his father had turned a blind eye to their antics for years, but he would not put up with it for one minute.

A thin-faced man of about forty opened the door to Duncan's demanding knock. The gamekeeper could only hold Duncan's probing stare for a few seconds before he dropped his head to avoid further eye contact. Without a word of common courtesy, Duncan brushed past the man into the room. There were three others, all gamekeepers, in the gloomy room, playing cards and smoking pipes. They immediately removed their caps and got to their feet. Duncan's eyes moved around the sparsely furnished quarters, partly to acknowledge to himself who was present and also to detect any signs of poaching. He finally revealed his purpose and asked the whereabouts of MacPherson. The four men looked at each other before one of them spoke.

"I think he has gone into Marnock to get stores. He should be back soon, sir."

"To get stores at this time? A whore more like. Tell him when he gets back that there's been a change of plan and any strays shot are to be buried on the hillside and not brought onto the estate. And no one is to mention this to my father or they'll be out of a job. Is that understood?"

"Aye, sir," they replied in a variety of mumbles. Duncan could feel their contempt on his back as he turned and marched out without another word. From the window, the bitter grey eyes of one of the men watched Duncan's fractious strut back across the cobbled courtyard.

"He's a real arrogant bastard!"

The cards were quickly put aside and a half-eaten salmon was placed back on the table.

The soup course was being served when Duncan returned to the dining room. He sipped the hot consommé with a satisfied grin. He was determined that his father's benevolent attitude would not interfere with the running of the estate; after all this was his inheritance and no disease from some ill-fed stray was going to devastate an important part of that inheritance. In future he would have to be more careful of what was said in front of his father. How often had he listened to the estate's accountants, trying to persuade the Laird of the uneconomic folly in allowing the profits from the coalmines to be eaten up subsidising the estate? He was adamant that Leaburn was capable of paying for itself, so long as the tenants' leases were renewed and rents increased to a profitable level. Those tenants who could not pay should be evicted and their holdings turned over to sheep farming; the profits from the mining company would not last forever! It was this part of the discussions with their accountants that worried him. It was Duncan's grandfather, Lord William Dunbar, who first invested in the Lanarkshire mines, which were now so profitable that they could be run by company managers and accountants with little input from the family. During his grandfather's time, the success of the coal company had resulted in much needed revenue being diverted into the restoration of the castle, with a new west wing and extensive stables being built when other estates were falling into ruin. Lord William had also increased the estate's land to what it was today. Duncan's admiration for his grandfather was boundless and he often spent a thoughtful moment under the great man's portrait, satisfying himself in their uncanny likeness; the deep set eyes and strong jaw line. He resembled the portrait so much that he often felt a sense of reincarnation when looking at it.

"What do you make of all this nonsense in Ireland?" asked Dunbar. "This Irish Home Rule Bill will be the beginning of the end."

"Of what?" Caitriona asked.

"The Empire of course! Once the Irish get their independence, they'll all be looking for it. Before you know it, India and the other colonies will be clamouring for their right to self govern."

"So you agree it's a right?" asked Fraser.

"Of course it's a right, but it doesn't mean they have to get it. Where will the British be without the Empire? No, give the Irish their sovereignty and in twenty years' time there will be no Empire."

"Well I think they should be allowed to govern their own country, if that's what they want," said Caitriona.

"It's not that simple. The Unionists are threatening civil war if the Liberals pass this Bill. There'll be a blood-bath there before the end of the year," said Fraser, his voice expressing real concern.

"They'll never get Home Rule through the Lords. Look what happened when they tried to do it a few months back; there was more than three to one against. And that will never change," argued Dunbar.

"Yes, but they can only delay the Bill. They can't stop it if the Commons is determined to pass it. They just don't have the power any more since the Liberals took it away," explained Fraser.

"You're not saying much, Duncan," said Caitriona.

"I've got more important things on my mind. Who really gives a damn, anyway? If the Irish think they can run Ireland, then let them. Within a year they'll have ruined the country and will be begging to be taken back. They're just a backward country of peasants and priests."

"Oh, Duncan, I think you just like being horrible to impress everyone," said Caitriona.

Suddenly, there was a clatter from the kitchen and Dunbar nodded to Roberts, who bowed his head in acknowledgement and quickly, but with his usual calmness, went into the kitchen to investigate. He was horrified to find his wife, who was also the cook, bending over a scattered tray of pork and apple sauce.

"For God's sake, Margaret, what happened?" he asked, standing over his flushed-faced wife and the panic-stricken maid who had dropped the silver salver.

"Never mind that now," scolded Margaret. "Just give us a hand tae get this lot picked up before the Master comes in. Here, Morag, take that other tray in and get started before they get tae wondering what's goin' on. And mind this time it's hot."

"I'm sorry, Mr Roberts. It burnt me hand."

"Be careful next time, Morag," he ordered. "And if the Master asks what's happened, just tell him an empty pot fell off the kitchen sink. Dae ye hear?"

"Aye, Mr Roberts. A' hear ye."

Mrs Roberts picked up the meat and washed it in hot water from the potato pot. The meat was then rearranged on a clean silver salver and a thick coat of piping hot gravy spread over it. The salver was put on the top tray of the oven awaiting Morag's return.

"Ye see, there was nae need tae panic," she said winking at her admiring husband.

"Aye, yer a terrible woman," he replied, returning his wife's mischievous wink. "What they don't see won't hurt them."

Morag nursed her throbbing hand in a damp napkin under the hot salver and proceeded to serve the main course. The conversation at the table had turned to Fraser's recent appointment as a junior doctor at the Royal Infirmary in Edinburgh. He had secured the post through his uncle, Dr Cameron Munro, a well-known surgeon, only three weeks after graduating from Edinburgh University with a first-class honours degree. The duties of a junior doctor, even if his uncle was chairman of the hospital board, were onerous and the hours long. Fraser's ambition to be a top surgeon was strong and he endured the less pleasant duties and the long hours as necessary burdens, making the ultimate achievement even more desirable.

As Morag attempted to serve Duncan, she suddenly felt his hand on the back of her leg. She instinctively drew back as his hand moved up her skirt, causing the salver to tilt to one side and hot gravy to spill onto the back of his licentious hand. Duncan screamed, jumping up from his chair and abruptly pushed Morag and the silver salver away. As Morag struggled to regain her balance, the hot gravy rushed back up the salver and ran over her arm.

"Stupid little bitch!" shouted Duncan as he took out a white silk handkerchief and wrapped it around the burn on the back of his hand. In spite of her own pain, and Duncan's abusive manner, Morag held on to the tray until she was able to place it on the dining table. Her legs then gave way.

"Oh! The poor girl's fainted," cried Caitriona as Fraser rushed past Duncan to catch her before she fell against the marble fireplace. On hearing the furore, Roberts returned from the kitchen to see what had happened, raising his left hand to his forehead at the sight of Morag lying in the arms of Caitriona, while Fraser used a napkin to carefully wipe the hot gravy from the pallid girl's sleeve and hand.

"Is the girl's arm badly burnt?" asked Dunbar.

"Yes it is," confirmed Fraser.

"Duncan, help the doctor to carry Morag into the other room."

"There's no need. I can carry her," said Fraser, lifting her without much difficulty.

"Damn you, Duncan, give the man a hand," insisted his father.

"Roberts! Give the good doctor a hand," commanded Duncan. Roberts glanced in the Laird's direction, who nodded his consent, furiously watching the smug grin of defiance appear on his son's face.

"How's your hand, son?" he asked in a mocking tone of over-concern.

"It's fine," replied Duncan, fidgeting with his handkerchief, which had come loose.

"Well I think you should let Fraser have a look at it when he's finished with Morag."

"No, it's not that bad."

"Well you've made enough noise about it. I insist the good doctor has a look at it."

94

In the sitting room, Fraser and Roberts gently laid Morag on a *chaise-longue* by the window as she gradually recovered from her shock. In spite of her obvious pain, she apologised profusely for spilling the gravy as the tears welled up in her eyes. "Roberts could you be so kind and fetch my medical bag from my room."

Once Roberts returned with the bag, Fraser applied some calamine lotion to Morag's arm, which took some of the throbbing pain away. "I'm sorry to be such a nuisance," she sobbed, as Fraser put a dressing over the lotion.

"Don't worry, Morag," reassured Caitriona, "just you rest there until you feel a little better. Roberts, can you get one of the other girls to sit with her for a while."

"Of course I will, Lady Caitriona."

When they were satisfied that Morag was comfortable, Fraser and Caitriona returned to the dining room, where father and son sat in stony silence.

"How is she?" asked Dunbar.

"Her arm is quite badly burned, but it will be fine in a few days," replied Fraser. "Let me have a look at that," he insisted as Duncan pulled his hand away.

"No it's fine. It only hurts a little.Sit down and eat your dinner before it gets cold."

"Don't be such a damn hero," barked Dunbar. "Let the doctor have a look. It may become infected if it's not treated properly. You can't have that silly handkerchief wrapped around it while you are eating."

Under the pressure of his father's insistence, Duncan held out his hand. Fraser carefully removed the handkerchief and stared incredulously at the faint pink mark. Duncan turned away, unable to bear the moment of denunciation. Fraser continued to look at the hand but said nothing. He then began to spread copious amounts of ointment on the tiny burn, before applying an unnecessarily large lint bandage.

"How is it?" asked Caitriona.

"He'll live," replied Fraser as Duncan gave him a contrived smile in grudging gratitude.

After serving coffee, Roberts set about preparing the library; he put more coal on the already blazing fire and placed a tray of liqueurs and a box of cigars on a large oval-shaped coffee table in the middle of the room. Young William, the stable boy, was sent to the cellar to replenish the brandy decanter. Once satisfied that all was in order, Roberts closed the heavy curtains and retired to his own quarters in the basement, where his wife was already undressing for bed.

"How's Morag?" he asked.

"She's in her room fast asleep. I looked in a few minutes ago to see if she needed anything, but she was dead to the world. That's a nice young doctor."

"Aye, there's no airs and graces with him," agreed her husband.

"What's that?" asked Margaret with a startled expression, straining her neck as though it would improve her hearing.

There was another rattle on the stained glass window at the end of the hallway. Roberts stopped undressing and pulled his braces back over his shoulders. He looked at his wife, who nodded for him to go and see what was making the noise. He gave a mocking laugh and said it was just the wind blowing some branches against the door. As he began to take his braces back off, there were three loud thuds at the door.

"Will ye go and see who it is!" she demanded.

Roberts opened the back door to find Callum Macnair standing there, soaked to the skin and still gasping for breath.

"What ails ye, lad?"

"It's Ewan, he's sick. I need tae get him a doctor."

"What's wrong wi' Dr Wilson. Can ye no … ?"

"No! He's away tae a funeral in Oban and will no' be back until tomorrow evening. His wife told me that there's a Doctor Munro staying wi' the Laird tonight."

"Can it no' wait until tomorrow?"

"No, ma thinks it's real serious."

"Com' in before ye catch yer death yerself."

Callum waited anxiously, while Roberts went into the bedroom and explained the situation to his wife.

"Well, you'll just have tae go up and tell the doctor. Betty Macnair is no' one tae go running after doctors unless there's something far wrong," she said, pulling on her dressing gown and following her husband into the other room. "Here, Callum, dry yerself wi' that," she insisted, handing him a towel.

The dinner party retired to the library. The formal room was stuffy and Dunbar tried to open one of the windows to let in some fresh air. The strong winds made the frame wrench in his hand and he quickly pulled it shut again. He then sat opposite his son, who was on the other couch, puffing a large cigar and drinking a glass of brandy. They were now both quite drunk.

"What shall I play?" asked Caitriona excitedly, taking a seat at the piano, while Fraser stood at her side.

"Do you have to?" mumbled Duncan unkindly.

"Why don't you go to bed if you're going to be in this mood," scolded his father.

"I might," said Duncan defiantly, resting his head back and blowing an exaggerated puff of smoke towards the ceiling.

"Play... play that one I like, darling," suggested Dunbar, the slur in his voice matching the blankness in his mind. "You know … you know the one. How does it go?"

"I don't think I want to play any more," she sulked, closing the lid back over the keys.

"Now, Caitriona, don't let that Phil… Phil..." Dunbar stuttered.

"Philistine," suggested Fraser, drawing a contemptuous glare from Duncan.

"Yes, Philistine. Don't let that … oh, Fraser, what is he?"

"Philistine," said Fraser, with an apologetic look towards Duncan.

Caitriona, with feigned reluctance, began to play Chopin's *'Etude in E Major'*, which she had only recently learned to play with any fluency. Fraser's eyes followed hers: reading each note as she played, before turning the music sheet with a practised flick of the wrist. Dunbar closed his tired eyes as he rested back in the spacious leather couch, his glass of brandy following each note on an imaginary score above his head.

Caitriona was almost halfway through the difficult piece when the library door slowly opened and Roberts entered, giving her an apologetic bow of the head, before stealthily crossing the room towards the Laird.

"Yer Lordship, I'm sorry to trouble you..." he whispered. The butler then explained the Macnairs' desperate need for a doctor. Dunbar listened, his face showing a sobering look of concern.

"Thank you, Roberts, you did right in telling me. Will you get some of the men to get the gig ready? Ask the lad to come in. He can dry himself by the fire."

"Yes, sir."

"What's wrong?" asked Caitriona as soon as Roberts left the room.

"It looks as though your services are required, Fraser. A young lad, one of my tenant's sons, is very ill. He has a fever. Unfortunately, Dr Wilson is away at a funeral and will not be back until tomorrow. Do you think you could see the boy?"

"Damn cheek," interrupted Duncan. "These people think …"

"No, it's all right. I'd be glad to see the boy. Do they have any idea what's wrong with him?"

"If they knew that they wouldn't need you," said Duncan sarcastically.

"Don't be so rude," snapped Caitriona. "I'm sure if you broke your leg you wouldn't need a doctor to tell you, but you'd still need one to set it for you."

"Oh! Come in, lad," Dunbar beckoned, turning to Callum, who was standing at the door with Roberts.

Callum would have stepped back into the hall only for Roberts's forceful push from behind. He walked towards the fire as directed by the Laird's outstretched arm.

"I'll only be a minute; I have to get my stethoscope from upstairs," said Fraser.

"Roberts!" shouted Dunbar.

"No, it's all right. I'll be quicker getting it myself," insisted Fraser, rushing out the room.

"I hope it's not too serious," said Caitriona, turning towards Callum, whose wet clothes were now emitting their dampness into the warm room.

"I don't know."

"How old is your brother?" she then asked, trying to make Callum feel less ill at ease than he looked.

"Thirteen," was Callum's laconic reply, still staring into the fire.

Caitriona realised that asking questions only made him look more uncomfortable. So instead she sat down again at the piano, but watched him curiously from the corner of her eye as Callum twisted his wet cloth cap in his nervous hands. A cold draught followed Roberts into the room.

"The gig is ready, sir."

"Good, the doctor will be with you shortly."

"I'm going as well," proclaimed Caitriona, when Fraser reappeared at the door with his brown leather bag.

"Don't be silly, darling," replied Fraser.

"You said the wrong thing there," laughed Dunbar, causing him to choke on his cigar smoke and immediately begin a fit of coughing and spluttering.

"I'm going!" Caitriona insisted, slamming down the piano lid.

"All right, darling, if you must," conceded Fraser. "But you can't go dressed like that."

"Oh, of course not," she said, turning to Callum instinctively.

"It's only a doctor he needs," said Callum, storming past Caitriona and out into the hall.

"What did I tell you?" laughed Duncan. "You offer to help them and they throw it back in your face. Take your coat off, Fraser. His own folk can look after the boy with their ridiculous herbs and potions. It's probably his brother who's infected the sheep," he added, slapping his thigh in acknowledgement at his own joke.

"Can you take me?" Fraser asked Roberts, who smiled and took the doctor's bag.

"You're a damn fool!" shouted Duncan in a drunken growl.

"Why don't you shut that stupid mouth of yours," snapped his father, slamming his empty brandy glass on the table.

Caitriona went to her room and took off her necklace; it felt heavy and unnecessary now. The rain was lashing against the window in relentless waves. She lifted back the heavy velvet curtains and looked out into the darkness. Why had he been so rude? She only wanted to help.

The gig pulled up alongside Callum, who had already run halfway home. Roberts insisted that he get in. So he clambered, almost reluctantly, into the seat beside Fraser, who smiled at him reassuringly. Roberts drove the gig against the wind in the direction of a pale yellow light, which stood out in the distant darkness of the hillside. The gig finally came to a halt at the bottom of a muddy pathway that led to the Macnair cottage. Fraser's mind quickly recalled his school day readings of Burns' *Tam O'Shanter*, when he caught the almost ghostly sight of a cluster of old women, wrapped in shawls, standing outside the cottage. They seemed to be chanting in some queer incantation as he rushed past them; his smile of introduction ignored by the few that even noticed him.

The rain had stopped again and now only the icy cold wind blew violently around the little cottage, before howling its way through the heather and over the mountains towards the west of the glen. Fraser followed Callum into the cottage and was surprised to find it so dark and smoky. The light from the fire cast ghostly shadows on the grim looking faces of those gathered in the front room. The womenfolk were sitting around the fire, trying to keep warm with cups of hot tea. The men stood in the corners, smoking and talking in whispers. Their murmurs fell silent on seeing the doctor standing at the door.

"Hello, I'm Doctor Munro," he said, seeking out the likely parents from the staring eyes that were fixed on him from the moment he stepped into the glow of the fire.

"Oh, doctor," came a pleading voice.

"Where's the boy?" he asked, straining to see through the nebulous glow from the scattering of candles. As he spoke, those standing to his left seemed to melt away into the darkness and a path opened up to a dimly lit box-bed, where a tearful Betty Macnair stood with a trembling hand raised to her lips. Callum put his arm around his mother and whispered something that made her lips part in a strained but hopeful smile.

"There's not enough light in here," said Fraser as he lifted back the coarse blankets from his young patient. "Is there an oil lamp in the house?"

"No, but me feyther has gone to get some more candles from the neighbours," said Callum.

"Good God, this will never do," mumbled Fraser. "I'll have to have some decent light."

"I can go back to the castle and get a couple of paraffin lamps," suggested Roberts, who was still standing at the crowded doorway.

"Good, and get some sheets, and ask Miss Dunbar to come with you. I will need some help."

"Aye, very good, doctor. Is there anything else you need?"

"No, that's all. Oh, there's not enough air in here. Can people that have a home to go to, please leave," he pleaded, looking around the crowded room.

Within a few seconds, all but a handful of close relatives were left. Fraser quickly removed his coat and dinner jacket. His orders were immediately followed and a large pot of water was placed over the fire to boil. With his sleeves now rolled up to his elbows, he continued with his examination, muttering curses under his breath at

102

the lack of light. Callum lit the only other candle that he could find. The extra light caused Ewan's frail, white body to look emaciated in the shadows cast by his own bony contours. The coarse blankets were saturated in sweat. When he coughed his whole body wrenched with the pain.

"How long has he been like this?" Fraser asked, already sure in his mind of the diagnosis.

"It's three days now since he became sick but this has been the worst day," said Betty, her chest heaving with every word she spoke.

"Has Doctor Wilson seen him at all?"

"No," said Callum, almost apologetically. "We thought he'd be fine and we don't have the money for doctors."

At that moment Jamie Macnair came in with an arm full of candles and food. He kicked the door shut with the heel of his boot and dropped the various items on to the table.

"How is he?" he asked anxiously.

"Light those candles so I can see what I'm doing. Ah, never mind, there's the gig back. Can some of you go and fetch the lamps and blankets," demanded Fraser as he re-engaged his stethoscope and listened to the faint murmurs of Ewan's heart and lungs.

Caitriona came in abruptly. She was followed by a gust of cold wind, which blew out most of the candles, leaving the room in virtual darkness. Fraser was about to use some colourful language, when he turned to see Caitriona standing in the weak glow from the fire, laden with the white sheets he had asked for. He smiled at her as the candles were quickly relit. She was shocked at the cold, damp room into which she had rushed. She could not help but notice the bare stone floor beneath her feet. The whole atmosphere was one of poverty. She quietly turned from the staring faces and went to Fraser's side.

"How is he?"

"Make a fresh bed with those!" he ordered, ignoring her question.

Caitriona touched her chest in shock when she caught a glimpse of Ewan's pale, gaunt face. As she looked away, her eyes met Callum's cold stare.

"Here, I'll give you a hand," he said, taking the sheets from her arms.

With the extra light, Fraser was now able to give Ewan a more thorough examination. The symptoms were all there: the lungs were inflamed and waterlogged; his temperature was high and he was perspiring profusely. The painful coughing and rapid shallow breathing all confirmed his previous, preliminary diagnosis. The boy was dying. Callum's own bed was quickly stripped of its heavy blankets and replaced with the fresh, white sheets. Then, Fraser lifted Ewan's shivering body onto the newly made bed. The heavy blankets were then heaped on top to keep him warm. After giving Ewan some morphine to ease his discomfort, Fraser announced that there was nothing else that he could do until the morning. There was a strained silence before Callum asked the question the others feared to ask.

"How bad is he, doctor?"

"I'm afraid he has pneumonia; lobar pneumonia, to be precise. You will just have to pray that he makes it through this night. I've done all I can. He's in the Lord's hands now."

"Oh no!" cried Betty Macnair, falling to her knees at the side of the bed.

The wind had now died down as Fraser led Caitriona back to the waiting gig. Roberts said nothing. It was not his place to inquire into the boy's chances of survival. He was not a religious man, but he said a prayer more than once as he trotted the gig back to the castle. There was no hurry now.

"Will he live?" asked Caitriona as she snuggled up to Fraser for warmth.

"He's too far gone."

Chapter 10

When Caitriona awoke the following morning, the waters of Loch Fay shimmered under a pale blue sky. The early spring sunshine was still too weak to take the chill out of the brisk sea air that still had a hint of winter in it. There were only a few of the smaller fishing boats still tied up at the quayside; the others having already cast their nets in the deeper waters beyond the peninsula where the loch merged with the sea. There was a sudden splash on the otherwise silent waters when an osprey dropped to the loch's surface to catch an unsuspecting fish in its talons. The bird then rose from the circles of water, shaking the wet from its magnificent wings as its prey struggled in vain. Caitriona opened a side window to get a better look at this rare sight, when a shot rang out. She watched in despair as the osprey fell like a stone on the far shore with the trout still wriggling in its dead grip. She screamed in disgust. "Duncan! How could you!" But her brother was on the other side of the loch and too far away to hear her. She watched despondently as he triumphantly waved his shotgun above his head.

There was a soft knock at the door and Morag entered carrying a breakfast tray. Caitriona rushed across the room to take it from the girl.

"You should not be carrying heavy trays; you had a nasty burn last night. Where's Mary?"

"Mary is off this morning; she's gone to visit her folks."

"How is your hand?"

"Oh, it's fine this morning. I can hardly feel a thing."

"Nevertheless, it will need time to heal."

"The kind young doctor gave me something to take away the pain and …" she began to ramble as she made the bed.

Caitriona was not listening; her mind was on the sick boy she had forgotten about in her comfortable dreams. It's such a beautiful morning, she thought, no one so young could die on a morning like this. Last night was different. The idea of death was so real but this morning it seemed impossible. Morag's nattering broke through her thoughts when she heard Fraser's name.

"Up early he was and away without a bite to eat."

"Is he back yet?"

"Not yet, miss. I haven't seen the gig come back yet."

"The boy …? Is there any news of the boy?"

Morag looked blankly back at Caitriona, her mouth open but no words coming to her lips.

"The boy that was ill. The one that Doctor Munro has gone to see this morning," explained Caitriona.

"No one told me anything about any sick boy, miss."

"Is my father up?"

"Aye, miss, up and away first thing wi' the doctor gentleman. Master Duncan has gone out shooting. The house is empty, except for you and me, miss. Oh and of course Mrs Roberts … and William who is … "

"Get my clothes. No, never mind. Go and get the stable lad to hitch up one of the gigs and tell him to wait for me at the gate."

"Aye, miss, I'll get William to do it right away."

Caitriona rushed to her closet, throwing aside silk and velvet gowns until she found a plain navy blue cotton dress she often wore when strolling along the hillsides. She heard the sounds of crushed gravel as the gig drew up at the front of the house. She rushed downstairs.

"Morning, William."

"Mornin', miss," he replied, doffing his cloth cap.

As she climbed into the gig, there was another barrage of shooting from the other side of the loch. Birds of various species scattered from the relative safety of the hedgerows and into the clear skies over the loch. Two of the gamekeeper's black Labradors swam out to retrieve the dead birds as they fell to the water.

"Is it not too early in the year to be shooting game birds?" she asked.

"It's no' birds they're after, miss. They're hunting deer. There's talk of a big stag in the woods and Master Duncan is oot tae get it. Where to, miss?"

"Take me to the Macnair's cottage. Do you know it?"

"Aye, miss. Ah know it fine."

The old horse neighed at the unnecessary tugging, which caused the bit to cut into its mouth. Caitriona suffered the uncomfortable ride, thankful that it was only a short journey that they had embarked upon. The horse and gig eventually came to a halt some fifty feet short of the dirt path leading to the cottage. When Caitriona asked why he had stopped, William took off his cap and solemnly pointed at a black shawl draped over the half-open shutters at the front of the house. Caitriona rushed from the gig and up the path. When she neared the cottage, she suddenly stopped and hovered at the door. There was a presence beyond that door of something she had not experienced and perhaps had no right to. She smiled with relief as the door opened and Fraser took her by the arm.

"Darling, what are you doing here?" he asked with a deep sigh in his voice.

"Is the boy dead?" she asked as he led her away from the door.

"Yes, he died a short time ago. There was nothing I could do. Your father and Roberts have gone for the Reverend. You had better go back home. I'll wait for them here."

"Should I not convey my condolences to the family?"

"I'll do that for you. They're washing the body before dressing it for the wake. It would be better if you pay your respects at the funeral tomorrow."

"Yes, I suppose you're right," she agreed as she climbed back into the waiting gig. "He was so young."

Within hours the sad news spread through the glen from croft to croft. Those working in the fields stopped whatever they were doing as a mark of respect to the bereaved family. Working clothes were changed and those that had them dressed themselves in their Sunday best. Soon a steady stream of relatives and neighbours began to make their slow walk over the fields and along the twisting braes to the solitary cottage on the hillside where they paid their respects.

The Laird's gig returned from the manse with the Rev. Knox, who had been planning a morning's fishing when he was surprised by the Laird's rare visit to the manse. After leaving the minister at the Macnair cottage, Charles Dunbar returned home with Fraser, sending Roberts back with six bottles of whisky and a basket full of freshly baked scones and bread for the wake that evening. But there would be no serious drinking at this wake as a mark of deep respect to the unnatural loss of one so young.

The solemn shadow of death that spread through the glen that day also cast its gloom over the household at Leaburn Castle. Mrs Roberts chided Morag to stop her crying.

"I told you not tae go tae the house. Now didn't I?" she said as Morag cried even louder. "Now there's a good lassie, dry your eyes now. You don't want tae be serving the Laird's dinner with tears running down yer face. Now do ye?"

When the Laird said grace at dinner that evening, he included a prayer for the boy's soul and confirmed that they would all have to attend the service and funeral in the morning. No one spoke for sometime until Duncan decided that he had enough silence for one night and began to tell of his unlucky shot at a stag that he had been stalking in the woods.

"Must you go around killing everything?" interrupted Caitriona.

"Isn't that a dead chicken you're tucking into?"

"Duncan! Enough," warned his father.

"Well, my sister seems to think the animals that we eat die of old age."

"It's one thing killing for food, it's quite another killing for the fun of it," she retorted.

"Indeed. But you did eat salmon last night. Did you not? And I had great sport in catching it."

Caitriona declined to answer and turned to engage Fraser in conversation.

The following morning the sky was overcast. Callum, his father and two uncles carried the coffin at the head of a slow procession of mourners. They walked the half mile to the graveyard at a respectful pace. Along the way, neighbours joined the end of the cortege, swelling the numbers and leaving virtually every cottage in the glen empty.

The Rev. Knox stood, bible in hand, at the Kirk gate as his church bells rang out their mournful sounds of solemnity. He knew that the power of the Lord's word was never stronger than at times of death. The dark line of mourners suddenly stopped as Jamie Macnair, blinded by the flow of tears that he could no longer control, stumbled for a second time. Angus rushed forward taking the weight of the coffin on his broad shoulders. He put his arm under the coffin and on to Callum's shoulder.

The Rev. Knox prayed in his gruff, monotonous voice. The coffin was lowered into the ground. His almost hypnotic praying seemed to ease the pain of those clinging to each other at the graveside. But as the damp, brown clay was shovelled into the deep abyss that was death, each thud caused cries and sobs to rise above the Reverend's words of spiritual justification. '... *Behold I show you a mystery; we shall not all sleep, but shall be changed. In a moment, in the twinkling of an eye, at the last trump: for the trumpet shall sound, and the dead shall be raised incorruptible, and we shall be changed.*"

Callum stood with his arm tightly around his mother; he felt her fragile body shivering in his strong embrace. His father stood beside her, his head stooped in a grief he could not endure. A damp breeze swept over the isolated graveyard causing Callum to instinctively look up at the rumble of thunder. Darker clouds were now tumbling over one another as they moved swiftly across the sky, casting a dark shadow over the glen. He turned to see Caitriona standing with her father, and quickly turned away again. He could not corrupt his grief with thoughts of her.

On the Tuesday morning, only a week after the funeral, Callum woke to what sounded like heavy sobbing from the other room. He sat up quickly, trying to make sense of it in his tired and confused mind. A feeling of panic gripped him when he saw daylight seeping through the gap at the bottom of the door. His mother had not woken him at his normal time. He stumbled to his feet, throwing his blanket over his bare shoulders. In the back room he found his father on his knees, his upper body lying across the bed. "What's wrong? Feyther, what's wrong?" he repeated, gently pulling his father from the side of the bed. His mind and body froze when he saw his mother's cold white face; her eyes were open and staring beyond this world and into infinity. He felt the coldness in her dead hands as he took them from his father's reluctant, tight grasp. No words passed between father and son as he helped his distraught father to his feet.

Still in a daze, Callum quickly dressed himself. Then, after a painful look back at his father, who sat in a trance in front of the unlit fire, he rushed from the cold misery of the cottage into the bright spring sunshine. He ran to the crossroads, still trying to decide in his mind whether to go for Dr Wilson or the Reverend. He knew that she was dead but still found himself running towards the old doctor's house.

The doctor pulled his braces up over his vest and quickly followed Callum back to the cottage, but it only took him a few seconds to know that Betty Macnair was beyond human intervention. He was able to confirm later that she died of heart failure and that she would have died very quickly and without much pain. The news of the death stunned Glenfay.

"Two deaths taking place in the one family within a week. What next for poor Jamie Macnair?" Mrs Abercrombie sighed, passing on the awful news to another customer in the village shop. "She died of a broken heart. Dr Wilson even wrote it on the death certificate," she exaggerated.

The funeral was a blur to Callum. When he thought about it afterwards, all he could remember was the constant shaking of hands and the low whispering voices of condolence. Among the voices and hands, there was only one person's touch and voice, which actually gave him comfort. Caitriona had paid her respects before returning with Fraser to Edinburgh. The remembrance of her touch was the only solace he could find in the blackness that followed.

In spite of his mental torment, Callum had not neglected his duty to the croft. Within days of burying his mother, he was back on the hillside, glad of the solitude and to be away from the constant awkward looks of his neighbours, most of whom found it difficult to know what to say to him now that their words of sympathy had been used twice in such a short space of time. It was another couple of weeks before he came upon the rotting carcase of another dead sheep. Until then, he had forgotten all about the three dead sheep and the blood samples that the vet had sent off to Glasgow for analysis. That was almost a month ago, he thought, dragging the dead sheep behind him. Surely the results should be back from Glasgow by now? When he finally reached the field behind the cottage, he threw an old sack over the carcase, leaving it unburied so the vet could examine it later.

Every morning Callum would be up and in the fields before his father was even awake and when he came home in the evening his father was already in MacTaggart's spending what little money he had on whisky. Even when they did find themselves in the cottage together, only words of daily necessity passed between them, as they both hid their feelings from one another and from themselves.

"Found two dead lambs this morning," Callum said as he returned home to find his father sitting hunched and silent by the unlit fire.

His father said nothing.

"I brought them down for the vet to have a look at."

Again there was no answer, only a nod of the head as his father continued to stare vacantly at the cold ashes scattered in the hearth. Callum opened the shutters. The burst of daylight exposed the litter of empty whisky bottles scattered around the room. The stink of whisky and tobacco smoke had now replaced the homely smells of cooking and sweet scented plants.

"Ye cannae sit like that every day."

"Why no'?" was the terse reply.

"Why no'? Because ye cannae just give up."

"Yer mother did."

"Ma never gave up in her life," shouted Callum in anger. "She died of a heart attack. Sure ye heard the doctor tell ye himself. She didn't lie about after Ewan died. She was still up every morning before anyone else."

"It was hard enough wi' Ewan dying but yer mother a week later. I don't see any point any more."

"Any point to what?"

"To anything."

"Well if you want tae lie doon and die, then go and do it in the byre. I'm goin' tae get this place cleaned. There's no use sitting feeling sorry for yerself."

"I should have put it on the door, not the barn," he mumbled to himself.

"What ar' ye gibbering about?"

"The corn dolly … I should hav' hung it on the front door."

"The bloody corn dolly … that's just superstitious nonsense!" said Callum, noticing for the first time the doll in his father's hand.

"Giv' me that and I'll put it in the bloody fire. If the minister hears ye talkin' like this he'll drum ye out the Kirk for being a pagan."

"Leav' it! It's not yours tae burn! And tae hell wi' the minister!" said Jamie defiantly.

"Please yerself!"

Callum rushed around the room, mumbling to himself; throwing rubbish into a tin bucket and pulling and pushing furniture this way and that. After a few minutes his father stood up, coughing amongst the disturbed clouds of dust rising from the floor.

"I'll give ye a hand, son. What do ye want me tae do?"

"That's more like it. You never mind the house. Just take this and get yerself cleaned up a bit," said Callum, handing his father a jug of water and a basin. His father took off his twisted braces and stripped to the waist, before going out to the back of the house to wash. Callum continued to clean the hearth and set about lighting a fire. There was a familiar knock at the door.

"Com' in, Angus," he called without turning.

"I thought it was about time ye came doon tae MacTaggart's for a drink," said Angus, before sneezing. "Good God, what are ye up tae?"

"I'm trying tae get this place cleaned and tae stop ma feyther from sitting about in a dream all day."

"Where is he?"

"He's out the back getting washed. Here, give me a hand," said Callum as he struggled to move the dresser to the other side of the room.

Once the cottage was cleaned and a fire was on, Callum made a pot of broth and left it simmering for his father to take as he pleased. Washed, Jamie was a different man and Callum felt a lump in his throat as he watched his father wipe the dust from his neglected fiddle.

"We're going down MacTaggart's for a few pints. Do ye want tae com' for a while?"

"On ye both go. I'll be all right. I've been drinking too much these days anyway."

"Are ye sure?"

"Aye, I want tae read the good book for a while," said Jamie, Bible in hand.

"Right, I'll see ye later," said Callum as he left with Angus to meet the Murray brothers in MacTaggart's.

It was a pleasant evening and they walked briskly towards the village and MacTaggart's bar. Many of the fields were showing the first signs of growth from the spring sowing and there was a strong smell of honeysuckle in the air. The loch was relatively calm and the daffodils were at their best along its banks, admiring their own beauty in the water below.

"How's Mhairi?" asked Callum, breaking a long silence.

"Oh she's fine. Aye married life's no' too bad. Ye might be thinking about doing it yerself soon."

"Wi' who?"

"Och, there's a few that might have ye … if ye showed some interest."

"Aye, well I'll show an interest when I have an interest."

Glenfay's vet, Donald Kirkland took another look at the fifty pounds before putting it into his wallet. He walked briskly down the gravel path leading him away from the castle, still considering whether or not to tell his wife about his unexpected windfall. It was not that he wanted to deceive her, but there was always the possibility that she would not agree with the nature of the deed that had earned him what would normally take the best part of three months of his veterinary skills to earn. He stopped every so often on his walk home to reconsider his dilemma.

Duncan Dunbar stood at the library window with a large glass of brandy in his hand, watching the vet walk down the road. He raised his glass to him in mockery; well satisfied with the clandestine bargain they had struck. As the vet disappeared over the brae, Duncan turned to the side window and pushed the curtain aside. He studied with a keen eye the position of the estate's wool mill and its proximity to the Macnair croft. There was only a couple of hundred yards between the two buildings. While taking another sip of brandy there was a short, sharp knock at the door.

"Come in," he called without turning.

The estate manager, Robbie MacPherson, came in with his head bowed and cap in hand.

"You were looking for me, sir?"

"No, I wasn't looking for you. I sent someone to find you," sneered Duncan with his practised sardonic wit. "I want you to go to the mill."

"Aye, sir," replied Macpherson as he turned to leave.

"Not yet! You bloody fool!"

"You're aware that we started using some new dyes a few months back?"

"Aye, that I am, sir."

"Well, I am not satisfied with them. We've had complaints from some customers that they fade too fast. I want you to stop using the new dyes and have the barrels that we have left stored in the shed at the back of the mill until I arrange for them to be uplifted. I want this to be done as quickly as possible. Do you understand?"

"Aye, sir, what do ye want me tae tell the women tae use instead?"

"There should be at least a couple of barrels of the old dye in the shed. Get them to use that. I'll order more in the morning."

The fifty pounds lay on the kitchen table as Kirkland and his wife stared at the crumpled notes in stony silence. Her mind was made up; it had to go back! Kirkland now wished he had never agreed to take the money in the first place. How could he now go back on his agreement with the likes of Duncan Dunbar? His wife was right when she said that agreeing to lie about the results of the blood tests was the most stupid thing he had ever done. Dunbar was so forceful, even aggressive, in persuading him to agree that he did not have the time to consider the full implications of such a pact, or muster the resolve to say no, even if he wanted to. He could not deny the money was hard to resist but, as his wife said, it was dishonest money that would still haunt their consciences long after it was spent.

All that night, Kirkland went over the contents of the report in his mind and although there was no doubt that the sheep died as a result of the toxin poison, there had to be some other reason for Dunbar paying such a sum. Why would Dunbar be willing to pay as much as fifty pounds to stop the Macnair's discovering that their sheep had been poisoned when he could buy their whole flock for much less? Why? He read the report again while his wife, his conscience, continued with her knitting in the chair opposite.

He took notes as he read on. The only source of the chemicals that poisoned the sheep was the dyes used at the mill up behind the Macnair's croft. Although the main stream, into which the residue dye was discharged, ran all the way down the hillside and into Loch Fay on estate land, it meandered its way only yards from the Macnair croft. There was no doubt that the samples he had taken from the stream contained the same toxic compounds found in the blood samples taken from the three dead sheep. Kirkland suddenly went into a cold sweat at the thought that he might have been seen at the stream taking samples. Why did Duncan Dunbar not just accept liability and pay the Macnairs the few pounds to replace their dead sheep? It was true that other crofters' sheep often strayed to that side of the hill, but not that many. These thoughts ran through his mind until the penny finally dropped. *Why had I been so bloody stupid? That's it!*

"What is it, Donald? What ails ye?" his wife asked.

"Nothing, I will tell you when I am sure."

"You sounded sure enough to me. What is it? You're not thinking of keeping that money?"

"No. I've just realised that Duncan Dunbar fears the same poisons that killed the sheep caused the deaths of young Ewan Macnair and his mother. The Macnair's well may have been contaminated by water from the stream. All the deaths have happened within a few weeks of each other. It's possible that both doctors failed to recognise the symptoms and wrongly diagnosed the cause of death."

"My God!" said his wife, putting down her knitting and going to the money that was still lying on the dresser. "You had better take it back now before Callum Macnair comes here tae get the results himself," she insisted, putting the money into his reluctant hands.

"It's late. I'll do it in the morning."

"It's not that late tae do it now. I won't sleep tonight if that money is still in this house. Take it back to him while ye can."

"What am I goin' tae say to him?"

"Just tell him ye have changed yer mind. What can he do?"

Kirkland breathed a heavy sigh, before getting up to put on his coat.

Duncan got up from his seat once Donald Kirkland had stopped talking and walked over to the window, turning his back on the nervous vet. After some silent reflection, he said, "If you don't do as we agreed, then you will never again be employed on the estate. You'll never survive on what you earn from the few crofters who can afford to pay for your services. What the hell are you worried about? All you have to do is say the sheep died of some virus and that's that. Who, in these parts, would even think to question your opinion?"

"But that's the whole thing. They trust me and I can't betray that trust."

"You're a bloody hypocrite, Kirkland! Only a few hours ago you agreed to do just that. There, take the money and don't be a bloody fool," insisted Duncan, pushing the money into Kirkland's lapel pocket.

"No, I'm not taking the money and I'm telling the Macnairs exactly what killed their sheep. It's no' a few poisoned sheep that you're worried about. If that were all, you wouldn't be in the least concerned. You're worried that the boy and his mother died as the result of this cheap dye that you've been using."

"Don't be bloody ridiculous. Two doctors signed medical certificates and they both died of different and identifiable causes," blasted Duncan.

"Maybe so, but you're still worried that at least one of the doctors may have got it wrong. The doctor who attended the boy was only recently qualified and we all know that Dr Wilson is not as able as he once was. That's why you're willing to pay me fifty pounds," said Kirkland, his voice becoming stronger as his confidence grew with each word he spoke.

"Well, Mr Kirkland, your true colours are beginning to show. For a minute I thought that you had a twinge of conscience, instead I see it's pangs of greed that have brought you back here. Well, name your price, man!"

"No, I don't think you understand, Mr Dunbar. There is no price. You can keep your money. I intend to advise the Macnair family of the true contents of the report. It's then up to them to take what they will from it. Good day, sir."

"Kirkland!" shouted Duncan. "I will leave the money in this

drawer until tomorrow evening. I think you should have a long talk with your wife tonight before you cut off the main source of your income. If you inform the Macnairs of the true contents of the report, then you will never treat another animal belonging to this estate."

Kirkland left without another word. He felt a chill as he walked out into the fresh air, his forehead was awash with sweat and his heart was beating fast, but he felt much happier than he had an hour earlier.

Chapter 11

Callum took a pinch of tobacco from his pouch and promptly dropped it from his fumbling fingers onto the floor. He was very drunk. The bar was now busy and there was a hum of voices rising through the clouds of tobacco smoke to the wooden rafters. He struggled under the table for a few minutes before finding his tobacco.

"Oh, ye bastard," he slurred, thumping his head off the table as he tried to get up from his confused, stooped position.

"Ye spilt half ma bloody pint," Angus complained, pointing to the dripping table.

"What was I saying?" asked Callum, still fumbling to roll a cigarette.

"Ye were saying ye were in love wi' somebody," replied Angus in a relatively sober voice for someone who had drank four pints of beer and six glasses of whisky.

"But yer no' goin' tae tell me who she is."

"Aye, ah would tell ye but..."

"Never mind, I know well enough."

"No, ye don't and ye'll never find out," Callum mumbled to himself.

"What was that?"

"Nothing. If I ever get married I want ye to be me best man."

"I should think so," replied Angus. "C'mon, ye better get up home, before yer no' able."

They staggered home, singing out of tune at the top of their voices. Angus had to bear most of Callum's weight as they criss-crossed from one side of the road to the other, coming very near the ditch on a few occasions. They embraced at the crossroads near the Lea Brig and bid each other a good night more times than was necessary, before parting to walk their separate ways home in the pitch darkness.

The next morning, Callum woke to the sound of excited voices coming from the back of the house. Bright rays of sunlight seeped through the cracks in the door and onto the flagstone floor. He looked over to his father's empty bed and was more than surprised to see that it was not only empty, but also made. There was also a fine fire burning with a pot of porridge left to simmer over it. For a moment he even expected his mother to appear and chide him for drinking too much the night before and sleeping late when his father and Ewan had been up for hours; if only. He forced himself to sit up and listened to the boisterous voices arguing outside. He could hear his father having words with Donald Kirkland. He dressed as quickly as his aching head would allow him, stooping every so often to listen. He could make out that they were talking about the dead sheep. Donald must have the report and, by the sounds of things, his father was none too pleased with it. He looked for a moment at the simmering porridge, deciding that his stomach would not be able to keep it down. He lifted the heavy cast iron pot away from the heat, before it dried up into an inedible crust, and went out the back to wash.

"Why didn't ye wake me?" he asked, reaching for the tin basin at the side of the house.

"Don't be putting any water in that," said his father. "The vet tells me that it's got some..."

"Toxins," assisted the vet.

"What the hell's that?" asked Callum, laying the basin back against the wall.

"It's like a poison of some kind," said his father.

Donald Kirkland explained to Callum what he had been telling his father, namely, that there was no doubt that their sheep were poisoned as a result of certain chemicals found in the stream. All three blood samples sent to Glasgow contained a lethal amount of aniline, a colourless oily liquid used in dyes. The only source of the dyes was the Laird's mill.

"There's another half dozen lying dead beside the byre, and who knows how many on the hillside," said Callum. "If it's the Laird's mill that's responsible, will he no' have tae compensate us?"

"Mind bury it deep and throw in plenty of lime," shouted Kirkland, ignoring the question and calling to Jamie, who was dragging one of the dead ewes away to be buried. "I'm sure the Laird will pay you for your loss."

"If the sheep were poisoned by dyes in the stream, then why haven't we been affected? The same water must go into our well."

"Yes. Well, I'm hopeful that the quantities found are only fatal to the likes of sheep. Of course, Dr Wilson will have to have a look at you. But I must say you both look healthy enough to me. I spoke to Duncan Dunbar and he has withdrawn the dye."

"For God's sake," shouted Callum kicking the tin basin off the side of the wall, "ye spoke to that bastard before ye told us. It took over a month tae get the report and ye tell him before us. While we're still drinking water that's been poisoned! How long have ye had the report, Kirkland?" Callum shouted, grabbing the vet by the scruff of the neck.

"For pity's sake," pleaded Kirkland, trying to catch his breath.

"Callum!" shouted his father. "Have ye gone mad?"

"Aye, maybe," said Callum, releasing the vet from his grip.

"I had to make some tests myself," explained Kirkland, fixing his ruffled collar and tie.

"Why did ye go tae Dunbar before telling us?" Callum again

demanded, not taking his eyes from the nervous vet.

"Who do ye think was paying for the report? You couldn't afford tae pay for it, so he agreed to pay for it. I didn't think there was anything wrong with that," he explained, turning to Jamie for support. "He had to be told anyway, so that the mill would stop using the dye before someone else got killed," he added before he could stop himself. At that moment, Kirkland wished that he had simply continued with his conspiracy with Duncan Dunbar and told them that the sheep died as a result of a rare virus. Even the thought of the illicit agreement caused beads of sweat to appear on his hot forehead.

"What do ye mean someone?" snapped Callum, well aware what he meant.

"Well..." Kirkland stuttered, "as I've said, there were likely only enough chemicals in the water to affect the sheep..."

"Aye, ye said that. But you also said something else. Ye were thinking about Ewan and ma, weren't ye?"

"No, I don't think... well I don't know," conceded Kirkland, taking a nervous step backwards. "Ye know yerself that both were seen by two different doctors and their symptoms were totally different, but ye'll both have tae speak tae Dr Wilson yourselves and get tests done. I'm not a doctor."

"We will!" shouted Callum, pulling on his shirt.

Duncan wiped away weeks of undisturbed grease from a window at the side of the mill as he watched Callum, gesticulating angrily in the direction of Donald Kirkland. He then produced a small silver box from his waistcoat pocket, from which he took a pinch of snuff, to clear his head, before turning to MacPherson.

"I want this mill cleaned from top to bottom. Look at these windows," he scolded, running the forefinger of his right hand down the window pane and then cleaning it on MacPherson's lapel. "You see?"

"You told me tae give the women the day off. Who is gonnae do the cleaning?"

"You have two choices: either you do it yourself or you can get the women in this afternoon. If they refuse, you have my authority to fire them. It's up to you, MacPherson. In the meantime you can take me over to Dr Wilson's."

Duncan followed Mrs Wilson into the parlour. MacPherson waited outside in the gig. The doctor's house had a homely feel to it, with the smell of baked bread coming from the kitchen and a good fire blazing in the hearth. The doctor was still wearing his dressing gown and had been reading *The Times* while finishing his breakfast. Duncan raised his hand to indicate to the surprised doctor that he need not get up.

"Have a seat, sir," offered Mrs Wilson, dusting down one of the chairs at the breakfast table.

"No thank you, Mrs Wilson. I prefer to stand. Do you mind if I have a word with your husband alone?"

"Oh, not at all. I've got plenty of work to do in the kitchen."

"I take it that this is not a social call, Duncan?" enquired the doctor, getting to his feet in spite of Duncan's wishes.

"No. It's not as a matter of fact."

"Is your father ill?" the doctor asked anxiously.

"No. No, it's nothing like that."

"Oh, I see. So what is it, Duncan? Are the stomach pains back again? As I told you the last time, if you eat rich foods ..."

"There's nothing wrong with my bloody stomach! Will you just listen for a minute and I'll tell you why I'm here."

Dr Wilson lit his pipe and cast a cold eye over Duncan, who was clearly under some kind of pressure as he began to explain why he was there. The doctor listened without interruption, not sure why he was being told about matters that seemed to have nothing to do with him.

When Duncan had finished saying his piece, Mrs Wilson came back into the parlour with a tray of tea and scones.

"Just leave them, Annie," said her husband, taking the pot from the tray and pouring himself and Duncan a cup of tea. "I was not aware that Mr Kirkland obtained a report ... never mind knowing anything of its contents. Aniline you say."

"He hasn't spoken to you?"

"No, but why should he? I'm not a veterinarian, unless, of course, he thinks these toxins got into the Macnairs' drinking water. Then that would be a different matter…a very serious matter indeed. The mother and young Ewan died very quickly after one another."

Duncan's eyes followed Mrs Wilson out of the room before he replied, "Your own diagnosis didn't show anything. All I'm asking is that you advise the Macnairs that there is no possibility that the water caused or in any way contributed to the deaths."

"I can only speak for Mrs Macnair as I didn't even see the boy. You know I was quite certain that it was a pulmonary embolism. However, now, after what you have just told me, I'm not as sure as I was."

"You didn't notice any signs of poisoning and what about the boy? Didn't he die of pneumonia? The two deaths are completely different and neither you nor Dr Munro noticed any signs of poisoning," rattled Duncan, trying to get the old doctor to stand by his original diagnosis.

"I've never come across aniline and I wouldn't know what to look for. The poison could have caused the symptoms that Dr Munro thought to be pneumonia. And it's quite possible that Betty Macnair's heart was too weak to put up the same resistance that her son had. I simply don't know. The authorities will have to be notified and the bodies may have to be exhumed for post-mortem."

"Good God, man, is this really necessary? You would think they had been murdered. If you simply tell the Macnairs that there is no question of poison being involved ..."

"I think you had better leave and take that with you!" said Dr Wilson, pointing to the roll of notes that Duncan had just placed on the table. "I will pretend that I never had this conversation with you, for your own sake! I intend to have a word with Mr Kirkland and to see this report. If I have doubts about the cause of death, I'll have no alternative but to report the matter to the Procurator Fiscal's office in Marnock. I would not attempt to bribe him if I were you."

"Very well, doctor. Speak to Kirkland if you must. I will just have to hope that your original diagnosis is accurate. Good day, doctor."

At Leaburn Castle, Callum demanded to see the Laird. When Roberts inquired into the nature of his visit, Callum told the butler it was none of his damn business, to which Roberts merely nodded his head and showed the angry young man into the parlour.

"Wait in here and I'll go and see if the Laird will see you."

"I'm sorry, Mr Roberts. I didn't mean to be rude ..."

"That's all right. I know you didn't. I'll get the Laird."

Callum stood in the centre of the room, his eyes shifting from one object of elegant finery on to another. A painting of naked women bathing in a spring of clear water caught his exploring eye. He had never seen such a painting and he felt slightly embarrassed to find himself staring at it when the door opened.

"A Caravaggio," said Charles Dunbar. "It's quite beautiful, don't you think?"

"I've no' come tae talk about paintings, yer lordship," replied Callum boldly. "Are ye aware that yer mill's been poisoning our

128

water?"

"No, I'm aware of no such thing. What makes you think the mill's doing anything of the kind?"

"Mr Kirkland told me he gave you the report..."

"What report?"

"The report he said he gave tae yer son."

"What's in this report?"

"Ye mean ye don't know?"

"Roberts!"

"Yes, sir."

"Where is my son?"

"He has gone out, sir. I don't know where."

At dinner that evening both Charles and Duncan remained silent, each waiting for the other to speak. Charles studied the serious frown on his son's face and was at least pleased to see that he was worried about the situation. The Laird asked for more potatoes, letting Duncan stew in his thoughts for a while longer.

"Why the bloody silent treatment?" Duncan finally snapped, pushing his plate away. "I know you saw Callum Macnair today. So why don't you say something?"

"I was hoping that you would say something. He was accusing me of polluting the stream at the back of their house with toxic chemicals from the mill. It's funny; I never even knew that the stream went through their croft. I also told him that the dyes we used at the mill had been in use for over fifteen years and that there hasn't been any known case of poisoning in that time that I'm aware of."

Duncan listened silently. He knew his father was enjoying this cat and mouse nonsense but he had no option; he would have to endure the humiliation. The Laird continued to unwrap his recently acquired knowledge, piece by piece. That afternoon he had already quizzed MacPherson, who had confirmed the recent change of dye being used at the mill.

"How was I to know that the dyes were poisonous? It's only a few bloody sheep that died."

"Well if that's all then you have nothing to worry about. As both Dr Wilson and Kirkland have told me, the two deaths at the Macnair home may be nothing more than just coincidence. But if there is a link, then you will have something to worry about."

"You're bloody enjoying this, aren't you?"

"Of course I am not. How many men in my position would like to see their only son in prison?"

"In prison! What do you mean?"

"I spoke with our lawyers this afternoon. George Rankin feels that criminal charges may be brought. You must have thought so yourself or you would not have gone as far as offering Donald Kirkland fifty pounds to keep the contents of the report to himself."

"The lying swine! I didn't..."

"It wasn't him that told me. In fact he denied it at first. After the Macnair lad left I had a look in your office and I found this lying in an unlocked drawer in your desk," explained the Laird, taking a small black notebook from his inside jacket pocket and throwing it across the table towards Duncan. "If you're going to try and bribe people, you shouldn't keep a record of it lying about. I suppose your visit to Dr Wilson this afternoon was for the same purpose? And although I didn't ask the doctor at the time, I am reasonably sure you tried the same thing with him. I can forgive you for trying to bribe Kirkland, but Dr Wilson? I would have thought that even you would be aware that if any man is incorruptible, it's that man."

"What if I did?" conceded Duncan. "What can we do?"

"I like that. You've made a complete mess of things and now you ask what can ...*we* do. Well, unfortunately, you are my son and I guess I will have to protect the family name from the scandal of having a criminal in the family."

"Why should I be blamed? What about the bastard that imported the stuff in the first place?"

"At this stage we just have to hope that any post-mortem produces a negative result. Then all we have to worry about is nipping the whole thing in the bud by paying the Macnairs a few pounds by way of compensation for their sheep. According to Kirkland, most of the flock are showing signs of poisoning. In the meantime our solicitor is looking into the possibilities of criminal liability for using these chemicals. From now on you will speak to no one or do anything without speaking to me first. God help you if the post mortems show that young boy and his mother were poisoned."

Burns Wallace & Co was one of only three firms of solicitors in the market town at Marnock. They were not averse to taking on cases outside their normal scope of expertise but as the senior partner, Malcolm Wallace, carefully explained to Callum and his father, suing the Laird was not a matter they could act in, as their past dealings with the Laird could give rise to a possible breach of confidentiality. By way of further impediments, Mr Wallace went on to explain the enormous cost involved in raising such an action and the difficulty in proving the case in a court of law. They would also have to consent to the bodies being exhumed and a post-mortem carried out. "Do you want that?"

"How much would it cost to take him to court?" asked Callum, in a direct, matter of fact tone, ignoring the lawyer's concerns.

"As I've been telling your father, we can't act! Even if we wanted to ..."

"So you don't want to act, is that it?" retorted Callum.

"You're not understanding what I'm saying, young man. We can't act due to the fact that we acted for the Laird in the past."

"But ye don't act for him now. Everyone in the glen knows that George Rankin does all his legal business."

"Yes, indeed," replied Mr Wallace, unable to hide his annoyance. Everyone in the glen was well aware that their best client decided to part company with his firm after Duncan Dunbar took over the running of the estate. "But, as I've tried to tell you, we have dealt with the Laird's estate for over twenty years and during that time we have had access to information that is strictly confidential. If such information was beneficial to your present action, then we would not be allowed to disclose it to you and therefore we would not be acting in your best interest. There would therefore be a conflict of interest and that would make our position as your solicitors untenable. Do you understand that?"

Callum turned to meet his father's perplexed expression. Jamie Macnair just shrugged his shoulders and said nothing. After a moment's silence, Callum got to his feet and thanked Mr Wallace for his time.

"I take it that Anderson & Co, up by the Kirk, shouldn't have this conflict of interest thing."

"No, I wouldn't have thought that Robbie Anderson has ever had any instructions from the Laird. You can try him all right. Remember what I've said about the cost of this type of case and the fact that there will have to be a post-mortem. Good day, gentlemen."

Robbie Anderson was a well-known character in the criminal courts of Scotland and in particular the Burgh Court in Marnock and the Sheriff Court at Lochgilphead. For thirty-five years he had practised law and he had the furrows of worry ploughed into his forehead to prove it. "The law changes every bloody day. Ye cannae keep up wi' it," he was often heard to mumble on his way back from court as his disgruntled client headed to prison. The truth of the matter was that Robbie wasn't too great when it came to the legal peculiarities of a case and the only clients he could get were those who could not scrape together enough money for anyone else. It was said that auld Robbie would get you six months for the price of a pint. He did win some cases but convictions were his forte, which was rather unfortunate for a defence lawyer.

"Don't worry about money," said the lawyer, peering over his broken pince-nez spectacles. "We can discuss that later. Now tell me, where is the report now?"

"I think the vet, Donald Kirkland, still has it," replied Callum. "Will you take the case?"

"I'm prepared to look into the case for you. Whether I take on the case or not will depend on what I come up with," explained the lawyer, excited at the thought of suing the Laird, although slightly apprehensive at conducting his first civil case in years. Just how many years he was not quite sure. The lawyer went on to ask a number of questions, which were intended to elicit as much information about the case as possible. He scribbled the replies and some of his own observations into a small notebook.

In mid June, Mhairi confirmed to Angus that she was pregnant. Within days of being told the good news, Angus cleared out the junk that had accumulated in the spare room, and set about converting it into a nursery. He spent ten shillings on a cot, costing nearly as much as their own bed had. He would never treat his bairn the ignorant way his father had treated him. He smiled to himself at the realisation of his dreams: soon he would be a father.

It was nearly a month after Callum had lodged his complaint at the police station in Marnock that a brown envelope arrived at the cottage. It was from the Procurator Fiscal's office. He read the letter slowly to his father. '... *After a thorough investigation into the complaint lodged at Marnock Police station on the second of this month, I can confirm that there is no evidence whatsoever to warrant the initiation of criminal proceedings against the Laird, Lord Charles Dunbar, any member of his family, or servants in his employ. I can confirm that I have spoken to both doctors involved and also the vet. In the opinion of this office, there is no evidence to warrant the disturbance of your relatives' graves and, until such evidence is forthcoming, the file on this case will remain closed...'* Callum read on, but by now the meaning of the letter was clear; there would be no criminal trial.

"Perhaps it's just as well," sighed his father. "We both used the water as much as yer mother and Ewan, and there's nothing wrong wi' us. I never did like the idea of their graves being disturbed. Let's try and put it behind us, son, and let them rest in peace."

"Aye, maybe yer right," sighed Callum, staring at the official letter, before crumbling it up and throwing it into the fire.

Duncan knew his father was enjoying his distress and it was obvious that he was in no hurry to discuss the real purpose of the lawyer's rare invitation to dinner. Dunbar had made it clear to his impatient son that he would deal with the matter at the appropriate time and not before. So Duncan suffered in silence, desperate to know the outcome of the police investigation, but in no position to bring the matter to a head. It was with relief that Duncan followed his father and their guest into the library.

"Well, you'd better put him out of his misery, George," said Charles.

"Well... the case has been fully investigated and the Procurator Fiscal has decided that there is insufficient evidence to take the matter any further."

"Why the hell could you not have told me two hours ago?"

shouted Duncan, getting to his feet and casting a contemptuous glare at the flustered lawyer.

"Oh... I would have, but..."

"But he told you not to!" Duncan interrupted, turning his anger to his grinning father.

"You're off the hook, that's all that matters. It's not often I get the chance to see you sweat," said the Laird, puffing on his cigar with a satisfied grin.

"Well to hell with the pair of you!" stormed Duncan as he rushed from the room, slamming the door behind him.

"Maybe we should have told him earlier?"

"Och, don't be worried about his little tantrums, George. He needs a lesson now and then."

The lawyer did not answer, but sheepishly sipped from his glass.

Duncan burst out into the courtyard. He breathed deep sighs of relief in the brisk fresh air. The last few months had been a nightmare. He had lived with the fear that one day the constable would appear with a warrant for his arrest. Now the weight had been lifted; he felt the burden of being under his father's power also lifting from his shoulders. *As for that bastard Kirkland, as soon as I'm Laird he's fired.* Duncan felt the resurgence of his strength with every breath that filled his lungs.

The following day Callum received a letter from Anderson & Co, advising that an offer of compensation had been received at his office in respect of the poisoned sheep. That afternoon he travelled through to Marnock to discuss the offer and the decision of the Procurator Fiscal not to take criminal proceedings. As Mr Anderson explained, forty pounds was a handsome price for such a claim and it was obvious to him that it was an inflated offer with guilt written all over it.

"What are ye saying?" snapped Callum.

"Exactly, what I have just said. The fact that the Crown has not found evidence makes it virtually impossible for us to benefit from their investigation. Without money to pay for our own experts to carry out tests then we have no case. You must remember it's over three months now since they were buried so any trace of poisoning has almost certainly vanished by now. I spoke with the fiscal and he's confirmed that the two doctors are standing by the death certificates that they signed."

"You think I should sign."

"I don't see what else you can do?"

Callum stared at the document for a moment and then, to the lawyer's horror, ripped it in two.

"We may not have the money to prove what killed them, but I'm no' taking their guilt money tae help them sleep easier. Thanks for yer help anyway, but ye can tell them that there are some people that even they cannae buy."

At Leaburn, the threat of war was now the main topic of conversation at the breakfast table, as the news of the assassination of the Archduke Franz Ferdinand and his wife quickly reached even the remotest corners of Europe. "There will be war in Europe before the year is out," sighed Dunbar, folding away his morning paper, as Morag served him his favourite breakfast of kippers with a poached egg.

"That can only be good for business," replied Duncan, unable to understand his father's apparent inability to see the opportunities a war in Europe would present.

"We would only see the benefit if this country becomes involved, God forbid."

"Why should Britain become involved in a war in Europe?" asked Caitriona.

"The Germans have their eye on our Empire and this ultimatum by Austria is the excuse they have been waiting for to start something. The Russians have already mobilised," explained her father.

"Well let them try," scoffed Duncan. "We will soon show them who they are dealing with. Anyway, if a war starts then our coal and livestock will triple in price overnight."

"That might be the case, but there is always a price to pay in any war and this one will be no different. Let's hope the British Government has the sense to stay out."

"Nonsense," said Duncan. "I hope they have the sense to put the Kaiser in his place if he starts anything."

"Be careful what you wish for," replied his father.

As Callum opened the door, he was surprised to see Mr Anderson standing there. The lawyer smiled and removed his bowler hat, "Good morning, Mr Macnair. Can I come in?"

"Of course, Mr Anderson, come in."

Callum led the lawyer into the room and offered him the chair by the fire. Mr Anderson took off his heavy grey coat and removed his gloves, before making himself comfortable.

"Is your father in?" he asked, taking out some papers from his worn leather briefcase.

"He's out back feeding the hens. Will I get him?"

"Yes, but after I speak to you first...You will recall the offer of forty pounds that the Laird made to you, by way of settlement for the loss of your sheep?"

"Aye."

"I must say that when you tore up the offer, I was initially stunned and I should add, very quickly impressed."

"I never tore it up tae impress you."

"Oh, I know, that's what impressed me. I did not mean to sound patronising. It worried me a great deal that you should have the unanswered questions of your mother and brother's deaths hanging over you, and so I made some investigations myself. I managed to obtain the toxicology report, which had been influential in the Procurator Fiscal's decision not to proceed further with the matter on a criminal basis. I had this report looked over by a friend at Glasgow University, who is a forensic scientist. I can tell you that the contents of the reports are accurate and that the findings of the report are that the sheep examined were poisoned by the toxins discharged into the stream from the Laird's mill. However the toxin in question was not concentrated enough in the water to kill a human being." The lawyer waited for some response from his silent client.

Callum got to his feet and walked over to the window. "Do you believe the report?"

"I have no reason to doubt it. It also backs up the medical certificates by both doctors."

"I don't understand. Why have you gone to all this trouble?"

"I'm a lawyer. You came to me for help and to be honest, I was quite looking forward to suing the Laird. That notion soon seemed very selfish and when you tore up the offer in my office that day, well I decided that if there was a case for the Laird, or more correctly his son, Duncan, to answer, then I was at least going to look further into what evidence there was available. It is now certainly the case that both your mother and brother died as both doctors had stated, and not by poisoning. You should now be able to let their memories rest in peace and not feel any guilt about not being able to get to the truth of their deaths. I have a copy of the report and a letter from my friend in Glasgow, giving his opinion on the matter. Here, take them and read them. You must put this whole thing behind you," added

138

the lawyer, handing Callum the papers.

"Ye must be thinking that I was a fool tae tear up that offer now," said Callum, flicking through the official looking report.

"Oh, not at all. You had every reason to refuse the money. We had no report then to refer to, but being a rather cautious man when it comes to money, I continued to negotiate matters on you behalf, while carrying on my own investigations. I managed to get the Laird to raise his offer to sixty pounds. And now there is no reason why you should not take the money."

"Why is he willing to pay so much if he's already seen the report and knows that no criminal proceedings are being taken?" asked Callum as his father came in and sat quietly by the window.

"Simple," said the lawyer, nodding his acknowledgement of Jamie's presence. "The Procurator Fiscal has advised the Laird that no criminal proceeding under the Toxic Pollutants Act 1894 will be taken against his son, so long as any claims arising out of the death of the livestock are settled and there is no repetition."

After some further discussion, Callum was satisfied with the lawyer's advice and the situation was explained to his father. The discharge form was finally signed.

"What about yer fee, Mr Anderson?" asked Callum as the lawyer got up to leave.

"Oh, don't you worry about that. As part of the settlement I made sure that they would pay my fees on top of any compensation. You'll receive your compensation within a few weeks. Good day to you both."

As the lawyer closed the door behind him, Jamie looked at his son and said in a soft voice. "At least we'll be able to get a decent gravestone."

Chapter 12

Autumn 1914

On the estate moors, at the other side of the loch, Charles Dunbar had already bagged twelve grouse, and a couple of quail. Only Lord Mortimer had achieved a more successful morning with nineteen birds. The party of eight had paired off into four teams, with Dunbar shooting alongside Sir Randolph Guthrie MP; a fine parliamentarian, but a poor shot. In between the bursts of gunfire, the Laird's two black Labradors retrieved the game from the dense heather, as the gamekeepers continued to flush out more birds into the line of fire.

Once the last of the birds were retrieved, the party celebrated the shoot with a dram of whisky before returning to Leaburn. Only Duncan looked miserable as they walked back over the moors to the waiting gigs. He had a bad day's sport, with only a handful of birds. His father's success with the gun only added to his own frustration. "Never mind, Duncan, there's always tomorrow," said Lord Mortimer, who offered him another nip of whisky from his hip flask.

Roberts set up a picnic table near the edge of the loch and a large tea urn was carried all the way from the castle by two of the stable boys. Roberts dressed the table with a white linen cloth, while Morag emptied a large hamper. She placed plates and cutlery beside the silver salvers containing joints of carved cold meat. When the hunting party returned in the afternoon, Macpherson and young Williams collected the sacks of birds from the gamekeepers and took them back to the castle for Mrs Roberts to prepare for dinner that night. Dunbar acknowledged Roberts hard work with a nod and a smile as he led his guest to the loch side picnic.

"What's the latest news, Randolph?"

"You'll know as much as me, Charles. I'm not in the War Cabinet, remember."

"You must have some idea of how things are going. Here, have some of this boiled ham."

"Thank you, Charles. Well, the only thing I'm hearing that is any different from what's being written in the papers, is that the number of casualties are much higher than reported, but that's to be expected, for morale you understand … oh that's quite enough," he added in his gruff voice, as Morag placed another slice of ham on his plate.

"Is it true that this damn thing might last a whole year?"

"The way things are bogged down at the moment it might be years. It certainly won't be over by Christmas, you can be sure of that."

"I'm worried, Randolph," said Dunbar, turning in the direction of Duncan, who was with the rest of the shooting party. "He's the only son I have and even though we don't get on well, I couldn't bear to lose him."

"Well unless he's foolish enough to sign up you have nothing to worry about."

"If the casualties continue to be so high then they'll have to bring in conscription, surely?"

"Well, maybe. At present there is no plan to do so. There's enough bloody fools around only too eager to get their heads shot off for King and country."

"I'm surprised to hear you being so cynical. I thought you Tories were behind the Liberals and the war a hundred per cent."

"If I knew one good reason for Britain to be in it then I might be. If you're worried about Duncan being drafted into the war, then don't. I can easily have him classified as holding a position of national importance. The coal that you're supplying the Ministry of War is essential and, as far as the Company papers are concerned, it's Duncan that's the named supplier. So don't worry about him being conscripted; he'll come through the war unscathed and probably financially better off."

In late October, Fraser received his commission to join his father's old regiment, and took the train to Marnoch to formally ask Dunbar for his daughter's hand. Caitriona was already making plans; sure in the knowledge that her father would be pleased they had finally named the day.

Fraser was met by Henderson, Dunbar's new chauffer. "I see the Laird has finally been seduced by the motor vehicle."

"Yes, sir, it's a fine machine, I am proud to drive it," said Henderson as he placed Fraser's suitcase on the rack at the back of the car.

When the car pulled up outside Leaburn, Caitriona rushed out to meet Fraser. They embraced. "You look so handsome," she sighed as she straightened his tie. "And they made you a captain already?"

"Oh, that's because I'm a doctor and not really a soldier. Is your father home?"

"No, he's out with a party of friends on a grouse shoot. He'll be home this afternoon. Oh, don't tell me you're still afraid of him?" she teased on seeing the strain appearing on Fraser's face. "He'll be the one that's afraid when he sees you in your uniform."

"Let's go for a walk," suggested Caitriona as she took his arm.

"Why don't we take the car?"

"No, I want to show you off in your new uniform."

They walked hand-in-hand, along the loch side with the late autumn sun on their backs. When they reached the crossroads at Lea Brig, Caitriona noticed Callum Macnair working in the fields. He was quite far off, but she knew it was him. His face and arms were brown from the long summer and he looked strong as he lifted forks of hay on to the top of a large haystack. She pretended to be tired and suggested they sit for a while. Fraser took off his jacket and placed it on the grass so she could sit on it. They watched a small boat in the shallows.

"Look! He's caught one," said Fraser as a creel was pulled on board and the lobster removed. The fisherman did not seem too impressed with his catch, and threw the young lobster back into the loch.

Caitriona turned to see Callum walking down the field towards the Macnair cottage. She turned back to the loch when she felt Fraser looking at her.

"That's the young fellow who lost his mother and brother. Is it not?"

"Yes. I think it is. Will you take me back now; it's getting a bit chilly."

At dinner that evening, Caitriona sat proudly opposite Fraser, as the others in the company offered their congratulations. A toast to the happy couple was followed by a toast to the King. The wedding was to be at the end of the month only two weeks before Fraser was due to leave for France. The news of the wedding was met with just as much excitement by the servants as it was spread through the castle in whispers and smiles. When it finally reached the kitchen, Mrs Roberts poured herself a sherry to celebrate, before sending up the next course of roast grouse in a blackberry and red wine sauce. She was already thinking about the menu for the wedding.

On the morning of the wedding, all sorts of vehicles drove up and down the glen road with whatever Dunbar thought was necessary to make his daughter's wedding day the talk of polite society for years to come. The ordinary glen folk looked on with curiosity at the comings and goings from Leaburn.

Callum stood on the hillside and watched the wedding procession on the narrow road from the Kirk to Leaburn. The villagers cheered the horse drawn carriage carrying the bride and groom as the church bells proclaimed their marriage to the world. Callum sat for much of the morning on the hillside watching from afar. "Tess!" he eventually said, as the last of the wedding guests disappeared into grandeur that was Leaburn castle. "Let's go home, there's no' much down there for the likes of us."

When the day finally came for Fraser to leave, a dread came to Caitriona's heart when she saw the fear in his eyes as he struggled to eat his breakfast. He smiled when he realised she was looking at him. "Don't worry, darling, by the time I get there it will probably be all over."

"Oh, I hope so," she said as she took his hand.

The train was already putting out steam. They embraced. The platform was crowded with hundreds of raw recruits from across the glen. Fraser held Caitriona as their final kiss was smothered in the steam from the noisy locomotive. They only broke their embrace when a sergeant major bawled out orders to the stragglers to get on the train.

Fraser waved to Caitriona from the crowded carriage. She watched the train disappear in a cloud of smoke before returning to the car. Henderson doffed his cap as he opened the passenger door. "He'll be fine, Miss," he said.

"Thank you, Henderson."

The trees along the loch side were almost bare and there was snow already on the mountains to the north. Poor Fraser, she thought as Henderson changed gear and turned into the next brae.

It was a cold winter's day, but Angus was determined to collect much needed stores from the wholesale shop in Marnock. He rigged up the cart he had borrowed from Callum and kissed Mhairi goodbye, warning her to stay in bed and not to be up and about in case she caught another cold.

"Remember what Dr Wilson said about taking things easy," he stressed when they parted.

"Och away and don't be so daft. It's only a bairn I'm having."

The remnants of the previous night's snow had turned into slush and the low winter's sun was quickly making the slush into puddles of icy water. The road became muddy the nearer he got to Marnock, and he had to keep a tight rein on the old donkey. The town itself was very busy as he pulled up outside the hardware store. His curiosity was drawn to the other side of the road, where a large crowd had gathered around the steps at the front of the town hall. On the top step, between two neo-classical pillars, stood a little man, in a pin-striped suit and bowler hat. Angus crossed the road to see what was going on. He watched from the back of the crowd, as the speaker waved his fists in the air and spat out well-rehearsed patriotic slogans. A bloody warmonger, thought Angus. The crowd stood in silence; most were unaccustomed to such a forceful manner of public speaking. Every so often, heads would nod in agreement to confirm the veracity of this gifted orator.

"... And in the fields of glory, the prime of our nation is holding back the might of the German army. The Hun is strong and our brave soldiers will need all the support and help that we can give them. You young men! You must search your conscience and consider whether or not you can sleep in your warm beds at night, while your fellow Scots cry out for your help! A dark cloud of evil has spread over the towns and cities of our allies, in Belgium and France. Men and women, young and old, are being butchered by these German monsters."

He then took off his bowler hat and held it to his chest. "God save the King!" he shouted. This was met with a mixed reaction from the crowd, some responded in kind, while others mumbled amongst themselves as the man beseeched those willing to serve their country to … "Sign up here and stand with pride against the evil Hun!"

Angus's eyes followed the man's pointing finger towards two soldiers sitting at a desk under an imposing poster of Lord Kitchener. There were half a dozen or so young men already in a queue in front of the table, which was draped in a Union Flag. "A shilling a day is a hero's pay!" the warmonger shouted, his face grinning in satisfaction as he led the cheers of the crowd at each new member to join the line of recruits. A burst of laughter erupted as an angry mother dragged one young, potential soldier from the queue. "War! I'll give ye war! Wait till I get ye home," she scolded as her son's face turned scarlet with the shame of his public humiliation.

When the crowd finally dispersed, Angus walked back to the store to pick up the supplies, and a bottle of whisky to wet the baby's head when the time came. After he had loaded the cart, covering the stores with a sheet of canvas, he went into a nearby ladies clothes shop to buy Mhairi a gift. The hat he finally settled on cost three shillings. Three days in the army, he thought cynically. Anyway, Mhairi had been complaining about not having any fine clothes for the Christening. At least this was a start, he thought to himself as he tucked the present under the seat at the front of the cart. Having completed his intended chores, he flicked open his watch and decided that an hour in the tavern by the market place would not do any harm.

There were only a few customers in the bar, and he ordered himself a glass of beer and a whisky. He sat by the window opposite a blazing peat fire, the heat thawing his cold hands. His thoughts were about the war and how foolish men were to sign up to get killed for the sake of a shilling a day or the boast of killing some foreigner. It's a crazy bloody world all right, he sighed as he tried to remember the reason for the war, but for the life of him he could not recall. Och, to hell with it anyway, he concluded, throwing back his glass of whisky with a satisfied grimace on his face. It's another bloody English war anyway. Those buggers are not happy unless they're fighting with somebody. Any Scotsman who joined up to fight under the Union Jack had a short memory after what they bastards did at Culloden! He ordered another drink.

After a while two soldiers staggered into the bar with two giggling girls clinging to their arms. The soldiers wore Douglas tartan trews and green doublets, the uniform of the Cameronians Scottish Rifles. They looked like complete opposites; one was small and fat, with a cheery red face, while the other was skinny, with a long, grey face and sunken eyes. The girls were the type that Angus had seen in many a foreign port; their faces covered in cheap make-up.

"Up the Scottish Rifles!" The skinny one shouted as he raised a full glass of whisky to his mouth, managing to drink half of it before spluttering and coughing in retreat. Angus sat quietly at the window looking out at the throng of activity in the busy main street. His mind was quickly going through the list of stores that he had bought, wondering if he had forgotten anything. It began to snow again and, as he contemplated the long journey home, he convinced himself that another whisky might be required to keep the cold out.

The temperature had dropped outside and the slush was beginning to turn to ice, allowing the fresh fall of snow to take hold. He wiped the condensation from the window and peered out to make sure the donkey and cart were still tied up securely. He took out his clay pipe and knocked the head of the pipe against the heel of his boot, emptying its crispy brown contents on to the floor. He lit his refilled pipe, inhaling briskly and puffing out the thick clouds of smoke at the same time, until he was sure that the tobacco was burning nicely. He promised himself that he would get off home as soon as he had finished his whisky and smoked his pipe, although he was in no great hurry to finish either.

After a short time, he reluctantly got to his feet and, after tapping the hot ash from his pipe into the smouldering fire, he took his empty glass over to the bar and made to leave.

"Och, don't be horrible," giggled one of the girls at the bar as she pulled at the other's arm. "Don't, Wilma."

"Shush," said Wilma, pulling her arm away from her friend's grip.

"How's Mhairi?" asked Wilma, her face filled with contempt.

"What?" Angus replied, surprised that she seemed to be addressing him.

"How's Mhairi MacDougall?" she repeated. "Are ye no' the big daft mug that married her?" She threw her cigarette on the floor.

"Wilma!" shouted the barman. "Leave the lad alone."

"What the hell are ye on about?" said Angus, his voice rising with anger. "Yer nothing but a cheap bit of trash!"

"Drink yer drink and shut up," said the skinny soldier, pulling Wilma back from Angus.

"Let go, ye bastard," shouted Wilma, pushing the soldier away. "He's got the right tae know about the cunning bitch."

"Know what?" demanded Angus.

"That it's no' yer bairn she's carrying! That's what," she hissed at him.

"What the hell ar' ye saying, ye lying whore?" shouted Angus grabbing her by the throat.

"Let her go!" shouted the skinny soldier, trying to restrain Angus from behind. "For God's sake, man! Yer choking her!"

Angus released his grip as she coughed and spluttered to gain her breath. "Yer a lyin' bitch," he said, pushing her hard against the bar.

"Ask her yerself?" she shouted after him. "Everybody knows it's

Toby Black's bairn. Everybody knows she's been coming through here tae bed him while yer out on that silly fishing boat trying tae catch fish. Ye bloody fool!"

Angus pushed the doors open and rushed out into the cold night. He felt sick and confused. He could hear her shouting and cursing after him. He crossed the slippery road to the cart, struggling to keep his balance in the icy slush. "Bitch, lying fuckin' bitch," he cursed, wiping the snow from the seat, before climbing on to the cart.

His mind was tormented as he tried to steady the cart, which slid on the ice under the fresh snow. He held the reins tightly, his knuckles turning white with the icy winds that cut into them. He took the bottle of whisky from one of the sacks under the canvas and drank from the neck of the bottle. As he drank, his defence of Mhairi's virtue turned on its head and he began to doubt her more with every mouthful, his mind soon in turmoil with the drink and his rage. The more he drank, the more he believed that Mhairi had made a fool out of him.

It began to snow heavily again, but he did not notice. He could hear Wilma's screeching laughter inside his crowded head. *"Everybody knows. Everyone but you, ye bloody fool!"* He could see all the faces in MacTaggart's, talking and laughing amongst themselves; laughing at him? Even Callum must have known! *"Everybody knows. Everyone but you!"* His mind began to run riot with rage. Wilma's twisted, ugly face screamed at him with a shrill laugh as the other girl and the two soldiers repeated her taunt. The bottle was soon empty and he threw it into the darkness, cursing Mhairi for a whore, at the top of his voice. He remembered the hat under the seat, and pulled it from its box, before throwing it with all his might into the wind, which caught the wide brim and blew it across the snow-covered fields and halfway back to Marnock.

By the time he reached Glenfay, his mind was full of the madness. Mhairi was resting by the fire when she heard the cart pull up outside the house; she smiled to herself, knowing fine well that Angus must have stopped off for a drink. She folded away the small blanket that she had been knitting and stirred the pot of stew hanging over the fire. She got a fright when the door opened with a bang, knocking a china ornament from the dresser.

"What in heavens is wrong with ye?" she shouted, kneeling beside the smashed fragments of the ornament. "Good God, yer roaring drunk!" she said as she watched him staggering into the room, his eyes wild and hateful towards her. She forgot about the broken ornament. "What's wrong? Why have ye got yerself so drunk?" she asked in a nervous voice.

He stared at her. "What's wrong?" he shouted. "What's wrong?" He made to grab at her but he was too drunk and he fell against the fireplace. "Ye damn whore," he shouted. "Ye've been making a bloody fool out ah me."

"What are ye talking about?" she said, moving near the door.

"I was talking tae one of yer friends. Aye one of them painted whores, like yerself."

"Who have ye been talkin' tae?"

"Ye bloody slut!" he shouted as he lunged forward.

Mhairi screamed and ran from the house.

"Aye, get tae hell and take Toby Black's bastard wi' ye," he shouted as he slammed the door after her. His rage turned on the furniture, pulling and kicking anything that reminded him of Mhairi and the wedding. He stopped to find a half bottle of whisky that he remembered was in the dresser. He opened it and took a hefty swig, before overturning the dresser, smashing its glass front and contents on the stone floor. "The Devil's whore," he shouted as he slumped on the floor in the corner of the room. He lay in the ruins of their home crying like a child until he finally fell into a drunken sleep.

Mhairi ran through what was now a snowstorm and found refuge in a neighbour's home. Although she wanted to go back after a few hours, Elspeth Murray was a very persuasive woman and made her stay the night.

"It's no' just yerself ye have tae worry about now," she said, looking at her husband, who nodded with every word his wife spoke. "What if he hits ye this time? What about the bairn? Yer more than welcome tae stay the night wi' us. The boys are able tae share a bed; ye can have Hamish's bed for the night. Angus will be a different man in the morning. That whisky can make the devil out of any man."

"Aye, Elspeth, maybe yer right. But ah don't want tae be too much trouble tae ye."

"That's a good lass. Ye'll be nae trouble tae us."

The following morning, Mhairi returned home and tentatively opened the front door. She turned in tears into Elspeth's open arms when she saw her furniture and things scattered and broken about the floor.

"Angus Campbell!" called out Elspeth as she moved into the wreckage of the room, with Mhairi still sobbing in her arms. "Where the hell are ye hiding, ye big, drunken fool?"

It was another two days before Mhairi finally gave up waiting for Angus's return. She was unable to make any sense out of his sudden change from a gentle, loving man to that of a foul-mouthed, drunken madman. She was expecting him to return, shame-faced and pleading for her forgiveness. At first she was resolute; he would not be forgiven and she would demand that he find somewhere else to live, but as the hours ticked away she became desperate for his return at any price. She knew someone had poisoned his mind against her, but she had told Angus about Toby Black and at the time he was not interested in the least, '*it's in the past,*' was all he said, and that was the end of the matter. She looked around at the wrecked house with chairs overturned and smashed glass from picture frames scattered about the floor. She had left it that way to show him the kind of monster he was in drink and to win a pledge that he would never drink again for the sake of her and the baby. His hurtful words began to run through her confused and tired mind again. She nervously picked up the broken china and glass; many of the shattered ornaments had been wedding presents. She felt the hot tears running down her cheeks as she tried to make sense of the madness that had stolen away her happiness. Where was he? she wondered, no longer concerned about the destruction all about her. She could not wait any longer and she threw her shawl over her shoulders and rushed from the house, stopping at every corner to make sure she did not meet any of the neighbours.

Callum knew immediately that there was something wrong when he opened the door to find Angus's heavily pregnant wife standing like a battered scarecrow in the biting December winds.

"What's the matter, Mhairi?"

"Can I speak tae ye for a minute?"

"Of course, come in and get heat at the fire, ye look frozen."

"Is yer feyther out?" she asked looking in the direction of the box-bed.

"Aye, he's away tae the village. He'll no' be back for a bit yet. What's the matter, Mhairi?" he asked with concern, as she let her shawl fall to her shoulders, revealing her tear-stained face and red sleepless eyes.

"What the hell is wrong?" he asked again.

She turned to look queerly into the flickering, yellow flames that jumped madly to catch the fresh peat that Callum had, only a few minutes before, thrown on top of the morning's red hot ashes. "It's Angus," she finally said, her voice broken with heavy sobs. "He's left me."

"What? When? What happened?" rattled Callum, getting to his feet.

"I thought you might know. Have ye no' seen him?"

"I saw him on Friday night, but no' since and he never seemed upset or anything. When did he leave?"

"Saturday night. He was at Marnock that day and everything seemed fine when he left, but he came home that night roaring drunk, cursing me and calling me a whore. Oh, Callum, ye know that's no' true."

"Whit got in tae him?"

"Somebody must have said something about Toby."

"Did ye no' tell him anything about you and Black?"

"Sure I told him, but he wasn't interested. Now he thinks I'm carrying Toby's bairn."

"Did he say who told him that?"

"Some painted whore, he called her. He was so mad that he smashed up the house and called me the devil's whore!" she sobbed.

"Hush," pleaded Callum. "But Black can only be out the jail a few months; the baby must be near due. Has he no sense? He must have been mad wi' the drink all right."

"He's no' coming back, is he?"

"He'll be back. Once he's cooled off and sees what a fool he's been. He'll be back. He'll no' want tae miss the bairn being born."

"But that's it; he doesn't think it's his bairn I'm carrying." She started to cry again. "He said he's no' staying around here tae have people laughing behind his back. 'Ye can look after yer ain bastard,' he shouted at me. The big fool, can he no' just count the months and see it's his bairn I'm carrying all this time. What am I goin' tae do, Callum?" she said, raising a trembling hand to her mouth. "Dae ye think he's away tae get a ship? Oh God, I feel sick."

"Here, lie down a while. I'll go into Marnock tae see if I can find him," he said and wrapped a blanket around her shivering body.

Late that night Callum returned from Marnock to find Mhairi lying sleeping by the fire. His father had come home to find her there and let her sleep.

"What's goin' on?" he asked in a whisper as Callum, looking exhausted, sat down to take off his heavy boots.

"It's Angus … he's disappeared. He's been missing for two days. They had some kind of row."

"Don't tell me he's had enough of married life already."

"Callum!" said Mhairi in a startled voice as she woke to see him sitting opposite her. "Did ye find him? Is he all right?"

"No, Mhairi. No one's seen him since Saturday afternoon."

"What am I goin' tae do? He's no' coming' back, is he? He's away tae Glasgow tae get another ship. Oh, my bairn," she cried in despair. "What about me bairn?"

"There, there," said Jamie, putting his hand on her thin shoulder.

"I'll go through tae Glasgow tomorrow," said Callum.

"Oh, will ye, Callum, will ye? Me bairn needs its feyther."

"Aye, but I cannae promise that I'll find him. Here, put on yer shawl and I'll walk ye home. I met Mrs Murray on the way home and she said she would get a good fire going for ye and make ye something decent tae eat."

"Oh, but I'm no' hungry. I'm no' hungry," she repeated.

Callum spent the next two days in Glasgow, but he could not find Angus. He returned home dejected. The weeks passed. His baby daughter was born three days before Christmas and christened at the

Kirk and named Fiona Campbell. Everyone said she had Angus's smiling eyes.

Chapter 13

Angus watched a procession of soldiers marching through the bitter cold along Sauchiehall Street in the centre of Glasgow. The sound of the pipes and the beat of the drums mingled with the cheers and whistles of the excited crowds that thronged the pavements. Only weeks ago he had sneered at a similar procession, but then he still had money in his pockets and food in his belly. His mind was made up; there was nothing to go home for but ridicule. He would take the King's shilling and take his chances with the rest that were marching off to France. At least no one would know him and he didn't care too much if he got killed or not. What better credentials do you need for joining the army?

After a cursory medical, he was enlisted as Private Angus Campbell, the newest recruit of the Argyll and Sutherland Highlanders. The following day he found himself in an army training camp in Stirling. As the alcohol was sweated out of him, his body was gradually forced back into fitness, but very few could get a civil word out of him and he spent at least two of his first six weeks of training behind bars for fighting with other recruits. He tried to get Mhairi out of his mind but he could not stop his dreams and his nights were tortured by the sneering taunts of Wilma McGonagall. None of the men in the barracks would dare wake him during one of these nightmares.

The battalion arrived in France on the 22nd of February 1915. They were deployed to support the 1st Argylls, who held a sector of trenches forward of Sanctuary Wood in Belgium. There were no offensives in the first few months and Angus settled down to the tedium and squalor of trench life. The routine was as mind-numbing as the constant bombardments; eight days in the trenches, with no more than a hole in the trench wall to sleep in, and then eight days in the reserve camp just behind the front lines. He manned a Lewis machine gun post along with a happy-go-lucky sergeant, by the name of Colin McNeil, who had served two years in India, putting down many an uprising in the Punjab. "If those crazy bastards got their hands on ye, they'd skin ye alive and feed ye tae the vultures," he told Angus, spitting out his chewed tobacco in their unsavoury memory. "It makes a bullet or a bayonet seem quite civilised."

An unexpected artillery bombardment suddenly pounded the trenches, causing men to dive for their lives in the rat-infested mud. Angus stayed at his post with the tobacco-spitting sergeant, who winked at him in his typical devil may care manner. "If yer name's on it, there's no' much use getting in tae a panic," he said and laughed as the shells exploded all around them.

When the bombardment stopped and those not killed or maimed picked themselves up. The sergeant slapped Angus on the back. "Yer no' got a death wish or anything like that?"

Angus did not answer, but turned away to look out over the parapet.

"Keep yer head down, lad!" shouted the sergeant. "Do ye want tae get it blown off? What's the matter wi' ye, lad? Every other new recruit is shitting in his pants every time there's a bombardment and you don't even budge a muscle to protect yerself."

"Ah don't see you diving for cover," snapped Angus.

"I've been at this soldiering game all my life. I'll know when tae duck when the time comes. I don't think you give a damn. Is it a woman that's eating away at ye?"

"I don't want tae talk about it," said Angus, suddenly feeling more vulnerable than he had when the shells were falling.

The sergeant saw the hurt in Angus's eyes and changed the subject. "Well, it's nearly time for bully beef and maggot pie," he laughed. "You can go and get yours first; if I'm lucky I might get hit with a mortar before I get hungry."

The following morning, the British heavy guns opened up an almighty bombardment on the German lines. The constant barrage made the air around the trenches heavy with the smell of cordite and fear as the battalion was ordered to stand ready and fix bayonets. The officers were in a state of high excitement and barked out orders along the trenches. 'No man's land' disappeared into a fog of smoke as the shelling continued for over two hours.

"Don't worry, men, there'll be no one left in the *Bosche* trenches but ghosts," shouted the company major, watching the bombardment through his field glasses.

Angus wiped his mud smeared bayonet on his kilt and fixed it to his rifle. The choking smoke from the exploding shells began to fill the trenches. Men were coughing and wiping the hot tears from their eyes when the whistles began to blow. The battalion emerged en masse from the sanctuary of the trenches into the churned-up wasteland of no man's land. The pipers played the regiment's battle tune, the *Skye Boat Song*, as the waves of men walked in staggered formation with their rifles upright. The Germans quickly re-emerged from their concrete bunkers and their callous machine guns opened up, ripping through the line of exposed soldiers as the advance quickly disintegrated into chaos. "Keep the line!" shouted the captain as some of the men began to turn and run back to their own trenches, while others threw themselves into the newly created shell holes for cover. Under constant fire, Angus could hear the bullets whistle past his head, but continued to advance with the main body of men. He saw his company piper felled by a spray of machine-gun fire. Without much thought for his own safety, he took the pipes from the dying piper's hands and marched on through the bedlam, playing one of the few tunes he knew well enough to get the pipes roused, *Mary O' Argyll*.

What was left of the battalion eventually reached the chaos of enemy front lines, where hand-to-hand fighting took place with bayonets, before the first few trenches were captured. In a well prepared plan, the Germans quickly withdrew to their heavily defended back-up trenches as their own field guns opened up on their captured front line. The only senior officer to reach the German line, Captain Milligan, looked with dismay at the exhausted remnants of his battalion, and decided that the advance was doomed. The captain ordered his men to retreat.

Under the cover of a smoke screen, the survivors, many badly wounded, crawled back into their own trenches with the merciless, enemy machine-gun fire claiming more victims. The Germans soon recaptured their briefly lost trenches and their heavy guns then opened up and bombarded the British line for hours.

By the end of the day, when the guns eventually fell silent, the battalion had lost over three hundred men and gained nothing. Other battalions along the British lines had suffered even greater losses. The offensive was a complete failure. The British trenches were now hastily preparing for a German counter-attack as the generals ordered reserve troops to the front to cover their losses.

In time, the fear of a German offensive passed and the rain began to fall in a torrent, turning 'no man's land' into a breathing quagmire. As night fell on the battlefield, the wounded were taken out to waiting ambulances and then onto the clearing stations just behind the front line. For no obvious reason, other than to show they were still there, a British gun battery began to send over shells into the German trenches.

"What are the bloody fools doing?" shouted Captain Milligan, coming out of his dug-out and looking back at the moonlit ridge where the shells were coming from. "Sergeant, send someone up to those bloody idiots and tell them to stop that racket and save their shells."

The battery continued to fire its 16 inch shells, whizzing over their own lines to the dismay of the exhausted men trying to get some rest and come to terms with the horrors of their failed attack. Angus watched the silhouette figures of the gunners against the large pale moon. Suddenly, there was an almighty explosion and the battery disappeared in a blinding flash after taking a direct hit from a very accurate German Howitzer. Captain Milligan shook his head and went back into his dug-out without saying a word. Most of the men in the trench were just glad the shelling had stopped and slipped off into a corpse-like sleep.

Callum took some peat over to Mhairi, who had not been feeling well since the birth of the baby. Her heart was broken. She wrote four times to the regiment, but after two months there was still no reply.

"Have ye heard anything?" she asked as he stacked some fresh peat on the fire.

"No, nothing … but he might not have got my letters."

"Oh, Callum, it's been months since he joined up. Do ye...?"

"Och no, don't be thinking like that. They'd soon tell ye if anything happened to him. How's the baby?" he asked, taking a chair by the window and looking into the cot.

"She's well; Angus's mother still comes over every day to help me with her."

"Has he still no' written tae his ma again in all this time?"

"She's said he hasn't, only that letter in February saying he joined up with the Argylls and was on his way tae France."

They fell silent for a while. Mhairi noticed that Callum was troubled about something; she hadn't seen him so agitated before. He sat staring out the window smoking nervously. The clock on the wall ticked loudly in the silence that had come between them.

"It will soon be summer again," he said finally in a faraway voice. "Mhairi, I'm goin' tae join up tomorrow."

"What! You're no' serious," she said in a startled voice.

"Aye, tomorrow morning, I've been thinking about it for weeks now. Someone has to tell Angus about that twisted bitch McGonagall that fed him wi' all those lies about you. I've written to him and explained everything, but if he's not getting or accepting his letters then what else can we do?"

"Callum, ye can't just sign up and go there, get him and then come back again. The two of ye might get killed."

"There's talk of conscription coming in anyway. I'm as well volunteering before they start dragging us out our beds to enlist. If I volunteer, I'll be able to pick the regiment."

"Oh, Callum," she said, crossing the floor and throwing her arms around his neck. He put on his cap to leave, and forced some money into her reluctant hands.

"Take it for the baby," he insisted.

The following day Tess followed Callum around the house, sensing that something was wrong.

"Don't let her follow me," he said to his father as he patted the anxious collie on the head. "And don't be fretting, lass. I'll be back in a few months."

"Here take this wi' ye," said his father, taking some of the compensation money from under his mattress. "I've got enough to pay for the headstone."

"Ah don't want it. You'll need it more than me," replied Callum, putting the money back into his father's hand.

When time came to leave, Callum wanted to hug his father but they were never able to show such feelings and even now the thought passed quickly.

"Bye then. I'll write when I get tae the camp in Stirling."

"Here, tak' this," said Jamie, offering the corn dolly to him.

"Feyther…it's only a wee bit of twisted corn stalks…"

"It will protect ye, son. I'll feel better if ye had it wi ye."

"All right, if it makes ye feel better," said Callum, reluctantly taking the corn dolly and putting it in his backpack. "Will ye be all right?"

"Aye, I'll make another one…look after yerself," said Jamie, turning away to stare into the fire. There was a lump in Callum's throat as he closed the door behind him and walked down the path. He could hear Tess barking and scratching frantically at the door and his father calling to the dog. "Come here, lass! It's just ye and me now. C'mon. There's a good girl." The dog, still whining, eventually went to Jamie and lay at his feet. But for the crackle of the fire and the constant ticking of the wall clock, the cottage was now still as a graveyard.

Hamish and Gavin Murray went through to Marnock to see Callum off. The three friends left a couple of hours early so they could have a few drinks before they said their goodbyes. In the bar opposite the recruiting office Hamish, uncharacteristically, bought the first round of drinks.

"They're doubles," he said with a grin as he placed the tray of drinks on the table. "Well, here's tae ye, Callum," he toasted cheerfully.

"Dae ye think ye'll find him?" asked Gavin, in a low, sad voice.

"Ah don't know. All ah know is that he's in the Argylls and that's the regiment I'm joining. I've got tae go tae Stirling for basic training before I get sent tae France."

"By the time ye get there he'll probably be back here on leave," Hamish grinned.

"Aye, Callum, what if he's wounded or something?" asked

Gavin.

"Well, I'll just have tae see what happens."

Gavin bought the next round of drinks; both he and Hamish insisted that Callum should save his money.

"Well, don't buy any more whisky for me. I'll have a pint of beer instead. I don't want tae be turned down for being a drunk."

"Och, don't be daft," laughed Hamish. "Everybody that volunteers is half cut."

"Ah wish I was going," said Gavin, swigging back his glass of whisky and shuddering with the taste of it.

"God, listen tae him, two drinks and he wants tae go tae war. I told ye that the bloody army is filled wi' mugs that go for a few pints and end up marching doon the road wi' a gun in their hands."

"Och, shut up, Hamish," replied Gavin. "Ah only said I wished I was goin'."

"Well, don't wish too hard," said Hamish. "They'll be bringing in conscription soon and we'll all end up collecting German bullets. Sorry, Callum. I didn't mean…"

"Don't be daft, Hamish. I'm well aware of what's happening over there."

"Dae ye want another drink?"

"Damn it, Hamish, get me a half…Yer as well to be hung for a sheep as a lamb."

"Mine's a half as well," shouted Gavin, before turning to Callum. "Ye might meet the doctor that married the Laird's daughter," said Gavin, the whisky making him slightly dizzy. "Ye mind the big wedding they had up at the castle."

"Aye," was Callum's short reply, his mind returning to the day of the wedding as Hamish came back with the tray of drinks.

"Ah told the barmen that the three of us were through tae enlist and he gave us these on the house," Hamish sniggered.

"Och, Hamish that's no' right," said Gavin. "Whit if he sees us through here at the market or something?"

"Ye just tell him ye failed yer medical," laughed Hamish, holding his mouth closed to try to stop a fit of laughing.

"I better get goin' after this one," said Callum reluctantly.

"Hell! Look what the wind blew in," said Hamish nodding in the direction of the door as Toby Black breezed into the bar with Wilma McGonagall dangling from his arm. Black's time in prison had only hardened his already tough appearance. There was a crooked scar over his left eye that he had collected in Barlinnie Prison after a fight over a card game. He was wearing a battered-looking bowler hat and a long black coat.

"That's the bitch that told Angus all those lies about Mhairi," muttered Gavin under his breath, hoping that Black's cauliflower ears were as hard of hearing as they were reputed to be.

"If he's that good at fighting, why does he look like a well-used punch bag?" scoffed Hamish, rather louder than he intended.

"Shut up," snapped Gavin, nervous that Toby was not as deaf as people made out.

With a sneer of contempt, Toby Black unbuttoned his waistcoat and demanded two drinks from the nervous-looking barman. "This place is like a bloody morgue," he said in a fractious tone, sneering at the few customers that were standing at the bar. One man put on his coat to leave. "What are ye doing?" barked Toby. "You don't like my company?"

"I was just headin' off home," said the man meekly.

"Sit on yer arse! You can pay for these drinks," ordered Toby.

"Here," said the barman, putting a bottle of whisky and some glasses on the table, "have a drink on the house."

164

"Shut up! He's buyin' them," Toby shouted, pointing aggressively at the frightened customer, who was now fumbling through his pockets for the money. When the man moved to the bar to pay for the drinks, his nerves got the better of him and he dropped the coins on the dirty, sawdust-covered floor. When he bent down to pick them up, Toby gave him a humiliating kick to the backside. This brought a shrill of laughter from Wilma.

"The bastard," muttered Hamish, wanting to do something but afraid to.

"Leave him alone!" shouted Callum, getting to his feet, to the horror of his friends.

Toby turned to Callum with a grin of satisfaction. "What did ye say?"

"He wasn't doin' ye any harm."

The customer, whom Callum was standing up for, took his chance and ran out the side door. Toby took no notice, now that he had someone else to pick on.

"It's all right, Toby, he didn't mean anything," intervened Hamish.

"You shut up!" Toby shouted. "Dae ye know who I am?" he boasted, turning back to Callum.

"Aye!" said Callum. "I know fine who ye are."

"Toby, let the lad alone," pleaded the barman. "He's away tae enlist tae day. What dae ye say? No harm done?"

"So ye want tae be a soldier," sniggered Toby, turning to Wilma, who laughed at the idea as much as her boyfriend.

"C'mon and let me see if ye can fight then!" Toby challenged, throwing off his coat and rolling up his shirt sleeves.

"Away and fight somebody yer ain size," shouted Gavin, shocked by his own bravery as he got to his feet with clenched fists. Toby laughed out loud.

"Would ye look at the size of that wee runt!"

"Stay out of this, Gavin," said Callum, moving forward to isolate himself from his friends.

"Don't worry, I'll have that wee runt after I beat the shit out of you."

The two men squared up to each other. Toby playing the exhibitionist with the deft movement of his feet and the quick jabs of his fists full of bruised knuckles. Callum moved clumsily in comparison, dogging punches, more by chance than design. Still keeping an eye on Toby's grinning face, Callum stumbled against a table, leaving himself open to a rapid succession of bare knuckles to his unprotected face. There was blood everywhere as Callum wiped his face with his sleeve and spat on the floor. Toby moved in to finish him off, but his over confidence led him straight into Callum's driven fist, which knocked Toby against the bar. "Ye bastard," he cursed, stunned by the blow. Another exchange of blows caused Toby to back off. Callum spat more blood from his cut mouth. "C'mon, ye bastard!" he shouted, seeing the fear in his opponent's eyes for the first time. "Have ye had enough?

"Right, lads! That's enough," shouted the barman.

"C'mon, let's get out of here," shouted Callum, dropping his hands as Toby continued to back off. As Callum turned to the Murray brothers, his cowardly opponent grabbed a beer bottle and smashed it against the bar. A fragment of the shattered bottle accidentally hit Wilma on the face, slicing into her cheek. She screamed hysterically as the blood poured down her face and neck. Callum stood his ground and lifted a chair. Black had had enough and threw what was left of the bottle at Callum. It smashed into the gantry as Black ran from the pub, shouting, "I'll get ye for this, ye bastard!"

With his heart still beating frantically, Callum sat on the steps outside the town hall cleaning the blood from his swollen face. "They won't take me lookin' like this."

"It's no' that bad now," said Gavin, trying unsuccessfully to clean the bloodstains from Callum's shirt.

"Never mind that, I've got another one in my bag," said Callum, pulling a fresh shirt from his rucksack.

"There, that's a lot better," Gavin lied as he wiped the cut above Callum's eye.

"Maybe ye should leave it for a few days before ye enlist. A couple of days will no' make any difference," suggested Hamish.

"No I can't. Once I get cleaned up I'm going. You two are as well heading home."

"No, we'll wait wi' ye for a while," said Gavin.

"Aye, we're in no hurry," agreed Hamish, looking around him to make sure that Toby Black was not still hanging around. "At least that bitch McGonagall got what she deserved," he added.

"She didnae deserve tae get her face slashed," said Gavin.

"Och, it was only a wee scratch," said Hamish. "Maybe it will stop her tellin' lies about people."

They sat for a while longer to let Callum recover from his ordeal. The cuts were more bloody than serious and they had now stopped bleeding. His left eye was slightly swollen, and his hands were bruised, but he felt a sense of satisfaction that he had made a coward out of Toby Black.

With the blood cleaned from his face and a new shirt on his back Callum didn't look too bad. The three friends sat quietly not saying anything, until out of the blue Gavin said emphatically, "I'm goin' tae enlist as well!"

"No yer no'," said Callum, just as forcefully.

"Ye cannae stop me," he said boldly. "I'm eighteen."

"Yer no' eighteen yet!" said Hamish.

"So, I'm nearly eighteen, and I'm enlisting. It's my life."

"Ma will go mad if ye enlist," said Hamish, "and I'm no' goin' tae be the one that has tae tell her. She'll blame me for letting ye."

"Ye don't have tae tell her. I can send a message back with Hector Macleod," he replied, pointing to Hector, who was loading up his cart outside Miller's hardware store.

"Ah don't want ye tae com' wi' me," said Callum.

"Ye cannae stop me if I want tae join up," he repeated, the whisky ruling his senses.

With a final draw from his Woodbine, Callum got to his feet and shook Hamish's hand before turning to Gavin. As he gave him a hug, he said, "You go home now and don't be giving me a hard time. Hamish, don't let him near that recruiting office. I'll see ye in a few months. The war will likely be over by the time I finish me basic training." He crossed the road to the recruiting office, while Hamish held his brother by the arm.

Holding a handkerchief to his cut eye, Callum sat in a small crowded room with a dozen other new recruits. The recruiting sergeant, with his pronounced pigeon chest expanded to the full, called out their names in alphabetical order. The first recruit responded with a lazy, "Aye", only to be immediately reminded that he was now in the army. "Aye, sir!" screamed the sergeant. Once the roll was called, the sergeant went on to explain, in his booming voice of military discipline that they would be boarding a train at 1800 hours and arriving at the training camp, near Stirling, at 1900 hours. He then looked at his watch and confirmed they had fifteen minutes to relax and have a smoke before they would be marched to the station.

168

The sergeant lit up one of his own cigarettes, taking long, slow draws, while thinking about the cold pint of beer he would have once he got these raw recruits on their way. As the sergeant stamped out his finished cigarette, the door behind him opened and a spotty-faced corporal stuck his head into the smoky waiting room and said in a broad Glaswegian accent, "Sergeant, two more recruits for the train."

"Send them in," bellowed the sergeant as though the corporal was on the other side of the moon instead of just two feet away from him. The other recruits looked up with natural curiosity, while Callum, already lonely in this room full of strangers, smiled with amusement when he saw Gavin enter the room followed by his annoyed looking brother. "Ah, more lambs to the slaughter," said the sergeant, immediately regretting the words as soon they left his mouth.

Callum felt a sharp sense of guilt at the profound truth of the sergeant's unintended remark and the smile quickly disappeared from his face. The two brothers listened to the sergeant's words of wisdom about the difference between a twelve-hour clock timetable and the one the army and the railways preferred. After which Hamish was none the wiser; his mind was still trying to come to terms with what was happening. *In the bloody army! What the hell's Ma going to say when she finds out?*

The barracks at Stirling was an eye opener for new recruits as they were drilled from morning to night, under the constant abuse of a bow-legged Sergeant-Major, with the unfortunate name of Willie Short, or Wee Dick as the recruits called him, but never to his face. He gave Gavin a particular hard time, taking a sadistic pleasure in making him bully up his boots until he could see his face in them. If the boots did not please the Sergeant-Major during morning inspection, then Gavin would be sent for a five-mile hike on his own with his full pack on, as the rest of the men tucked into their breakfast. Exhausted, Gavin would then have to join the rest of the squad in the afternoon for another five-mile hike over the same rugged countryside. Callum had to pull back Hamish on a couple of occasions as he threatened to *'Take the bastard's head off!'*

The three months of training was suddenly reduced to six weeks and orders were posted confirming the new battalion would be heading to France in two weeks' time. A strange mood suddenly gripped the barracks that night and the joking and banter of the previous nights all but disappeared as the reality of the situation began to sink in. When the lights finally went out, men who had not prayed since they were children began to pray in the stillness of the night, while others settled for the relief that masturbation gave them.

The week before they left, the squad was given a weekend pass to go into the town and let off some steam. Dressed in the regimental uniform, Callum and the Murray brothers walked, with the rest of the squad, the two miles into Stirling. They began to whistle the *Skye Boat Song* when they reached the outskirts of the town and locals stopped to watch the splendid sight. After a walk around the town to impress the girls, Callum and the brothers decided to get their photograph taken in a shop that was making a roaring trade from new recruits eager to pose in front of the camera in their new uniforms. Although they paid an equal share of the cost, Hamish claimed guardianship of the photograph and, after they all had a good look at themselves; he put it in an oil-skin wallet for safe keeping. They then crossed the road to the King's Head to get drunk.

After only six weeks of training, the new 11th battalion of the Argylls arrived in France to man the Allied lines near the Par du Calais town of Bethume. At every new hardship, Hamish would seize the opportunity to blame Gavin for getting him into this *bloody nightmare*.

"Naebody asked ye tae join up!"

"If ye weren't so bloody daft, I wouldnae have joined up! Ah was mair scared of telling Ma that you joined the army, than any bloody

Germans at the time. How could I have gone back and told her ye buggered off tae the war."

"Ye didnae have tae tell her and ye know it. Hector told her anyway. Ye were just bloody scared that Toby Black would be waiting for ye on the road home," said Gavin, scraping a piece of mud off his rifle butt and throwing it at him.

"Give it a bloody rest," snapped Callum as Hamish made to throw some of his own mud at Gavin.

Every day there was talk of another offensive. One minute it would be rumoured that the Germans were about to mount a major attack and when nothing happened, the rumour would change to a planned Allied offensive, which also came to nothing. In the meantime the only enemy the men had to face was the constant battle with the ubiquitous lice that plagued them day and night.

"Right, lads," shouted the sergeant, "the reserve will be here in a few hours, get yer kit together. You can take your chances with the French whores in the village for a couple of days."

"Thank God," said Hamish as the sergeant disappeared back into the nearest dug-out. "I thought we'd never get out of this hell-hole!"

That night, the company were deloused and marched back to the town of Bethune, some two miles behind Allied lines. The small town had not been touched by the shelling, although most of the inhabitants had long since left to safer parts of the country. It was a warm summer's evening and they marched down the narrow country lane with the rumble of heavy guns in the distance. As they entered the town, a column of Canadians passed them on the way to the front. "You'll only get the pox from those French tarts," shouted one of the Canadians, hanging from the back of a truck as their convoy splashed past the company of grinning Scots. "Who cares?" shouted one of the men back. They all laughed. Life seemed worth living again, if only for a few days.

The medieval town was inevitably turned into a military headquarters for the General Staff in the sector, with officers and the military police hovering in and out of the town hall. The French Tricolour was draped over the balcony, alongside the Union Flag fluttering in the breeze. Two sentries, in the kilts of the Seaforth Highlanders, stood on guard at the entrance of the town's only other municipal building, the public library. When the order was given to break ranks, Callum and the brothers walked cheerfully down the main street. The first thought in their minds was to get some decent food; weeks of eating their meagre rations of stale bully beef and hard biscuits had left their stomachs raw with the pain of hunger. They counted their silver francs and agreed to use at least half of their joint funds on whatever food they could buy. Apart from the two pubs in the square, the only shop they could find open sold nothing but ersatz coffee and thin slices of rye bread.

As they walked about the town and its boarded-up shops, Hamish noticed two laughing soldiers coming from a house on the other side of the street. "They look as if they've found something," he said, walking over towards the soldiers.

While Hamish spoke with the two soldiers, Callum and Gavin stood back on the pavement and watched a line of horse-drawn ambulances that had just returned from the front and were now on their way to the field hospital on the outskirts of the town. One dying soldier's head hung over the end of the cart; the side of his face had been blown away and raw, red flesh clung to shattered bones. Blood gargled from his open mouth with every jolt of the cart.

"Oh God!" said Gavin, grabbing Callum's arm.

"The poor bastard," said Callum. "You'd think they'd shoot him and put him oot of his misery."

They watched wagon after wagon pass with their cargo of human misery and unbridled suffering. Some of the less seriously injured men forced a smile through the pain; a shattered leg or arm meant home for them. The column stopped for a moment and Callum gave one man a cigarette. The man coughed and spluttered blood as he inhaled; he wiped his face and smiled, taking another draw. "Welcome to hell, lads," the man said with an Australian accent. The column moved off again.

"C'mon!" shouted Hamish, his face flushed with excitement from the other side of the muddy road. "C'mon, I've found somewhere," he added, pointing to the house, which the two soldiers had just left. It was a big house, with large bay windows and an imposing oak door with large brass fittings. It must have belonged to someone quite important before the war. Ivy still clung to the wall under the windows and clematis, with soft pink flowers, bloomed over the doorway. There was an outlined mark on the door, left by the owner's missing nameplate.

They ordered food from a handwritten menu and Callum gladly paid the six francs from their kitty as a rather fat French woman laid a plate of chicken and bread on the shaky little table in the corner of the front room. The food was greedily devoured.

"Are you boys looking for pretty girls?" the woman eventually asked in her recently acquired English as she lifted the empty tray from the table. She nodded towards the stairs. "Pretty girls."

"No," Callum flustered. "No… just a bottle of wine."

She smiled and said something in French that they could not understand. She returned to the table with the bottle of wine and had another laugh to herself as she took the money from Callum.

"Ye need tae be fair drunk tae want tae fuck that auld thing," sniggered Hamish. "She must be nearly forty and she's got a face like a pig's arse. I would'nae ride it into battle."

As they continued to drink the wine and talk about what they would do that night, the woman returned to the table followed by a pretty young girl, dressed in a thin, see through nightgown and suspenders. She shouted to the shy looking girl to hurry and then spoke to Callum again, no doubt influenced by the fact that he

173

seemed to be the one with all the money. "You like her?"

While Callum stared at the girl in silent embarrassment, Hamish was nodding his approval with wide eyes fixed on the small nipples that peered through the flimsy nightgown. "You like?" she repeated, rubbing her thumb and index finger together to indicate that money would be the only element of courtship required to have her.

"How much?" asked Callum, in a low nervous voice.

The woman turned to the girl and said something in French and the girl turned and went back up the stairs, while the three friends watched her slow, seductive movements. The woman turned back to Callum. She indicated to him to show her the moneybag that he had in his tunic pocket. Callum opened the small pouch and spread the silver coins on the palm of his other hand. She pointed to the money in a circular fashion and then pointed individually to the three of them. Gavin's heart was pounding. He was afraid and was hoping that Callum would immediately refuse. He had no desire to go upstairs but was too frightened to say anything. To Gavin's relief and Hamish's obvious disappointment, Callum shook his head and put the money back into the pouch. She threw her hands up in the air and cursed in her own tongue. She was about to lower her price when a drunk soldier, in the regiment kilt of the Argylls, stumbled down the stairs, a bottle of wine in one hand and his shirt in the other. A girl, in scant underwear, was shouting and screaming after him, before throwing a hairbrush down the stairs, hitting the drunken soldier in the back.

"Go tae hell, ye whore," he shouted back.

"Mademoiselle soldat!" shouted the irate girl, followed by a further string of abuse.

"He only wanted to talk to her about his wife, again," laughed the older woman. "Mademoiselle, soldats," she added, pointing to Callum's kilt.

"Angus!" said Callum in a stunned whisper. "Angus!" he

174

shouted, as he got to his feet to meet the soldier's drunken glare. Callum went to embrace him, but Angus pushed his way through the shabby curtains that hung over the side door and ran from the house. Callum stood motionless for a moment and turned to the Murray brothers. "It was him. It was Angus." He rushed into the street after him, pushing his way through the weary-looking ranks marching along the muddy road. He was stopped by an officer on horseback, who took his whip to the back of his neck. "Get back or I'll have you flogged," the stern face officer shouted. Callum stepped back on to the pavement as Hamish and Gavin came out at his back.

"Where did he go?" asked Gavin, as glad to be out of the whorehouse as he was to have found Angus.

"Ah don't know," said Callum, still scanning over the marching troops to the other side of the road. "I'm sure it was him."

"That's the fuckin' gratitude ye get for tryin' tae save that daft big bastard's marriage," said Hamish, spitting into the soft mud in anger.

"He's drunk," said Callum. "He probably didn't recognise us in these uniforms. Com' on I'm goin' tae see if I can find him."

"You can go if ye want. I'm goin' back in," said Hamish, nodding back at the whorehouse door. "Give me ma share," he demanded, his intentions plain. Callum threw the money pouch at him and hurried down the street towards the other side of the town, with Gavin running after him.

The madam took the four francs from Hamish, and he nervously followed her up the stairs, through a heady miasma of scent and cigarette smoke. He could hear girls giggling in one of the rooms as he was led along the hall. The bathroom door was open to the left and he turned to see a naked girl washing betwcen her legs. The girl stopped what she was doing and smiled at Hamish. He grinned inanely at her. The fat woman pulled the bathroom door closed and shook her head. She then opened the door at the end of the hall and nodded for Hamish to go in. He hesitated at the threshold and she had to give him a gentle push before she was able to pull the door closed behind him.

Hamish looked around the room which was in semi-darkness and scented with an overpowering array of perfumes. The bed was made, and covered with a thick red bedspread, which was badly worn in the middle and frayed at the edges. "Take your clothes off, soldier," said a female voice, in English with a harsh French accent. He turned towards the source and could see someone moving behind a lattice screen in the far corner of the room. "Don't be shy, young man...I won't bite you...unless you want me to," she added, with a guttural laugh that unnerved Hamish. He slowly unbuttoned the top of his shirt as the whore appeared theatrically from behind the screen, with a cigarette in her mouth and a feather scarf around her neck. Hamish stopped at the third button on his shirt as he looked at her large, vein-scarred breasts that spread across most of her upper body. She was in her late forties, and caked in bright, garish make-up, which failed to mask her advancing years. Hamish's eyes were drawn down the folds of flesh around her waist to her unruly bush of black pubic hair. "You a virgin, soldier?" she asked, with a slight tease in her voice as she touched her ample breast and nodded for him to get on the bed.

"No, I can't do this," said Hamish as he lowered his hands from his shirt. He turned and left the room with a cackle of laughter following in his ears. He rushed downstairs and confronted the madam and demanded his money back. She shook her head and said something to him in French, which he did not understand. He again demanded his money. She shook her head again and beckoned him to follow her back upstairs. He refused. She then shouted upstairs and a girl appeared at the top of the landing wearing a white basque and suspenders. Hamish smiled at the girl and decided to try his luck again. The madam barred his approach halfway up the stairs and began to rub her fingers together again, demanding more money. Hamish looked at her disdainfully then back to the landing to where the girl was smiling at him and seductively undoing the top of her basque. He asked the madam how much; a question she instantly understood as she raised four fingers. Hamish, still shaking his head, gave her four more francs as she stood aside to let him pass.

Angus was nowhere to be found and, after an hour or so, the two dejected friends returned to the whorehouse to get what was left of their money from Hamish. The door was locked so they kicked and banged it for a couple minutes before giving up and sitting down on the damp steps at the front of the house.

"Dae ye think he's still in there wi' them?" asked Gavin.

"Who cares?"

The sounds of heavy field artillery caused a flurry of activity around the Town Hall. Callum and Gavin sat unperturbed, smoking the last of their tobacco in quiet indifference to the commotion around them. The door opened behind them and Hamish appeared, still pulling his braces over his shoulders and grinning with the thought of his lost virginity. "Auld Hun must be getting a pounding," he said, getting down to sit beside them, "Ah take it ye never found him?" he asked.

"No," replied Gavin. "No thanks tae you!"

"Oh shut up. Why should I go running after him? I had better things tae dae wi' ma energy," he laughed, sticking his fingers in Gavin's face.

"Fuck off, ye dirty bastard!" shouted Gavin, jumping to his feet,

"Where's the rest of the money?" asked Callum.

"Here," replied Hamish, taking a few coins from his pocket and handing them to Callum.

"Is that all that's left? Ye didnae pay sixteen francs for one fuck!"

177

"It was eight francs."

"So where's the rest?" demanded Callum.

"Ye took that long tae get back."

"The dirty bastard's done it twice," interrupted Gavin. "I hope yer dick falls off the next time ye have a piss."

"Here, Gavin," said Callum, giving him ten francs, "at least we'll be able tae get a few drinks and something tae eat later."

"Ah, c'mon, I thought the money was between the three of us?" complained Hamish.

"It was, but you spent yours and some of ours, ye greedy bastard," said Callum coldly.

"Yer no' goin' tae buy food and beer and no' give me any."

"Just watch us!" said Gavin.

That night Callum and Gavin bought bread, cheese and a bottle of red wine from a small farmhouse on the outskirts of the town. Hamish followed around like a hungry dog, hoping that they would take pity and throw him something once they had had their fill. The earlier bombardment had stopped and, apart from the occasional flare shooting into the sky, the night was quiet. They sat beside a decaying haystack where Callum and Gavin settled down to enjoy their banquet as a grim-faced Hamish sulked quietly beside them. When the bread and cheese began to disappear, Hamish reopened negotiations and promised to give two shillings from his next pay if one of them gave him even a small bit of bread and cheese. They ignored him and kept on eating until the bread and cheese was safely in their stomachs. With nothing left to lose, Hamish got to his feet and bombarded the two of them with a torrent of verbal abuse. As he stormed up and down the field shouting and swearing, the other two laughed themselves into a fit.

"Ye pair of bastards," shouted Hamish, cooling down a little, when he remembered the bottle of wine sitting against the haystack. As the joke petered out, Callum took a lump of cheese and some bread from under his tunic and threw it towards Hamish. "There, the next time don't be so bloody selfish."

Hamish devoured the food, praising Callum for his generosity, while keeping one eye on the wine bottle that Gavin was now raising to his mouth. The fun having gone from depriving him any further, the bottle moved freely between them. After a few minutes, Gavin asked the question that he had wanted to ask all night. "What was it like?"

"What the first or the second time?" asked Hamish boastfully.

"Get tae sleep!" said Callum. "He's probably got the pox anyway."

It was not long before they all fell silent. The tiredness of the day crept over them; Gavin was thinking about the beautiful girl in the whorehouse and promised himself that he would save eight francs for the next time they got leave. Hamish was checking himself between the legs, wondering if the pox really made your penis fall off. Callum was trying to understand why Angus had run from them, if only he could speak to him for five minutes… God, the poor bastard's mind must be demented with the shame he must feel, if only he could get a hold of him before he did something stupid.

Mhairi stood at the upstairs window with her baby daughter in her arms and stared at the thousands of bright stars that were sprinkled across the cloudless sky. As she stood there, quietly humming an old Celt song to her sleeping child, a shooting star fell from the heavens and raced across the sky before disappearing behind the blackness of the hills to the east of Glenfay.

Chapter 14

Fraser received orders to deploy to a field hospital near the town of Ypres. In April, Caitriona received a letter from him. The postmark was scored out but the envelope had the French national emblem stamped on the front, which made her heart race a little as she opened it.

My Darling Caitriona,

April 15th 1915

I am missing you terribly already. I keep your pendant in my breast pocket so that you are always close to my heart. I hope that you and your family are all well. We arrived in ....last night and reached the town of... this morning. The station was very busy with soldiers arriving every hour, while the wounded were being stretchered onto the empty trains (which are no more than cattle trains). I have been told that I will be moved up to the field hospital at... this afternoon. The front is only a few miles away and you can clearly hear the thunder of the guns in the distance. I still haven't got used to the idea of being a captain and I feel rather awkward every time one of the men salutes me. It's all rather strange. I have been billeted in a little office behind the station and intend to get some sleep before we leave this afternoon. There are three other doctors with me here and they are as tired as I am; two of them are already asleep and the other, like me, is writing to his wife. I will write again as soon as I get to... Don't worry!

Caitriona folded the letter back into the envelope and put it under her pillow to read again later. She then stood by the window and looked over the loch, its surface so calm and beguiling. She then looked across the glen towards the Macnair croft and the gorse bushes that were blowing wildly in the wind.

It had been raining for days. The front lines had turned into a muddy quagmire of misery. Most of the men in the trenches were exhausted with tedium and poor rations as the generals dithered on both sides as to the best way to break the stalemate.

"Where have ye been, corporal?" asked a tired-looking soldier as Angus slipped into the muddy trench beside him. "The serge has been looking' for ye."

"Where is he?"

"He went back tae the dug-out."

"Here," said Angus, pulling out a bottle of wine from under his muddy coat.

At the sight of the wine, two other soldiers gave up their struggle to get to sleep.

"There's talk of a German push tomorrow," said Private Gray, handing the bottle to the man next to him and wiping the blood-red wine from his lips and mousy moustache.

"Look, Moony, they say that every bloody day and nothing happens," snapped Angus.

"But, corporal," said Moony, a nickname he hated as much as the acne that was responsible for it. "I heard the lieutenant telling..."

"What the hell does that yin know? He's in there crying fur his mammy every time there's a bombardment. I'm goin' tae get some sleep," groaned Angus, climbing into a dug-out in the side of the trench. "Wake me up if Jerry gets too near," he said sarcastically, before pulling his heavy coat over his head.

Exhausted, Angus was sleeping within minutes and dreaming of life before the war, when he cared about things. It had taken a long time for his hatred of Mhairi to leave him, but when it did the longing for her returned like a hunger. His dreams, as always, turned to Glenfay, its high snow-capped mountains and lush green fields, its beautiful sea loch and its peace. He felt the warm sun on his neck as he drew the scythe through the dry hay, while laughing and joking with Callum. As the darkness came to his dreams again, he could feel Mhairi's moist lips forced against his and her hands touching him. He kissed her soft breasts and felt himself inside her. Then the dawn broke with the sound of officers' whistles and the shouts of men running to their posts in the strained light of early morning. Angus woke grudgingly from his sleep. His face was smeared with muddy water from the feet of soldiers running along the duckboards in the narrow trench. "Oh God," was all he could think to say, his head thumping with the cheap wine.

"Get tae hell out of there, corporal," shouted the sergeant. "The Bosch has moved their heavy stuff on to the ridge."

"What?" groaned Angus, getting to his feet.

"You crazy bastard, ye were in that bloody town again!" shouted the sergeant, his eyes blazing with anger at Angus's glazed expression of indifference. "I've a good mind to report you this time!"

"Serge, if ye had a good mind ye wouldn't be here."

"What's goin' on down there?" shouted one of the officers, emerging from the dug-out further along the trench.

"Nothing, sir," replied the sergeant.

"Well hurry up and get the men to their posts."

"Aye, sir."

Within seconds the German artillery opened up with their heavy field guns, the prelude to an offensive. So the bastards are going tae attack, thought Angus, running to man his machine-gun post, his head still throbbing. There was a cluster of small explosions from the German lines and within minutes the sky over 'no man's land' was green with toxic clouds of gas. Panic gripped the British trenches, as

182

the miasma of poison drifted towards them. Angus quickly wrestled out his bulky gas mask from its tin container and pulled it on, as the gas engulfed the trenches. He choked for breath at first, but soon caught enough air to stop from suffocating. Every breath he took caused him fear; fear that the mask would block up or even worse leak in the gas, which could burn out lungs in seconds. He lay face down in the mud and waited for the all clear. If only there was some wind. His heart was beating hard, each breath had to be sucked through the thick filter, and he was beginning to feel sick. He desperately tried to think of something else. If he vomited, he would die.

A month ago he would not have cared, but a change had come in him and he wanted to live! To see Mhairi and the baby he now knew was his! Why was he so stupid? Why didn't he think? It was only when he was drunk one night that he finally told Sergeant Harrison the whole story. "If he was in prison when ye say he was, then how could it be his baby? For God's sake man, can ye no count?"

The green fog was still visible through the mud-smeared glass of the mask. Don't be sick. He held his breath, which seemed to help for a while, until he exhaled and had to breathe even harder to replace the air his lungs had polluted. His mouth was dry and there was a strong smell of stale wine from his breath. He buried his head in his hands and prayed, but could not bear it much longer. He was going to be sick!

The bombardment startled Hamish and Gavin awake; Callum was already standing halfway up the toppled hay stack, watching the smoke rising from the fields off in the distance.

"We had better get back," he said as the other two struggled to their feet. "That's our lines they're shelling."

"What do ye mean, we had better get back?" said Hamish, climbing up beside Callum to get a better look. "We're on rest leave."

"Don't be daft. The Germans will be attacking as soon as they stop pounding our trenches."

"So?" said Hamish. "That's no' our problem."

"It is now," said Gavin, pointing to their company lieutenant, who was waving frantically at them from the roadside.

"Just our bloody luck," moaned Hamish as he sat down to put on his boots. "We should have sat on the other side of the bloody haystack."

The offensive continued unabated and word soon reached the Allied General Staff that the Germans had broken through at three points along the Allied lines. After confirmation was received, General Sir Horace Smith-Dorrien, the commander of the third army holding the region, demanded an explanation from his flustered subordinates, who blamed everything and everyone but themselves. "General!" interrupted his secretary. "The Field Marshall's on the line." The general reluctantly took the telephone receiver and embarrassingly offered the same excuses that he had himself rejected only minutes before. The line abruptly went dead and the flushed-faced general turned to the assembled section commanders and said in a quiet, dejected voice. "There is to be no retreat. Any men caught retreating are to be shot as deserters. I want roadblocks set up to ensure that every position is held."

"But, sir, it will be impossible to stop a retreat if the Germans have already broken through," insisted an alarmed-looking officer.

"That's the Field Marshall's orders. No retreat. Now return to your duties…Oh, Travers!"

"Sir?"

"I would like a word." The general waited for a few minutes until the other officers had left the room, then said in a gruff voice, "Travers, it doesn't look too good, the bloody Germans are swarming all over the place. I think you had better make arrangements to evacuate all essential and sensitive material on a minute's notice. If the Germans break through at this sector, then we'll have to be ready to move all Staff back until the hole in the line is plugged. Remember, Travers, try and do it quietly. I don't want any panic."

"Yes, sir. I'll make the necessary arrangements."

The groans and screams of wounded and dying men increased during the day with the continuing bombardment, which shook the worms from the ground. A grey fog of smoke threw a curtain of uncertainty on the horizon as orders made in the safety of oak-panelled rooms in Paris were put into fruition. The sickly sweet smell was overwhelming in the hot afternoon as Fraser stood and looked at his morning's work with fresh blood still dripping from the small jagged teeth of the amputation saw. His eyes were dark and sank deep into his haggard, exhausted face. He turned to the nurse and shook his head before taking off his bloody apron and wiping the dirt and sweat from his forehead, while she finished stitching and bandaging the soldier's raw stump. Fraser needed a break from the carnage and handed the saw to Jenkins, one of the auxiliary male nurses, who was just as skilled at sawing through rotten, gangrene flesh and shattered bone. Fraser lit a cigarette as he emerged from the stifling heat of the tent into the green field which was still out of reach of the enemy's heavy artillery.

He looked at the beauty of the blue sky and the small white clouds drifting overhead, while blowing the acrid smoke from his lungs with a congested cough that turned to a convulsion before he finally regained his breath and some degree of composure. The smells of decaying, rotting flesh, chloroform and iodine permeated his sense of taste as he spat the corrupted mucus from his mouth. His temporary paroxysm caused hot tears to run down his pallid cheeks while the sun blinded what little vision he had left in his tired eyes.

"Are you all right, doctor?"

"Yes, nurse. I'm fine. I think I may have inhaled some chloroform. I'll be all right in a few minutes."

"Here, doctor," she said, handing him a handkerchief. "Maybe you should have a rest for a while."

"Thanks, Rachel, but I'm fine," he said with a rare smile on his cracked lips as he wiped his face. "You go back in and keep an eye on Jenkins in case he cuts off some poor soldier's good leg."

Fraser held the canvas flaps open as the nurse went back into the exhausting heat and nauseating smells of the makeshift field surgery. He was still not ready to go back to the butchery that had become his trade and he lit another cigarette, walking to the back of the tent to get a better look at the never-ending stream of men heading for the front lines some three miles to the north beyond the meandering River Somme. The road had been churned up with a hundred thousand boots, the wheels of heavy-laden horse-drawn carts, and the lines of grunting trucks struggling to get munitions to the hungry guns. The ground trembled under his feet with the thunderous roars in the distance as a small British biplane flew overhead, spluttering smoke from its noisy engine.

He turned to go back into the surgery, when he was startled to see the tarpaulin covering the dismembered limbs moving. He thought that his tired eyes and mind were playing tricks on him as he gradually lifted the edge of the grotesque shroud, his heart beating fast with apprehension. He raised his handkerchief to his mouth and nose, cursing the large bloated blowfly larvae that fed on the rotting flesh. The adult flies buzzed around the discarded human carrion, drunk on the intoxicating methane aroma from the decaying limbs that once had walked and danced with life. The tarpaulin moved again and he stepped back, wondering if the ghosts of some of those who had not survived the trauma of amputation had returned for their missing limbs. Even with all his education and scientific learning his mind was still able to play superstitious tricks on his logic and he had to take a deep breath before pulling the tarpaulin back with all his strength. He fell back on to the ground, recoiling at the sight of a scrawny, ginger cat gorging itself on the maggot-infested flesh. He quickly got to his feet and shouted at the feral animal which hissed and spat at him with the memory of its recent weeks of starvation screaming in its wild eyes. "Get away, you monster," he shouted, picking up a stick to chase the brazen animal. The cat stared at him defiantly, tearing at a piece of raw flesh before scampering away with its ragged, blood-soaked tail in the air. As Fraser pulled the tarpaulin back over the dismembered arms and legs, the barrage of heavy guns stopped. The sudden silence was like a distant echo from another time.

He returned to his work, ordering two orderlies to arrange for the immediate burial of the severed limbs, while relieving Jenkins who was having difficulty cutting a patient's femur bone just above the knee. The bloody muscles and nerves were already flayed from the bone as the nurse tightened the tourniquet to slow the loss of blood, but the bone cracked under the strain. The patient groaned in spite of the anaesthetic and Fraser ordered the nurse to apply more chloroform as he pulled down the severed nerve ends, tying and crushing them, before finally cutting through the remains of the fractured bone. The nurse injected clear alcohol into the nerve endings and pulled the loose skin over the gory wound before stitching the skin around the stump. The bloody operation over, Fraser put his hand on the young soldier's chest to feel his heart beating faintly. For the first time he looked at his patient's face, which was glazed like marble. The soldier's heart suddenly stopped and Fraser put his hand on the nurse's shoulder.

"You can save the bandages; he's dead."

That night Fraser lay in his quarters drained and depressed with the constant strain. The amputations were now carried out on an industrial scale and even when he was lying on his bunk, trying to rest, he knew there were still dozens of surgeons working through the night to try and save the broken bodies of young men who only a few months ago may have been dreaming of the glory of war. He tried to think of Caitriona, but even her beauty could not rid him of the horrors that quickly returned to his mind.

Fraser was up early the next morning, unable to sleep with the constant noise from the Front and the agonising cries of soldiers wrecked with shrapnel. The retreat was already in progress in some places by the time Field Marshall's orders were relayed to the front lines. On the roads back over the Belgium-French borders, tens of thousands of men marched with the sound of heavy German artillery pounding at their heels. But for some reason, the Germans decided to halt their advance after only two miles into the Allied lines. The crisis was over and the British dug in. The stalemate was resumed.

Caitriona was now beside herself with worry. The tone of Fraser's letters had changed and his once flowing and gratuitously embellished handwriting had gradually deteriorated over the months to erratic scribbling, much of which was illegible. At first she told herself that the conditions at the Front were not helpful to letter writing, but the steady decline convinced her that all was not well with Fraser and the strain he was under was increasingly evident with every new letter she received. His brave words could not hide the torment in his mind.

"Don't worry, darling," said her father, reading one of the letters. "He must have very little time to write and he has simply written the letters very fast. I'm sure that he'll be all right."

It was a dull morning when the news Caitriona had been dreading for weeks finally came. She felt faint as Mrs Roberts, with tears coming to her eyes, handed her the brown, Government-stamped envelope, which the police constable had delivered. There was little doubt in Caitriona's mind about what this could mean. Her father rushed downstairs after seeing the constable walking up the path. Charles put his arms around his trembling daughter as she struggled to open the thick brown envelope. The heavy black type was blurred with the stream of tears that flowed down her face. Her eyes could only focus on the words 'Missing in Action', which were underlined in red. She pulled the letter to her chest and turned to her father. "He might still be alive," she said in a broken voice, relieved for the little hope that those words gave her. "Look!" she added, handing her father the letter.

"Yes," he agreed. "At least there's hope. He must have got caught up in the retreat from Ypres."

As the weeks passed into months, nothing was heard of Fraser's fate. There was still no confirmation that he was killed and Caitriona finally received a long-awaited letter from the Red Cross, confirming that there was no Captain Fraser Munro on the lists of those hospitalised or held prisoner by the Germans.

If only she heard something of his fate, even knowing he was dead would be better than nothing. She could not stand the waiting, day after day. She had to do something. If she was doing something she could get her mind off the constant worry. Looking at the letter from the Red Cross again, with its embossed emblem at the top of the page, the answer suddenly stared her in the face. That's it, she thought. She would join the Red Cross and serve her country as Fraser had done.

Chapter 15

It was a warm day as Charles Dunbar wandered through the grounds of the castle with Macfie, the head gardener, at his side. Since Duncan had taken over the day-to-day management of the estate, Charles found more time to spend doing the things in life that gave him most pleasure. Every morning before breakfast he would go for a long walk along the loch road and then spend the rest of the day reading the books he had bought as a young man but never had the time to enjoy. At least once a week he would accompany Macfie around the rambling gardens, testing his own limited horticultural knowledge with Macfie's undoubted expertise.

"The dahlias are looking a treat this year," he said, gently touching the plant with his walking cane.

"Aye, yer lordship, they've come up well this year all right."

"Get one of the lads to cut some of these for the house," he said, pointing his cane at the flourish of red and yellow roses covering the trellis at the back of the rockery.

"Aye, sir, I'll get young William tae do it right away."

Before he could decide on further cuttings for the house, the sound of a car horn stole his attention. "Oh, Caitriona," he muttered to himself, raising his cane to let her know that he was in the garden. The car struggled up the steep path to the greenhouse, the engine roaring as she forced it into second gear.

"Still trying to get the hang of the damn thing?" he said, as he opened the car door for her. "I can't see how these noisy things will ever take the place of a good reliable gig."

"Oh, it's just that I haven't driven for such a long time and the gears are a bit stiff, but I'm getting the hang of it again," she said, adjusting her light summer hat as it caught the breeze.

"Any news?" he asked softly, taking her hand.

190

"No. He's still missing."

"I'm sorry, darling."

"Oh, Daddy, I can't stand it much longer. If only I knew one way or another."

"Yes I know, dear, but you have to be strong. What kind of day did you have at the hospital?" he added, changing the subject.

"I don't think I'll ever make a nurse," she said, reflecting on the long shift she had spent at the Red Cross convalescent hospital in Stirling. The hospital provided training for those young women who wanted to make their own contribution to the war by enlisting as voluntary auxiliary nurses; the nearest many of them could be to their loved ones serving overseas. Caitriona had enrolled in the hope of being posted to one of the many English hospitals receiving the flood of casualties from France.

Dunbar had been shocked the day she announced her intention of joining the local Voluntary Aid Detachment. At first, he could not understand why his daughter would wish to take on the unpleasant job of a nurse, when there were so many other, more lady-like, occupations she could involve herself in. He soon realised that Caitriona was not the kind of person to content herself with joining one of the many women circles dedicated to the knitting of woollen socks and balaclavas. Caitriona's strong feminist ideals came to the fore in this time of national crisis and she had made it clear that, if the young men of this country were prepared to lay down their lives for their country, then she would at least nurse those who came back broken and wounded.

The first few weeks of training soon taught Caitriona to forget her privileged life. The work she had chosen was onerous and despite her dedication, the matron was never slow to remind her of her shortcomings.

"Yer no' the Laird's daughter here! Take these bed pans and make sure ye clean them properly."

"Yes, matron," replied Caitriona, biting her tongue as she took the bed pans from the matron, determined to show that she was not afraid of hard or even unpleasant work.

So it was, under the stern eye of the matron, Caitriona scrubbed floors, washed blood-stained clothes and changed bedclothes soiled with human waste. Of the ten women volunteers who started training at the same time as Caitriona, only three remained to sit the First Aid and Home Nursing examination. To her surprise, matron smiled at her when she told her she had passed the final exam with merit, "Well, ye proved me wrong. Have a seat and I'll make us both a cup of tea to celebrate."

So far, the war had been profitable to the estate, with Duncan using all his influence to secure high prices from the Ministries of War responsible for supplying coal and fresh meat to the army. With such profits to be made, he was determined to utilise as much land in the farming of sheep as possible, but his plan to raise the rents of the tenant farmers (as a prelude to inevitable evictions) was scuttled when the Laird was approached by a group of crofters, angered by the letters they had received intimating the increases. Charles Dunbar immediately reduced the rent increases from the fifty per cent mentioned in the letter to five per cent, apologising for the anxiety caused by an unfortunate clerical error.

"I will not have you making trouble like this," scolded Charles. "What if the press got a hold of this? Don't you realise there's a war on? My God, some of the people you were trying to force out have sons fighting at the Front. I would have thought you'd have had more sense."

Duncan did not look once at his father during this dressing down but sat brooding over his half-eaten quail as Morag tentatively removed the plate. Normally, he would have stood up to his father and given as good as he got, but he had other things on his mind. That morning he had received a brown envelope containing a white feather, the second such token of this kind he had received that week. It was clear that others now perceived him to be a coward and were determined to make that fact known to him. To hell with them, he asserted to himself, taking another drink of wine as his father watched in a curious silence.

In the autumn of 1915, in a wood just outside the town of Chateau Thierry, some ten miles behind French lines and not many more from Paris itself, a naked man was found living like a wild animal. A retired professor of Botany from La Sorbonne discovered the man. The professor, with his butterfly net still in his hand, watched in disbelief as the naked man sat like an ape on the other side of the river picking berries from a tree and eating them after a cursory examination with a lick of his tongue. The professor's first thought was to run and get the police and have the man arrested, thinking he must be a deserter or an escaped lunatic. As he continued to watch the strange bearded creature, the scientist in him took over. He followed him for more than an hour before the naked creature disappeared into the mouth of a small cave high in the rocks overlooking the woods. So that's where you live, the Professor thought, hurrying back to the town to fetch his friend, the village doctor.

The doctor was all for informing the local gendarme, but his old friend persuaded him that Claude Petain was a clumsy fool, who would shoot the man dead before they got a chance to question him. After much discussion, the two men decided to capture the man themselves. The doctor loaded his small handgun which he was keeping for any Germans who managed to break through the French lines. The professor agreed that some form of protection was necessary in the event that the man was dangerous.

They stood at the mouth of the cave, suddenly apprehensive about going into its blackness. The doctor took out his gun, his hand shaking with the fear of actually having to use it. The professor nervously lit a match as they edged forward and peered into the shadows that now flickered on the rocks. At the far end of the cave, the naked man sat with his knees pulled under his chin, his body rocking with the fear of discovery. The man's face was gaunt; his eyes glazed and frightened. They asked him if he was all right, but the man did not seem to hear the question, and simply stared back at them, rocking his body so violently that his head was now banging off the wall of the cave. The doctor put away his pistol and gradually moved towards the man with soothing words of comfort. "There, there. We will not harm you."

By the time spring 1916 arrived, the armies on both sides had endured a long miserable winter. During an early thaw, the generals decided to test each other's defences. For three days the German and British relentlessly pounded each other with heavy artillery bombardments. The killing season had come around again. During the bombardments the men crouched down in the besieged trenches as heavy shelling indiscriminately exploded all around. Gavin held on to his brother's arm, his nerves shattered with the constant fear of being blown to pieces.

Every so often there would be screams along the lines when some unfortunate section received a direct hit. The huge explosions drowned out the sounds of the men's fears as prayers were mumbled hypnotically until the all clear was finally given and the pounding ceased for a while. The men gradually got to their feet as the officers checked for any signs of a German ground offensive through their field glasses. As night fell the men waited for the next onslaught. Fields along the River Somme were now laid waste in a sea of mud and decay. Broken, lifeless trees stood out like haunted silhouettes against the pale sky.

On the fourth day the guns fell silent and an eerie calm settled along the front-line trenches. Through bleak, grey skies the weak morning sun gradually melted the last of the frost, which covered the vast, lifeless soil. Only the ugly, man-made defences broke this homogeneous landscape of nothingness. Rolls of barbed wire crisscrossed the killing fields in vulgar uniformity, with the occasional machine gun post positioned on muddy knolls, fortified with rain-sodden sandbags.

A small kingfisher flew down from the colourless sky and perched itself on the broken, limp branch of a dead tree. The bird chirped frantically as though distressed at the barren wasteland to which it had returned by instinct. On seeing the iridescent bird, Callum nudged Hamish awake. "Look!" he said, still peering carelessly over the parapet of the trench. Hamish rubbed his puffy red eyes with his frost-bitten fingers and followed Callum's stare. The bird was now singing incessantly as it groomed itself with mechanical-like precision in the pale sunlight. "What?" grunted Hamish, still half asleep and staring beyond the ethereal tree stump to the German lines. The bird then flew away into the greyness as Callum slumped back against the wet mud. "Nothing," he said, sinking back into a mood of melancholy. Hamish looked at him strangely for a moment but said nothing.

The rumours of another offensive faded with the onset of darkness. The weeks in this sector of the front had been the most miserable that the battalion had endured since arriving in France. The food was even more sparse and foul than they had previously become accustomed to, and the idea of catching rats and roasting them over a fire, was becoming more palatable by the day. Gavin had become very quiet; his eyes heavy with fatigue and his young face now gaunt with hunger. He only spoke when he had to and his left hand developed a nervous tremor that got markedly worse whenever they were under bombardment.

"Macnair!" shouted Sergeant Watt, splashing along the trench towards them. "I need four men tae come wi' me. Captain Harris wants paths cut through the wire and ye don't need me tae tell ye what that means." Hamish got to his feet and stood beside Callum. Gavin, afraid to be left behind, joined them, hiding the tremor in his hand in the pocket of his long coat. Some of the other soldiers turned away as the sergeant scanned their reluctant faces for the fourth man. "Clark! It's been a while since you showed the Germans that ugly mug of yours." There was a burst of laughter; many of those laughing were more relieved than amused. "Right, you four, com' wi' me," ordered the sergeant, pushing his way back along the crowded trench.

They followed the sergeant into the captain's dug-out. Captain Harris stood in the dimly lit bunker, his fingers nervously drumming on the table he was leaning over. He was a thin pallid-faced young man, the product of a public school and more at home holding a cricket bat than a gun. He was the sixth new captain the company had been given in as many months; the German snipers found their soft heads exploded better than those with less education in them. Harris signalled to his valet to leave and greeted the sergeant with a reluctant smile. "Are these the best men to do the job?" he asked in a tone of voice that did not seem to care about the answer.

"Aye, sir! They're all experienced men."

"Well, sergeant, you'll take this sector," said Harris, running his finger down a recently drawn map.

"Right, sir, how far do we go?"

"As far as you can," said the captain, pausing for a moment. "These men are all privates."

"Yes, sir," replied the sergeant.

"Don't you have any corporals left in your company?"

"Well yes, sir, but these men work together like a team and they've been in 'no man's land' wi' me often enough."

"Well tell me, sergeant, who takes over if you're...?"

"Macnair, sir, I've every faith in him," said the sergeant, nodding towards Callum.

"Well, Private Macnair, from now on you take the rank of acting corporal and if the sergeant falls, you are responsible for ensuring that as much of this sector is opened up as possible. Do you understand?"

"Yes, sir."

"Good. Now corporal take your men outside until I have a word with the sergeant and good luck." Once the men had filed back into the trench, the captain handed the sergeant a cigarette. "Now, sergeant, I hope you haven't mentioned the planned offensive to the men."

"Oh no, sir."

"Good, I don't want any of them caught by Jerry and blabbing their mouths off. You know how important it is that as much of this wire is cut as possible without the Hun knowing what we're up to."

"Yes, sir."

"Here, take this flare and fire it when you come back over our lines. I'll make sure that all the men hold their fire until you and your men are safely across. Remember to let the other men know of the signal in case you are… you know what. Good luck, sergeant." When the sergeant had gone, Captain Harris took another mouthful of whisky and slumped himself down on his bed. It was the only way he could get any sleep.

"Right, corporal," said the sergeant, slapping Callum on the back, "you follow up at the rear; there's no point in the two of us getting too close. If I'm hit then take this; it's the signal to get back in. It's bad enough getting shot wi' Germans but it's an awful waste of bullets getting shot by our ain men." He gave a hearty, but hollow laugh.

As night fell, Sergeant Watt, wire cutters in hand and a quick prayer on his lips, slipped over the parapet. Callum counted to fifty before following. Once over, the men crawled through the mud on their stomachs, using their elbows to force themselves along. They cut through the barbed wire as they went, invisible in the dark moonless night. As they got further into 'no man's land', the stench of rotten flesh became nauseating. Callum came across one headless corpse, which was mangled in the reels of clinging barbed wire. He rolled the decaying body into a shell crater without the slightest thought of its origin. It did not matter to Callum if it was German or British; dead is dead. There was a sudden sound of wire recoiling against itself. The men all fell flat into the squelching mud. Within seconds there was a burst of yellow light overhead as a flare went up from the German trenches. The flare was immediately followed by excited German voices as their machine guns opened up along the line.

The sergeant was caught in the barbed wire he was cutting and struggled frantically to free himself. The machine bullets peppered the mud around him. Callum rolled into the same crater as the headless corpse and helplessly watched the sergeant's entangled body being shot to pieces against the fading yellow light of the flare. As darkness came again, the Germans opened up with mortars and sporadic bursts of machine-gun fire splattered the mud and anything that moved on it. Callum's heart was pounding hard against his chest as he clung to the earth when a mortar exploded in front of the shell hole. He looked back at his own trenches which were only a few hundred yards away but each inch was possible death. He strained to the edge of the slippery crater and pinpointed the direction of the machine-gun fire before throwing a grenade as hard as he could in that direction. The exploding grenade had little effect on the concrete bunker and the Germans simply opened up with further mortar fire. It looked like only one or maybe two machine-gun posts and not, as Callum had initially feared, the German front line. The German guns stopped as quickly as they had started. Callum assumed they were saving their ammunition to pick them off at daylight. In the sudden silence he could hear the sound of moaning. Clark lay in the quagmire of mud, groaning in agony; his body ripped to shreds with shrapnel as blood oozed from his torn and mutilated flesh. Callum slipped back into the crater, "Gavin! Hamish! Are you okay?" he shouted, his voice nervous with the fear that there would be no reply.

"My leg, I've been hit in the leg," replied Gavin in a pained voice.

"Clark's got it wi' the sergeant. I can't see or hear Hamish," shouted Callum.

"Hamish's lying a few feet from me; I can hear him moaning. I think he's in a bad way."

Callum climbed back to the rim of the crater and peered through the darkness. He could just make out the slumped body of the sergeant, tangled in the barbed wire. Clark had stopped groaning, his face sinking in the soft mud.

"Gavin! I can't make out where you are."

"I'm in a shell hole to the left of the sergeant and about six yards behind him. Hamish is in front of the hole; he's still alive."

"Can ye no' try and pull him in?" shouted Callum, scanning the darkness in front of him and to the left of the sergeant's body.

"I've tried to reach him, but me leg is..."

"It's all right. Stay where you are."

Callum slumped back into the muddy crater, trying to think. He had to try and get Gavin out at least, but what about Hamish? He couldn't carry the two of them. He looked back at his own lines but there was no sign of anyone coming to their aid; *they probably think we're all dead.* As he agonised over what to do, there were mumbled voices and the clatter of equipment from the German bunkers. He waited, expecting the crack of machine gun fire …but it never came.

"Callum! Callum!" shouted Gavin. "They're pulling back. Please help me get Hamish, I think…"

"Stay down. It might be a trick."

A barrage of German heavy artillery began to blast the British positions. Callum knew instantly why the Germans had pulled back. He scrambled over the edge of the crater and moved deftly through the line of broken wire. He rolled into the shell hole beside Gavin who was lying in water up to his waist; his eyes gave a faint smile. Callum patted him gently on the shoulder. "I'm goin' tae get ye back tae a nice warm bed and a pretty nurse, so hang in there, while I see how Hamish is."

Callum took another deep breath before climbing out the crater and crawling on barbed wire, which tore through his uniform and skin. One look at Hamish was enough. He was in a bad way. Callum touched his friend's bloody face, but there was no response.

"We'll send someone back for him," he said as he slid back into the shell hole.

"Is he dead?" asked Gavin. "He's dead, isn't he?"

"Come on. You've got tae help me here," said Callum, pulling Gavin from the muddy water. "We need tae hurry," urged Callum as the morass of mud shuddered underfoot with the exploding shells. The black sky was being torn apart with jagged white and yellow flashes of man-made lightning as the pulverised landscape appeared in the hot colours of hell. Callum threw off his backpack and lifted Gavin on to his back.

"Callum," said Gavin, his voice broken with tears. "I'm all right. Get Hamish. Don't leave Hamish."

"Just hold on, only a wee bit tae go. We'll come back for Hamish."

"Callum, I've wet myself. I'm sorry."

"Don't be daft. Ye were lying in water. It won't be long now, just think of that warm bed. For a moment Gavin's mind returned to the brothel and the pretty girl he had watched on the stairs. He took her hand and walked with her into the darkness. As they neared their own front lines a shell exploded just behind them knocking Callum to his knees. Two stretcher-bearers rushed to their aid.

"Ye wasted yer time, son," said one, as they lifted Gavin onto the stretcher, his back ripped open with shrapnel. "He's dead."

Callum, in a daze, got back to his feet and staggered the few yards to the mouth of the trench before collapsing into it with despair and exhaustion.

The bombardment lasted all night, but once again as the dawn broke the heavy guns on both sides fell silent. The British High Command decided to call off the planned offensive and fresh orders were relayed to each sector along the Front to ensure that the defences were made secure again. Callum made his report to Major Cruickshank. The Major simply nodded solemnly, the grave responsibility of sending the men to their death etched on his face. "If you get me the men's details, I'll write to their families."

"Sir, if it's all right with you, I'd like tae write to the Murray brothers' family."

"Yes, of course, they were your friends. There's a pen and paper here if you need it, corporal."

When Callum returned to his post, the other men were quietly drinking tea and smoking, waiting for the morning canteen to arrive. Some were re-reading letters from their loved ones, hoping there would be mail soon to give them something new to read from home. Empty stomachs, which only a few hours earlier were too nervous to hold food, now rumbled loudly as the men watched two planes high above the trenches engaged in a dog-fight. The German pilot seemed to have the upper hand and was aggressively tailgating the British plane, while spraying it with machine-gun fire. Soon there was a black trail of smoke coming from the doomed plane, which then nose-dived towards the ground behind the British trenches. The explosion was followed with cheers from the German trenches, as a plume of black smoke rose into the crisp morning sky. "Bastards," shouted one of the company sergeants, slumping back into the hole in the trench wall he was resting in. "Where's that lousy canteen?"

The quarter-master had obviously been ordered to feed the front-line men well that morning, to fortify them for the task ahead. Thankfully, the canteen had reached the lines before he was aware that the offensive had been called off and had a chance to order the cooks to reduce the rations to their normal meagre level. The extra cigarettes and tobacco, along with a double helping of rum were distributed. Callum could not eat; his mind was on the letter he would have to write to Hamish and Gavin's mother. What could he write? They died bravely for their King and country?

"Captain Harris, get Corporal Macnair back down here," ordered Major Cruickshank, peering through his box-periscope over 'no man's land'. "There's someone still moving out there."

Callum followed the captain along the muddy duckboards to the major's dug-out and observation post. The major was still on the observation step, scanning the German lines, when the captain tapped him on the shoulder. "Corporal Macnair, sir."

"Yes, corporal... I think one of the men from your aborted reconnaissance mission is still alive out there. Here! Have a look for yourself," said the major, stepping back down onto the duckboards. Callum took the periscope and looked across the churned-up ground, still smoking like molten rock from a recently erupted volcano. He saw Sergeant Watt's body lying over the wooded stakes and barbed-wire, where he perished. Callum scanned the ground around the sergeant, and his heart began to pound in his chest when he saw something moving slowly near to where he thought Hamish was lying.

"There's someone moving out there, sir. I think it might be Hamish...I mean Private Murray, sir."

"That's what I thought. But if he keeps moving a German sniper will soon pick him off."

"It might be just rats eating at the corpses," said the captain, who was now looking through the periscope.

"But it might not…sir!" said Callum, unable to control the anger in his voice. "I'd like to try and bring him in, sir."

"So would I," said the major, "but you'd just get yourself killed. Once it gets dark you and two men can see if you can reach him. The men will have to volunteer; I'm not ordering anyone out there to put their lives at risk for someone who might be beyond saving anyway."

For the rest of the day Callum urged the light to fade from the sky. Two stretcher-bearers had already volunteered and he was now feeling guilty at putting their lives at risk. The afternoon canteen was the usual fare and he took some bully beef and mixed it in his tin mug with a few dry biscuits. The tea made it bearable and the hollow feeling in his stomach was fooled for a while. The daylight eventually began to fade and the sun sank on the horizon in tortuously small increments that put Callum's nerves on edge.

"Corporal, get your men together and if you get into trouble don't expect any help," said Captain Harris. "Good luck. We'll hold fire for ten minutes along the line. After that, be sure you make yourselves known before you try and bring him in. If the Germans open up, then you're on your own."

"Yes, sir."

Callum decided there was no point in carrying his rifle and slipped over the parapet into the soft muddy ground followed by the two stretcher-bearers. He crawled towards the faint outline of Sergeant Watt's body and through the gaps in the barbed wire that they had opened up the night before. The sky was dark; thankfully there was no moon. He continued to crawl, stopping occasionally to listen for any sounds coming from the body now only a few feet away. He passed the shell-hole where the headless corpse was being sucked into the mud, and indicated to the two stretcher-bearers to shelter in it while he cut the barbed wire that was between him and Hamish. As he cut the wire, it suddenly recoiled violently. The sound echoed in the still night and Callum sank his face into the mud, and waited for the sound of machine-gun fire. After a few seconds he lifted his head and continued to move through the breached defences until he could reach out and touch Hamish's leg. The lack of response left Callum cold. He continued until he was lying alongside his friend and able to move him. He looked dead. Callum put his hand inside Hamish's tunic to feel for a heartbeat. There was a faint pulse. Callum shook Hamish, who groaned and opened his eyes.

The following morning, reinforcements were brought up, relieving those who had survived the long nights of shelling. The wounded, including Hamish, were transported in ambulances to the Casualty Clearing Stations, a few miles behind front lines. The dead, who could be reached, were buried in mass graves with words hastily spoken over the gaping pits and their gruesome, butchered contents of humanity. The bodies were wrapped in tarpaulin sheets and tagged with their details in the hope that they would be recovered and reburied when it was safe to do so. Callum helped shovel the earth over the mass grave where Gavin was buried with twenty other men from the battalion. In an army that now numbered in the millions, he suddenly felt all alone.

A long, desolate line of exhausted and wounded soldiers followed a caravan of ambulances along the road of mud and shattered trees. The advancing fresh-faced companies shouted words of comfort, while some promised revenge on the Hun, but the retreating soldiers simply forced a smile at their naivety. Hamish was semi-conscious and, as he was jolted around the crowded cart, his mind wandered through surreal images of his mother holding out a bowl of hot soup to a smiling German, with his spiked helmet and grey uniform covered in blood. He tried to run but his legs sank into the ground as the German turned to him with the face of his brother. For a moment he smiled but the face became distorted and decayed to rotten flesh as the German laughed insanely and ran at him with his bayonet dripping in blood.

"It's a trick! It's a trick," he shouted as one of the medics held him down and gave him another shot of morphine.

Chapter 16

It was a few days before Hamish finally emerged from his darkness. The first thing he saw was the vaulted ceiling of the field hospital, which had been a Benedictine Abbey before the war. Now cleared of its holy relics and pews, it was the main ward for those soldiers recovering from surgery. He gradually regained his other senses as the sound of mainly female voices mingled with the moans and groans coming from some of the other beds. He had no memory of being in 'no man's land' as he struggled to make sense of his surroundings.

Soon, the smell of iodine and other less familiar hospital odours attacked his fragile senses and he began to feel sick. The tight bedclothes caused him to panic as his weak body wrenched itself violently with each spasm from his stomach, his vision blurred with the tears and pus that each attack forced from his eyes. He vomited yellow bile over the bed.

"Now that wasn't very clever," said one of the nurses as she pulled the tight blankets from the bed. She then put a tin bucket on the floor and held Hamish over it as he emptied what little his stomach had left. "There that's better," she said as he fell back on to his pillow. "Here, have a sip of water… and try and get some rest, you been very ill."

"What happened to me?"

"Your leg was shattered with shrapnel," she said, looking at the medical card at the bottom of the bed, before tucking the rough woollen blanket under the thin army mattress. She had now dealt with so many men waking from their delirium to find themselves crippled for life that she was convinced the sooner they know what was wrong with them, then the sooner they would come to terms with it. "You're one of the lucky ones; you still have one good leg…"

"One good leg, you've taken me leg off…my God."

"You'll be off to England in the next few days…A war hero…think of it…"

"I don't want to be a bloody war hero," he cursed, as he gently lowered his hands under the blankets. His right leg was gone. All that was left was a stump, bandaged and numbed with morphine. He passed out.

It took over a week before Callum was allowed an afternoon's leave to visit Hamish in hospital. The Battalion's casualty list had been posted a few days earlier and confirmed that Hamish had survived the ordeal of surgery.

Callum got a lift in an ambulance that was on its way to the hospital from the Front with two soldiers who looked near to death. The roads were treacherous, with shell holes, and the remains of dead horses. On a couple of occasions the driver had to be careful not to end up in the ditch, as he crunched the gears and swerved around the tight corners. Over the groans of the two wounded men, they could still hear the thunder of heavy guns to the north as the Abbey finally came into view.

"You'll need a hand to stretcher these two in," offered Callum.

"No, yer all right, I'll get a couple of the orderlies to give me a hand. They'll know where to take them."

"Anyway, thanks for the lift."

"You're welcome…hope your friend's all right."

Once in the Abbey grounds, Callum was directed to the main ward in the chapel, where one of the nurses pointed Hamish out to him. The smell of urine and gangrene almost turned his stomach, but Callum was more worried about how he was going to tell Hamish about Gavin. In spite of the putrid smell, he took a deep breath to steady himself, before walking along the rows of camp beds. Most of the men in the ward were in a bad way, many with horrific injuries that made death seem kinder. The doctors and nurses were overwhelmed with the grotesque nature of some of the men's injuries, although they did what they could for them, most would not live very long. At the far end of the ward, Hamish was sitting up, staring at the wall opposite.

"How ar' ye Hamish?" asked Callum, putting his hand on his friend's shoulder to bring him out of his trance.

"Callum!"

"Sorry, Hamish. I couldn't get here sooner. They were expecting another offensive from Jerry, and wouldn't let me come until today. How ar' ye?"

"Callum, they took me leg off."

"They had to; otherwise you'd have died…"

"I'd have rather died! I will be nae use tae anyone now. Nae use…I wish they had just let me die. No woman is going tae look at me now!"

"Don't say that, Hamish. You'll be going home soon."

"How can I go home without me leg? Where's Gavin? You'd think he'd visit his…What's the matter, Callum?"

"I'm sorry, Hamish…Gavin didn't make it…he's dead."

"Oh God…good God… no…! I can't go back home without Gavin! Dead …he's dead."

"He got killed the night you were wounded…I'm sorry, Hamish."

As the tears ran down his pallid cheeks, Hamish slowly drifted back into a deep stupor. Callum tried to encourage him back, but soon gave up. After a few minutes, he was asked to leave by one of the nurses as she put a screen around the bed.

"He needs to rest, corporal. Come back another day when he's come to terms with losing his leg, some take it worse than others."

With the constant fear of a German offensive, Callum could not get leave for another couple of weeks. The day before his next visit, a letter from Hamish's mother arrived addressed to both brothers. He wondered if this letter had crossed in the post with the one he had sent a few weeks earlier. He took the letter with him as he walked the six miles back to the hospital the following morning. When he arrived at the ward, Hamish's bed was being stripped down by a young nurse. He rushed up to her.

"Where's Private Murray? This was his bed!"

"The soldier in this bed died during the night, corporal. He's in the morgue."

"The morgue?" Callum recoiled, the blood draining from his face as he dropped the letter onto the floor. The nurse picked it up.

"I'm sorry, but so many die in here every day. I'm sure they'll let you see him, if you want to."

Still stunned, Callum followed one of the orderlies around the back of the hospital to the horror that was the hospital morgue. There were rows of bodies covered in white sheets, lying on the grass waiting for their turn to be sewn into canvas shrouds. The air was rancid. The orderly lifted away the top of the sheet. Hamish was lying with his eyes wide open, as though he was still in a trance. Callum bent down and closed them.

"Why is he naked?"

"They need the pyjamas," said the orderly, shaking his head.

"Where's his uniform, his kilt?"

"They'll be with his bag over there."

"Get them! He's no' getting buried like that!"

"What does it matter?"

"It matters tae me! Will ye get them and help me get him

209

dressed?"

"All right, but we better hurry up as they'll be burying this lot this afternoon."

Once Hamish was dressed, Callum remembered the photograph. He stared at it long and hard, the brothers smiling faces unaware of the fate that awaited them. He found it too painful to endure for long, and put it back in the sporran to be buried with Hamish.

Within the hour, Hamish was put on to the back of a horse-drawn cart with other corpses in various stages of decomposition. Callum followed the ghastly convoy of carts to a mass grave in a field not far from the hospital. The bodies were laid out in a row, in a deep trench, by a handful of orderlies, as the hospital chaplain prayed over them. Callum watched, with a lump in his throat, as the mechanical digger covered the corpses with black earth not unlike the rich soil of Glenfay. He would have to write another letter to Mrs Murray. The thought made him feel physically sick.

Callum never got a chance to write that letter. The following night he was caught in an explosion when the Officers' dug-out took a direct hit, killing Major Cruickshank and Captain Harris outright. Callum, like many others, was buried under the earth that the shell had lifted high into the air, before falling back into the open trench. He thought he was going to suffocate, before he was dragged from the soil, coughing and spluttering, but alive. He did not feel the shrapnel in his leg until he tried to stand up, only to fall back into the collapsed trench.

After a six- hour bombardment, the Allies fell back under a sustained onslaught by German infantry who began to advance through the abandoned British trenches. A full retreat was ordered.

During the chaos of the retreat, Callum was taken to a field hospital a few miles behind the front lines.

The ground shuddered as the German bombardment advanced and the shells began to land in nearby fields. "Hold him still!" ordered the surgeon as he prodded the gaping wound in Callum's leg. "Thankfully, it looks like the corporal has only a small piece of shrapnel in his thigh and the bone looks fine…"

"We will have to get the wounded on ambulances as soon as possible," said the nurse anxiously.

The surgeon ignored her and continued to cut into Callum's leg to dig out the twisted shrapnel. "Give him some more chloroform; I think he felt that. I'm nearly finished…We can start to get these men out of here. "

Still unconscious, Callum was taken by ambulance to the village station. There was a slight drizzle as two burly stretcher-bearers lifted him onto the scrubbed floor of a cattle wagon. The rain on his face revived him a little, and he opened his eyes for a moment. He was still too drowsy to make sense of what was happening to him, and soon slipped back into morphine induced dreams, as the train rattled through the French countryside towards the coast.

At Le Havre, the quayside was awash with wounded, and hundreds of stretchers lay side by side as the victims of the war waited in the rain for the troop ships to disembark. Callum was now conscious, and the first thing he did was check he still had both legs. His left leg was getting painful as the morphine began to wear off, but at least he still had it. He sat up to watch the ranks of fresh troops flooding the quayside. He remembered the sergeant's slip of the tongue at Marnoch Station when the Murray brother's entered the waiting room. *More lambs to the slaughter.*

The voyage across the Channel was rough and many of the men were sick. The sea air soon cleared Callum's head from the residue of the morphine and he cried with the pain in his leg and at the thought of leaving both Hamish and Gavin behind in France.

It was late in the evening when the hospital ship arrived at Southampton. The fear of a U-Boat attack only lifted when the ship was safely in port. From there, the wounded were taken by train to various hospitals in Hampshire. Callum and at least a hundred other wounded men were taken to a convalescent hospital just south of Salisbury. Once in the hospital ward, he was given another shot of morphine; it eased the pain in his leg, but nothing could take away the torment every time he remembered his dead friends.

Caitriona read the letter from Duncan a second time. She then folded it away and stared blankly out at the lush green lawn at the front of the hospital. It was a warm summer's morning and the more able-bodied men were making the most of the pleasant sunshine. "Oh, Daddy," she sighed, her mind running through the contents of the letter again.

"Nurse!" called a stern-faced sister, her voice sharp with reproach. "Hurry up with those blankets."

"Yes, Sister," replied Caitriona, the tears freezing in her eyes as she rushed past the sister and into the ward. Many of the beds were lying empty as their usual occupants strolled around the grounds.

"What kept you?" asked Nancy Jones, a volunteer from the Welsh valleys. "She's been up and down the ward like a mad dog for the last ten minutes."

"I went back to the room to change my shoes."

"Nurse, get on with your work and stop chattering," ordered the Sister from the entrance to the ward.

"Oh, I can't stand that old cow," whispered Nancy as she caught the other end of the sheet and tucked it under the side of the mattress. "Are you all right? You look a little pale."

"It's my father. He's had a stroke..." said Caitriona, breaking down in tears.

"Oh, I'm sorry," said Nancy, rushing to comfort her. "Come and sit down for a while."

"What's goin' on?" demanded the Sister.

"She's had some bad news from home," explained Nancy. "I can manage the rest of the beds myself, Sister."

"Well get on with it…Nurse Munro, come with me."

Caitriona followed the Sister into the small dispensary, shaking her head against the Sister's indication to sit down. The Sister took a buff file from her desk drawer and opened it without looking at Caitriona. "Well, what's this news you have?"

"I got a letter from my brother. My father's had a stroke."

"How bad is he?"

"I don't know."

"I suppose you'll be wanting to give up nursing and go home to look after him?"

"No, I don't want to give up nursing. But I would like a couple of weeks to…"

"A couple of weeks? I take it that you are aware that there is a war on?"

"Of course, Sister."

"Well if every nurse took a couple of weeks off every time one or their family became ill, where would the hospital be then? I take it you were awake when the Surgeon General addressed the staff last week?"

"Yes."

"Then you'll know about the casualties that are already mounting up and waiting to be shipped back. In a few days we will be overrun with wounded soldiers and…" The Sister stopped for a moment as she studied the file. "I see your father's a Laird, the Lord of Glenfay no less. What are you doing nursing?"

"My husband's a doctor. He was a surgeon in a field hospital and has been missing for more than nine months. I wanted to do something to help."

"Why did you not stay in Scotland? They're plenty of hospitals in your own country that I'm sure would be glad of another nurse."

"I wanted to be where…I would be most needed."

"Well that's all very noble, but what use are you if you're not here when you're most needed? Wait here!"

The Sister returned after some minutes, an uncharacteristic smile on her thin white lips. "I've spoken to Doctor Jenkins, and the expected flood of casualties has not come to anything so you can have a week. You can leave as soon as you can, but I want you back no later than a week today. Is that understood?"

"Yes, Sister. Thank you."

As Caitriona left the room, the Sister continued to read her file. She could not understand why a person of Caitriona's class wanted to be, not even a nurse but an auxiliary nurse. It must be the Florence Nightingale sense of duty that these toffs have when the King's honour is at stake. She shook her head as she put the file back in the drawer.

Caitriona sat patiently in Folkestone Station; her mind on her father. She then looked at the last paragraph of Duncan's short letter, which was cold and dictating, *'There's no need to come home. He has a nurse to look after him.'*

On the platform a paper boy was shouting the latest headlines, but Caitriona could not make out what he was so excited about. His papers were selling like hotcakes as he turned from one customer to another. Caitriona beckoned the boy, who smiled at her, taking the

214

halfpenny she handed him with a cheeky doff of his cap. A sudden feeling of guilt overwhelmed her as she read the bold headlines, *'A Massive Allied Offensive Began This Morning'*.

It was late in the evening when Roberts met Caitriona coming up the path to the house.

"Why, miss, we had no idea you were coming home tonight," he explained, taking her small suitcase from her grateful hands. "We didn't get your telegram. I could have sent Henderson to meet you at the station."

"I didn't send one, Roberts. I only knew myself this morning. The Reverend Knox was in Marnoch and was kind enough to give me a lift to the village."

"Only to the village? Your brother will not like that."

"I asked him to leave me there. It's only a half mile walk and I needed time to think."

"Caitriona!" called Duncan from the front door. "You should have let us know you were coming."

"I only got your letter this morning. How's Daddy?" she asked with some hesitation in her voice.

"Why don't you come into the library," he said taking her gently by the arm.

Duncan poured himself a large glass of brandy as Caitriona stood impatiently with her arms folded, waiting for him to speak. "Well?"

"There was no need for you to come home…"

"Who the hell do you think you are?"

"I'm only thinking of you, Caitriona. He's not..."

"I want to see him," she said, turning to leave the room.

As she rushed up the stairs, her heart began to beat fast when she saw a nurse sitting outside her father's room reading a book. The sound of her footsteps penetrated the nurse's concentration and she immediately got to her feet to stop Caitriona entering the room. "His Lordship is sleeping," she said, moving between the door and Caitriona.

"Get out of the way. I want to see my father!" demanded Caitriona, brushing the nurse's outstretched arm away.

"Oh, I'm sorry, miss. It's just that the young master ordered me not to let anyone disturb him."

"It's all right. I won't disturb him," said Caitriona, as she let herself into the darkened room. She then moved anxiously towards her father's bed. He was sitting up against the headboard with his eyes open but glazed and unmoved by her presence. She stepped closer to the bed on seeing a faint smile come to his lips. "Daddy," she said in a broken voice, thankful he seemed to recognise her. She lifted his trembling, cold hand and sat on the edge of the bed. "It's me, father. It's Caitriona." But he simply stared straight ahead. The thin smile, if it was ever there, was gone from his tired face. She began to talk to him about anything she could think of; hoping against hope that his vacant, lost look would pass and he would be his old self again.

That night, with Caitriona sitting by his side, Charles Dunbar smiled for the last time as he took his leave of the world.

After only a few weeks of convalescence, Callum was discharged from the hospital and sent home to recover from his injuries. Although he now walked with a slight limp, he could manage quite well with the aid of a walking stick. He knew he was one of the lucky ones as many of the wounded soldiers he had befriended at the hospital would never walk again. He counted his blessings as he travelled to London, spending a night in the capital before catching the early morning train to Glasgow.

Exhausted after a poor night's sleep in a cheap hotel, he slept for most of the second stage of the journey, as the Glasgow bound train rattled past the countless English stations until it finally crossed the border into Scotland. He sat up when the train pulled into Lockerbie Station, where he could smell the peat rising from the station house chimney.

When the train finally moved again, the Scottish countryside seemed to open up before it. To the west, clouds were casting gloomy shadows over the hills and fields; rain was in the air, but he did not mind one bit. He could make out the familiar bluish grey smoke of burning peat streaming from houses scattered along the lower slopes of the hills, with their purple and red hues of heather. Down the gullies, water, black with peat, was cascading into a fast flowing river below, which frothed with a frenzied excitement as it swelled over its banks. Sheep grazing close to the railway line scattered as the train rattled by. He would soon be home.

"Glasgow Central in twenty minutes," called the porter as he passed through the carriage. Callum rested his head against the window again and tried to get back to sleep.

He was eventually brought out of his uncomfortable slumber when the train finally screeched to a halt in the noisy confusion of Glasgow Central Station. He gave himself a shake before lifting his rucksack on to his back and following the other passengers onto the platform. Sitting for so long made his bad leg stiff and a little sore, and he became self conscious of his limp as he wandered around the station looking for the ticket office. There was a sudden blast of bagpipes and he stopped to watch the columns of new recruits that followed the pipers on to the main concourse. A red-faced sergeant major, his chest sticking out and proudly displaying his military ribbons, shouted the soldiers' names in alphabetical order from a clipboard. The men broke rank as their names were shouted and rushed to say their goodbyes to their loved ones. The reality of the war was now evident on their faces as tears of fear and grief replaced the cheers that Callum remembered from when he had passed through the same station only the year before.

The next train to Marnock was not for another hour and Callum found a bar nearby to pass the time. It was now raining hard and he watched the deluge from the pub window. He was half drunk when he finally crossed the platform and boarded the north bound train. Glad to find an empty compartment for the two-hour journey, he took out a half bottle of whisky to dull the pain in his leg and to keep his mind from wandering back to France. He put his bag on the seat next to him, hoping it would deter unwanted company. It was another ten minutes before the locomotive let off a violent burst of steam and slowly pulled away from the station. Thank God, he thought, opening his tobacco tin to roll a cigarette. The train slowly travelled through the smoky city, and Callum began to feel tired again, and he rested his head against his canvas bag. In spite of the whisky, or maybe because of it, images of Hamish and Gavin flashed through his mind again. Too painful for him to endure, he sat up again, and took another drink.

The train began to pick up speed as it gradually freed itself from the city. It had stopped raining, and a weak rainbow appeared over the grimy tenement skyline, contrasting sharply with thousands of chimneys puffing out ragged lines of black smoke. "Tickets, please!" Callum jumped, as though he had been doing something wrong, but relaxed again as the cheery faced conductor nodded at him without looking at the ticket. "Some bloody day this has been," said the conductor. "You wouldn't think the sun was splitting the trees only yesterday."

"That's our Scottish summers for you," replied Callum as the conductor looked him over.

"On leave?"

"Aye, I've got a couple of weeks."

"Well, make the most of it. I hear it's not too pleasant over there."

"Aye, I will."

The train pulled into Dumbarton Station, and Callum watched the people standing on the opposite platform as they picked up their cases and bags when the Glasgow bound train pulled alongside. He sat up sharply when he noticed Caitriona Dunbar sitting in one of the carriages. She was looking straight at him with sad, fixed eyes. He smiled, but she stared back without any hint of recognition as his own train began to slowly move off. He sank back into his seat and cursed the thought of his stupid grin, as though she would remember him. Just as he was drowning in embarrassment, the compartment door opened with a bang, and a small, stout man forced his way into the compartment, behind a large, brown suitcase. "Oh, I'm sorry," he said as he pulled the door closed and lifted the case on to the rack above the seats. Callum ignored the man's clumsy entrance and looked out the window, trying to bring Caitriona's face back into his mind, but all he could see was his own reflection.

"Terrible weather," said the man, taking the seat opposite.

"Aye."

"Home on leave?" continued the man, cleaning his glasses with a large white handkerchief.

"Aye."

"Oh, I envy all you young men, marching off to give those damn Germans a bloody nose."

"Why don't you enlist then?"

"Oh, I would. I would, but it's my eyes you see," he explained, thankful in his mind for the myopia that had been a curse all his life, but now was a blessing.

Callum turned his head back towards the window and closed his eyes. The man took the hint and settled back in his seat to read his newspaper. Callum was glad to see the broadsheet screen going up between them; the last thing he wanted was to have a stranger pry into his thoughts.

It was dark when he arrived at Marnock station and as he stepped from the train, clouds of steam covered the empty platform like a thick fog rolling in from the sea. He threw his backpack over his shoulders and went into the waiting room, with its beacon of flickering, yellow light diffusing into a watery haze through the rising steam. The waiting room was empty and he checked his pocket watch with the clock on the wall; they agreed that it was 10.05 pm which meant the train was five minutes late. He walked around the back of the station building to see if his father was waiting there with the cart, but there was no sign of anyone. He then wondered if his father had got the telegram he had sent at the weekend. He rolled a cigarette for a minute and considered what to do. He looked down the road towards Marnock itself; why the hell did they no' build the station nearer to the town, he thought, looking at the faint lights in the distance against the blackness of the surrounding hillside. Marnock was a good half a mile away from the isolated station and Glenfay another five miles beyond that. It was a very dark moonless night and the stars sparkled in their thousands as he looked up into the infinite sky, blowing the last of his cigarette smoke in three chasing circles before stubbing it on the ground with the heel of his boot. So much for the hero's welcome. He got to his feet for the long walk home.

When he neared the outskirts of Marnock, he heard the sound of a cart rattling along the stony road, and then his father's voice cursing the old donkey as it trotted at its own slow pace. Tess was walking alongside and broke into a run when she heard Callum shout her name. He knelt down to catch her as she jumped up to lick his face in her frenzied excitement.

"Callum! Is that you?" called his father, pulling up the cart and screwing his eyes up to make out the dark, crouched figure up ahead.

"Aye, it's me. What kept you?" he shouted, walking to the stationary cart with Tess running around him in circles.

"Och, for God's sake, is that all ye have tae say tae yer feyther after over a year away?"

"How are ye?" asked Callum, throwing his backpack on the back of the empty cart.

"I'm fine and how are you, son?" asked his father as he watched Callum struggle to lift himself on the cart. "How's the leg?"

"I'm all right…the leg's a bit stiff…that's all."

"Here, give me yer hand," said Jamie as he helped pull his son on to the wooden seat. "There, we'll have ye home in no time."

The cart rattled along the dark road as fast as the donkey wanted it to go. There was a strong smell of peat burning in the damp air that reminded Callum of happier times before the war. "It's good to be home," he said.

"Aye, it's good tae have ye home. That's a fine beard ye have there, I wouldn't have recognised ye only for Tess. Com' on ye old bugger, get a move on... It's a shame about the two boys. Their poor folks..."

"Aye." It was all Callum could and wanted to say.

"We've a new Laird now. Old Dunbar passed away a week ago," said Jamie, giving the donkey a slap with the reins to get a move on. "He was a decent man, but that son of his will ruin the place before he's through."

Callum said nothing; he now knew why Caitriona looked so sad when he saw her on the Glasgow train. The cart trundled on over the brae into the darkness of the night with only the noise of the cartwheels on the stony road breaking the silence. He lit a cigarette as the cart turned onto the road running alongside the loch. The dark loch seemed to stretch into infinity as it gently lapped against the shore. The ghostly shadow of Leaburn Castle then appeared on its craggy outcrop of rock.

That night he tossed and turned violently in his sleep; his troubled mind wandering through the grotesque and haunted landscape of the Somme, where dark, green coloured clouds fell from violent skies. He began to cough and choke in a burning sea of fog, which began to engulf him, clinging to his throat as he struggled to free himself. He felt his feet, heavy and weak, being sucked into the soft, brown earth, pulling him, deeper and deeper into the hell below him. A hand reached out and grabbed him by the arm. He could see that the hand belonged to Gavin, who looked at him with a distorted, bloody face, disfigured but still recognisable. The hand began to lose its slippery grip as Callum tried to maintain a hold of its brittle fingers. He watched in horror as Gavin fell into a black abyss which seemed to have no end.

"Wake up, son," said his father, shaking Callum from his nightmare. "Yer been having a bad dream, son." With his heart still thumping and his body soaked in sweat, Callum freed himself from the fatigue that tried to suck him back into the darkness.

"I'm all right, Dad, just go back tae bed. I'll be all right in a minute," he urged as he took a rolled cigarette from his tobacco tin. Jamie reluctantly went back to bed. Callum lit his cigarette and tried to collect his thoughts. It felt like the nightmare had lasted forever but it was still not morning. He lay awake shivering; afraid to go back to sleep, but his fatigue eventually overcame his fear.

Chapter 17

When Callum woke again, the cottage was still in pitch darkness and for a moment he thought he was back in the trenches. Slowly his confused mind cleared from its deep and troubled sleep and he gradually recognised the dark shapes as furniture, pots, and other objects that were once so familiar to him. He lay back in the bed, his eyes heavy with sleep, afraid the nightmare was waiting to capture his mind again. He began to shiver with the sudden feeling of coldness and wrapped the top blanket around his shoulders. Tess jumped from the bottom of the bed and pushed her head under his hand. "How ar' ye, lass," he said, patting her thin head gently.

He was soon desperate for a smoke, and lit a cigarette as the first rays of daylight began to seep through the cracks in the wooden shutters. He thought of Caitriona again, she looked so unhappy, but her face soon faded from his mind. *She's married, ye damn fool!* Shaking his head of her memory, he got out of bed and dressed in civilian clothes, which were in his rucksack, leaving the damp uniform lying in a heap on the floor. He found his old boots behind the door with the mud still caked on them from the last day he had worn them.

"Let's get a fire on," he said to Tess as she followed him around the room, her eyes on his every move.

"Callum!" called his father from the darkness of the other room. "Are ye up already?"

"Aye, do ye want some porridge?"

"What are ye doing up at this time?" said his father, still half sleeping and staggering into the main room.

"I can't sleep and I feel like going for a walk. Ar' ye wanting some oats?" asked Callum again, taking a small pot from the rail above the hearth.

"I'll get that, son."

"No, it's all right. I've missed making porridge. Get dressed while I get some water from out the back."

It was a sunny Sunday morning but the ground was still soft underfoot with the heavy rainfall of the last few days. Callum looked at the high cirrus clouds that streaked the pale blue sky. It was going to be a fine day, he thought, as he gazed over the loch towards Leaburn Castle.

After breakfast, he packed his kit bag with Hamish and Gavin's belongings so he could return them to their mother, something he had been dreading since he came home. He decided to go for a long walk to build up the courage before facing the poor woman with her grief. He walked along the familiar hillside with Tess by his side, throwing a well-chewed stick for the dog to retrieve as they made their way through the heather. It had been a long time since she had gathered sheep on these hills. She seemed quite content with her early retirement and ignored the few grazing sheep they passed along the way. Callum identified his neighbours' sheep by the coloured dye on their rump and was surprised how many bore Dunbar's mark so far away from the Laird's own fields.

The sun was now quite warm and he took off his jacket throwing it over his shoulder, feeling a sense of peace he had not experienced for such a long time. He sat down beside the old stone dyke at the edge of the field and rolled another cigarette. After finishing his smoke, he folded his jacket into a pillow and laid it against the dyke, lying back to rest in the pleasant warm sunshine. He soon fell asleep with Tess lying patiently at his side.

It was over an hour before he woke from his deep, dreamless sleep, his eyes blurred with the brightness of the sun. He could hear the distant peal of the Kirk bell and looked down the hillside to see a steady stream of dark figures walking towards the Kirk. He could just make out his father, who was standing on the grass verge near the crossroads with bible in hand, waiting for the Laird's gig to pass before stepping back onto the road.

Callum got to his feet and walked down the hillside.

The service had started when he reached the Kirk and Ian Craig, the senior church elder, gave him a stern glare as he opened the creaking, oak door.

"Morning, Ian."

"Oh it's yerself, Callum," whispered the old man, his wrinkled face exhibiting a rare smile.

"Aye, Ian," said Callum as he broke free from the elder's tight handshake. Heads turned with nods and smiles of recognition as he took a pew at the back of the crowded church. The Reverend was already fired up and his voice was filled with its usual tones of righteousness. "Now turn to chapter three and page number six hundred and thirty six of the Good Book," said the minister, as he turned to the well thumbed page in his own bible. "To everything there is a season..." He began with his voice slow and almost melodic. Callum's eyes left the Reverend's performance and darted from one familiar head to another. He noticed Duncan Dunbar sitting alone in the family pew, his thick neck and flushed face, giving him the appearance of a tethered bull in a field of heifers.

Callum's wandering thoughts were abruptly brought back into focus as the Reverend pounded his fist on the pulpit and repeated. '...*A time to love, and a time to hate, a time of war, and a time of peace...This is a time of war and there is no sin to have hate at such a time. God's words are clear and the righteous must wage war on the wicked and that is why I ask you young men of this parish not to flinch from your duty to your King and country. The devil is in the black hearts of the Germans and they must be stopped in their evil tracks.*"

The minister was now flushed and his dark eyes surveyed the congregation, avoiding the new Laird's pew to his left, where

Duncan sat impatiently waiting for the service to finish. Callum had had enough and got up to leave. The church door closed with a bang as the congregation followed their preacher's silent stare down the aisle.

"That looked like your lad, Jamie. Ah didn't recognise him at first wi' the beard and all."

"Aye, Reverend. He got home last night."

"Has he turned pagan on us?"

Jamie did not answer, but lowered his head. There was a buzz of whispers around the congregation as the Reverend closed his bible with a dramatic thud; immediately silencing his obedient flock with the collective words of God. This brought a disdainful smile to Duncan's face.

Callum walked around to the graveyard at the back of the church. There was now a granite gravestone on his mother and brother's grave and he stood there for a moment with his thoughts of the past. There was a rose in a bottle at the side of the headstone. He picked up the tiny bottle and touched the withered flower; its crispy, thin petals immediately disintegrating. As he placed the bottle back down on the bed of white, sun-bleached shells that covered the grave, he suddenly remembered that it was his mother's birthday at the beginning of the month and he fought back the tears as he imagined his father cutting the little flower from her rose bush at the back of the cottage, carrying it along the road to the Kirk, before placing it on the grave to mark a day that passed unnoticed when she was alive.

The sun was now warm on the back of his neck and he turned to look over the loch, which looked as calm as he had ever seen it. All the town's fishing boats were tied up along the quayside. No one fished on a Sunday, well except for otters and poachers. The seagulls and the smaller black head gulls of Glenfay did not keep the Sabbath either, as they flew in bursts of furious excitement at every scrap of gutted fish they could find among the lobster creels and fishing nets scattered along the cobbled quayside to dry. He took a deep breath to fill his lungs with the fresh, salty air he had so often dreamed of in the stench of the trenches. He then turned to see the Reverend shake hands with the first few parishioners leaving the church and watched the steady stream of people spill onto the road, making their way home. He noticed Elspeth Murray with her daughter Eileen and waited until they had moved away from the Kirk before making after them. "Mrs Murray!"

Elspeth, dressed in black from head to toe, pulled her shawl back and stared at Callum without speaking.

"Ah brought this back," said Callum, pulling a brown paper parcel from his backpack. "It's their clothes and things," he explained.

Elspeth did not say anything, or offer to take the parcel. Callum handed it to Eileen, who took it with nothing more than a nod.

"It was your fault," Elspeth finally said, with a mixture of pain and anger in her voice. "They only signed up because of you. Why did ye have tae take ma bairns wi' ye?" she sobbed, pulling her shawl back over her head and turning away from him.

"Mrs Murray!" he called after her. "I'm sorry!" But she simply walked on.

After what had happened with Mrs Murray, Callum had put off going to see Mhairi until the following day. She was no longer living in the fine, big house at the quayside. It was not long after Angus had enlisted that the rent arrears brought the bailiffs to the door. The warrant sale that followed broke Mhairi's heart as she stood in the rain, child in arms, watching people from the surrounding towns pay next to nothing for her precious things. The local folk from Glenfay would not bid and they watched in disgust as strangers filled their carts with the furniture that she and Angus had bought only a few years before. There was a disapproving murmur among the locals as Jamie Macnair bid two shillings for the cot and bedding. There were no other bidders.

Jamie carried the cot and blankets through some hostile women who had moved into the glen to work in the new meat processing plant. He ignored the obvious hostility and walked over to his cart.

"Mhairi! C'mon there nothing for ye here," he said. "There's nae point watching this. I'll take ye up tae yer folks. At least ye'll have a cot for the bairn." As he walked to the cart, Jamie turned to the hostile crowd and said, "Did ye think I was goin' tae sleep in it meself?"

Callum gave the door another loud knock before Walter, with part of his chin still covered in soap from his aborted shave, opened the door. Walter's angry face mellowed when he saw him.

"Hello, Walter. Is Mhairi in?"

"Aye, com' in, Callum, she's tending tae the wee yin at the minute. It's terrible what happened tae Hamish and Gavin, and poor Elspeth no' that long a widow. It's a damn shame, all right."

Callum just shook his head, and followed Walter into the untidy house; there was a smell of urine and sickness in the small damp room. He was surprised by Mhairi's scrawny appearance; her beautiful mane of fiery red hair was dull and straggly, hanging over her sad, thin face.

"Callum!" she said in a soft, strained whisper as she got up to meet him.

"How are ye?" he asked, but could see for himself.

"I'm fine. And how are you?"

"Great."

"I'm away tae finish me shave," said Walter. "Put on the kettle,

Mhairi."

"Aye, feyther," she replied in an irritated voice. "Away and have yer shave."

"Have ye heard anything from Angus?" Callum asked hopefully.

Pulling her shawl over her shoulders, Mhairi went over to a dresser and took out a tin box from a drawer. She sat back down on the bed beside her young daughter, who was shyly looking up at Callum.

"Here," she said as she handed him two envelopes, "I got the first one just over a month ago, the other one this morning."

"I can't read these."

"I want ye tae...Yer the one that went tae France tae look for him, who else should have the right tae read them."

.

When Callum began to read, it was as though he could hear Angus's own voice in his head. He sat down by the window.

Mhairi,

I was glad tae get yer letter. I'm sorry I sent the others back unopened. Maybe if I never let myself get so damned drunk that day, I might have seen sense. That bitch really got to me...I've been a bloody fool.

I was gassed a few weeks back. The thought of dying without seeing you or the baby was awful, but the doctor told me I must have only inhaled a small amount of gas, and that my lungs are not that badly damaged. My nose and throat still feel like they are on fire, but it's not as bad as it was. Most of the gas patients in here are in an awful bad way. So I've been very lucky. Anyway, I should be getting home soon to convalesce for a few weeks. I can't wait to see you and the bairn.

P.S. I never did run into Callum or the Murray brothers. Their battalion is in another sector. Now I'm in hospital there's not much chance of getting to meet up with them. Maybe when I get back out here after my leave, I could apply for a transfer to their unit. Then the Four Musketeers will be back together again. Anyway, I can't wait to see you... Kiss Fiona for me and write soon...Angus.

"Do you forgive him?" asked Callum.

Mhairi did not answer at first but turned to her young daughter and brushed the child's hair away from her eyes. "Of course I forgive him, what else can I do?" she said eventually. "We were so happy for such a short time. I love him and I want him to come back to us."

"He was still in France when he sent this," said Callum, looking at the postmark on the envelope. "He may be in a hospital in England by now, or even on his way home."

"They're not letting him home," said Mhairi, indicating to Callum to read the second letter, which also had a French postmark on it.

Mhairi...I'm sorry, my leave was cancelled. I was due to get ten days to recover from the gas attack, but they cancelled it. Someone reported me for drinking the night before I was gassed. They blame that for making me sick and causing me to pull off the gas mask before the all clear was given. They even threatened to court martial me. They passed me fit to return to active service shortly after I sent you my last letter. I don't think they'll ever let me get out of this war.

I can't stop thinking about Hamish and Gavin Murray. I saw their names together on the Regimental casualty list. Give my condolences to their folks; losing one son is bad enough. I still haven't found out where Callum is stationed, I hope he is all right. My battalion has moved about so much in the last few weeks that I have no idea where we are, never mind Callum's battalion. I could not bear it if something happens to him. Let me know if you hear anything. ... Kiss Fiona for me and write soon.

"They've blocked his leave, after being gassed…The heartless bastards!" he said, handing the letter back to Mhairi. "At least he wasn't badly gassed. You have tae be grateful for small mercies in this damned war."

"Is the tea made?" asked Walter, now cleanly shaven.

"I had better be going."

"Och, don't be silly," protested Walter. "You've only just got here. You'll need tae tell us all about it. We hear nothing in these parts."

"I've got tae get back home, Walter, maybe some other time."

"Callum, surely this war can't last forever," said Mhairi, combing her daughter's hair.

"No, but it feels like it will."

With the summer well and truly over, the fields around Glenfay were once more in need of the scythe. The fine weather had some in the glen out early in the season, and bales of hay began to appear in the lower fields. The sound of gunshot could also be heard echoing over the moors as the grouse were driven into the line of Duncan Dunbar's fire. It was a time of plenty in the glen, and the folk made the most of it before the winter months took hold.

One morning Callum received two letters in official War Office envelopes. He read the first letter, which directed him to attend a medical examination at the army barracks in Marnock the following Tuesday. The second letter was more of a surprise to him. He looked at it again. The letter was signed by the regiment's commanding officer, General Howard, and was short and to the point. He had been awarded the Military Medal for bravery shown under enemy fire. He could not make up his mind whether to be pleased or angry with the letter. Being caught in a cross fire in 'no man's land' was not very brave and neither was carrying Gavin back to the trenches, that was instinct. Gavin might even have survived if he had left him for the stretcher-bearers to retrieve once the shelling had stopped, and Mrs Murray would have had at least one son to comfort her in her old age.

"Here," he said as he handed the envelope to his father. "They're giving me a bloody medal!"

"Good God," replied his father, quickly reading the short letter. "That's great."

"What's great about it? They'll be ten a penny by the time this war's over."

"It's a Military Medal. They don't give them to anyone, son. I'm proud of ye. And at least ye survived wi' yer life. That's more important. With a Military Medal pinned tae yer lapel, ye can walk down any street wi' yer head up high. No one can say that ye haven't done yer bit."

"Feyther, the war's no' finished."

"Aye, but at least it's finished for you."

"No, it's no' finished for me either."

"What dae ye mean?"

"I've tae go for a medical next week and, if I'm passed fit; I'll be back in uniform within days."

"But yer leg...yer still limping...how can they pass ye as fit? They can't be taking wounded men back when the country's still full of young, fit men, who have no' even lifted a finger."

"Well, we'll wait and see," said Callum, sure in his mind that he would be passed fit. He was actually restless now and found the last few days long and without meaning. MacTaggart's bar was not the same without his closest friends and the people drinking in there only wanted to talk about the bloody war.

It was a dull day but at least it was not raining. He lit a cigarette as he walked down the road to the village shop. "Mornin', Callum!" shouted Billy Wallace as he heaped a fork full of dry hay on to the stack he was building at the bottom of his field.

"Mornin', Billy. That's a fine stack yer building."

"I want tae get it covered," said Billy, wiping the sweat from his forehead with the back of his thick, weather beaten arm. "It looks like it might rain," he added, nodding over towards the low clouds over the far end of the loch.

"Och, it will no' rain the day, Billy," said Callum, walking on towards the village.

In the grocer's shop, Mrs Abercromby was her usual talkative self and asked Callum how he was doing and whether he was glad to be home and said how she was sure his father must enjoy having him back to run the croft. He bought a copy of the *Daily Record* and handed her a sixpence, wishing that he had the correct change as he stood nodding to her constant chattering about things he had little or no interest in. At least twice she stopped to put the sixpence in the till only to turn and open a new line of gossip that she was sure he had not heard.

"Aye, there's a lot being goin' on since you've been away at the war. It's a terrible war right enough. Ah! Poor Elspeth Murray losing her two boys like that… and buried out there in that awful country that they had no business being in the first place. The French, why can't they fight their own…?"

"Thank you, Mrs Abercromby," he said dryly as she gave him the change from her puffy fat hands.

"Who would have thought Miss Dunbar; oh I can't get use to her married name…Munro isn't it?"

Callum shrugged his shoulders, trying to be nonchalant, but he was suddenly frozen to the spot.

"Aye, I'm sure it's Munro," she reflected. "Who would have thought that she'd become a nurse."

Callum put the coins into his pocket, but wished he had not been so eager to get away and pretended that he had forgotten to buy some tobacco.

"Ah, it must be the loss of her poor husband," she finally added, lowering her voice to a whisper. "He's missing now; it must be nearly a year. Och, they should put her out of her misery and tell her the truth. Is it a quarter ounce yer after?"

Callum could not control his desire to hear more, but she stopped speaking and just stared at him as if he was stupid. "Is it a quarter?"

"Aye... aye, no give me a half ounce."

"That will be thrupence."

Callum paid her the thrupence and, as she turned to put the coins in the till, he asked with an awkward hesitation in his voice. "Where is she a nurse?"

"I think she went tae some hospital in England. Poor girl, she must have been hoping her husband would be brought in and she'd be there for him. Ah, well it's a terrible war."

Before he could ask another question, someone came in and reluctantly he said his goodbye. He walked back home and was caught in a heavy downpour which made him smile to himself as he passed Billy Wallace's tarpaulin-covered haystack. Billy was right about the rain. Callum began thinking about what Mrs Abercromby had said, and felt a tinge guilty about the news of Caitriona's husband. The fact that Fraser was more than likely dead made him feel happy inside. Thousands were dying every day and he did not know Fraser any better than the Germans he had shot for King and country. Death did not seem to have the same meaning to him any more, and he no longer thought about it with the fear and dread of his childhood, but now as the ultimate escape from life's miseries. *Those who die should not be pitied; it's the living that has to suffer that should be pitied. He was alive and Fraser was dead. Who should pity whom?* He reasoned and argued with himself all the way home.

Duncan Dunbar adjusted his tie, smiling at himself in the long dressing mirror. He walked away from the mirror and turned to salute himself. He was very pleased with his tailor-made uniform. Sir Randolph, his friend at the Ministry of War, had ensured that his new uniform would not be stained by the unpleasantness of war and that his posting to the regimental headquarters at Stirling would enable him to return to Glenfay on a regular basis.

"They've come up a treat, sir," said Roberts as he entered the room with a pair of long, shiny, black leather boots.

"Not bad," said Duncan as he sat down and raised his right leg for Roberts to pull one of the boots on.

"They're rather tight, sir," said Roberts, having difficulty getting Duncan's large foot down the narrow leg of the boot. The butler struggled for a few fruitless minutes before Duncan impatiently pushed him away with his other foot.

"Out of the bloody way, I'll do it myself!"

"I'm sorry, sir," said Roberts, but he was not in the least bit sorry.

"There!" said Duncan as he stamped his foot on the floor.

"It looks very smart indeed, sir. Would you like me to put the other one on?"

"No! Give it here."

"Very well, sir."

"Get William to get my horse ready. I think I'll go for a ride."

"Yes, sir."

"There," said Duncan as he pulled the second boot on and then resumed his parade in front of the mirror. *This will put an end to those bloody white feathers.*

Roberts went out to the stables where he found William sitting on an upturned tin bucket daydreaming.

"Get off yer backside!" Roberts ordered, giving the lad a slap to the back of the head.

"Och," groaned William. "What did ye do that for?"

"The master is going out riding to show off his new uniform, so ye better get his horse ready."

"His uniform? He's joined the army?"

"Aye, it looks like it."

"Good, so he'll be goin' tae the war in France. Maybe he'll get taken prisoner and we'll no' have him back for years."

"Ah wouldnae be hoping for too much. He's too damn happy looking tae be going anywhere near the war."

"He'll have tae go if he's in the army."

"We'll have tae wait and see. Now hurry up and get that horse ready."

Chapter 18

The following week, after a brief examination by an army doctor, Callum was passed fit for active service. He was given orders to report back in another week for retraining before joining a new battalion of the Argylls. While he was at the training camp, his decoration came through and the brigadier made much of the occasion, presenting the medal during a full parade. His rank of corporal was also confirmed at the same time. Most of the men in this new battalion were either conscripts or men who had recovered from wounds that they once thought signalled the end of their war. Apart from these two groups, there were a handful of men, who, even at this late stage, joined as volunteers. Callum soon became friendly with Ronnie Walker, a young conscript from the East End of Glasgow.

"If it's a capitalist war and you're against capitalists, why did you join up?" asked big Jock Murdoch, a miner from Lanarkshire.

"I didn't. The capitalists used their laws of oppression to force me here. Conscription," declared Walker, looking uncomfortable in his uniform.

"Ye could have refused like those... what are they called?" stuttered Murdoch.

"Conscientious objectors," said Callum.

"I considered that, but thought I would do more good fighting the capitalists and their bloody war from within their ranks, rather than preaching to the converted and the convicted in one of their stinking jails. Look at poor John MacLean, rotting up in Peterhead Prison, while they force feed him with rubber tubes stuck down his throat. What good is he there?"

"But whit good are ye here?" asked Murdoch, scratching his thick neck.

"The audience that matters is here, training to fight their fellow workers for their capitalist masters to get even richer from the inflated prices and the sale of munitions for the war effort."

"If the officers hear ye talking like that, they'll shoot ye for treason," interrupted another soldier, by the name of Billy Auld. "They'll call ye a German spy and shoot ye, and anyone daft enough tae be sitting listening tae ye. So, if ye don't mind, keep yer talk of revolution and the like tae yerself!"

"Aye," agreed Callum. "It's no' the kind a thing tae be saying tae just anybody."

"There's time. It's all a matter of time," concluded Ronnie.

In late November 1916, the new battalion sailed to France. By then Callum no longer had a limp and, apart from the occasional twinge, marched as well as the next man. The battalion then travelled from Le Havre by train to Rouen, where the railway station was in chaos. Wounded men lay in stretchers all along the platforms as a few dedicated Red Cross nurses tried their best to tend to the wounded men's desperate needs.

The battalion waited in the town square as the major and two of his officers entered the town hall, where they received fresh orders to march on to the town of Albert, at least fifty miles further inland and just behind the British front lines along the River Somme.

The road and the pavement had long since lost their individuality and the main street had been trampled into a river of mud. A line of Red Cross trucks and horse-drawn carts lined up outside the station with more wounded. "Jesus Christ!" said Ronnie, as they passed one man who had lost both legs and an arm; the stumps red with the blood-soaked bandages.

"Don't look at them," said Callum, passing more badly wounded men.

Once out of the town, the battalion followed a line of trucks carrying fresh ammunition to the front. It began to rain hard and the narrow country road soon became waterlogged. They marched over sixteen miles before they entered the ruins of another small town. The Germans had held the town for two months before the British counter attack forced them back and completed its destruction. Callum was shocked when he recognised the large oak door of the whore-house, hanging from its brass hinges. Only part of the building was still standing while the rest lay in rubble. He wondered what had happened to the madam and her girls; he hoped that they got out in time. They marched on; the mud making their boots heavy, and sapping their energy with every step. They passed through the town on to another road of mud and decaying corpses; the sickly sweet smell of death was nauseating. The stuttering sound of aeroplanes could be heard over the distant pounding of field artillery, but the men were more worried about their blistered feet. "Get down!' shouted one of the officers, jumping from his horse and into the ditch at the roadside. The rest of the battalion dived for cover as an enemy plane dropped from the clouds and opened fire with its machine-gun spitting lead into the ground and soft flesh of a few dead horses lying at the side of the road. A second plane followed, but this one had time to correct its attack and sprayed the far side of the road and ditch, killing two men and wounding three others. The new battalion had had its first casualties and after a few prayers by the Padre, the dead were buried in the ditch they fell. The war had been kind to them. Their suffering was short, thought Callum, as he lit a cigarette and threw his shovel in the back of a cart.

That night the battalion were billeted to an abandoned farm. "This is terrible," said Ronnie, as the men found shelter in one of the large barns. "Ah bet the officers don't eat this pig food," he added, watching Callum break a hard biscuit into a tin of condensed milk. "You'd think they would at least give us something decent tae fuckin' eat."

"What were ye expecting?" asked Callum. "In a few weeks even this will taste like ambrosia."

"Well, you can have mine, I'd rather starve."

"I'll keep it for ye. For when ye decide you've starved yerself enough."

The shelling intensified. Callum fell asleep, while Ronnie lay next to him, his eyes wide awake as he listened to the thunder of shells exploding only a few miles away to the north. He began to scratch. The lice he had heard about had finally infested his clothes.

"Who's that?" groaned Callum as he fought to waken from his deep sleep.

"It's all right. It's me, Ronnie."

"What the hell are ye doing?" snapped Callum, shaking himself awake, still holding Ronnie's wrist.

"I didn't want tae wake ye. I was hungry, that's all."

"Stealing from a fellow worker," said Callum sarcastically.

"It's mine anyway," replied Ronnie.

"Now yer sounding like one of them capitalists that yer always on about," laughed Callum, taking out the biscuit from his top tunic pocket. "Soak it in yer milk. If you try and eat it like that, ye'll break yer teeth. I'm going for a walk."

The bombardments continued and the dark sky occasionally lit up with the yellow flares that burst over 'no man's land'. Callum lit a cigarette and drank some water from a canteen that was left hanging by the door. He spat. The canteen had warm wine in it. He walked over to a well in the courtyard. A bucket lay nearby. It was full of rainwater and he scooped up a mouthful of the cold, clear water in his cupped hands, quenching his thirst. It began to get light, so he went back to the stable and wrote some verses inspired by the silent night.

Some of the men were now getting washed, while others sat about smoking and quietly talking. Ronnie was fast asleep in his bed of damp straw. Callum gave him a gentle kick. "Ye better get up before they put ye on a charge, comrade."

"Ah, fuck off will ye, yer worse than a bloody officer."

The mud was rock hard with the early morning frost as the battalion marched behind the major's white stallion towards the desolate horizon. By the time they reached the Front it seemed that the generals on both sides had decided that it was time to wind down for the winter. Apart from the occasional bursts of shelling in the mornings, the threat of a further offensive seemed over for another year.

With Christmas only days away, it began to snow along the front line. Falling in the silence of the early morning, it quickly lay a white mantle on the frost-hard mud. The snow brought a temporary madness to the bored soldiers as snowballs were thrown and little snowmen appeared on the parapets of the trenches.

"Why don't we have a snowball fight wi' Jerry?" laughed one soldier as he lobbed a snowball over the parapet in a vain attempt at hitting some unsuspecting German.

"Don't start that," shouted another soldier. "Those bastards will start throwing back grenades."

It had stopped snowing and a German plane flew overhead. A salvo of rifle fire greeted the roaring engine as it swung over the British lines. The plane did not return fire and quickly turned back towards its own trenches. A cheer went up.

"Must have been a reconnaissance flight," said Callum.

"Don't tell me, Fritz's planning something," said Murdoch.

"No, I don't think so; they're just making sure we're not up to anything."

Suddenly a cheer went up and the men that were not already standing at the parapet of the trench got up to see what all the fuss was about. Callum climbed up beside Ronnie who was laughing and pointing into 'no man's land'. A rabbit was running around the snow in a panic. It did not know which way to run to escape the noise of cheering men on both sides. A shot rang out and the rabbit's blood splattered across the white, virgin snow. There was a hushed silence. Hungry faces on both sides peered over their trenches and looked with watered mouths at the fresh meat lying only yards away.

"Tommy!" shouted someone from the German lines. The soldier then held up his rifle with a white flag tied to the bayonet. "Tommy! I'll get the... what do you call it? *Das Kaninchen*, and if you do not shoot I'll throw half towards you," he shouted in broken English. There was no response for a moment and then one of the British soldiers shouted in a broad Glasgow accent. "Aye, but if ye don't throw half, I'll blow yer fuckin' balls off!"

The British soldiers laughed.

The German, in his long, grey coat, climbed out with a nervous grin. "Now you don't shoot!" he shouted, walking slowly towards the rabbit. A laugh went up from both trenches as the big German slipped and fell in the powdery snow. He got up again and mocked his own embarrassment. He walked on carefully.

"God, he must be hungry," said Billy Auld, his rifle sight following the German's every step. The German reached the rabbit and picked it up by the long ears, its blood was still warm and dripping on to the snow. He then pulled out a knife from his long coat, before putting the rabbit back on the ground and cutting it in half. To a cheer of approval, he threw one half of the rabbit towards the British trench. The bloody carcase landed beside Ronnie, who grabbed it and waved it above his head in triumph. The German turned back towards his own trenches to cheers from both sides of the barbed wire.

"What the hell's going on!" demanded the major as he burst out from his dug-out. He pulled one soldier down from the parapet and climbed up the wooden steps to see for himself. He saw the big German walking nonchalantly back to his trenches, holding half a rabbit up by the ears. "Shoot him!" ordered the major to the soldier standing next to him. "Shoot! Damn you!" he screamed, pulling the rifle from the reluctant soldier and taking aim. His first shot missed by a few feet, as the German turned towards the British lines and held up his rifle with the white rag tied to the bayonet. "No don't shoot!" he shouted as the major's second shot ripped into his shoulder, knocking him to the ground. The major's took aim for a third time as the German tried to get to his feet. In his panic the wounded soldier slipped again, letting go of the rabbit.

"C'mon get up," urged Callum. The men along the trenches willed the soldier to get to his feet.

The major fired again but this time the gun jammed. The sound of the rifle jamming echoed in the tense silence as men on both sides shouted on the wounded soldier to run. The major fired again, ricocheting off the German's gas mask. A cheer finally went up along the trenches as the German dived head first into a shell hole.

"Shut those men up!" demanded the major, his face flushed with anger and a little embarrassment at his poor marksmanship.

"Hey, Tommy," shouted the big German. "That was not cricket. Very bad."

"Give me that!" said Callum, taking the half rabbit from Ronnie.

"What the hell are ye doing?" demanded Ronnie. Callum did not answer but thrust what was left of the rabbit high into the air, which, as it landed, skidded across the snowy surface, stopping only a few feet from the shell hole.

"Is this another trick?" called the German as he spiked the rabbit meat with his outstretched bayonet, pulling it into the crater.

The major had already returned to consider the contents of General Patterson's letter. Only the captain followed him back into the dug-out. "Here, Armstrong, what do ye think of this?" he asked, handing him the letter.

"Corporal John Hamilton and Sergeant Angus Campbell."

"The 9th Battalion; is that not the ragamuffin outfit we relieved on Friday?"

"Yes, sir. What was left of them."

"Well, General Patterson wants me at the court martial."

"When is it, sir?"

"Thursday morning. You'll have to run the show for a few days."

"It's not a very pleasant business."

"Nonsense, Armstrong! It's what we need right now. You saw how the men behaved five minutes ago, letting that bloody Kraut walk into 'no man's land' and then cheering the lucky bastard."

"I think it was all just a bit of sport."

"Sport, my arse. I'm surprised at you, Armstrong. I would have expected you to have at least taken a shot at the Hun."

"Oh, I couldn't do that, sir. It was your bird, so to speak. I was sure you would have bagged him."

"Well..." coughed the major, "he's got a hole in him now that he wasn't born with." He laughed.

"It was damn unlucky that your last shot hit his gas mask."

"Anyway, it showed me what we're up against now. This time last year every man would have put a hole in any German that was fool enough to pull a stunt like that. They're sending out conscripts now that have dodged the war for the last two years. They don't have the stomach for war. The French Army is plagued with agitators and

244

thousands have deserted in the last year. We have to nip this cancer in the bud before we have the same problem. We'll give these two a fair trial and then they'll be shot like the cowards they are. If we have to execute a thousand to stop the rot, then so be it. I want this letter pinned outside. It won't take five minutes for this to spread along the lines. The men must know that it's Jerry or them and there is no in-between...Armstrong! Send in that runner. I'll have to reply to the general."

"Yes, sir."

The major was right; it did not take long for the contents of the letter to spread along the maze of trenches. Bad news travels fast.

"Are ye sure?" asked Callum. "Are ye sure that it's Angus Campbell?"

"Aye, I'm sure, Corporal John Hamilton and a Sergeant Angus Campbell, both for desertion," said Auld. "They'll be shot for that. I heard the major was to be on the Court Martial. Poor buggers don't stand a chance with that bastard."

It was dark now and the snow had stopped. Callum walked along the crowded trench. He lit a match to read the letter posted outside the major's dug-out. It was true. He dropped the match as it burnt down to his numb, frozen fingers. At that moment a magnesium rocket shot up into the air, followed by a burst of machine-gun fire. Callum turned with a detached interest as the bright yellow light faded with another burst of machine-gun fire. Another patrol had been caught in 'no man's land', but this time it was German.

The court martial was held in a school commandeered for that purpose, the basement was secured with steel doors and iron bars. The two prisoners were held in separate cells under constant guard as they waited for the staff officers to arrive.

The door at the side of the room suddenly opened. "Attention!" The soldiers' hobnailed boots made a thundering noise on the wooden floor as Angus was marched, at the double, to the gymnasium in the main building. There were three judges sitting at a long table draped in the Union Flag; Major Bryce and two captains. General Patterson was too busy to deal with such matters. The court martial lasted an hour and fifteen minutes. A young officer, who had only just finished his legal training the week before his commission came through, represented both accused. This was his first case and it showed. Both men were found guilty. Each time the young lawyer tried to speak in mitigation, Major Bryce interrupted him, "Good God, man! These men are cowards. All this rubbish about being good soldiers...Good soldiers don't desert their posts!"

The nervous lawyer's pleas for mercy fell on deaf ears and the sentence of death by firing squad was read out. Both soldiers stood ashen-faced as the major ordered their stripes to be torn from their uniforms. They were then marched back to their cells. As the heavy iron doors slammed behind them, the reality of the judgement quickly set in. This time tomorrow they would both be dead. They would be killed by British bullets, fired by British soldiers, on the orders of British officers. Angus threw himself down on the straw mattress under the barred window. *Coward! Those bastards are the cowards.* He lay there in the cold damp cell scratching the lice that would soon have to find someone else to torment. He could hear muffled sobs from the other cell. He shouted to Hamilton and the sobs immediately stopped but Hamilton did not reply. Angus shouted again. Still there was no reply. He lay back down on his bed of straw.

Angus took his clay pipe and tobacco tin from under the flimsy mattress and had a smoke before falling into a deep sleep. He had not been able to sleep all night with the worry of the court martial but now, without much thought, his tired eyes closed out the nightmare of reality and he slipped back to his childhood in Glenfay. He ran through the green fields with Callum running behind him; their arms spread apart like aeroplanes. The smell of the salt sea air and burning

246

peat filled his senses. The loch was in full tide as the fishing boats brought home their catch of herring. He could see men mending their nets and his mother standing on the cobblestoned quayside, in her silk shawl that came all the way from the Argentine. Mhairi stood on the steam-filled platform at Marnock, with a young child in her arms. He threw down his heavy rucksack and embraced them both. The war was over and he had come home to stay. But then the dream began to change. Mhairi and the baby were gone. He called out but he made no sound. He ran but could not move. A green smog covered the station and he coughed and choked as he fumbled to put on his gas mask. He could not get the mask on and he fell into the morass of mud and water, sinking into the brown, clinging earth. His hands dug into the mud, which turned into the flesh of some decaying corpse and he screamed again. He woke suddenly to the sound of keys rattling in the iron door. He thought for a moment that he had slept through to the next morning and a sick feeling came to his stomach. The guard put his head around the door, his face was solemn and his voice subdued. "There's someone tae see ye, sergeant."

Angus sat up. The daylight was fading and the cell was in shadows. He lit the stump of a candle and screwed his eyes to try and make out the figure beside the guard.

"Angus, how are ye?"

"Callum! God, is that you?"

"Aye, it's me," replied Callum, slowly entering the cell.

"Mind! Fifteen minutes," said the guard, pulling the door closed with a clatter of keys.

"How are ye?" asked Callum again, struggling for words.

"I'm all right. I'd be a lot better if I wasn't going to get shot in the morning...How did ye know?"

"It's posted. Why did ye do it?"

"Two years. That's why I did it. Two bloody years of killing and living like a rat in a sewer. I just wanted tae go home. Is that so bad that they have to shoot ye? I wanted tae see Mhairi and the baby. I was such a damned fool leaving her because of what some jealous bitch said. Ah guess ah don't have tae tell you that."

"I got ye some tobacco," said Callum, offering the stick of dark brown pipe tobacco.

"Here," said Angus, returning half of the block. "I'll never finish it. There's no point wasting it."

"I'll give it to Corporal Hamilton."

"He doesn't smoke. He's not a corporal now either."

"Well, I'll just leave it wi' ye. Is there any chance?"

"None! The major said they've got tae make an example of cowards! The bastards."

"There must be a way to appeal this? To Field Marshal Haig?"

"Haig!" Angus laughed loud, but it was a cynical laugh. "Callum, it's that bastard that's sending thousands to be slaughtered every day. They're shooting deserters to make sure no one is brave enough to question them. I deserted and I didn't even try to deny it. Tae hell with them and their bloody war!"

Callum lit a cigarette. The candle was struggling to stay lit in the cold breeze that ran through the cell. He did not know what to say to Angus. He had only another five minutes and he could not think of anything. Every thought he now had seemed so trivial. He smoked in silence as Angus stared out through the cell window and took a long draw from his rolled cigarette. "Remember the Rev. Knox caned me for poaching from the Laird's river…The Laird's bloody river, what right did he have tae it more than anyone else? Fish that had swum halfway around the world suddenly belonged tae the bloody Laird and no one else. There's one law for those bastards and another for the rest of us."

"Did ye know Duncan Dunbar has evicted three families from

248

their crofts since the auld Laird died? We're out here fighting the bloody Germans and those bastards are back home throwing our folk off their ain land. They can shoot me tomorrow. I'm no' fighting their war any longer. I'm tired, Callum. I'm just so tired. Let them shoot me."

The door opened again and the guard came back in with a bowl of soup and two slices of bread. He laid the tray on a chair beside the door. "It's time up. Ye'll have tae go before we change guard. Ye know yer no' supposed tae be in here."

"All right, but just a couple of minutes longer."

"Okay, but hurry up. Ye'll get me into trouble."

The guard pulled the door over but this time he did not lock it closed. Callum could hear him shuffling about impatiently outside. "I had better go," he said in a restrained voice unable to look Angus in the face.

"Och, don't worry about me," said Angus with a feigned cheer to his voice. "Look! They treat ye like a bloody king in here," he added, pointing to the tray of soup and bread. "If they fed us that at the front then maybe they'd get the breakthrough they're so desperate tae get."

Callum pretended to laugh but the sound stuck in his throat. The guard gave the door a bang with a key.

"Here, can you to take this back tae Mhairi wi' this letter?" asked Angus as he took his silver pocket watch from his tunic pocket.

"I was going to ask one of the guards to send them, but you can't trust anyone, and I would rather you didn't post the letter, you know what these censors are like. I want Mhairi tae know the truth about this bloody war. Maybe she could sell the watch and get some money for her and the bairn. Will ye dae that for me?"

"Of course, I'll get them back tae her."

The guard opened the door. Callum, with tears in his eyes,

hugged Angus for a short moment, afraid to let him go, before Angus pushed him away. "Don't worry about me, they'll probably miss!"

Callum followed the guard out into the courtyard of the building. He tried to thank the guard but could not speak. He put the pocket watch and letter into his breast pocket and stood for a moment in a daze. In time, he managed to get a lift in an ambulance back to the front before anyone noticed he was missing. He still could not believe that in a few hours Angus would be dead and there was nothing he could do about it.

Angus did not sleep again that night and, as the morning light flooded into the grey, cold cell, his anxiety grew with every sound. He could hear the noisy engines of troop trucks as they passed through the town on their way to the front. The guard came in with a bowl of water, some soap and a towel. Angus washed and put on the rest of his uniform. Ten minutes he was told. He refused to see the chaplain. The iron door closed again with a bang. He had faced death so many times over the past two years, but this time it was different. This time the element of chance had been removed. He instinctively stood up as he heard the sound of heavy boots marching down the corridor and the jingle of keys. His heart was pounding heavy. He took deep breaths and stood to attention. He tried to swallow but his throat was too dry. He would show them that he was no coward! They had stopped at Hamilton's cell. The clatter of keys opened the cell door. Angus could hear the chaplain praying with Hamilton repeating the words, his voice struggling to keep up as he gasped for breath after every few words. Hamilton stopped praying; he realised his time had come. Then, in a moment's panic, he refused to go like a 'good' soldier and there was a struggle before the guards dragged him kicking and screaming from the cell. They frogmarched him down the corridor. There was a further scuffle outside while Hamilton was tied to a chair. Angus could hear the sound of his own heart, beating hard in his chest. He heard the orders being given to the firing squad. He held his breath as he heard the clicks of the breechblocks. "Fire!" Hamilton was dead. Gone from this world to who knows where. His body was now just flesh and bones; it was slumped like a rag doll, oozing the blood that had given him life.

The bright purple and yellow shades of dawn began to creep over the horizon as the clear night sky clouded the coming morning. Callum's eyes were now heavy with sleep but his anxiety would not let him close them. He rolled a cigarette, his hands shaking as he dropped most of the tobacco. He lit the thin cigarette anyway, but it burnt out very quickly and he threw it away after only a few long draws. A pale yellow sun began to rise through the thin streaks of clouds. It was very quiet. The hard ground had turned to slushy mud where he had been walking up and down. It must be after eight by now, he said to himself, repeating this over and over as though he was trying to pass through some invisible pain barrier. His breathing became heavier as he felt the cold silver of the pocket watch in his hand. He opened the ornate silver cover. Five to eight! He snapped the watch cover closed and put it back into his pocket. His hands were now shaking violently. He blamed the cold and rubbed them together. He needed to piss and he urinated into a tin bucket lying outside the dug-out. He opened the watch again. Just over a minute to go. He was in a trance as he watched the second hand tick methodically around the bold Roman numerals.

As they marched Angus out into the cold grey morning, a British bi-plane flew low overhead. The soldiers in the courtyard all instinctively looked up. Hamilton's bullet-ridden body lay on a stretcher to the side. A soldier threw a bucket of water on the ground to wash away the blood. Angus was forced down on to a wooden chair; his hands were tied behind his back. His breathing became violent. He thought he was going to suffocate as a hessian hood was tightly pulled over his head; he had to open his mouth wide to breathe as the coarse canvas was sucked tight to the contours of his face. He could feel the soft touch of Mhairi's hand as the rifles' barrels clicked.

Chapter 19

It was early March 1917 when the battalion received orders to join the British First Army under General Horne. It took a four and a half hours long march before the battalion reached the outskirts of Arras. The town had all the scars of war and many of its buildings were reduced to rubble. Hundreds of tents covered a nearby field. It was clear that something big was being planned. "Out of the frying pan and into the fire," said Callum as they watched the constant parade of fresh troops from every corner of the Empire. There were hundreds of wagons loaded with munitions; heavy guns drawn by teams of mules; tanks which churned up the road and more troops, always more troops. At least conditions at the camp were not as bad as they had been at the front. The tents, although crowded, were dry. The food was only slightly better, but the men were now guaranteed one hot meal a day. The build-up continued and it was clear to everyone that a major spring offensive was not far off.

The tender beauty of the spring was shattered by the commencement of five days of Allied shelling. The barrage continued day and night. On Good Friday the battalion was moved up to a small, abandoned village, less than a mile from the front line. The bombardment stopped for a few hours on Easter Sunday and a service was held in the town square. Many of the men received communion and the tone of the sermon was desperately solemn.

Within an hour the battalion reached the front-line trenches. Callum was unexpectedly promoted to sergeant, a promotion he was not comfortable with and would have refused if he had an option. The lieutenant gave him his stripes, which had taken from the tunic of the last unfortunate man to wear them before a sniper took off the top of his head.

"This is as bad as the last bloody hole they stuck us in," said Ronnie, settling down to eat his lunch of cheese and bread.

"At least it's no' full of mud and rats," replied Private Murdoch, fixing a photograph of his pretty, but rather plump wife into the side of the trench. "Only two bloody days we had…Two bloody days!"

"Ye were only married for two days before ye left?" laughed Ronnie.

"Aye, and I don't know what ye think is so funny."

"Sorry, Murdoch, it is just that ye didn't get much time tae get tae know her…ye know what I mean?"

"I know fine what ye mean. Don't start the smut with me, Walker, or you will get me bayonet up yer arse."

"I'm only joking with ye," said Ronnie, scraping mud from his boots. "I'm glad that I don't have a wife tae worry about. Ye don't know what they're up tae when yer stuck out here."

"Whit the hell ar' ye saying?" demanded Murdoch.

"Well, we've all heard the story about Corporal Hamilton. He only deserted because he got a 'Dear John' letter from his wife."

"What ar' ye trying tae say, Walker?"

"Nothing, don't be daft, Murdoch. I'm only thinking about myself. All I'm saying is wi' my luck, if I was married, I'd be waiting every day for one of those bloody letters tae come. Dear Ronnie, it wi'd say*, I'm no' prepared tae wait till you're finished playing at soldiers so I've moved in wi' the milkman,"* he said, with a mocking female voice. The others laughed, except Murdoch, who was still not sure if Ronnie was having a go at him or not. "Aye, I'm glad I've no' got a wife waiting for me, because I don't think she'd wait that long."

The sun was now warm and the mud was beginning to dry on their uniforms. The shelling had stopped for a while and Callum closed his eyes and laid his head back against his rucksack. "Ah, this is the life, and they think we're having a terrible time back home."

254

"We should have been told to bring our swimming costumes," added Ronnie. "Oh, damn," he moaned when a slow moving cloud blanked out the sun.

"There's something up!" said Murdoch. "There's a whole swarm of red hats buzzing around the major's dug-out."

"They've no' been shelling for the last five days for nothing," said Callum, getting up and looking down the trench.

"Sit down the pair of ye," said Ronnie, "yer blocking out the bloody sun."

The spring day faded into a chilly evening and the shelling resumed as confirmation of the planned offensive was passed down the ranks.

"Tomorrow!" said Murdoch, not expecting it to be so soon.

"It's very Christian," said Ronnie. "The bloody day after Easter…very Christian," he added, spitting his disgust into the mud at his feet.

"Well, ye knew it had tae happen some time," said Callum. "The only problem is that we've been pushed right up to the front and when it starts we're the mugs that have to go first."

"What if we all refuse tae go?" said Ronnie. "They can't shoot everyone. Can they?"

"They'll shoot you if anyone hears ye talking like that," said Private Auld. "I'd rather take my chances wi' the Germans, at least ye can fire back at them."

"Callum," said Ronnie, hoping for some support.

"Billy's right. At least out there ye have some chance. If ye don't go over when they blow those bloody whistles, then they won't even bother tae court martial ye, they'll shoot ye on the spot."

"What chance do ye think we've got?" asked Ronnie, showing

signs of fear for the first time.

"You've got the same chance as me," said Callum.

"I'm goin' tae make it!" said Murdoch, emphatically. "Ye have tae believe that yer going tae make it. God will look after ye, so long as ye believe in him."

"God!" Ronnie sneered. "If he cared a damn, then there wouldn't be a bloody war."

"It's no' God that made this war," replied Murdoch angrily. "It's man who made this war."

"Aye, but why does God no' dae something tae stop it. I'll tell ye why, because he doesn't bloody exist. That's why," shouted Ronnie, his fear quickly disappearing with the chance to get on his soapbox. "Why does the church not tell all the soldiers to lay down their arms? We're all supposed to be Christian. *Thou shall not kill!* Whit happened tae that commandment? The church! It's those bastards wearing dog collars that are the real war mongers."

"Shut up!" shouted Callum. "Here comes the major." They stood to attention as Major Bryce came along the trench, stopping to speak to the occasional soldier, before moving on.

"At ease, men," he said when he reached Callum and the others. "You've no doubt heard that we're having a go at Jerry tomorrow. I expect you're eager to get a crack at him."

"Aye, sir," lied Callum.

"Good man. You men, I'm sure you won't let the regiment down. Will you?"

"No, sir," the others responded. Only Ronnie said nothing.

"I didn't hear you, soldier!" barked the major.

"No, sir," said Ronnie.

"No, sir, what?"

"No, sir, you didn't hear me."

There was a tense silence as the major's face flushed scarlet. "Why not?"

"Why not, what, sir?"

"Are you trying to be funny, soldier?"

"No, sir."

"Stand to attention when you address me! What's your name?"

"Private Walker, sir."

"Well, Private Walker, I'll ask you again. Are you going to be a credit to the regiment?"

"No, sir. I'm going to be blown to bits, sir!"

The major turned to the other officers at his side. "It seems that you have a troublemaker in your company, lieutenant, but I know what he's up to." He then turned back to Ronnie and put his horsewhip to his neck. "You think that you'll get out of your duty by being insubordinate. What do you take me for? You'll remain here with these other men and you'll be the first to go over the top. Do you hear me?"

"It's hard not to."

"You'll pay for this, young man."

"Lieutenant, if he refuses to do his duty, shoot him."

"Yes, sir, it will be a pleasure!"

"Don't think this is the end of it, soldier," said the major, turning back to face Ronnie. "As soon as this offensive has runs its course, I'll be dealing with you…We will have no cowards in this regiment."

"Aye, sir…if you say so."

"I bloody well do say so. You'll pay for this, mark my words. Remember, Lieutenant, if he fails to go over, shoot him. Do you hear?"

"Yes, sir."

As the major and his cortège of officers moved on, a shell exploded near the trench showering it with earth and stones. A leg was grotesquely exhumed in the explosion and landed beside the major and his officers. The rotten limb was still shod in a fine German boot. The major retreated back into his bunker.

"It's a pity we can't have men like him flogged, Major," said Captain Armstrong, when they returned to the dug-out.

"It may be against army regulations, but I'll have him flogged to an inch of his life at the appropriate time. He's not getting out of the line as easy as he thought. Damn conscripts!"

Ronnie's insubordination was whispered along the trenches through the lips of soldiers who, although prepared to face German bullets, were still excited by the daring of one private's courage to say what he was thinking to the Major.

"You're off yer head," said Murdoch, shaking his own head in disbelief at Ronnie's grinning face.

"To hell with him…What are ye so afraid off? He's only a man like the rest of us. No sir, yes, sir, three bloody bags full, sir. To hell wi' him! You won't see him tomorrow. That's for sure."

"You're no' giving' yerself much of a future," said Callum. "Even if ye get through the next few days, as soon as the advance comes to an end, the Major will have yer arse in a sling. You'd be better tae have bit yer tongue like the rest of us."

"Right now I really don't give a shit. The chances are that we're all goin' tae get shot or blown to bloody pieces tomorrow anyway."

"If ye think like that ye will," interrupted Murdoch. "I'm goin' tae make it," he added as he looked at the picture of his wife again as though he were reaffirming a promise to her.

"The Russians had the right idea," said Ronnie. "Put the bastards up against a wall and shoot the lot of them."

The British heavy guns opened up again, pounding the German lines in a final effort to destroy as much of their defences as possible. The Germans responded in kind as the men fell silent. The noise was unbearable as the two armies created even more mud. It was after midnight before the shelling stopped. There was a full moon throwing its reflected light on the miles of trenches. Many of the men were smoking cigarettes or puffing away at clay pipes; others wrote letters and postcards to their loved ones. No one could sleep as the tension of the coming morning hung over the trenches like a thick fog of anxiety.

At dawn a double ration of rum was distributed.

"Dutch courage," said Murdoch, who declined his ration.

"At least the Dutch were no' so fucking daft as tae get involved in this bloody war!" shouted Ronnie, happy to take any unwanted rum that was going.

As the sun emerged on the horizon, the order to stand ready was relayed down the trenches. Major Bryce emerged from his dugout to survey what was left of the German defences through his box-periscope as his officers returned to their units.

"Remember, don't stop for wounded!" shouted the lieutenant, trying to control the fear in his voice. "As soon as you hear the whistle, get going." The lieutenant then counted down the minutes on his pocket-watch…"Ten minutes, men, keep your heads down," he urged as the German machine guns sprayed bullets along the parapet. Callum watched as a rat scurried along the duckboards and into the major's dug-out…"Nine minutes!"

As the British bombardment continued to pulverise the German lines, the ground beneath Callum's feet shuddered like a morass of jelly. He looked at Murdoch who was talking to the picture of his wife as though she had some supernatural power to save him from the horrors that waited above…"Eight minutes!" The tension was unbearable and some men urged for the whistles to blow. The lieutenant held his nerve, determined to do his duty as mud splattered on his face from another spray of bullets…

"Seven minutes!" Even through the noise of the bombardment, it was possible to hear the mumbled prayers of men preparing to die…

"Six minutes!" The order was given to fix bayonets.

"Remember! Stick the bayonet into the gut, don't get it caught in the ribs or you'll no' get it back out!" Five minutes!" A single clear shot rang out as a German sniper dispatched one of the officers, who forgot to keep his head down.

The lieutenant lifted his handgun in the air…"Four minutes! Keep your heads down, men!" The British heavy guns suddenly fell silent.

"Three minutes! Get those bloody bayonets fixed," ordered the lieutenant, putting his whistle to his dry, nervous mouth. He wondered if he had enough breath in him to even blow it…

"Two minutes, men! Wait for the whistle!" Callum fixed his bayonet and shook hands with Ronnie, Auld and Murdoch and wished them luck.

"One minute!"

All along the British front line, the sound of hundreds of officers' whistles signalled the attack as thousands of men emerged from the trenches. Within seconds bullets ripped into the bodies of young men who died before they had lived. Shrapnel from mortar shells tore others to pieces. Soldiers were made corpses, wives became widows and children became orphans. The brown mud was now red. Bits of human flesh hung from mangled barbed wire, in what was now a human abattoir of unimaginable carnage. The Major watched the slaughter as the first line of attack was cut to pieces. "Bloody conscripts," he muttered, giving orders for the next wave to follow.

Before he got a hundred yards, Callum took the blast and shrapnel from a German shell. He was fortunate enough to be blown back towards the trench he had come out off and was recovered from the carnage before the next wave of troops went over. Close to death, he was stretchered back to one of the many field hospitals, where the pieces of German metal were removed from his body. Then, along with hundreds of other seriously wounded men, he was left in a nearby field. The doctors could not waste any more time on him as more and more casualties arrived from the front.

An orderly checked through Callum's kit bag for identification. He found the silver watch and was tempted to steal it, but put it back into the bag when he noticed one of the nurses watching him. After looking at the shrivelled remains of the corn dolly, he found the letter addressed to Mhairi, with Angus's name and rank on the reverse. He wrote out a name tag and fastened it to Callum's wrist; at least they would have a name for his grave, he mused.

While Callum lay close to death, the war raged on without him. He was semiconscious; his pain numbed for a while with the morphine jabbed into his shoulder. He could smell the smoke from the battlefield and the strangely calming smell of lavender. There was a constant buzzing sound in his head, which drowned out the shelling as bloated flies took advantage of the human carrion in the warm sun. How long had he been here? His eyes were open but he could not see anything. Was this the death he had feared as a child? After surviving two days at the Clearing Station, the decision was taken to send him to a field hospital further down the line.

The arrival of the first American troops on French soil, under Major General 'Black Jack' Pershing, caused great excitement.

Caitriona and her friend Nancy joined the huge crowds that had gathered at the port of Saint-Nazaire to cheer the smiling soldiers ashore. It was a bright summer's day and the sun sparkled on the officer's silver buttons.

"Aren't they just marvellous," said Nancy, waving her scarf over her head.

"They look very confident," said Caitriona, not prepared to show the same enthusiasm as Nancy. "We had better get back soon."

"We've got plenty of time," said Nancy, stealing a glance at the watch pinned to her uniform. "It's not very often that we get a chance to get away. Oh! Look at him. He's so tall and handsome. I can't wait until we get some of their wounded bodies to wash."

"Nancy! What if anyone heard you say such a thing?"

"Oh, never mind them," said Nancy. "If their English is as good as my French, then they won't have a clue what I'm on about."

"You never know."

One of the American soldiers, under the weight of his new kit bag, tripped and fell head first down the wooden gangplank. He was helped to his feet by two other soldiers. His forehead had been split open and blood poured down the front of his face.

"Come on," said Nancy, pulling Caitriona's reluctant arm. "Let's get our first American casualty." They pushed their way through the slightly amused French crowds; Nancy shouted out her status and held her Red Cross bag high above her head as confirmation. "Help him over to the side," she ordered, pointing towards a wall. "That's right, sit him up there and we'll soon have him back on his feet. Here!" she said, turning to Caitriona and handing her the medical bag. "You're better at this, I'll keep him amused."

"Oh, thanks very much," replied Caitriona. "If it was the top of his leg that got cut, you'd soon have his trousers off."

"Now, Caitriona, remember they speak English in America," laughed Nancy, smiling teasingly at the two soldiers standing over their injured comrade.

"What's your name, soldier?" asked Nancy as Caitriona carefully wiped the blood around the raw wound.

"Rosenberg. Private Charles Rosenberg, ma'm...aaaah!"

"I'm sorry. It will be over in a minute," said Caitriona as she cleaned the wound with a strong antiseptic.

"Rosenberg? That doesn't sound very American," remarked Nancy.

"It's as American as any other name, unless you were expecting an army of Red Indians to come over."

"Very funny," said Nancy. "It sounds German to me. What do you think, Caitriona?"

"Well, I'm sure there are plenty of folk with German names in America. It doesn't make them any less American."

"My God! You'd think I was a spy or something. It may be a German name but I'm a soldier in the U.S. army and that's all that should concern you. Are you finished?"

"In a minute."

"And where in America are you from?" enquired Nancy.

"The Badger State...Wisconsin."

"Never heard of it!" said Nancy, bluntly.

"Are you finished yet?" he asked again, giving Nancy a cold stare.

"There you are," said Caitriona as she fixed the bandage with a safety pin. "You look like a war hero already."

"Thanks, ma'm. I'd better get back to my company."

As the soldier walked towards the column of marching troops, Nancy gave Caitriona a nudge in the side. "What do you think? Not bad looking? Even if he is a German spy."

"You forget that I'm still married!"

"For God's sake, Caitriona, it's nearly two years since he disappeared. There's thousands killed and buried here in mass graves. You've got to accept it some time. He's not going to come back."

"Come on, let's get back before we're late," replied Caitriona, fastening the strap back down on the first aid bag before handing it back to Nancy.

"Oh, don't be mad with me," said Nancy, rushing to follow Caitriona, who was already walking briskly towards the station.

"Don't be silly. I'm not mad with you. My heart's given him up for dead a long time ago, but my mind can't accept it without at least some idea as to what happened to him. You see I checked with a lawyer and was told that there is a presumption in Scots Law that a person is presumed to be alive unless he has been missing for at least seven years."

"So if you meet someone else you couldn't get married? My God that's awful."

"Well, I could go to court and get what's called a "Declarator of Death". It sounds bad but that's what I'd have to do. Anyway, I've no intention of getting married again, not for a long time. Let's hurry or we'll miss the train."

They showed their passes and climbed on to the packed train as the clock in the town spire struck the hour. When they entered the nearest carriage, two French soldiers immediately stood to give the nurses their seats. Nancy quickly accepted but Caitriona shook her head, as she saw that one soldier had an arm missing and the other was badly scarred down one side of his face. The soldier's smiles and insistence embarrassed Caitriona into taking the seat beside Nancy. To Caitriona's relief, both soldiers got off at the next station.

"I felt terrible," she said as they watched the two wounded soldiers leave the train.

"You're too sensitive. They both had good strong legs to stand on. Now if they had only one leg each then I might have been a little reluctant," said Nancy with her usual attempt at shocking Caitriona.

The train stopped at another three stations before it reached the town of Montbert, just south of Nantes. They had a further two miles to go on foot. The sun was still very warm and they picked wild flowers along the roadside to cheer up their room at the hospital. The main building of the hospital was a deserted convent where the more seriously injured soldiers were given time to recover before making the arduous journey back to England. The recent sinking of two hospital ships by German submarines had made an evacuation of the wounded much more dangerous.

It was Caitriona who had volunteered for overseas service and Nancy only signed up when she failed to persuade her friend to change her mind. They had been at the hospital for nearly three months and had survived their first real test when thousands of wounded arrived during and after the Arras offensive. Caitriona had become very hardened by the human suffering that she saw every day; men in their blood and urine-soiled blankets, some screaming as their mangled limbs were removed with insufficient doses of chloroform or morphine to dull their tortured senses. The matron was so pleased with her two new nurses that she gave them the day off to recover from the exhausting few months that they had just endured.

Now that the Battle of Arras was effectively over, only a few hundred wounded remained at the hospital, the rest having been sent back to England or patched up and returned to the front. Matron met Caitriona and Nancy at the gates of the nunnery. She was a thin woman in her mid-forties, with years of worry etched into her face. Her frown caused the returning nurses a little panic, but they relaxed as she smiled at them, holding her hand over her eyes to keep out the sun.

"Did you have a nice day? You had the weather anyway."

"Yes, thank you, matron. It was lovely," replied Caitriona.

"We watched a ship full of them Yanks arrive," said Nancy.

"Well, I'm glad you had a nice day."

"What's it been like here?" asked Caitriona.

"Oh, it's not been too bad. After you have your dinner I would like a word with you both in my office. Oh, it's nothing to worry about," she added, on seeing the expressions of concern appear on their faces.

The matron was sitting in quiet meditation, in what had been the mother superior's room, when Caitriona knocked gently on the door.

"Knock again," urged Nancy as Caitriona's rather timid knock failed to solicit any response. She knocked again, hurting her knuckles in the process.

"Com' in!" called the matron, slowly lifting her head from the mass of papers spread across the large table. The walls were now bare, but they still bore the marks where paintings and other religious icons once hung. Caitriona was struck by the outline of a large cross behind the matron.

"Yes, it's a bit spooky, but you soon get used to anything," said the matron, indicating, with a nod, for them to sit. "This is a list of all those who died in this hospital in the last six weeks," she said, holding up a long sheet of paper with hundreds of names on it.

266

"Makes you wonder if there are any men left in England..."

"And Wales," interrupted Nancy.

"Oh, I didn't mean anything by that, it's just that everyone here refers to back home as England. It's easy to forget that there are Welsh, Scots and Irish dying over here in their thousands...The reason I wanted to speak to you is that I've been asked for two volunteers to go with Doctor Chalmers to a small hospital just north of Paris. Don't worry it is still well behind the front lines. The French have agreed to let us have it for some of our more serious casualties; those that are still too ill to make the Channel crossing. We have orders to get as many beds cleared here as possible before there is another offensive. I am sure you will get the chance to visit Paris when you get some time off. "

Both Caitriona and Nancy smiled.

"I see that I might not have to look too far," said the matron. "The powers-that-be have arranged for Doctor Chalmers to take charge of the hospital and he has asked for two nurses to go with him. I have suggested you both. Caitriona, you speak French I understand."

"Yes."

"And Nancy, since you are both friends, I supposed you'd like to stay together. You have also shown yourselves to be fine nurses. I can tell you now that he has agreed with me and if you are happy to volunteer, then that's that, what do you say?"

"Yes, of course, we'd love to."

"I don't think it's something that I'd expect you to love to do. What about you, Caitriona?"

"Won't you need us here?"

"Don't you worry about us. There are ten more nurses due to arrive within the week. Remember, you're not getting an easy option. The twenty patients that Doctor Chalmers is taking are some of our worst casualties and they'll need plenty of nursing before they're well enough to risk the journey across the Channel."

"Well in that case, of course I'll volunteer."

"Good, Doctor Chalmers has given me a list of the wounded he intends to take. Here! Take it and make sure that each patient fits the name on the list. The train is leaving tomorrow morning at eight."

Once they were back in the ward, Caitriona divided the list between them. "Here, take this and make sure you record a full note of their wounds."

"Isn't this exciting?"

"Yes, Paris, it's been a long time since I was there...What's the matter?"

"I see you gave me the ward with all the gas cases. That's not fair; you know how they make my stomach turn with all their spitting and grunting."

"Oh, stop moaning. You're supposed to be a nurse! Here, give me that list and you can take this," said Caitriona, exchanging the two lists.

Most of the men were to be found in the chapel of the nunnery, which had been cleared of its wooden benches to allow nearly a hundred camp beds to take their place. The church, now re-christened Ward One, retained its solemnity, the shape of the roof and the stained glass clearly revealing its true identity at a glance. Caitriona showed the ward sister the list and explained the matron's orders. The sister carefully looked down the roll, studying each name, and taking a pen from a concealed pocket at the front of her uniform, she scored out two of the names. "Johnstone died last night and we lost Lieutenant Henry this morning."

"Follow me," said the sister. "Do you know that most of these

268

men are gas casualties? Some of them are very bad."

"What type of gas, sister?"

"Chlorine and Phosgene; the Germans are not fussy which one they use."

Caitriona followed Sister Milligan down the lines of beds. Some men looked at her with long hungry stares; others either could not look or had long since been relieved of such basic human desires. There was a sense of order restored that had been missing during the chaos of the Arras offensive.

"We'll have to have most of these men out of here by the end of the week. There's talk of another offensive. There seems no end to this slaughter," said the sister. They stopped as she took the list from Caitriona. "Private MacKay," she said, ticking the name on the list. Caitriona looked at the man, his face was gaunt and yellow, his eyes glazed. He looked dead but his chest was still moving. By the time they had gone around the ward, ticking off each patient, he was dead.

"I'm afraid you've got your hands full there. I don't suppose many of them will last the journey, never mind make a full recovery, but Doctor Chalmers is a very Christian man and must think there's at least some hope if they're given proper care and attention, something we just don't have time for here. Anyway, I'll make sure that they're taken to the station in good time. God be with you."

"Thank you, Sister."

Caitriona walked out of Ward One into the bright evening sunshine. She had forgotten that it was such a beautiful day. She had only two more patients to account for, both of whom were in the small green tent, which was for the men with mainly blast trauma injuries. A feeling of dread ran through her as she pulled back the canvas flap, with its metal lace hole hot to the touch from the sun.

"Is the sister or nurse here?" she asked, her voice uneven and nervous as she surveyed the staring faces.

"She was here a minute ago," said one of the men, blowing a funnel of smoke towards the ray of sunlight that she had let into the tent. She took a deep breath and forced herself into the hot, smoky tent.

"Which of you is Private Wallace?"

"He's dead; he died two days ago...They took him to have his foot amputated and that was the end of him," said a soldier as he threw the end of his cigarette in a bucket at the bottom of his bed.

"Is there a Sergeant Campbell here?"

A few heads turned to a bed at the far end of the tent. "That's the sergeant lying up there," said the same soldier, who had been doing the talking. "You won't get much change from a pound out of him. He's been like that since they brought him in."

She moved through the rows of beds and took the sergeant's papers from a folder. He had a number of shrapnel injuries; including a fractured skull, and loss of sight in both eyes and possible brain damage caused by trauma from an explosion at close quarters. She was beginning to feel the strain of her new responsibilities. Only six out of the ten were still alive. She feared that there would be none by the time the train arrived at its destination. *What was the point of all this*?

She met Nancy on the way back to the matron's office. Nancy was just as despondent. "This is going to be a lot of fun," she said with her usual tinge of sarcasm. "Ten men and each one of them has something missing. One poor soul's lost his bits; the whole lot blown off with both legs."

"His what?"

"You know."

"You mean his...oh, that's terrible. Four of the men on my list are dead."

"You lucky devil! That's only six you have to look after. You

270

take two of mine and that's…"

"Sometimes I don't understand why you joined the Red Cross. As soon as I tell the matron, she'll simply add four new names."

"But that's it don't tell her and…"

"Don't be stupid, Nancy. How do I explain four missing patients to Doctor Chalmers?"

"Maybe you're right."

"Anyway, we will have to look after them all together, no matter how many we end up with."

The matron showed no surprise when she was told of the four dead men on Caitriona's list. She was well aware that the twenty on the list represented the most seriously wounded in the hospital. She added another four, less seriously wounded.

It took nearly three hours for the slow moving train to reach Senlis. The ambulances were waiting at the station as organised by Doctor Chalmers, who had arrived a couple of days earlier to ensure the facilities were sufficient to take seriously wounded patients. The building had been a girl's private school and the dormitories and classrooms made excellent wards. Ten locals had been taken on as auxiliaries and porters. Doctor Chalmers arranged for the twenty British patients to be divided into two adjacent wards and placed Caitriona in charge of one and Nancy in charge of the other.

For the first time, Caitriona could here the boom of heavy guns in the distance.

Chapter 20

In the second week, another two of the gas patients died. Each day was just one long chore as few of the badly wounded men could do anything for themselves. Many of the men were incontinent and the bedclothes had to be changed as a matter of routine; this unpleasant task took up most of the morning.

"They're better off dead," said Nancy, covering the gaunt hollow face of another patient with the bed sheet.

"How can you say that? What about their families?"

"Oh, Caitriona, would you like to live if you were them?"

As they entered the corridor between the wards, Beatrice, one of the French nurses came running towards them, her face excited and a little frightened as she rattled out something in her strong Breton dialect that completely passed over Nancy's head. Even Caitriona, with her fluent command of the French language, had to ask her to slow down and repeat what she was trying to say.

"The man with the bandages on his eyes," she said, breathing heavy and indicating with her hand circling her own head. "He's gone mad."

"Come with me!" Caitriona told the nurse in her own language, rushing past her towards Ward One.

"What the hell's the matter?" called Nancy, hurrying after them.

"There's a problem with one of the patients."

When they reached the ward, three porters were desperately holding Callum down on the bed as he struggled violently with them; shouting in a language that everyone, except Caitriona, thought was German. She quickly dabbed some chloroform on to a piece of lint and held it against his mouth. He continued to struggle for a few minutes, and then gradually lost his strength as he was forced back onto the bed.

"He's as strong as an ox," said Corporal Simpson, who was sitting up in the next bed smoking his pipe. Although he had lost his right eye and suffered a near fatal wound at Arras, he was the only patient in the ward who was making any real progress. "You'll have to get him tied down or put in another room. It's no' very safe for the rest of us if he has another turn when that drug ye gave him wears off."

"Thank you for your advice, Corporal, and put that pipe out or go to the dayroom. You know you're not supposed to be smoking in the ward!" replied Caitriona sharply, before turning to one of the porters. "Go and fetch the doctor. The rest of you can continue with your duties, but don't stray too far in case we need you again."

"He's soaking in sweat," said Nancy. "Why do you think he was shouting in German? Don't tell me, he's . . ."

"Don't be silly, Nancy. It wasn't German. It was the Gaelic."

"It sounded like German to me. Remember those wounded German prisoners spoke the same way."

"It was Gaelic, I tell you."

"How can you be so sure?"

"Because I can speak German quite well and I know a little Gaelic."

"English, French, German and Gaelic, you should be working for the government instead of emptying bedpans. What was he screaming about anyway?"

"He was shouting something about a pocket-watch."

"A pocket-watch, you'd think that would be the least of his worries. Your Gaelic must be a bit rusty. He's been spoon fed like a baby for the last two weeks, and you think the first thing he's

273

worried about when he comes round is the time," mocked Nancy with a forced laugh. "You'd think he'd be at least a little concerned that he can't see."

"You can laugh if you like. When I was holding the chloroform to his mouth, I heard him shouting that someone had taken his watch. He's been on morphine since his operation and there's no telling where his mind is. He may have to be strapped into the bed for his own safety, not to mention the other patients. I'll let the doctor know what's happened if you wait here with him."

"I'll get the doctor! At least if he comes 'round, you can talk to him," said Nancy, taking the clipboard from the bottom of the bed. "Maybe you can help him find his pocket-watch!"

"Maybe I will," retorted Caitriona, unable to find anything wittier to respond with. She always felt defenceless against Nancy when she was in one of her sarcastic moods. Anyway, it was a pocket-watch the sergeant was upset about, she reaffirmed in her mind. As she tucked the blanket under the mattress, she felt there was something familiar about him.

Doctor Chalmers looked at the clipboard at the foot of the bed. *Sergeant Campbell.* "It seems we have a Scotsman under all that hair."

"Beatrice was feeding him when all this happened," explained Caitriona.

"Maybe you should deal with him in the meantime," said the doctor as he carried out some tests while Callum was still under the influence of the chloroform. The bandages were removed from his eyes and the doctor tested their response to light. Both his eyes dilated normally but the cornea was still clouded with a thin film of whitish fluid. The eyes had no response to movement and the chances of their recovery seemed slim. He could not determine if there was any permanent brain damage. "There's no need to keep these bandages on, the scarring around the eyes seems to have healed up quite well. There might be some improvement if they're exposed to light."

"What about the straps, doctor?" Nancy asked. "He was like a madman and he's frightened the other patients."

"I think we should take him out of the ward and put him into the small room, between the wards, over-looking the garden, and make sure the door is locked until we get a better idea about him. He's had serious head injuries and he may well be very violent. Nurse Munro, I'd like you to ensure that there's a porter with you at all times when you're dealing with this patient. Let's see how he is when the chloroform wears off."

"Yes, Doctor," she replied.

"Caitriona thinks he was shouting about a watch," said Nancy.

"About a watch?" he asked, turning back to Caitriona as she removed the empty syringe from Callum's arm.

"Yes, doctor. He's a Gaelic speaker and he seemed to be distressed about a watch when we came in."

"Where are his things?"

"They're in a haversack under his bed," replied Caitriona as Nancy disappeared under the bed to retrieve it. The doctor rummaged through the bag of clothes and papers.

"Mm, no watch…What's this? It seems our sergeant is a bit of an artist," he added, flicking through a manual of pencilled drawings of life at the front. "Here, Nurse Munro, there's a few pages with notes on them. See what you can make of them…There's a letter to his wife…I wonder if we should post it for him? There's also a strange looking straw doll in the bag, must be something he made in the trenches," said the doctor, handing Caitriona the haversack. "Please remain with this patient in case he comes around. Nurse Jones, you can go about your duties, we have another seventeen patients to look after. I'll be back shortly."

As the doctor left the ward, Callum began to moan softly. Caitriona felt quite frightened for a moment and had to stop herself from calling after Nancy. He then settled back on his pillow and closed his blank eyes and mumbled something she could not make out.

"I'd give him some more of that chloroform, if I were you," advised Simpson, sitting on the edge of his bed, ready for action.

"Please stay in your bed, Corporal, everything is under control."

"If he makes a sudden move on ye, you'll be glad of my help. Those porters are no' much use. The only thing the French know how to do is retreat."

"Thank you, Corporal, but I don't think he is going to be any trouble. Isn't that right, Sergeant Campbell? Are you able to hear me?"

There was no response from Callum. She checked his pulse. It was normal but his temperature was high. Then he suddenly grabbed her hand in a tight grip. Her heart jumped as she tried to struggle free.

"Let go of my hand, Sergeant!"

"I told ye tae be careful!" shouted Simpson as he came to her aid, but Callum had already let go of her hand.

"Get back to your bed, Corporal!"

"The watch … someone stole my watch," said Callum, this time in English, in a faint, rasping whisper.

"Who stole your watch, Sergeant?"

But Callum did not answer. His mind had already drifted back into the darkness of the trenches as he lost consciousness again.

The corporal was already on his way back to his bed when he turned to Caitriona. "That young porter was at the bed this morning. I thought it was a bit strange when he pulled the screen around the bed. Maybe he stole the sergeant's watch?"

Caitriona did not answer. She had suddenly recognised her patient. There was a doubt for a moment, but now the bandages were removed and she had time to look at him, she was sure. She looked into the abyss of his blind eyes, which showed no emotion as though the soul had deserted the body. She tried to make sense of the name on the clipboard, Angus Campbell, but could not. She then heard the sound of footsteps and turned to see Doctor Chalmers coming along the corridor, with the hospital administrator, Monsieur Rennie, following close behind. She turned to Callum again.

"Who stole your watch?" she asked, but there was no response as Dr. Chalmers and M. Rennie arrived at the bedside.

"Is he conscious?" asked the doctor.

"He was a minute ago, but he seems to have passed out again."

"M. Rennie's agreed to let us have use of the empty room in case there are any further problems. Get two porters to move the bed along the corridor. I think we should strap him down for his own safety. If he's going to be a problem then we'll have to get him transferred to the asylum."

"The asylum!" said Caitriona. "But..."

"No buts, nurse. If he stays like this then we'll have no choice. We can't deal with these types of cases."

"He mentioned his watch was stolen and this time he spoke in English. The corporal in the next bed saw young Jacques pull a screen around the bed this morning...why would he have to do that? Maybe the sergeant's not so crazy after all."

"I'll look into this," said M. Rennie.

"We'll have him moved in the meantime. We don't want to take any chances with the other patients," added the doctor as he turned to leave. "Remember, I don't want you to be treating him without a porter close at hand and keep the boy away from him until we find out if he's got anything to do with this missing watch. The last thing we need is a thief in the hospital. But it might be all in his head, so don't mention anything about the watch to the porters or other nurses until M. Rennie's had a chance to deal with it."

"Yes, Doctor," replied Caitriona.

The doctor sent along two of the older porters and the bed was wheeled into a room that was once the school's headmaster's office. The room was south facing and bright with sunshine. Caitriona closed over the curtains to protect her patient's eyes, although she thought that it probably would not make much difference. One of the porters brought in two thick leather straps and Callum was strapped into the bed. When she left the room, Caitriona locked the door behind her.

That evening, while the nurses and porters were at dinner, M. Rennie carried out a search of their lockers, but no watch was found. After some discussion with Doctor Chalmers, M. Rennie decided that Jacques would have to be questioned directly about why he was at the sergeant's bed that morning.

After dinner, Jacques stood with cap in hand, looking nervously from the doctor to M. Rennie, who stood at the window with his back to the boy, carefully thinking through his first few questions.

"How are your mother and father?" he asked with a friendly smile, turning to face the boy.

"Fine, they are fine, Monsieur Rennie."

"Good… and you? Are you happy with your work here?"

"Yes, Monsieur, I'm very happy here."

"Good, good. Now, we are very concerned about the sergeant,

the one that went a little crazy this morning, do you remember?"

"Yes, I remember."

"Did you see what happened to make him act like that?"

"No, I was washing the floor in the corridor when I heard him shouting. I ran into the ward… Beatrice was at the bed trying to hold him down."

"Beatrice?"

"Yes. As I got to the bed, the sergeant had managed to push Beatrice away, so I grabbed him and held on to him just as the other two porters came running in. They managed to keep a hold of the sergeant and Beatrice went to find Nurse Munro. The sergeant was still shouting."

"Did you know what he was shouting?"

"No. I think he was shouting in German. I did not think it was English. I'm not sure, I only know a little English, not much."

"What happened then?"

"Nurse Munro came in and put something over his mouth and in a few minutes he was unconscious. That's all that happened."

"But you don't know what made him go crazy?"

"No, Monsieur."

M. Rennie thought for a moment and glanced at the doctor before asking, "Did you see anyone with a pocket-watch this morning?"

"No," said the boy, glancing over to the doctor, then back to M. Rennie.

There was silence for a moment, M. Rennie was wondering whether or not to come right out and accuse the boy when the doctor spoke in French. "Jacques."

"Yes, doctor."

"Did you have to place a screen around the bed this morning for any reason?"

"Yes. I had to shave him. Nurse Jones told me to."

"You had to shave the sergeant?" said M. Rennie, determined to resume his role as chief interrogator. "Is it not old Laurent's job to shave the men who are unable to do it themselves?"

"Yes, but Nurse Jones said I should learn, and that's why she told me to shave the sergeant first."

"Only him?"

"Yes. She said I should practise on him because he would not be a problem to shave. Laurent gave me his scissors and razor."

"But I don't understand. When I saw him only ten minutes ago he still had a full beard?" said M. Rennie, twisting the end of his moustache.

"That's because I didn't get a chance to shave him. He was moving about every time I tried to cut his beard. I asked Nurse Jones what I should do and she told me just to leave him, for Laurent."

"Ah," said M. Rennie, "but why did you need to put a screen around the bed? You were only giving the man a shave."

"Because I had not shaved anyone before, I did not like the other men to watch me, so I put up the screen. I did not think I was doing anything wrong, Monsieur Rennie. I won't do it again. I didn't think it would cause so much trouble."

"Don't worry Jacques," interrupted the doctor. "You haven't done anything wrong. You can go back to your duties."

"Yes, doctor, I won't use the screen again."

As the boy closed the door behind him, M. Rennie turned to the doctor. "Well, what do you think?"

"I've no doubt that even if the sergeant has had his pocket-watch stolen, it wasn't the boy. He was not in the least bit aware that we were asking him questions that related to a theft, even after you mentioned the watch. If he had been the thief, he would certainly have suspected that we were on to him and behaved differently. No, I am certain the boy is not a thief."

"Well, where does that leave us?"

"I think we should wait and see how the sergeant is once the full effect of the chloroform wears off. One thing that puzzles me is the fact that a man, who for weeks has been barely conscious, comes to life when he thinks someone has stolen his pocket-watch. How would he even know anyone had taken it? It may very well be the case that his mind is so disturbed with the trauma that he's suffered, that he was merely hallucinating in a fit of semi-conscious hysteria. That's why I think we should let this matter of the watch rest for a while. We don't want to be seen accusing innocent members of staff on the possible ravings of a lunatic. Do you agree?"

"Yes. I think you're right, but for my own peace of mind, I'd like to confirm the boy's story about being asked to shave the sergeant."

"I'll ask Nurse Jones to come along and see you."

Over the next couple of days, Callum was continually drifting in and out of a semi-conscious state, and was having difficulty telling whether he was awake or simply dreaming. The morphine kept the pain in his body subdued but left him weak and unable to fight the darkness he felt constantly around him. Occasionally he would hear voices, but most of the time he was unable to understand what was being said. Sometimes when the sun warmed his face through the bay windows, he would feel a sense of peace as though he was floating free from his heavy body, content in a world of nothingness. He had thoughts, but they were so confused they left his mind before he could grasp any meaning in them.

Nancy smiled as she poured Caitriona a cup of tea during their morning break. "How's the crazy sergeant today?"

"I wish you wouldn't say that, Nancy. It's not very nice."

"I'm only joking. Sometimes you take things too seriously."

"It's just that I think it's awful that they are sending him to a French Asylum. He's not French and he should be sent home with the other men."

"It's only until after the war."

"Oh, Nancy. I don't know what to do."

"What are you talking about? It's not your problem."

"But it is! I know him."

"What do you mean?"

"I recognised him the day we removed the bandages."

"But why haven't you said anything?"

"I couldn't. I didn't know what to do."

"You're not making any sense."

"His name is not Angus Campbell. It's Callum Macnair. He lived on my father's estate. I didn't want to get him into trouble until I knew why he was using another name, so I decided not to say anything."

"Not even to me!"

"I'm sorry, Nancy. I wasn't sure what to do for the best."

"You obviously didn't trust me," sulked Nancy. "You should have told me."

"I know. I'm sorry. What do you think we should do?"

"What can we do? The fact that he's got the wrong name tag doesn't matter much. It's obviously a mistake made at the clearing station. I don't think it's anything more sinister. If you tell Doctor

Chalmers now, he'll want to know why you didn't say anything before. You should have told me. Anyway, in his condition, it really doesn't matter much what his name is."

"At least we can write to his folks. I'm sure his father will still be alive...I just think it's so sad. It's like he's being abandoned. He's got no one to care if he's alive or dead."

"He's blind. You have to feed him like a baby and he rarely speaks."

"It's funny, but since we stopped using the eye drops his eyes seem less cloudy and this morning I noticed him flinch when I pulled open the blinds."

"Did you tell Doctor Chalmers?"

"No, I wanted to wait to see if they improved more."

"Even if he got his sight back, what's the difference? He's probably got permanent brain damage and he'll likely be a vegetable for the rest of his life."

"He will be if he's stuck in some French asylum. Look at this."

Caitriona handed Nancy the manual. After a few minutes, Nancy gave the sketchbook back with an exaggerated grimace. "They're horrible!"

Caitriona began to read one of the poems that had stuck in her mind after reading it earlier that day.

We waited in the station as we said our last goodbye

I saw my own death inside your tired eyes.

The rain is falling now on this bloody Flanders field

It washes bright white bones, crushed by coal and steel...

They both sat with their own thoughts, drinking tea and looking out at the freshly cut lawns around the pond. Two wood pigeons flew on to the windowsill, one pecked continually at the windowpane. The birds were regular visitors to the garden and had lost their fear. They fluttered their wings but did not fly off as Caitriona gently opened the window and dropped pieces of bread on the ledge. Nancy got bored looking at the pigeons; she was thinking about Doctor Chalmers. She occasionally glanced at herself in the mirror at the other side of the room and wished she were as pretty as Caitriona. It was obvious whom the doctor preferred. She exhaled loudly.

Caitriona was still thinking about the poem. She wondered who the girl was he had left at the station and even though the words were of sadness and loss it was still strangely romantic. The thought of his loved ones not knowing what had happened to him troubled her. She decided she would write to Roberts to pass on a letter to the father. She would also have to tell Doctor Chalmers, who their sergeant really was. Nancy was probably right; it must have been a mix up at the clearing station. Now her mind was made up, she returned the sketchbook to the rucksack and changed the name on the medical card to Callum Macnair, before going to see Doctor Chalmers.

On the morning of his transfer to the Asylum, Callum woke, oblivious to his fate, to the sound of birds chirping and the smell of fresh flowers. His mind was clear for the first time as he listened to the morning chorus. He no longer wished to linger in the safe world to which his mind had retreated, and for the first time-felt strong enough to break free from the heavy pressure on his arms and chest. He tried, but could not move the weight from his body, when he heard the familiar sound of doors opening and then closing. There were whispered voices speaking which made no sense to him. Then a sweet scent filled his head with the pleasant sensation that made him incredibly content.

"How are you this morning, sergeant?" asked Caitriona, her usual introduction as she untied the straps and helped him to sit up against his pillow to feed him. She was shocked when he answered in a soft, whisper. "I'm fine. Where am I?"

"Jacques! Go and get the doctor," she called, turning to the porter. "Hurry!"

"Yes, nurse."

"You're in hospital. You were wounded four or five weeks ago," she said looking closely into Callum's eyes. "Can you see how many fingers I'm holding?"

"No, I can't even see your hand. Am I blind?" he asked, without any panic in his voice.

"Can you see anything, shapes or light even?"

"I felt the light when you came in."

"Good, that was when I opened the shutters. Is it still light?"

"It's bright, not as bright as it was a moment ago."

"Is it brighter than it was before I came in?"

"Yes."

"How about now," she asked, getting up and pulling the shutters closed again.

"It's gone dark again."

"And now?"

"It's light again."

"Am I goin' tae see again? I'm no' goin' tae be blind!"

"I hope not."

The porter returned with the doctor. Callum had gone quiet. The doctor introduced himself. "You've been floating in and out of consciousness for a long time, sergeant. How do you feel?"

"Weak."

"Do you know where you are?"

"Yes, I'm in a hospital, somewhere."

"I told him that, doctor."

"Well, what's your name and rank, soldier?"

After a slight hesitation, he replied as though he had just remembered who he was. "My name is Callum Macnair…my rank is sergeant."

"Do you remember how you got wounded?"

"No. My head's a bit blank at the minute."

"Not to worry, it's not unusual to have a temporary loss of memory with this kind of trauma. Not to worry," he repeated. "It will gradually come back over the next few days."

"Can you see anything in front of you?"

"No, nothing…The nurse has already tried that, doctor. I can't see anything. Do ye think I'll see again?"

"Possibly, possibly, you need plenty of rest and who knows. You're in a lot better shape than I thought you were. We'll just have to be patient and see how we get on. He can remain in this room in the meantime."

"Yes, doctor," she replied, following him into the corridor.

"Nurse, it seems that the sergeant is not mad after all. I'll obviously cancel his transfer to the asylum. His timing is impeccable; the ambulance is already outside…I also noticed that his eyes do not look as cloudy as they had been. Have you noticed this?"

"Yes, since we stopped using the drops there seems to be an improvement."

"Maybe the drops were doing more harm than good. It still looks like permanent damage to the cornea but you can never be certain when there is some improvement taking place. Now his mind has returned maybe his eyesight will too. I want you to check them every day and keep me informed."

"Yes, Doctor."

"And, Nurse, I'd like you to have dinner with me tonight," he said, his invite sounding more like an order than a request.

"No thank you, doctor. I normally have dinner with Nurse Jones. I wouldn't like to leave her on her own."

"Why can't she have dinner with the French nurses?"

"She can't speak French and none of them speak English very well."

"She's a big girl, I'm sure she'll manage without you. You deserve a night off…"

"But!"

"No buts, Nurse Munro, you need some light relief. There's a small cinema in the town, maybe we can go there afterwards. I think they'll be showing one of those Charlie Chaplin films. They're hilarious. Have you ever seen one?"

"No, I'm afraid not."

"Nothing to be afraid of," he laughed, pleased with his own sense of humour. "I'll meet you at the gate at six o'clock then!"

"Yes, all right."

Caitriona was still a little annoyed with Doctor Chalmers as she dressed to go out. The fact that Nancy lusted after him made matters worse.

"Honest! I didn't want to go."

"Why are you goin' then?"

"What do you expect me to do?"

"Not go. He can't force you to go."

"I tried to."

"You didn't try hard enough. You knew how I felt about him," sulked Nancy, lying on top of her bed staring at the shadows on the whitewashed ceiling. "It's not fair! You're already married to a doctor."

"Sometimes I can't believe the things you say. It's not that long ago that you told me to accept that Fraser was dead."

"I'm sorry, Caitriona. But if you don't even like him, why are you going out with him?"

"I'm hungry and nobody else has asked me," replied Caitriona. "Don't worry, no doubt he's only asking me out to find out about you."

"Do you think so?"

"Yes, but I'll tell him what you're really like."

"Oh, don't be cruel," said Nancy as she threw her pillow across the room at Caitriona. "You make sure you tell him how nice I am."

"I'll do my best," laughed Caitriona, throwing the pillow back, "but I hate lying."

"Very funny."

"What do you think?" Caitriona asked, dancing a twirl.

"Oh, it's a lovely dress," exclaimed Nancy, sitting up in the bed. "Where did you get such a beautiful dress?"

"I brought it with me. A girl must have at least one nice dress tucked away."

"I don't have anything nice to wear if he asks me out. It's not fair."

"Well, you can wear this."

"I can't wear that after you've worn it."

"Then I won't wear it."

"What!"

"I won't wear this, I'll wear something else," said Caitriona, genuinely excited that she could prove to Nancy that she was sincere in her lack of interest in Doctor Chalmers.

It was a warm evening but it was raining as Caitriona hurried to the gate, where she could see Doctor Chalmers standing impatiently under a large black umbrella, looking at his watch. He was wearing a brown tweed suit, with brown brogue shoes. He reminded her of Duncan. She slowly walked towards him. "I'm sorry I'm late."

"It's all right, woman's privilege and all that."

Nancy watched from the window as they walked down the road towards the village. She cursed the rain that made them share the same umbrella and for a moment she blamed Caitriona for not taking her own. *She knew it was raining before she went out.* Nancy then reproached herself when she remembered the dress. She then went along the wards checking that all was well before looking in on Callum.

"Well, sergeant, I guess I'm left with you and those other poor souls that cough and splutter from morning to night," she said as she began to hand feed Callum. He immediately took the spoon from her hand.

"I'll manage myself," he said. "You're not the usual nurse."

"No, I'm not. She's off to dinner with the doctor. So I'm afraid you're left with me tonight."

"Is she pretty?"

"Well, it's not something for you to be concerned with. She's a married woman."

"Oh."

"Eat up now and I'll be back in later to put out the lamp."

"Can you no' leave it on? It gets too dark at night."

"I'm sorry, sergeant but all lights have to be put out after dark. So eat up and get some rest."

Chapter 21

Callum awoke the next morning and waited patiently for the darkness to lift from his eyes. As the daylight flooded into the room he was able to make out the shape of the vase of flowers on the window sill. Relieved that he may be getting some sight back, he lay back on his pillow and listened to the sounds of footsteps on the gravel path below his window. Soon there was a clatter of keys at the door and the rustle of clothes as Caitriona passed by the bed to the windows.

"How are you this morning?"

"Hungry."

"Good! I'll get your breakfast in a minute," she said, wiping his eyes with a ball of cotton wool dipped in salt water. "Your eyes seem much better this morning. Do they feel any better?"

"Aye, a wee bit."

"They're certainly looking a lot better...I guess I should introduce myself to you, since I seem to have you at a disadvantage. You might even remember me from Glenfay where we met a couple of times."

"Glenfay?"

"Yes, my name's Caitriona."

"Caitriona?"

"Do you remember me?"

"Aye, you're the Laird's daughter... I remember," said Callum, trying to sound as nonchalant as possible as his heartbeat began to quicken.

"Yes," she said, recalling her father for a moment, before placing her hand on his forehead. "Your temperature is still quite high."

"Is that bad?"

"Not really, you have a slight fever, nothing to worry about after what you've been through. Apart from your eyes you seem to have made a remarkable recovery."

"I was sorry tae hear about yer husband….is he still missing?"

"Yes….How did you know he was missing?"

"I heard about it when I was back in Glenfay on leave."

"Your memory seems to be getting better. I'll send one of the porters in with your breakfast," she said as she left the room.

"Damn," he groaned. "Why did I ask her that?" He lay back unable to think straight. The person he had dreamed about so often was now his nurse. Was he still dreaming? He looked at the window again to make sure he had not imagined the vase, but it was even clearer to him now.

In the afternoon, Jacques was instructed to fill a bath tub with warm water and help Callum have his first real bath in nearly two months. Jacques poured a bowl of warm water over Callum's back as he sat in a large tin tub covered in soapsuds. The water felt good against his body, which was thin and weak from lack of activity. Jacques laughed as Callum pretended to be drowning under the water being poured over his head. Callum shook himself, splashing soapy water all over the floor. "Non! Non!" shouted the porter, through a fit of laughter. He stopped laughing when Nancy entered the room with two towels and a fresh pair of pyjamas.

"You're making a mess all over the floor, sergeant!" she scolded.

"Sorry, nurse, this silly bastard just…"

"Do you have to use that kind of language?"

"Sorry. I was in the trenches too long."

"Well, you're not in the trenches now. There are two towels on the bed. I'm sure you can dry yourself but, if you have a problem, you can always get the boy to dry you," she said, pulling the door closed. Callum got to his feet and walked, dripping wet, to the blurred shape of his bed. Although he was now able to make out the shape of things, the detail was left to his imagination. He found his kit bag at the side of the bed and took out his tobacco tin and rolled a cigarette. "Can ye get me a light from somewhere?"

"Non! Non…Nurse Jones…no smoking," Jacques scolded.

"Don't you worry about Nurse Jones. Can you see if you can get me a light?"

"Nurse Jones no' like smoking in ward," insisted Jacques as he continued to dry the floor.

Callum put the rolled cigarette back into the tobacco tin before dressing in the fresh pyjamas that lay on top of the bed. He could still smell the carbolic soap from his skin; it reminded him of Nurse Jones. As he put the tobacco tin back into the rucksack he remembered the letter and the watch. He found the letter easy enough but not the watch. He went through the bag again. "Jacques, has anyone been in this bag?"

Jacques did not understand, and shrugged his shoulders.

Callum got up from the bed and made his way to the door, and into the corridor. "Nurse…Nurse," he shouted.

"What's the matter, sergeant?" demanded Doctor Chalmers, who was making his way along to corridor on his morning rounds. "Doctor, someone has stolen a pocket-watch from me rucksack. I have to get it back."

"I think you better go back to bed. Here, let me help you….You've already told us about the watch, don't you remember?"

"No, I just know it's not in me bag."

"We've already searched for the watch, we couldn't find it. You

293

must have lost it or had it stolen before you ever got here. It must mean a lot to you?"

"Aye, it does…it does…"

Breathing erratically, Callum began to feel dizzy and lay back down on the bed, his chest wheezing. Dr Chalmers opened Callum's pyjama top and placed the cold chest-piece of the stethoscope over the heart, which was beating normally. "You just had a rush of blood to the head; it will pass in a few minutes."

"Can ye hear it?" asked Callum as the distinctive chimes of Angus's watch filled his mind. "It's Angus's pocket-watch."

"I can't hear anything. You're still suffering from the trauma of your injuries, just get some rest and we'll have another look for this watch."

The chimes of the watch suddenly stopped only to be replaced by the rat-tat-tat of machine gunfire in Callum's head as he lay there in torment.

In the afternoon Doctor Chalmers was just finishing off his morning reports, when the phone rang. "Another twenty tomorrow…Yes sir, we will be ready for them." He put the phone down and continued with his paperwork. There was a knock at the door. "It's open come in…Ah, you're back already, any luck."

"No, nothing," said M. Rennie, who had just carried out another search of the staff lockers. "It could have been taken from the sergeant's bag long before he arrived here."

"Yes, I know, but it might well have been stolen here. We cannot have a thief roaming the wards. Who knows what could go missing next."

"Well, I don't think I can start questioning the nurses or porters without any evidence. Jacques was one thing, but the others will not be very happy if they think they're being suspected of stealing."

"I agree, there's nothing else gone missing that we know of, so I think for the time being, we can assume the watch was stolen from the sergeant before he got here. The fact that he was raving about it in his delirium proves nothing. He actually thought he heard it chime this morning…Well I'm finished with this lot, will you join me for lunch M. Rennie? We can let the sergeant know we've carried out a further fruitless search and put an end to the matter."

"Very well."

Callum had no option but to accept the loss of the pocket-watch. The doctor was right. It could have been stolen from his bag at anytime after he was injured. Although he felt bad, there was nothing he could do. Shortly after Dr Chalmers and M. Rennie left for their lunch, Jacques appeared at the door with something that seemed to have a mind of its own. "Wheelchair!" he declared, after having repeated the word to himself all along the corridor. He then tried to explain that the doctor wanted the sergeant to sit in the sun for a while.

"What are ye gibbering about?"

"Wheelchair!" he repeated as though the word had magic powers.

"All right, I get you. It's a wheelchair." Callum put on his dressing gown, before taking Jacques's guiding hand and sitting on the ancient contraption. "Let's go then."

Callum was left on a grass verge, overlooking the pond, where he could listen to the sounds of summer: bees buzzing from flower to flower and the occasional flutter of leaves in the gentle breeze. He called for Jacques to move him forward to get more of the sun on his face, but Jacques was already on his way back to the ward. Impatiently, Callum tried to move the wheelchair by himself, but it would not budge. He eventually drifted off to sleep.

His mind soon wandered back to the war as he twisted and turned to free himself from the horrors that engulfed him. The rat-tat-tat of machine guns was now only drowned out by the exploding shells and screams of dying men. The darkness of his mind was now torn apart with streaks of lightening, and the roar of heavy guns. Then the whistles began to blow along the lines. Fix bayonets...rat-tat-tat...over the top...rat-tat-tat. He ran alone through the smoke and deafening noise, sure he would die, but the bullets whistled by his head until he was lifted into the sky on an eruption of earth. Now he could feel himself sinking deeper and deeper into the wet mud that had devoured so many.

"Where have you been all morning?" asked Nancy, stripping down one of the beds in the main ward.

"Did Doctor Chalmers not tell you?"

"I haven't seen Andrew this morning...So where did you go without telling me?"

"Nowhere exciting, I went into Senlis with the ambulance. That's three patients less for us to worry about."

"I forgot about them. I'm glad that horrible Corporal Simpson was one of them. I pity the poor woman he's going back to."

"Nancy, you say such terrible things, sometimes...How's our sergeant this morning?"

"Your sergeant you mean. He has been acting like a spoilt child. I can't see what you like in him."

"When did I say I liked him?" asked Caitriona, blushing slightly.

"You never, but I think you do."

"I told you that he comes from Glenfay and that I met him a couple of times. That's all there is to it! I think he's got a girl or even a wife back in Scotland waiting for him."

"What makes you think that?"

296

"The poem I read the other day. It must be about someone…I better go and see how he is."

"He's out by the pond. The doctor asked Jacques to take him out for some sun…Well, now you're back, I had better get going. I'm seeing Andrew again tonight and I want to see if I can find something nice to wear in the village. Thanks again for letting me wear the dress; I think it's done the trick. But I have to find something different to wear tonight."

"Good luck, there's not much choice in the village, try the little shop near the church."

"I will. Bye."

"Bye."

With the warm sun on her back, Caitriona walked along the gravel path towards the pond and smiled when she saw Callum sitting in the wheelchair. It was a beautiful day. She was wondering how his eyes would be, when she suddenly noticed him moving violently from side to side, causing the wheelchair to move slowly down the grass verge towards the pond.

"Sergeant!" she shouted, running towards him. "Sergeant, the wheelchair!" she called desperately. The wheelchair continued to roll towards the pond with increasing speed. She shouted again.

Callum awoke on hearing her voice and quickly realised what was happening. As he struggled to stop the wheelchair, it swerved to the side, throwing him on to the gravel path only a few feet away from the edge of the pond. The wheelchair tumbled on and splashed into the water.

Caitriona ran towards his motionless body, lifting his blood-stained head in her arms. "Callum, are you all right?"

"I'm fine," he said, lifting his hand to the cut on his forehead. She held him in her arms as she looked at the wound. He could feel her softness. She was still breathing heavily. He feigned a groan of pain as she attempted to clean the blood.

"Oh, I'm sorry. I'll have a word with the porter for leaving you so dangerously near the pond. He must have forgotten to put the brakes on."

"It's not Jacques's fault, so don't be giving him a hard time for nothing."

She continued to wipe the cut above his eye, noticing for the first time the small fading scar beside it.

Callum made no effort to get to his feet. Her body was moving gently against the side of his face. Then to his horror, he felt himself becoming aroused. He began to panic as she tried to help him to his feet. "No, just leave me here a minute."

"It's only a small cut."

"I can't get up," he lied. "My legs…I think…"

"Oh," she said, immediately dropping his head onto the path. "I think you'll be fine," she proclaimed, getting back to her feet. He faked another moan.

"Help me up will ye," he pleaded as the crisis in his pyjamas subsided.

"Are you all right now?"

"I'm all right," he replied, touching his forehead again.

"Let's get you back to the ward before you do yourself an injury."

Over time, Callum's sight continued to improve and he became more and more anxious at the thought of seeing Caitriona without the security of his partial blindness. At night he thought about her with the same longing he had felt for her when he watched her from afar in Glenfay. He tried to convince himself that she liked him, but he would immediately dismiss such an idea as mere foolishness. Anyway, she was still a married woman.

One day he was sitting by the large bay window, looking out at the gardens, when there was a knock on the door.He immediately got up, hoping it was Caitriona.

"Aye, who is it?" he asked, wondering why she would knock.

"Guess who?" said a familiar voice as Callum turned to see Ronnie Walker's grinning face peering around the slightly opened door.

"Ronnie, what the hell are you doing here? I didn't think I'd see you again."

"How are you?"

"Oh, I'm all right. How are you?"

"Couldn't be better, I managed to get a weekend's leave out of the bastards so I thought I'd come and see you on my way to Paris. How are your eyes? They told me that your sight was pretty bad when they brought you here."

"It was bad, but it's getting better every day. There's just a slight haze in both eyes but I can see enough to get about. The doctor thinks it will be back to normal within another few weeks."

"There, I brought ye a bottle of whisky that I stole out of a supply truck that gave me a lift here. I think you deserve it more than any of those generals it was meant for back at H.Q," he said, unscrewing the top. "Have ye anything tae put it in?"

"Aye, my mouth," laughed Callum, taking a swig from the bottle.

"I'll go and see if one of those good-looking nurses will give us a couple of cups."

Ronnie returned with two mugs and filled them with the whisky. "Here! That will put some hairs on yer chest."

"How are things at the Front?"

"Oh, fucking awful! But I don't think I have tae tell ye that."

"What about Murdoch and Auld?"

"Murdoch only lasted tae the day after ye left."

"Dead?"

"Aye, dead…so much for all that rubbish about God looking after him. Billy was lucky he got a blighty when he lost a foot."

"And ye think that's lucky."

"If ye saw the other guys that were in the field hospital, it was like a fucking abattoir. Even Billy seemed to think he got off lightly."

"It seems to me that you're the only lucky one. I thought ye'd be at least facing a firing squad by now. How the hell did ye get out of that one wi' Major Bryce?"

"Remember that fucker?"

"Aye, for God's sake, what happened?"

"You'll never believe it. His bunker got a direct hit wi' a monster of a shell during the first day of the offensive. You should have seen the size of the crater it left. He was probably spread over most of the battlefield like the chicken shit he was."

"What about Lieutenant Young?"

"Even better, he got a bayonet in his guts. The stupid bastard was so busy trying tae keep an eye on me that he ran into some big German fucker. Most of our officers got killed in the first few hours. Ah, tell ye, the Germans did me a big favour that day. To the Kaiser," he laughed, lifting up the cup of whisky.

"You're a lucky bastard."

"That's no' the best of it. Wait till ye hear this," said Ronnie, taking another drink from his cracked mug. "One of the other

300

officers from another battalion, saw me leading the charge all the way tae the German lines, and guess what? He thought I was a fucking hero and recommended me for a medal. How was he tae know that the fucking lieutenant was running behind me wi' his pistol aimed up my arse, waiting tae shoot me if I stopped. Can ye believe it?"

"You're having me on."

"No, honest, he recommended me for the military medal. Is this no' a fuckin' crazy war or what?"

"Are ye going tae accept it?"

"Why no'?"

"I thought you were against this capitalist war?"

"I am but it's easier tae have people listen tae ye when they think you're a bloody hero. If ye speak against the war, the other men think you're just scared. They'll no' think that if they see me wi' a medal pinned to my chest. You should know that. Look how the other men always listen tae you."

"I suppose so, but ye need tae watch yerself if ye go about bad mouthing the war. Ye'll end up getting a court martial for treason, medal or no medal."

"Don't worry. I'm no' so naive now. I know I'm no' going tae stop this bloody war. It will have tae run its course. Here, take some more," he slurred, his speech beginning to show the effects of the whisky.

"No, I've got enough. I'm half blind as it is. I don't want tae end up blind drunk as well."

Ronnie stayed for another hour or so and left, staggering down the road to catch the next train for Paris, where he intended to spend every penny he had on more drink and one or two pretty French whores. Callum went back to lie on his bed, his head light with the whisky. He laughed to himself as he imagined Ronnie's lucky escape from a court martial.

When Caitriona came in to see him that afternoon, she could smell the whisky but said nothing.

"The doctor said that you're fit enough to go for a walk."

"There's nothing wrong wi' my legs," he replied with a slight slur in his voice.

"Well, why don't you get up and give yourself a shave. I can get you a uniform from the laundry."

"Why? Where am I going?"

"Into town…I have an idea where we might find your watch."

"Where?"

"I'm not telling you until we get there," she said teasingly.

Caitriona returned a few minutes later with a uniform someone no longer needed. He put on the trousers, which were too big at the waist and too short in the leg.

"You look terrible," she said and laughed. "I'll see if there's a better pair in the other ward."

"I'll need boots. I can't wear these," he said, looking at his slippers.

"Finish your shave…I'll be back in a few minutes."

Caitriona came back into the room with a pair of boots and another pair of trousers. "Here, these should fit you a little better. We'll have to order you a new uniform tomorrow…Let's hurry," she said, their eyes catching as they both smiled at each other. "I have to be back by three."

The road to the village was baked dry with the strong sun. It had not rained for over a week and the dust powdered up around their feet as they walked along the road. A cart, pulled by a lame horse, trundled along behind them as a bony-faced man in a cloth cap gently urged the tired animal on. Two women sat in the back beside their salvaged pieces of furniture and bundles of clothes. The refugees did not say anything as they passed, their misery etched on their faces. The old man spat his tobacco chew into the ditch and cursed the Germans under his breath.

"They must be from Compiegne," said Caitriona as they stood aside and watched the overloaded cart slowly pass.

Callum said nothing; he did not want to think about the war. It seemed like another lifetime away from the warm sun and the pleasure of Caitriona's company. They walked on together, quietly for a while. The sky was a deep blue and the sun was now very hot on their backs. Their step quickened on seeing the spire of the village chapel dominating the skyline in the distance.

When they entered the village, some children in dirty rags ran towards Caitriona and began shouting in French. Callum could not understand what was happening. Then he saw Caitriona give each child a coin. They ran away shouting even louder. "They're very poor here. I always keep some coins in my purse for the children."

"What are they shouting and laughing about?"

"They're saying that I've got myself a handsome soldier."

They smiled at each other and walked on.

Customers with real currency were rare in the village and many eyes followed their progress across the road, before they stopped outside an old shop front, which was littered with all kinds of junk. The shopkeeper must have seen them coming and was at the door to greet them. "Bonjour," he said with a smile of desperation as he rearranged things for his two potential customers to get the best possible view of the more expensive items. Caitriona spoke to him in French; Callum listened and was only able to make out the negative nature of the shopkeeper's response. She then lifted a book from the counter and paid the shopkeeper one franc, which he seemed delighted to get for what looked like a very old second-hand book.

"What was all that about?" asked Callum as they walked away from the shop.

"I asked him if he'd bought a watch in the last month. He said he hadn't but that there was a pawn shop at the other end of the village."

"But why did you buy this old book?"

"He was so desperate to sell something that I thought I'd buy you a present. Don't worry, it's in English."

"You paid a franc for this?"

"That's only the cover. It's what's inside that matters...It's a good book; read it."

"Tale of Two Cities...How do you know I haven't already read it?"

"Well, have you?"

"No."

When they arrived at the pawnshop, Caitriona eagerly pointed to the cluster of objects stacked in the little shop window. "There's some watches, is it one of them?"

He looked from one watch to another, and shook his head. "No, it's not there."

"Well, there may be more inside," she said as they entered the shop.

"What's the point," he said despondently. "The doctor's right, the watch was probably stolen long before I got here."

"But if it was stolen here, then the person who took it might have sold it. And this is the nearest village to the hospital."

"All right, I guess there' no harm in looking."

The shopkeeper smiled at them through a long fringe of grey hair. "Bonjour," he said as Caitriona asked him the same questions that she had asked the other shopkeeper. The man hesitated for a moment before shaking his head and repeating, "Non, mademoiselle. Désolé." Caitriona then asked him if he had any other watches apart from the ones in the window. He produced a box of assorted timepieces. Caitriona went through them one by one as Callum shook his head. "Is that all?" she asked the man, who shrugged his shoulders before taking the box away. She thanked him for his time. "We had better go," she said sadly. "I was sure we would find it here."

"He looks a bit shifty, maybe he did buy it and has sold it to someone," said Callum, staring at the nervous-looking shopkeeper.

"Well, he's not going to tell us if he bought it. Even if he had no reason to think it was stolen, he must think it is now…" she stopped speaking and quickly turned back to the shopkeeper. "*Quelle heure est-il?*" The pawn broker instinctively put his hand on a brass chain that hung from his waistcoat.

"*Quelle heure est-il?*" Caitriona repeated as Callum grabbed the man's reluctant hand, pulling Angus' timepiece from the waistcoat pocket. The shopkeeper began to rattle his contrition, confessing that he bought the pocket watch from a soldier wearing an eye patch. "That's my watch, ye thieving bastard!" shouted Callum.

"Simpson," said Caitriona. "He's the thief." She turned to the man and told him that the watch was stolen and that she would have to get the police. He pleaded with her just to take the watch; he did not want any trouble.

Callum was studying the ornate engravings on the silver case; he thought of the cold winter's day when Angus gave it to him to take back to Mhairi. He quickly put the watch in his pocket.

"Let's get out of here!"

They sat at a small table outside a cafe across from the pawnshop and ordered coffee. The sun was still very hot but at least the cafe was shaded by a row of yew trees. The dapple shade was made even more pleasant by a breeze, which took the intensity out of the sun. Most of the villagers seemed to be avoiding the midday heat and the shops nearby began to close. An old woman in a black shawl came towards them and spoke pitifully to Caitriona as she held out her wrinkled hand. Caitriona gave her a few coins.

"She lost her husband and two sons at Verdun and she has to beg in the streets…it's awful."

There was a distant rumble of thunder from the front lines as another bombardment started. Callum tried not to think about the carnage that must be taking place in the trenches, but at least Ronnie was safely on his way to Paris. A scruffy black and white dog barked at the back wheel of a passing army truck which roared up through the village. A soldier, in the back, threw some spent cartridges at the dog. It whimpered, running off with its tail between its legs. Callum lit a cigarette, still looking over the watch. It was working perfectly. "I'm glad to get this back."

"It means a lot to you," she said as the waiter returned with two cups of very dark coffee.

"I've got to give it to Angus's wife. I promised that I wouldn't let him down."

"You've never told me what happened to your friend."

"He was shot."

"Oh I'm sorry."

"There's nothing for you to be sorry for. You didn't shoot him."

"It's a very unusual watch."

"Aye, he bought it when he was in Argentina. It's worth a few bob. He wants his wife tae sell it tae get some money for her and the bairn. I'm hoping tae get home soon so I can give her this and the letter."

"Why don't you just send the letter?"

"He didn't want it to go through the censor so he gave it to me. He wants her to hear the truth from him."

"The truth about what?"

"The truth as to how he died."

"How he died?"

"Aye, ye see, Angus knew when he was going tae be killed; he was shot by a firing squad. I went tae see him the night before they murdered him."

"That's terrible, why was he shot?"

"They called it desertion…He just had enough of the killing. They shot him after he fought for them for nearly two years. He was gassed twice and wounded in the arm. They cancelled his leave twice. He just couldn't take it any more and wanted tae go home tae his wife and bairn. And they shot him!"

"His poor wife and child…this is an awful war."

"Aye, it's no' the Germans we should be fighting," he said, thinking of Ronnie's desire for a class war.

"What do you mean?"

"Och, nothing, I'm just gibbering tae myself."

"We'll need to get back soon."

"Ye'll be surprised tae know that you were at Angus's wedding. Do ye remember?" he said, hoping to keep her talking a while longer. "It was about four years ago. Ye were there wi' yer father."

"Oh, yes, now I remember, the bride had lovely red curly hair?"

"Aye, that's Mhairi all right. Do ye remember seeing Angus?"

Caitriona thought hard for a moment but she could not recall what the groom looked like. "I was only there for a short time, and I'm surprised you remember seeing me there at all."

"Oh, I remember ye all right. Do ye remember myself and Angus meeting you and yer brother one day on the hill near yer father's mill?"

"Yes, so that was Angus?"

"Aye, that was Angus."

"You were both very rude."

"We were only kids. We were not used tae hearing other children speaking the way you and your brother spoke."

"So you thought we spoke funny?"

"Aye, not so much you, but your brother had us in fits."

"It's funny now, but I remember asking my father at the time why the village children spoke so differently and he said it was because they were common folk," she retorted with more than a hint of retaliation.

"Common! Is that it? Is that how you see folk that are no' as lucky as yerself?" he said, unable to control the anger. "Ye think yer something bloody special."

"Oh, I sorry, I didn't mean to offend you. I'm only telling you what…"

"Yer only telling me ye think I'm nothing but a bloody servant and you're Lady Muck. I should have known what yer like," he said touching the small scar above his left eye. "We had better get back to the hospital."

They walked back to the hospital without speaking. They both wanted to apologise but the silence became hard to break. Callum fumbled with the watch in his pocket as he cursed his quick temper. He stole a glance at her when she bent down to pick some cornflowers growing alongside the road. Her arms and legs had taken the sun. They passed more refugees on the road. The sound of shelling could be heard over the hills to the north and, by the time they reached the gates of the hospital, it began to cloud over.

On impulse, Callum took hold of her arm, "I'm sorry for losing me temper back there."

"That's all right, I'm sorry for saying ..."

"Let's forget it."

Callum was unable to hold back his overwhelming desire for her and, as she turned to him, he kissed her. As their lips parted they looked at each other, neither sure what to do or say next. "I've wanted to do that for a long time," Callum finally said, as he brushed the hair away from her eyes. "I better get back to the ward," she replied, turning to open the gate.

Chapter 22

After the death of his father, Duncan lost no time in putting his eviction plans into operation. Within days of the funeral, all the tenants on estate land received notice of substantial rent increases, making it clear that failure to make the new payments on time would result in summary eviction. He refused to see a delegation from the crofting community, referring to them in his curt letter as a bunch of communist troublemakers. Even the Rev. Knox was shocked by the new Laird's plans to turn great swathes of land over to sheep and the rest to the tractor. His condemnation from the pulpit only reached Duncan, who no longer attended the Kirk, through MacPherson.

"To hell with him!" he roared. "The bloody minister is only worried for himself. There's sheep and there's sheep. His sheep cost too much."

As the sheriff officers moved in to evict the first families, calls of outrage from the pulpit soon reached the local paper in Marnock and a campaign to stop them was led by the local Labour Party. Duncan went too far when he attempted to evict the Murray family.

"There's a call for you in the study, sir," said Roberts, his tone curt and lacking the respect shown to the previous Laird.

"Who the hell is it?" grumbled Duncan.

"It's Sir Randolph. He sounds rather agitated."

"I'll take it in a minute. Agitated? What the hell has he got to be agitated about?" he muttered to himself.

"Randolph. How are you?"

"Have you read a copy of the *Times* today?"

"No, not yet."

"Well, I suggest you do! How could you be so bloody stupid?"

310

"Hold on there…"

Click!

"Randolph… Roberts, get me this morning's *Times*."

"It's in your study, sir."

"I know where it is. I want you to get the bloody thing!"

Duncan had forgotten that the Murray family had lost two sons at the Somme and he could feel the beads of sweat on his forehead when he read the condemnation his actions had caused. In the House of Commons, the Prime Minister ordered an inquiry into the matter. In a fit of rage, Duncan threw the newspaper across the floor.

"Roberts! Get me Sir Randolph on the phone!"

"It's Sir Randolph," said Roberts, with a curt bow before leaving the study. Duncan stubbed out his cigar and wiped the sweat from his brow before answering. "Randolph, old boy, the line must have been cut off. I've read the *Times*. It was all a misunderstanding. The eviction notices were not meant for the Murray croft, but the Macnair croft. It is just a simple misunderstanding, that's all. I'll order the evictions to stop for a while until things cool down a little."

"I don't think things are going to calm down that easily. The Labour Party has taken up this cause as an act of treachery by the ruling classes against the soldiers fighting at the Front. It's political dynamite and I want nothing to do with it…nor do my colleagues."

"Listen, Guthrie, my father paid off your gambling and whoring debts when you were in trouble and you still have not paid a penny of it back. I have the promissory notes in my desk and if you do not back me in this matter and explain the misunderstanding that took place then you will receive a writ within the week demanding payment. Do you understand?"

"Blackmailing me is not going to make this go away. I helped secure lucrative government deals with your father for coal and meat production. He made it clear that my debt had been satisfied."

"Well, he never mentioned that to me and the promissory notes were inherited by me without any conditions attached to them. So, as far as I'm concerned, the five thousand guineas are still outstanding…and substantially overdue. If you help me in this matter then I will write off the debt once and for all."

"What can I do that will make any difference?"

"According to the *Times,* there's to be a parliamentary debate in the commons tomorrow… all I want from you is to explain that this was all a misunderstanding and that the evictions have been called off."

The following day, as Sir Randolph tried to defend Duncan's actions, the Labour Party demanded him to explain his connections to the Laird's estate and coal mining business. Unable to answer these questions with any real conviction, the embattled minister left the chamber to jeers and calls for his resignation ringing in his ears.

The storm over the evictions had turned Sir Randolph into a political leper. He was soon dropped from the coalition cabinet by Lloyd George and returned to the Conservative back benches. In spite of Duncan's desperate withdrawal of eviction notices, the damage had been done. Within weeks he received orders transferring him from his desk job in Stirling to a training camp in Dumbarton, where the Argyll's new battalion was in the final stages of preparation for active service in France. The uniform immediately lost its appeal for him.

In time, with Randolph's forced resignation and subsequent suicide, the scandal lost its bite, and before leaving for France,

Duncan made a substantial contribution to the Liberal Party. In return, he avoided a battalion command at the Front and was given a non-combatant role as personal secretary to General Hubert Hall. Although General Hall was notorious for his arrogant bad temper, he liked the young captain and treated him with the respect that, in his opinion, a Scottish Laird should receive. At the end of July 1917, the general received orders to move his troops to the town of Armentieres, and on the 20th of August, after a relentless British bombardment and weeks of torrential rain, the third Battle of Ypres began. Duncan was placed in charge of keeping the communications open to the front lines, although he relied on the regiment's hard-pressed signallers and sappers to actually do the dangerous work of ensuring telephone lines remained in constant repair throughout the offensive. Duncan even began to enjoy the war from the relative safety of Headquarters.

"Captain Dunbar!" said the general as he concluded another staff meeting. "Wait behind; I would like a chance to speak to you."

"Yes, sir."

"Take a seat, my boy," he said with genuine affection. "You've been doing a damn good job keeping these lines going," he added as he poured two large whiskies.

"Thank you, sir."

"Less of the sir, I told you only use that when there are others around. How would you like a little break from all this?"

"A break?" mumbled Duncan, suddenly fearing a more life-threatening posting.

"Oh, nothing too risky," said the general, with the hint of a laugh in his hoarse voice. "In fact it's a bit of an easy wicket, old boy. I'd like you to go to Paris tomorrow. I want Field Marshall Haig…"

"Field Marshall Haig?"

"Yes, I want you to fully brief him on the conditions here and the losses we are suffering. Here, take this," he added, handing Duncan a red folder. "Make sure you read it fully."

"Why me?"

"Why you? Because I trust you."

"Thank you, sir, I won't let you down."

"He'll see you the day after tomorrow. That will give you some time to see Paris. Have you ever been there?"

"No, sir."

"It's a beautiful city. The women are…well you don't need an old soldier like me to tell a young man like you about women," he said with a boisterous laugh.

"No, sir," said Duncan, his own laugh forced, but convincing.

"Oh, you could stop off and see that sister of yours. What's her name?"

"Caitriona."

"Is she still nursing at…? What's the name of the place?"

"Senlis... yes, she is."

"Remember, my boy, make sure that bastard listens to what's in that report. I don't want my name tarnished with this bloody futile massacre of men," he stressed with his hoarse cough and a mouthful of cigar smoke.

Doctor Chalmers carefully examined Callum's eyes and was more than pleased with the patient's progress. The corneas were now clear and both eyes were focusing as normal. "Remarkable, you're well enough to get a ship back tomorrow," smiled the doctor. Callum gave an anxious look towards Caitriona, who turned away. "But unless you're desperate to get home, I think it's best that you rest here for at least a couple of weeks."

"I'm in no hurry," said Callum, feeling a twinge of guilt about the letter and watch he had promised to get to Mhairi.

"Well, get as much of this fine weather as you can. I hear it can be pretty cold in Scotland."

"Yes, doctor," he replied, feeling the word 'yes' as it left his lips. He had made up his mind that he was going to learn to speak with less of an accent. He did not want to sound English, but he was determined not to sound uneducated. He wanted to be educated, like Caitriona. He was in awe of her fluent use of French and her love of books.

"Darling, it's a beautiful day, why don't we go for a walk?" she said as she pulled open the shutters. "Nancy said she would cover for me. I don't think all this reading you're doing can be very good for your eyes."

"Come here," said Callum as he grabbed her around the waist and pulled her on to the bed.

"Don't do that," she said. "Someone might come in."

"You weren't so worried last night," he teased.

"You shouldn't try and embarrass me," she complained, pulling herself free.

"Och, don't be silly."

"Now, get dressed," she said, her humour restored, as she threw his clothes on the bed. "I'll be back in ten minutes."

They walked for a while around the grounds. Caitriona was very nervous that some of the other patients might be watching them and kept her distance.

"Com' here," he said.

"No, don't be silly. There are two of those American nurses.

315

They might suspect."

"So, why do you care what they think?"

"It's not what they think that worries me. It's what they might do. They might report me for having a relationship with a patient, and then I'll be dismissed and sent home."

"Why would they want to report you?"

"They don't have to have a reason, darling, we must be careful."

"But, God I love you!" he said with the pain of the words on his face. "I want to be with you all the time and touch you without worrying what might happen."

"I know, darling. And I love you, but we mustn't do anything that might separate us. I couldn't bear to lose you now."

They wandered as far from the main building as possible, eager for the shelter from the cluster of trees at the edge of the long landscaped grounds. As though tempting fate, they fell into each other's arms in a raging passion, out of sight of the hospital windows. They kissed hard without restraint. He kissed her lips and then her closed eyes as he felt her breasts through her white uniform. "No, not now," she pleaded as he opened the top of her uniform and felt her nipple, hard and erect between his fingers. "No, stop," she moaned, without conviction as they continued to kiss and touch with an insatiable passion for each other. She could feel him hard against her thigh and wanted him.

Nancy asked the young captain to take a seat.

"She will be back in a few minutes."

Duncan gave an impatient look at his watch before taking the chair offered. After about five minutes he got to his feet and went back over to Nancy.

"Has no one gone to fetch my sister?"

"I'm sorry, sir. I had to deal with one of the other patients."

"Never mind! I'll find her myself..."

"I will go now," said Nancy, an obvious panic in her voice.

"Don't be silly, girl, you have more important things to do here. If she's only walking a patient in the grounds, then I can speak to her there. I don't have any time for sitting around."

"But, Captain."

"Where's the back door?"

"Just to the left of the kitchen, sir," she said, pointing along the corridor.

He marched along the corridor and through the ward as though he were on a parade ground, walking briskly past the beds where men lay with missing limbs and other horrendous injuries as though they were of no importance to him. He went out into the warm sunlight and raised his hand to block the sun, surveying the grounds for Caitriona. "Damn, where the hell is she?" he muttered to himself.

"Soldier," he shouted abruptly to a man in a wheelchair, with a tartan blanket over his lap.

"Have you seen Nurse Dunbar, I mean Nurse Munro?" The man did not answer; he was still looking off into the distance. "Damn," muttered Duncan, turning and walking over to a group of patients who were sitting at a small table, playing cards. "Have any of you men seen Nurse Munro?"

There was a silence for a moment, and then one of the patients pointed across the long, freshly cut lawn towards a cluster of conifers. "She went over that way."

Duncan followed the man's pointed finger. "What the hell's over there?"

"The sergeant," sniggered another man at the table.

"What did you say?" demanded Duncan.

The man played the two of hearts and blew a puff of cigarette smoke towards Duncan, but did not say anything. Duncan was about to repeat his question when he noticed the man's missing legs for the first time. He coughed and turned to walk across the lawn. He could feel the hot sun on his face and he was beginning to perspire under his tight uniform, "What the hell can she be doing way over here," he mumbled, the sweat now running down his face as he struggled for breath. He stopped near the row of conifers, wiping his face and neck with his handkerchief, before walking on. He pushed through the long flimsy branches, and was surprised to find nothing but a six-foot wall on the other side.

"Bloody hell," he cursed, walking along the line of conifers and other small bushes.

"Duncan!"

He turned to see Caitriona halfway down the long lawn, waving to him to come back. He felt a bit of a fool as he walked towards her.

"What were you doing down there?" she asked as Nancy walked back to the hospital with Callum.

"I feel like a complete fool. The men were obviously taking a hand at me. Oh well, I guess when you've got no legs there's not much to keep you amused."

"Oh, Duncan! That's a terrible thing to say."

"Well, I guess it is, but it's true, poor buggers. Anyway, I never came here to feel guilty for another soldier's bad luck. How are you?"

"I'm fine. Why are you here?"

"Well that's nice, I must say. I'm here to see you."

"What else?"

"I'm on my way to Paris and... was that a sergeant I saw you standing with?" he suddenly asked, noticing the top buttons of her uniform open for the first time.

"Yes. Why do you ask?"

"Well those men seemed to think it rather amusing that you were over this way with a sergeant. I hope that you've not forgotten that you're still married."

"How dare you!" she reproached as she slapped him hard on the face.

"It seems I've touched a nerve," he said coldly, raising his hand to his stinging face. "I hope you're not going to bring disgrace on your father's memory by causing a scandal?"

"It's absolutely nothing to do with you. Fraser's dead and I'm alive. I can be with anyone I choose."

"I can only hope that this is one of those temporary things and you'll come to your senses. It's one thing you playing at being a nurse, but once this war is over you'll find little in common with your sergeant."

"Have you quite finished?"

"For the moment, I'm sorry that this could not have been more pleasant for us. I did want to be friends with you; after all you're all the family I've got."

"Goodbye, Duncan," she replied tersely.

Duncan marched back across the lawn and into the ward. His face was wet with sweat. Callum was sitting with some other patients by the window. Duncan's face was a blaze of rage when he recognised him. They stared at each other for a moment and then Duncan threw Callum a look of utter contempt before storming out of the hospital.

Still seething, Duncan boarded the train to Paris, pushing his way into an empty compartment. *How could she do this? My God, he's nothing more than a bloody tenant! The silly little fool, she has no idea how much damage this kind of thing can do! Let's hope it only a temporary fling she's having.* Anyway, he couldn't deal with it just now. *Women! And they think we should give them the damn vote! They're more trouble than they're bloody well worth.* He put the matter out of his mind in the meantime, opening the red folder that was now sitting on his lap. The train was quiet enough for him to read the report. He wanted to be as well prepared as possible, taking copious notes as he read the detailed analysis of the recent debacle on the front lines.

It was only a thirty-minute journey and when the train arrived at the station, his hands began to sweat at the thought of having to speak to Haig. He asked for directions from a porter, dismissing the man abruptly as soon as he got the information he wanted. It had been raining, and the long Paris boulevards and avenues had a glass-like sheen to them as the sunlight struggled through the clouds. He crossed to the south bank of the Seine, standing for a moment in the Champ-de-Mars, looking up at the strange iron structure, which he had read and heard so much about. He could not understand why the people of Paris would want such an ugly structure. He shook his head disapprovingly, walking on to his hotel.

The following morning, he sat nervously outside the Field Marshall's Office. When the door opened, Duncan could hear Haig's gruff voice before the door closed again. He noticed that a general, who had just left the room, looked distressed as he opened a window for some fresh air and to steady himself.

"Are you all right, sir?" Duncan asked, getting to his feet.

"I'm fine," said the general, lighting the cigarette that he nervously put to his lips, taking a long draw, before turning to Duncan for the first time. "You're young for a captain. If you're waiting to give a report to Haig," he said bitterly, "don't be foolish enough to tell him the truth. If you even mention the word retreat, you'll be on the next boat back to Civvie Street with me. Don't look so frightened, young man; he only gets a kick out of sacking generals."

Duncan stood aside, saluting, as the general straightened his tie before turning to walk down the corridor with his head held ridiculously high. "The Field Marshall will see you now," said a stiff looking secretary. Duncan picked up his red folder from the chair and marched into the room behind a long-faced official.

"Captain Dunbar reporting on behalf of General Hill, sir!"

"Don't make so much noise, young man," said Haig.

"Sorry, sir."

"Well, it is a shame that Hill is not able to be here himself," said Haig, taking the folder from Duncan.

"The general asked me to…"

"Please be quiet for the moment, Captain, until I have a look at this report of yours."

Duncan watched as Haig turned page after page with only a cursory glance. The Field Marshall then stopped at the last page, which contained the conclusions and recommendations, including the fatal word. Duncan had read that page so often he almost knew it off by heart and his mind ran through the last sentence.

"Absolute rubbish!" barked Haig as he slammed the folder down on the table. "No wonder he didn't have the guts to bring it through himself. I take it that you have read the report, Captain?"

"Yes, sir."

"Were you also involved in the writing of it?"

"No, sir." Duncan could feel the beads of sweat on his forehead as he looked the Field Marshall straight in the eyes and said, "I don't altogether agree with the contents, sir."

"You don't? And what don't you agree with?"

"Well, sir, I have been in charge of the communication lines and have seen much of the front lines. It is my opinion that the men are as keen as they have ever been to make a breakthrough and instead of retreating, we should keep up the momentum along the Ypres salient and strengthen it with reinforcements. The Germans are already showing signs of battle fatigue and a further push by our chaps might be enough to force them to pull back. Once they start to retreat we will have the advantage and could very well force them out of Belgium."

Haig looked at Duncan long and hard before speaking. "Have you made your thoughts known to General Hill?"

"Yes, sir," lied Duncan, feeling the sweat running down the side of his face. He had to go all the way now. "The general has made it clear in the report what he thinks our chances are of holding the line."

"Well, young man, your views of things are similar to my own. So the general is saying we both don't know what we're talking about. I would like you to wait outside. I intend to draft a letter to Hill and I would like you to deliver it to him personally."

A week after Duncan's short visit, Caitriona stood by the window with tears in her eyes. Callum looked at the letter she had handed him. She could feel a lump in her throat as she tried to speak. "I suppose that had to happen sooner or later. There are now enough American nurses to staff the hospital twice over. But I can't understand why Nancy has not been ordered back."

"Well, that's it! Why don't you swap with Nancy?"

"Don't you think I haven't tried that? Doctor Chalmers has lost interest in Nancy and was keen to have her transferred. He thought there would be no problem until he phoned to Headquarters to arrange it, and was told bluntly that Nancy was to stay and under no circumstances were we to change places."

"That all seems a bit strange."

"It's not very strange when you know my brother. I didn't want to tell you but when he was here last week he found out there was something going on and I'm sure he's behind this."

"But how could he have found out anything?"

"One of the other patients made some silly remark."

"Who was it? What did he say?"

"It doesn't matter now, but it's likely that we were not as careful as we thought. Anyway, when Duncan confronted me with it… well I wasn't very wise and simply told him it was none of his business."

"Don't cry," he said softly, putting his arms around her. "He can't stop us that easily."

"But he has, don't you see? He'll never let us be together."

"Don't you have any leave due?"

"Yes!" she exclaimed, her voice immediately more cheerful. "That's it! I can take a week's leave and stay near the hospital, but I couldn't come to see you."

"No, but I could come and see you. I'm fit enough to get about and the village's not that far away. I could…"

They began to make plans and the gloom of their separation was gone. In its place was the excitement of being together for another week.

After telling Nancy of her plans, Caitriona went to see Doctor Chalmers to put in for her week's leave. He listened quietly as she pleaded for his help. He turned away and looked out into the gardens with mixed feelings, as he was still hoping that she would show some interest in him.

"I don't think they'll be too happy about this. It's such short notice. In fact it's not really giving them any notice. Are you prepared to tell me why you need to take next week off?"

"No, Doctor, I'd rather not."

"I see," he said, getting up from his seat. He had suspected for a while that there was something going on between her and Callum, but he wasn't sure. He could see in her eyes that she had been crying, and it was now obvious to him why. "I must warn you, Caitriona, that it's unlikely that you'll get leave without some strong reason being given. I have noticed that you've been very pale looking recently. Have you been feeling well?"

"I feel fine, thank you, sir."

"Well, I think that I should be the judge of that,' he replied with a smile. I think that a couple of weeks' rest is in order. You're certainly suffering from nervous exhaustion," he added as he picked up the receiver. "I'll put you in for sick leave."

"Thank you, Doctor, thank you," she said, having to restrain herself from kissing him.

"Caitriona, be careful," he said as she turned to leave the room. She walked briskly along the corridor, smiling with the happiness she felt at that moment. For two weeks they could be together every day on their own and free from the prying eyes of the other nurses and patients.

Chapter 23

The village had only one small family hotel, which had seen no guests cross its threshold since the outbreak of the war. The owner, Mme. Bissette, looked in shock when Caitriona asked her for a room for two weeks. It was ideal, thought Caitriona, as she followed the stooped woman across the courtyard at the rear of the building. Mme. Bissette turned to grin at Caitriona every few seconds, making sure her guest was not simply a figment of her imagination. The room was damp and very bare with only a bed, a thin mattress and two chairs under the window's broken shutters. Caitriona did not mind and accepted the woman's promise that it would be fine once it was cleaned and aired. Caitriona took the room and paid the first week in advance. Mme. Bissette put the money into her empty purse as her granddaughter, a girl of about ten, thin and barefoot, came into the room with a broom and started to sweep the dust from the floor.

Mme. Bissette came back a short time later with a pot of coffee, a plate of bread and strawberry jam. She insisted that Caitriona sit at a weather beaten table in the courtyard and eat, while she and her granddaughter prepared the room. Caitriona looked at the thin girl and wondered if she would be insulted if she offered her a slice of bread. With hungry, but proud eyes, the girl refused the bread and Caitriona did not insist. An old man with a short grey beard appeared with a round table and placed it in the room. Caitriona drank the bitter ersatz coffee and ate one slice of the very dry, almost stale bread. The sun was warm on her face and she was very happy as she closed her eyes to think of Callum. She felt herself drifting into a pleasant state of peace near to sleep when she heard the woman call to her. "Mademoiselle!" she said, bringing Caitriona out of her stupor. Mme Bissette stood at the door of the room and beckoned her guest to enter. The room had been transformed. The broken ribbed shutters did not look half as bad when open and bright sunlight filled the room, now sweet with the scent of freshly cut lavender flowers. The old man reappeared with Caitriona's luggage and placed it at the foot of the bed. She gave all three smiling faces two francs each. They were very grateful.

In the afternoon Caitriona met Callum and Nancy at the little cafe across from the pawnbrokers. "I had better get back," said Nancy as Caitriona kissed Callum and took the seat beside him.

"At least stay and have a coffee with us," insisted Caitriona, placing her hand on Nancy's arm to show that her plea was genuine.

"All right, then. Five minutes, but then I'll have to get back. What kind of place did you get?"

"It's very basic but it's nice," said Caitriona, turning to the waiter and ordering three coffees.

Nancy felt a little awkward as she sipped her coffee and watched Callum and Caitriona holding hands and looking into each other's eyes as if they were already alone. She drank her coffee quickly. "You'll have to be back by six tomorrow, and not later," she said turning to Callum.

"What difference does it make if I'm back at six or not."

"You'll get me into trouble! That's the difference. What do I say if you're not in your bed when one of the new doctors…?"

"All right," he conceded.

"Don't worry, Nancy," said Caitriona. "I'll make sure he's at the hospital in plenty of time."

"I had better go now," said Nancy as she got to her feet.

"Thank you, Nancy," said Caitriona.

Caitriona took Callum's hand again as they watched Nancy walking down the road. "She's a good friend," she said.

"Aye, but I don't think she likes me much."

"Don't be silly. She's going to all this trouble for us."

"Not for us, for you."

"Well, anyway she does like you. I think you should book into the hotel once you've finished your coffee."

"What do you mean book in?"

"Well that's the best thing to do. You'll not have to sneak in and out. I'm in room two, so try and get one or three. Have you enough money?"

"It depends on how much the hotel is going tae be," he said, collecting coins from every pocket in his uniform. "I haven't been paid anything for months."

"Don't worry; I've plenty of money in my purse."

"I'll have enough. How much was it?"

She told him and he counted out his francs. "Two short," he said.

"Well, there's ten francs. You can pay me back when you get the pay you're owed," she explained, seeing the reluctance on his face to accept the money.

He went across the street to the little hotel and booked into room three. Mme. Bissette was beside herself as he counted out a week's advance payment. He followed the happy little woman to the other side of the sunny courtyard. He nodded in ignorance as she explained that the room would look much better in no time. The granddaughter came in with her broom as Callum told Mme. Bissette he would be back later, not sure if she understood a single word he said.

Caitriona's room door was lying open and she was putting fresh flowers in a vase when he pulled the door closed behind him.

"Do you like it?" she asked as he took a seat beside her.

"It's fine."

"What will we do now?" she asked excitedly.

"Anything we like!"

The following morning Callum groaned as Caitriona gently shook him awake.

"Darling, wake up. It's after five. You'll have to get back to the hospital."

He rubbed his tired eyes, but quickly felt awake when he touched Caitriona's naked body. "You're beautiful," he said, kissing her neck.

"No, I'm not. No one's beautiful this time in the morning," she protested, pulling the covers over her head. He continued to kiss her and she struggled for a moment.

"You have to get up," she moaned before he smothered her lips with kisses. The morning sun was warm and it filtered through the broken shutters on to the white sheets as she gave up her futile resistance.

Duncan folded his copy of the *Times* and put it aside to read later. He called back his valet after cracking open his egg to find it hard-boiled. "Take this back and bring me a three minute egg," he snapped.

The week after he had returned to the field headquarters at Albert, General Hill was replaced with General Kerrigan. Even though Duncan wished for the war to end so he could return home, he was not envious of General Hill's early 'retirement' from the war, nor did he feel any guilt. He convinced himself that he had to disassociate himself from the report otherwise he might have found himself transferred to the front line. General Hill had already written his own resignation in the report as far as Duncan was concerned. "Generals get replaced and sent home, captains are transferred," he reconciled to himself.

One of General Kerrigan' first acts, on the direct orders of Haig, was to promote Duncan to major. Duncan was relieved that the promotion did not necessitate a change of duties and he continued to be responsible for the communications in the Albert sector. *I'll have to go and see how Caitriona's coping without her bloody sergeant*, he thought as he smiled to himself for being so clever in arranging her transfer back to the field hospital at Montbert. *She'll thank me for it in a few months' time.*

"Wilkinson! Where is my bloody breakfast?"

"Coming, sir."

The valet returned with the perfectly timed three minute egg.

Each morning Callum woke and forced his tired body from Caitriona's warm bed to make the two-mile walk back to the hospital before the doctors made their morning rounds. The hospital was now full of American doctors and nurses as the wounded from the U.S. army arrived in increasing numbers. Callum smiled when Nancy entered his room each morning, her face relaxing when she saw he was sitting up in his bed.

"You must be very special," said one of the new American doctors as he read the clipboard at the bottom of his bed. "Nurse, why has this man got a room to himself?"

Nancy explained the situation and the doctor frowned. "Well, he's no longer a risk; he's the fittest looking man in the whole hospital. I would like him moved into the main ward immediately."

"Yes, sir."

"By the way, Sergeant, you'll be glad to know that you're out of here on Friday. You'll finish your convalescence in England before you start your retraining. I'm sure you'll be glad to be getting back to your own country for a while."

"England's not my country," replied Callum dryly.

329

"Remember, Nurse, have this soldier transferred to the main ward this morning. We'll need this room for our own officers."

"Yes, sir. Right away."

That evening Caitriona sat looking out at the wet courtyard. Callum walked from one end of the room to the other, not saying anything. She turned to him. "Why can't I simply go back with you? I'm only a volunteer nurse; I can get a transfer back to..."

"I won't be in a hospital for long before they pass me fit to return to retraining. Within a couple of months I'll be back at the Front."

"But it's so unfair. You've been through so much."

"Well, getting wounded isn't good enough in this damned war. They want you to die for King and bloody country."

"Please, don't say that."

They sat in silence for a while with all the joy gone from their minds. Only two days and they would be parted. For how long neither had any control over. Their lives no longer belonged to them. Callum was a prisoner of the war and it seemed the only escape from its misery was the death that seemed to be awaiting him.

"What time do you leave?" she asked in an absent voice.

"Half past nine in the morning. At least we had this week alone together. Here, there's no point in crying. Who knows the war may be over before the year's out."

"This war is never going to end."

"It will end. It can't go on much longer. It might even be over before they get me retrained," he said, not believing a word he was saying.

"I love you," she said as they held each other tightly. The rain and wet autumn leaves fell on the little courtyard as the thunder of heavy field guns boomed in the distance. She shivered in his arms.

330

Their summer was over.

Caitriona returned to the hospital that Friday to report back fit for duty. She wanted to be there when Callum and the other men left. Doctor Chalmers insisted that she go to the station with the ambulance in case she was needed. She sat beside Callum in the front of the wagon while one of the porters drove the battered vehicle over the muddy road to the village station. She slipped her hand in his and they stole a smile from each other. The driver looked away. The station was crowded with soldiers and they stood together while the other men were helped onto the train.

"You had better go now," she whispered as the last of the injured soldiers were lifted on to the floor of the carriage.

"Look at that poor bastard," said Callum, his voice bitter. "What kind of a life is he going back to?" he said as they watched the legless man being carried by two struggling porters. For a moment, Caitriona thought that the same fate could so easily befall Callum and she turned away so he could not see the tears that were welling in her eyes. One of the guards blew a whistle and another raised a red flag to signal to the driver.

"You have to go," she said, squeezing his hand tightly. He looked into her eyes, his heart beating fast as he pulled her into his arms and kissed her.

"I love you."

"I love you, please come back to me," she said as he released her and turned to push his way through the crowded platform towards the moving train. He wanted to, but he could not look back. He climbed on to the slow moving train and wiped the tears from his eyes.

When she returned to the hospital she was informed that her previous transfer orders had been rescinded and that she and Nancy were to stay at the hospital to train the less experienced American nurses in how to deal with badly injured men that were now arriving at the hospital. Caitriona found it hard to smile, even when Nancy tried her best to cheer her up with a bottle of red wine after dinner. She went to bed early so that she could be alone.

Duncan stared out at the rain as it splashed relentlessly onto the waterlogged parade ground. He held a buff-coloured folder in his left hand, slapping it against the side of his leg. His face flushed with anger as he thought of what he had just read. There was a knock at the door.

"Come in!" He grunted as a nervous looking lieutenant entered with a sheet of paper.

"The information you asked for, sir."

Duncan snatched the paper from the lieutenant's hand and indicated with a flick of his finger for him to get out. He studied the sheet of paper before placing it into the folder, marked clearly in black ink '*Sergeant Callum James Macnair*'. He poured himself a large glass of brandy. Thinking for a moment about his most recent visit to his sister and how his initial hopes that the affair had ended were dashed when she shamelessly boasted of her love for the man. "The silly little fool! This war's to blame," he muttered to himself, opening the file and looking at the most recent communication between them. At least he now knew the sergeant's battalion. Duncan looked hesitantly at the black telephone on his desk and then aggressively lifted the receiver. "Baxter! Get a hold of Captain Conroy for me."

Captain Nick Conroy had to control the smile that threatened to appear on his lips as he listened to Duncan; he always knew Dunbar was an insufferable snob. *What difference does it make if his sister has a fling with the fellow? There's a war on after all.*

"So you see something drastic has to be done before this sordid affair becomes even more serious."

"I don't understand why you're telling me this."

"I need your help. It's as simple as that."

"I'd be glad to help but I can't see how I can be of any help. You're not looking to have the fellow killed?" asked Conroy, jokingly.

"Oh, good God no, nothing so drastic," scoffed Duncan at such a ridiculous notion, although it had crossed his mind. "You recall I mentioned my sister's husband and the fact that he has been listed missing for over two years. Well, I want to be sure he is not simply being held prisoner in some German hellhole, unable to communicate his predicament. If you can provide me with concrete proof as to what happened to him, I will be willing to pay fifty pounds and if you find out he's alive, I'll double that to one hundred."

"A hundred pounds?" said Conroy, sitting up with rekindled interest.

"Only if he's alive and you have definite proof. If he's dead, then there's fifty pounds in it for you. As I've said, we tried all the usual channels with no success."

"What makes you think I'll be able to do any better?"

"There's no one else I know with so many contacts in this part of the world. If anyone can find out what happened to him, it's you. Here is all the information you will require to begin your search."

"This sounds like a bit of a long shot. Two years is a long time to be missing. There are tens of thousands killed and buried in mass graves. I feel you may be wasting your money."

"Well, it's my money. Do you want the job or not?"

"Of course I do. Is there any chance he might have deserted?"

"I wouldn't have thought so; you'll see from the papers that he was a doctor."

"Yes, I haven't heard of many doctors deserting yet. Anyway, for a hundred pounds, I'll do my best."

"Remember, Conroy, keep this to yourself or you will forfeit your money."

"Don't worry, Duncan, but I'll need some money up front, for expenses."

"There's twenty pounds, you'll get the rest when I'm satisfied this matter is at an end, one way or the other."

As soon as he was back on British soil, Callum sent the watch and Angus's letter to Mhairi, now that the censors would not get their hands on them. He also wrote to his father to tell him he was still alive and not to worry about him. After only three weeks in a convalescent hospital in Sussex and six weeks at a retraining camp, Callum was back aboard a troop ship with his new battalion. It was a stormy winter's morning and the rusty old merchant ship lay in port at Dover, waiting for the swell to settle. Hungry gulls flocked overhead; they dived after anything, even cigarette ends that the cold and bored men threw into the tumultuous water, splashing violently against the ship.

"It's too dangerous to try and cross in this weather," said the ship's captain, a stout man with only a grease-stained white cap to identify him from the rest of the crew.

"I have orders to get these men over today. We'll give it another hour," said the battalion's colonel.

"What about your soldiers?" asked the skipper. "They'll be soaked to the skin," he insisted, pointing to the wall of grey sleet moving in from the sea. The colonel nodded his head and turned to his subordinates.

"Major, have the men disembark for an hour. Try and find some place for them to shelter until this weather blows over."

"Yes, sir."

As the men disembarked, the rain lashed the port and everyone on it, but the mainly conscripted soldiers' spirits were high with the thought of one more night on the safe side of the Channel. The men were marched into one of the massive warehouses, along the docks, to shelter as rum rations were distributed to give them the illusion of wellbeing.

"That's on for the rest of the day," said one sergeant to another as they stood at the open warehouse doors looking out at the downpour.

"Aye, maybe," said Callum, turning to the other sergeant, an Irishman with a thick Belfast accent. "But I still think we'll sail today."

"No, no. It's too damn risky. Anyway, what difference can a day make to this bloody war?"

"Not much, but I still say we'll sail today, Cassidy."

"A shilling says you're wrong."

"A shilling says I'm right," replied Callum, taking the coin from his pocket. "We'll let Gemmell hold the stakes."

It was another two hours before the battalion marched back up the gangplank. The heavy rain had passed. Sergeant Gemmell handed Callum the two shillings as Cassidy shrugged his shoulders and said. "You win some, you lose some." They climbed onto the wet deck of the commandeered cargo ship as a pale yellow glow of sunlight broke through the dreary skies causing a rainbow to appear on the otherwise bleak horizon.

"There's a good omen, lads," said one of the officers.

"Good omen, my arse," muttered one of the men.

The crossing was rough and most of the battalion suffered violent bouts of seasickness. Those not hanging over the side throwing up gave a cheer as the ship finally reached the French port of Le Havre. There were no crowds to cheer them ashore. The people of Le Havre had seen too many foreign soldiers marching through their town to take much notice of another shipload of Tommies. They marched behind a long line of slow-moving, horse-drawn gun limbers. They could soon hear the heavy guns and see a pall of black smoke on the horizon.

Caitriona lay on top of her bed reading Callum's most recent letter with the same excitement she had felt when she had first read it that morning. Her head was filled with mixed emotions. She was fearful now that he had returned to France and the war, but glad at the same time to know he was now only a few hours away if he managed to get leave. She touched her stomach; she would tell him then that she was carrying their child. With this thought a sudden panic gripped her. *What if he's killed?* All the doubts and fears she had since discovering she was pregnant came rushing back to her mind. *What will he do when he knows about the baby?* Even if he wanted to marry her, they could not until she was legally classed as a war widow. She would have to see a lawyer as soon as possible about getting a declaration of death for Fraser. Poor Fraser, she thought of him for a moment. She felt guilty at the lack of grief she felt for him. She made up her mind that she would write to an old friend from Edinburgh. Oh, I hope he's not in the army, she sighed as she looked through her things for her address book. *Douglas K. Weston, Advocate, Parliament House. Edinburgh.*

It was over two weeks before she received the official brown envelope with its Edinburgh postmark and six pages of meticulously handwritten text. She had to re-read parts of the letter, with its inherently pedantic words suffocating the page. She smiled to herself when she read his introduction. '*I hope this letter clearly explains the situation. I have written my opinion as simply as possible, in order not to confuse you.*' I wonder if he would have bothered with the preamble if he was writing to a man, she mused. She then read his opinion: '*... although it is the law that a man who has gone missing is presumed to be alive, this can be rebutted if he has not been heard of for at least seven years. The period may be considerably reduced if the missing person disappeared in circumstances where his life was in great danger. I am reasonably hopeful that the circumstances of Fraser's disappearance and the lapse of two and a half years will be sufficient for a decree to be granted. However, you will require a solicitor to take on the case and instruct me to pursue your petition in the Court of Session. May I recommend the firm of Wallace, Horne and Bryce? I must also warn you that, with the war, there has been a dramatic increase in these types of cases and it may take a number of months before your case reaches the court...*' Months! She put her hand on her stomach again and then buried her head in her pillow. "Months! I don't have months."

She was still sobbing when Nancy came into the room.

"What's the matter?"

"I don't know," sobbed Caitriona, her eyes red and puffy. "I just feel so miserable."

"Have you been sick again?"

"No…only this morning."

"Caitriona, you've still got time to..."

"Nancy, don't you understand? I want the baby."

"Then what's the matter with you?"

"I don't know. I guess I'm just frightened. I still haven't told

Callum, I don't want to tell him in a letter. I want to be with him when he finds out…This came this morning," she added, handing Nancy the lawyer's letter. "It may take months for the decree to be granted and by that time I'll be too far gone to hide the fact that I'm pregnant. I wish Callum would write and tell me he has got some leave. I have only had one letter and I've sent him over ten. Maybe he's found someone else."

"Don't be silly, he's back at the Front now and you know how long it can take to get a letter out. Don't worry; you'll get a letter from him soon."

"Yes, you're right," said Caitriona with a sigh as she wiped her eyes and forced a smile. "It must be the pregnancy that makes me feel like crying."

"That's more like it. I think you had better wash your face before you go back on duty. You don't want anyone getting suspicious."

"Oh, I hope no one suspects," said Caitriona, her fears returning as she studied herself in the long mirror. "Do I show?"

"Not at all, I look more pregnant."

"How long do you think I should risk it?"

"Another five or six weeks, perhaps eight at most. You could gradually let out your uniform."

"Promise me, Nancy; promise me that you'll tell me when I begin to show. I'd rather leave sooner than risk being found out."

"Don't you worry, I'll keep a close watch on you," said Nancy, taking Caitriona in her arms. "Don't worry; everything will work itself out in the end."

"I hope so."

Chapter 24

As the weeks passed, Caitriona became more and more susceptible to bouts of depression, which only lifted when she finally received another letter from Callum. She was pleased to read that there was not much fighting at the Front due to the terrible winter weather. She was slightly annoyed that he never mentioned the gloves and balaclava, which she had spent so long knitting for him. Maybe he never got them, she mused, immediately redeeming him from her displeasure. She almost jumped with joy when she read that he was travelling through to Paris on escort duty for the battalion's top brass, who were attending a conference in the French capital at the end of the month. He would be three days in the capital and was desperate to see her. Still trying to contain her excitement, she immediately put pen to paper, confirming that she would meet him. She wanted to write and tell him that she was pregnant, but again decided that it would be better to tell him when they met. She got up and looked at herself in the mirror and anxiously touched her stomach wondering if the bump was becoming obvious. The door opened and Nancy came in looking exhausted.

"You're not even dressed? You had better hurry up or you'll be late again."

"I don't care," said Caitriona, smiling uncontrollably. "This came this morning. Callum's going to Paris in two weeks and I've decided to give the matron a week's notice. I'm going to find a place to live in Paris until the baby's born."

"That's great. I told you everything would work out in the end. I'll miss you when you have gone," added Nancy, slumping down on her bed with the letter in her hand. "I wish it was me that was going to Paris."

"But I want you to come and see me once I'm settled. Promise you will?"

"Of course I will."

The road to Paris was thick with icy grey fog and the car carrying Duncan and Captain Conroy moved slowly towards the outskirts of the city. Duncan was impatiently drumming his fingers on his knees as he looked out the side window for some indication of their whereabouts.

"How long now, Corporal?"

"Another six miles, sir, it may take another twenty minutes in this fog."

"Don't be so impatient," said Conroy. "He'll be there waiting for you."

"Are you sure it's him?"

"If the photograph on the file is him, then he's the same man. He's a lot thinner and his hair is now quite grey, but he's the same man. I'm sure of it."

"And he doesn't say anything?"

"Not a word."

"I still can't believe you managed to trace him so quickly."

"It wasn't hard. I noticed that the Red Cross only checked military hospitals in France and England. I just widened the scope and checked a few asylums. I discovered three patients whose identities were unknown, so I paid all three a visit. This fellow is the man in the photograph you gave me. He looks quite different but it's him all right."

"Does he look insane to you?"

"He doesn't do anything; he just sits by the window staring out into a brick wall opposite. The doctors say he's been like that for the last two years. If that's not mad, then I don't know what is."

"How long now, Corporal?"

"It shouldn't be too long now, sir."

"Maybe your sister would be better off with the sergeant after all," said Conroy, taking Duncan's cold stare in his stride. "You might even agree when you see him."

The car drove up to the front gate of an old sandstone building, which was heavily interned with high walls, rimmed with broken glass embedded in a two inch layer of mortar. An old man in a baggy blue uniform opened the cast iron gates with a struggle. The car roared past without acknowledgement of his efforts.

Duncan briskly shook the doctor's hand and followed him into a long ward, its walls and ceiling yellow with tobacco stains. Very little daylight managed to penetrate the ward's unwashed windows and their cold iron bars of confinement. One bulging-eyed man in a long food-stained dressing gown stood in the corner urinating into a tin bucket. Duncan turned from one face of madness to another. *If Fraser is as bad as these lunatics, he can stay here.* The doctor stopped beside a bed at the far end of the ward and held out his hand by way of introduction.

"We've been calling him Claude as we assumed he was French. Claude, there are two gentlemen to see you."

The man in the bed slowly turned from the window and looked blankly at his visitors. He moved a shaking hand to brush away his long hair, streaked with grey, revealing two glazed eyes with the black circles of depression contrasting sharply with his flaky white skin.

"Good God, Fraser! What the hell's happened to you?" Duncan grunted, stupefied by what he saw before him. "We'll get you out of here and have British doctors look at you." Fraser continued to look at him blankly. "It's me! It's Duncan…Duncan Dunbar, don't you recognise me?" Fraser quickly lost what little interest he had in his visitors and turned back to stare into infinity. Duncan looked at the doctor accusingly. "This man is a British Officer. I will have him transferred to a British hospital as soon as I can make the necessary arrangements. I don't think this place can be doing him any good. Good day, Doctor."

Duncan ordered his driver to go straight to Senlis so that he could inform his sister that her husband was still alive, and to insist she end her affair with the sergeant. The extent of Fraser's obvious insanity worried Duncan, but he was still her husband and she would have to do her duty. At least any fear of Caitriona marrying Callum Macnair was over in the meantime. Once she knew Fraser was still alive she would come to her senses, he concluded, before urging the driver to go faster.

Caitriona grabbed hold of Nancy as Duncan told her of Fraser's two-year incarceration in an asylum .Feeling faint, she sipped the glass of water Nancy had poured for her. "Are you sure it's Fraser?" she pleaded weakly.

"I tell you, I saw him with my own eyes. He's going to need a great deal of nursing to get him well again."

"How bad is he?"

"He's in a poor way, but I don't think those French doctors know how to treat him. Wait, you'll see a difference when we get him home to Scotland. A few months at home will get him well again."

"Poor Fraser, how awful. How is it possible that the French doctors didn't notify the army that he was alive?"

"They didn't know who he was. He was discovered naked, living like a wild animal in a forest behind the French lines. He wouldn't or couldn't speak and the doctors assumed he was a French deserter suffering from shell shock. They never reported him to the French army for fear that they would put him up against a wall and shoot him for deserting."

"Can he speak now?"

"No…no, he hasn't said a word in the two years he's been at the hospital. He didn't seem to recognise me. I don't think that damned hospital or its doctors have been any help to him. I'm making arrangements for him to be taken home as soon as possible. You'll have to resign here to accompany him home."

"I can't," she replied firmly.

"Do you mind leaving us for a moment?" said Duncan, turning to Nancy.

"Caitriona?" queried Nancy.

"It's all right, I'll be fine."

"Of course she'll be fine, now run along."

"I'll be outside if you need me."

"Good God, what's wrong with that woman. You'd think you were frightened to be alone with your own brother. Now what's all this about not resigning? I'll have a word with the right people and there'll be no problems. It's not as if you're in the army or anything like that. Once I tell them about Fraser, they'll certainly agree that your place is at home looking after him. But don't worry we'll get a nurse in. So you see there's no problem."

"Oh, but there is. I can't go back with Fraser, not now. I'm in love with someone else and…" she broke off, pulling her long cardigan over to cover her stomach.

"Nonsense! You're married to Fraser and that's that. You'll have to put this damned fellow out of your mind," he stormed, walking up and down the small room in his agitation.

"I can't. I love him. Can't you understand?"

"What's there to understand? Fraser's the man you married and he needs you to fulfill your duties…the promises you made to him before God. You can't run off with some common soldier. And stop that sniffling; you'll soon get over this other fellow."

Caitriona fell onto her bed, crying uncontrollably. *What was she going to do? She couldn't go back with Fraser carrying another man's child and would Callum still want her with her husband still alive? What a mess her life was in. If only she didn't have to wait another full week before seeing him again.* As she lay there, she heard the door slam closed and the heavy footsteps of her brother fading along the corridor.

Captain Conroy was waiting in the car when Duncan slumped down beside him. Duncan ordered the driver to get going, pulling the glass partition closed at the same time. "How did it go, old boy?" asked Conroy, offering Duncan a cigar.

"Not as well as I hoped. No thanks," he added, rejecting the cigar.

"She still wants her bloody sergeant? He must be a good looking man."

"I'm not interested in what he looks like!"

"Maybe now is the time to have him shot," Conroy joked.

"If only it was that easy."

"His luck can't hold out forever, maybe he'll catch a German bullet before long."

"Well, we'll have to think of something."

Callum helped push the heavy trunks onto the end carriage of the waiting train. He was with Sergeant Cassidy and Sergeant Macgregor; all hand-picked by their battalion major for this assignment. Even being stuck in the luggage carriage for the three-hour journey was light years away from another long, freezing day in the trenches. The train slowly rolled away from the station, its whistle blasting two short toots as the steam filled up the platform. Cassidy turned one of the trunks on its side and took a pack of cards from his tunic pocket.

"Any of you suckers got any money?"

General Douglas and his three subordinates enjoyed a fine lunch while the train rattled along the snow-covered tracks. He scoffed to himself, reading his copy of *The Times*.

"Who does this fellow Wilson think he is? He wants to let the damn Germans off the hook. They come in at the last minute and then try and dictate the terms of an Armistice. Thank goodness our Government's got more sense. We've got to make the Germans pay for this war and then they'll not be in such a hurry to start another one." The three other officers nodded their agreement.

In spite of the cold, beads of sweat began to appear on Callum's flushed face. In only twenty minutes he had lost almost three weeks' wages. He had only ten francs left.

"What's wrong, Macnair?" sniggered Cassidy, who was winning most of the pots. "It's only money," he laughed, dealing Callum a low pair.

"I'm out!" said Callum, throwing his hand in.

"Hard luck," mocked Cassidy, dealing fresh cards to Macgregor, who was worrying about his own losses. Callum pulled a blanket around him and sat by the window in the carriage, ruing his bad luck. He tried to cheer himself up by re-reading Caitriona's long letter, the scent on the pages making him ache for her touch as he tried to imagine her waiting for him under the wrought-iron girders of the Eiffel Tower. The train rattled on and he stared out at what little he could see of the snow-covered countryside. An argument finally ended the card school.

"I'm not in the business of lending money," said Cassidy, who was gleefully counting his winnings.

"For God's sake, ye cleaned me out, at least give us a loan of a few bob until I get my next pay," pleaded Macgregor.

"There's Macnair, maybe he'll lend ye something."

"Tae hell with ye Cassidy," said Macgregor, before slumping down beside Callum, quietly lamenting his losses and thinking how miserable it was going to be in Paris without even the price of a drink, never mind the money to pay for the services of that French whore he had been dreaming about. Cassidy was showing his gratitude to the pack of cards by shuffling them in every way he could before returning them to their tattered cardboard box. Callum, incensed by his gloating, got up and sat opposite him.

"Eight francs! The highest card wins," challenged Callum, slapping the coins onto the leather trunk.

"I thought you were the smart one," said Cassidy, taking the cards back out of their box.

"Just cut the cards."

"I'll let you cut first."

"No, after you," insisted Callum, shuffling the deck before slapping the pack on the makeshift card table. Macgregor, desperate to see Cassidy lose, sat behind Callum and watched. Cassidy nonchalantly turn over the Jack of Hearts, grinning as he put it to the bottom of the pack. "Beat that Macnair!" Callum, with a desperate pray on his lips, shuffled the cards, and then placed them back on the trunk. He lifted the card from the top of the pack. There was a groan from Macgregor as he turned over a ten of spades.

"You win some, you lose some," laughed Cassidy. "I tell you what. Paris is not going to be much fun with you two bums walking around with nothing but holes in your pockets. I'll give ye back thirty francs each, but you pay me back thirty five..."

"Thirty five francs!" Macgregor complained.

"Take it or leave it."

"You should be wearing a black mask," said Callum, holding out his hand to take the loan along with Macgregor, who had no intention of paying Cassidy back a penny.

After unloading the officers' trunks at the hotel, the three sergeants were given the rest of the day to see Paris. They found a quiet café down a narrow, cobbled street just off the Champs-Elysees. They sat by the window and drank beer, watching the pretty girls walking past in their long winter coats as it began to snow.

"Three more beers!" shouted Macgregor who wanted to have his fill before he risked his manhood in the dubious sanctuary of a Paris brothel. The waiter returned with glasses and a jug of beer.

"Want eats?" he asked, indicating his meaning, with his fingers coming up to his open mouth.

"What have ye got, Frenchie?" asked Cassidy, with his usual lack of diplomacy. "We don't want any of them snails you lot eat."

"*Voila*," said the waiter, handing each man a handwritten menu.

"God, look at the bloody prices," complained Macgregor.

"The war," said the waiter, holding up his hand to show it was not his fault.

After the harassed waiter had tried his best to explain the menu, Callum and Macgregor, each ordered a croissant and a hard-boiled egg, the cheapest thing they could find on the menu. With his winnings, Cassidy ordered two eggs and three slices of bacon, and laughed heartily when the waiter returned with the food.

"Thanks, boys, I wouldn't be able to afford this without you."

"Aye, very funny, just eat it and shut up," insisted Callum, now getting pretty tired of Cassidy and his boasting.

As the clock behind the bar chimed the half hour, Callum got up to leave. He had drunk more than he had planned and he staggered a little as he shook Macgregor's hand. Cassidy grunted his goodbye. As more drinks arrived at the table, Callum could not resist a final cognac to keep out the cold. The others, including the waiter, cheered as he emptied the glass, slamming it on the table, before turning to the door. "Don't spend all yer money in the whorehouse; we've got another couple of days here."

"Don't worry about us, Macnair, we'll be in and out before they know we were even there," said Cassidy, emptying his own glass of cognac with an exaggerated burp.

"Speak for yerself," said Macgregor.

Outside the cold air hit Callum, he felt uneasy on his feet and slipped on the icy road. He was too drunk to feel in the least embarrassed and he picked himself up, before staggering on towards the tower he could now see on the other side of the river. He took a few deep breaths to try and sober up but the cognac was stronger than he thought and he began to feel sick. He stopped at a street pump and washed his face in the icy cold water, which sobered him up a little. As he neared the tower he heard the cathedral bells, it was already six o'clock; the walk had taken longer than he thought. He took another deep breath and tried to clear his head. *Why did I drink so much?*

When he finally found himself under the tower he looked around but couldn't see Caitriona. "I hope she's not going to be too late," he mumbled, lighting a cigarette and stamping his feet to keep warm.

He watched a French soldier and his girl kissing under the shelter of one of the girder legs of the tower. He smiled to himself as he crushed the cigarette under his heel. French trains are always late, he reassured himself, shivering and stamping his feet even harder to stop his toes from going numb. A tall, thin man in what looked like a postman's uniform, came over to him and said something. Callum smiled and shrugged his shoulders. "I don't speak French."The man grunted his displeasure, before walking away. Callum strolled over to one of the other iron legs of the tower to have a better look across the park. There was still no sign of Caitriona.

It began to snow again, and he watched the flakes as they landed near his feet, instantly disappearing on the wet ground. The man in the uniform came back and lit a gaslight at the foot of the tower, grumbling to himself as he passed by. Callum ignored him and lit another cigarette. The Cathedral bells then tolled the half hour. What's keeping her?

Frozen to the bone, he waited another twenty minutes before it was obvious to him that she was not coming. His hands and feet numb, he reluctantly walked back towards the café. *Maybe she got the date mixed up, but he knew she hadn't. Maybe she just couldn't get here for some reason and wasn't able to let him know. Maybe she changed her mind.* Through the café window, he saw Cassidy and Macgregor, now roaring drunk, and still drinking. He turned and walked back to the hotel.

While he waited in vain, Caitriona was already on her way back to Scotland with Fraser. Duncan had made all the arrangements, insisting on accompanying them on the long journey home.

Henderson was waiting with the car at Marnock station. The chauffer helped Duncan guide Fraser into the back seat as Caitriona sat beside him. Fraser was now a stranger to her, and she to him. Although she pitied him and was distressed by his condition, his madness had divorced them from each other in a way no legal decree could ever achieve. When he muttered incoherently as though recognizing Glenfay, she put her hand on his, and was struck by its cold, almost deathlike feeling.

As the car drove along the loch road, Caitriona's mind was almost as lost as that of her husband's. The terrible words repeating in her head as they had done the day she had received the letter…'Killed in Action.' She felt the baby again as she turned to look out at the haunted trees along the loch side. The only sound she could hear above the noise of the engine was the incessant caws of crows. 'Killed in Action…'

Chapter 25

As the cold winter gave up its long hold on the fields of the glen, the sounds and smells of spring filled the air. Green buds reappeared on the trees along the banks of the loch, and hardy spring flowers pushed their way through the soft, damp soil. Small animals emerged from months of hibernation to scurry through the decaying, wet undergrowth, looking for morsels of food to fill their empty bellies. A flock of wild geese circled the loch twice before landing on its mist-covered waters. On the hillside, Norman Campbell followed the plough, calling out to the two Clydesdales to keep the line steady as the land once again opened itself to the blade. He stopped to look at the rig behind him, and lit his pipe as he looked over the glen. Cottages were lying abandoned and fields fallow from the Laird's neglect. Most families had long since moved from the crofts to the towns to make way for the Laird's precious sheep that now roamed the Howe. There was still smoke coming from Jamie Macnair's chimney, but the man himself was rarely seen. Norman wiped the sweat from his brow and took up the reins as the horses slowly got back into their stride again. A rumble of thunder echoed in the distance.

On the Western Front, British intelligence discovered that the German army planned a massive spring offensive on the Somme. Callum's battalion had been moved up to the front line at San Quentin, to await the expected onslaught. Within days the Germans began pounding the British defences relentlessly. Callum's raw battalion was ordered to hold the line and repel the pending attack when it came. Now the most experienced soldier in his company, he was trying to keep the frightened young recruits alert to the threat of snipers as the creeping enemy barrage moved inextricable towards the British lines. So many fine officers were lost in the first few years of the war that boys were now being sent to take their place. Their youth and inexperience undermined their brave attempts at leadership as their weak voices melted into the clouds of smoke and churned up earth. The battalion's latest officer had none of the qualities of his predecessors.

Lieutenant Dawson was shivering like a nervous kitten in a corner and unable to hide the horror in his eyes. Only a few months ago he was playing cricket on the fields of Eton and dreaming of glory; now he had the lost his nerve and deferred to Callum's will. The terrified conscripts buried their faces into the soft mud of the trench walls and clung to their rifles, impotent against the heavy shells that blew up the criss-crossing lines of barbed wire, throwing great mountains of earth high into the air. The rotten nameless corpses of previous battles were scattered in every direction. This diabolical hell was even too hideous for the squealing, bloated rats as they scurried along the duck-boards and mud at the soldiers' feet, looking for somewhere to hide. There would be more human flesh for them to gorge themselves once the heavy guns fell silent. Soldiers prayed incessantly, bowels turned to water and previous lives flashed before terrified eyes as they waited for orders to fix bayonets.

Callum had looked through the lieutenant's box periscope to see the devastation in 'no man's land'. He then ordered Corporal 'Ginger' Johnstone, to take two magazines to the men manning the Lewis guns, who were calling out for more ammunition. The corporal hesitated and looked for confirmation from Dawson, until Callum barked the order again; the lieutenant nodded weakly in acquiescence. The machine-gun post was just in front of the officers' dug-out and more exposed to a sniper's bullet. Ginger held his breath, climbing over the parapet and scurrying to the sandbags that offered the two gunners questionable protection. "Stop firing at fucking nothin'. I'm not coming back for no fucker once this lot is gone…Wait till they at least get out of their fucking trenches!" he ordered before crawling back through the churned-up ground.

The German barrage stopped as suddenly as it had started. The men were ordered to fix bayonets as Callum again looked through the box-periscope expecting waves of German soldiers to be rising from their trenches through the clouds of smoke. None came and the agony of waiting became as unbearable as the fear of death itself. As the hours passed, men were so tired that they fell asleep standing up with their heads pressed against the muddy walls. Sleep was ephemeral, men were not able to tell if they had been dreaming or merely dazed into a stupor of bewilderment.

Callum let them rest and ignored the angry stare of one captain looking out from his dug-out at a sight that only a few months earlier would have resulted in men being put on a charge. The threat of a German push diminished with the fading daylight and orders were passed along the trenches for the men to stand down. Exhausted, Callum sat on an upturned, ammunition box and held his head in his hands. He was surprised how calm he was and how eager he had been to get it over with. He no longer gave a damn about the war. The last few months had been unbearable. His letters had been returned unopened and he had received none from Caitriona. His imagination considered every possibility and, in the worst days of the long winter, even thought that their affair had all been some morphine-induced dream. The war had in some way detached him from reality. The letters! He would reassure himself. Then he would read them, rereading the last one over and over again. They were real all right. *She could not have written such words of anguish just to fool him into thinking that she loved him. No one could be so callous or cruel. Something must have happened. She may be ill? Why didn't she write?*

He felt the cold for the first time and took a cup of tea from Lieutenant Dawson, who looked sheepish as he offered him a cigarette.

Every so often the rat-tat-tat of the German machine guns would open up on the unfortunate British sappers who were ordered into 'no man's land' to carry out futile repairs on the defences. The terrible beauty of the Very lights burst in the sky to catch the silhouettes of men dragging heavy rolls of barbed wire across the wasteland of gaping craters…rat-tat-tat. As the light faded, all that remained was the hellish sounds of wounded men abandoned in the mud.

When dawn broke, the barrage resumed and the trenches of exhausted men stirred into life. Orders were shouted to confused soldiers still trying to come to terms with the reality of the nightmare they thought they had merely dreamed. Bayonets were fixed with shaking hands and curses of despair. The barrage had moved from the destruction of the twisted and torn defences to the trenches. A heavy shell made a direct hit further down the line throwing up dismembered bodies of men only half awake when their end came. The bombardment continued for two hours as both sides exchanged thousands of shells on each other's devastated front lines. The German whistles could be heard as the heavy guns fell silent, and thousands of men in their grey-blue uniforms marched, shoulder to shoulder, into the killing fields. Orders were screamed along the British trenches and the men took to the firing steps and opened up indiscriminately at the lines of advancing soldiers. The Lewis guns were soon red hot. The ammunition was fed into their greedy barrels as it mowed down soldiers like ducks in a shooting gallery. But still the hordes of German spectres emerged from the morning mist. The order was given to pull back.

All along the British lines the German offensive overwhelmed the once seemingly impregnable Allied defences and a full-scale retreat was ordered by General Gough. Callum ordered his men out of the trench; some were too frightened to leave its shelter until another shell landed only a few feet away showering them with clay and rocks. The men scrambled onto the duck-boards that linked the front trenches with those further back. Bullets were being fired in all directions as men fell with both German and British bullets in them. The wounded were left where they fell. Heavy backpacks and long coats were cast aside as the soldiers scurried back to a dirt track that led to the nearest village. A team of horses made terrible sounds of distress as shrapnel tore into their flesh and they sank, still harnessed to an abandoned field gun, into the suffocating mud. Callum continued to fire back at the advancing German infantry, who were now using the British front line trenches as they set up machine gun posts to mow down the fleeing mass of Haig's routed Fifth Army.

Lieutenant Dawson had thrown away his revolver and was running ahead of what was supposed to be his company. His blond hair was matted to his head with sweat and the uniform that had been tailor made in London only a few months before was covered in mud and blood. Callum called on him to slow down but there was no response.

"Look at that fucking coward," shouted Corporal Johnstone.

"He's not a coward, just a better runner than us," replied Callum, still trying to hurry the rest of his tired and disorientated men on as the bullets continued to fly by his head. He suddenly felt a burning sensation in his upper arm and fell to the side of the road. The corporal took some field dressing from his bag and cut open the sleeve of Callum's tunic, and he quickly applied the dressing.

"You'll live," said Ginger, helping Callum to his feet as more bullets whizzed by. "Let's get the fuck out of here."

The road to Amiens was thick with trucks, horse-drawn wagons and thousands of exhausted troops. In the fields, heavy batteries were being disabled and abandoned by their crews. German planes flew overhead firing into the chaos of the retreat. Callum lost count of the hours they marched before they could rest up for a while on the outskirts of a village, where a field hospital nurse redressed his wound and confirmed that the bullet had gone right through only nicking the bone. When he returned to his company he realised that most were dead or missing. At least six were confirmed to be casualties. Those missing could be anywhere in the sea of troops that swarmed around the French countryside. No one had seen Lieutenant Dawson since early that morning when he was last seen retreating with undue haste. The battalion was now mixed up with other regiments and officers were as lost and bewildered as the ordinary soldiers.

Within an hour, fresh orders to march on were shouted by officers as the exhausted soldiers rested in the wet fields around the village. It took a half dozen shots into the air to rouse the men as an irate major rode around on his black charger telling his officers to get the bastards moving. The men were calling for water, but there was none to be had anywhere and, with the barrage of British guns pounding the advancing Germans, they got back on their blistered and bleeding feet to continue their desperate retreat in the direction of their own artillery. Callum continually urged what was left of his company on as the rear-guard tried to slow down the German advance. More and more equipment was being dropped by men no longer able to carry it. German planes continued to fly overhead, indiscriminately spraying the retreating troops with bullets. Callum again urged his men on.

Once they reached the relative safety of the British reserve lines, they were ordered to dig in and stop the advancing German infantry at all cost. Callum could no longer hold a rifle or use a spade and one of the battalion captains relieved him of his duties, ordering him to join the other wounded at the railway station awaiting to be taken to the clearing stations. He refused to leave his men but the captain was in no mood for his heroics and ordered him at gun point to get going.

When he eventually climbed aboard an overcrowded cattle train, he had only one thing on his mind. He could bear it no longer and now he had the chance, he would take it. To hell with the war, now he knew how Angus must have felt when he deserted. *I owe my life to no one.* The cattle train was destined for Paris with hundreds of wounded men lying virtually on top of one another, some dying quietly, some already dead. He stayed near to the open doors of the slow-moving carriage, preparing himself mentally for the jump he would have to make when the time came. He was sure that the men around him were all too far gone to take any notice of his desertion.

As darkness began to fall, he took his chance and jumped into the blackness below, rolling down the grass embankment until he crashed into the trunk of a tree. He lay still for a moment and then tried to get to his feet, but he was unable to. His wrist was broken. To his horror, he heard the train screeching to a halt and the shouts of men running back along the line. Still dazed, he struggled to his feet and staggered across the open field. The shouting became almost frenzied as two shots rang out. One bullet was so close to his head that he heard it whistle past and ricochet off a stone dyke only yards in front of him. He fell to the ground; sure if he ran the next bullet would be in his back. As he lay gasping for breath, his heart was pounding so hard in his chest that it hurt more than his arm. Then, in his confused mind, he could hear Angus's angry voice urging him, "Get up! Run!" He was back in the fields of Glenfay, with the bailiffs at his heels.

Another shot came close, more shouting. He was again on his feet, running for the cover of a thicket of bushes at the other side of the ploughed field. His feet were heavy with the thick, wet soil clinging to his boots. Unable to keep his balance, he fell again. *Get up! Get up!* The pain in his wrist was numbed with the fear of death as he ran frantically towards the blackness of the bushes, pushing through the clinging branches until he could struggle with them no more, dropping to the wet undergrowth, exhausted. He lay in the darkness listening for any sound of his pursuers, but he could hear nothing except his own heavy breathing. He lay exhausted, his chest heaving hard for every breath. He thought of Angus and the salmon they poached as boys; was it so long ago? Was Angus dead? He thought of Caitriona and tried to get up but his legs were too weak. He listened again, but could hear nothing but the wind in the trees. He sank back into the wet bushes. Long, desperate minutes passed and still nothing. Then his body convulsed with the relief on hearing the train moving off. He wretched violently, vomiting the little that was in his stomach. He got back to his feet and continued into the cold night.

For hours he walked in the blackness of the French countryside, not even sure if he was going in the right direction. He only knew he was directly behind the French lines and that he had to be careful not to be caught up in their retreat from the advancing German armies. The barrage of artillery to the north gave him some bearing and he continued to walk in the opposite direction from where he had jumped from the train. The bone in his left wrist was now cutting through the skin. Holding his arm, he stumbled on through fields and along hedgerows.

He scurried into a ditch as he caught sight of a small farmhouse off a dirt track. There was a warm yellow glow from a window at the front of the house. He sneaked up to it and peered through the tattered net curtains. Two women, in thick woolen clothes, were sitting by the fire. He thought they looked like mother and daughter; there was no sign of anyone else. As the old woman got up to stir a large black pot hanging over the fire, she reminded him of his own mother. He knocked at the door, shouting what little French he had picked up. "Bon soir! Je suis ami, ami." There were sounds of hurried panic from behind the door and Callum heard something heavy banging against it. He knew the women must be frightened. "Je suis ami," he repeated. "Parle English?"

"Go away, English. I have gun."

"Good, you speak English. Don't be frightened, I only want some directions."

"Then you go away?"

"I must find the town of Senlis. Is it near here?"

There was no answer, and then the daughter turned and spoke to her mother in French. They spoke too fast for Callum to make out anything.

"Is it near here?" he asked again.

"It is far from here," said the daughter, "...ten kilometers, maybe more."

"Ten kilometers," echoed Callum, dejectedly. "How far is the next village?"

"About three kilometers, keep to the road by river."

"Thank you," he added, pushing himself away from the door. He staggered back towards the dirt path, now drunk with exhaustion. He could no longer feel his legs and they buckled under him. He fell to the ground with a thud. The cottage door opened slowly. Then the daughter emerged, holding a lamp above her head, its pale glow falling on Callum's prostrate body. The older woman came out with a shotgun over her arm.

"You're too weak to go much further. Come into the house and rest for a while," said the daughter, no longer fearful of the stranger.

Too far gone to resist, Callum walked with their guiding hands on his arms. His head spinning, he slumped onto the seat by the fire. The pain in his wrist and lower arm was now excruciating. The bone must have fractured again when he collapsed. Both women began to busy themselves around him. The daughter helped him off with his coat, but she had to cut the sleeve from his tunic to get near the shattered limb.

"Here, drink," she said, taking a cup from her mother and handing it to him. "It will help stop the pain."

He sipped the hot, brown liquid. It tasted horrible. "Och, what is that?" he moaned. "Yer no' trying tae poison me," he said, suddenly fearing in his confused head that he had come upon two witches.

"It's herbs. It will help the pain," explained the daughter. "Drink it."

"Have ye no' got any whisky?" The daughter again addressed the mother, who seemed to be complaining as she fetched a bottle from the kitchen. The bottle was handed to Callum, who smiled at their generosity, biting the cork off and taking a mouthful. As he drank, the daughter pulled the two splints she had put on his arm, cracking the bones back into place. The old woman grabbed the bottle from his other hand as he screamed and mercifully passed out.

After an hour or so, he came around with the vapours of some other herbal remedy at his nose. His left arm was now in a sling but it was still throbbing painfully. Again, the daughter offered him the herbal draught, which he took this time without question. It tasted just as horrible. He swallowed it anyway, looking around for the bottle of cognac to kill the taste in his mouth. The old woman reluctantly handed him the bottle, seizing it back before he emptied it. He was given some bread and thick white cheese, which he quickly ate in his unnatural hunger. "You had better go now," said the daughter. "We have nothing else to offer you here."

All through the freezing cold night he walked. One deserted village after another. The dawn was breaking before he saw the familiar church steeple of Senlis in the distance. His legs were weak but his step quickened. The village was deserted. He walked on through the narrow streets, passing the old bookshop with the little corner café opposite. His mind returned to the warm summer; it seemed like years, not months had passed. On he walked, down the narrow country road to the hospital. A dark foreboding came over him as he reached the grounds of the hospital.

"Caitriona," he called, throwing a small pebble stone at the darkened window. "Caitriona, it's me, Callum," he called again. A flickering light came to the window and the shutters opened abruptly.

"Who the hell is shouting down there?" complained a tired female voice. "What do you want?"

"I'm looking for Nurse Munro. That was her room. Do you know where she is?"

"Who the hell are you?" she asked again.

"Please! Is she there?"

"Whoever she is, she's not here. You look in a bad way, soldier," she added as she noticed the sling on his arm and the pain on his face. "Wait there."

He waited for what seemed like an eternity. He then saw the American nurse, now in her uniform, walking towards him. She led him away from the building.

"What's your name?" she asked.

"Callum Macnair."

"I spoke to the matron and she said that Nurse Munro has gone back to Scotland with her husband, about eight weeks ago."

"Her husband!"

"Yes…Are you all right?"

Without answering, Callum, physically and emotionally exhausted, dropped to his knees in despair.

Chapter 26

The sea was rough and the ship rolled in the swell. Men who had once marched off to war with such vigour lay broken on the open deck as the rain poured down. Callum lay in a huddle of men, his arm strapped tight to his chest and his mind delirious. He was soaked to the skin, but his body craved for water to drink to quench the thirst that was adding to his torment. He tried to call out but his voice had left him and he prayed for death to release him as he vomited up the bile in his stomach.

"Are you all right, soldier?" asked a young Red Cross nurse, lifting his head from the wet deck and placing a makeshift pillow under it.

"Water….water…"

"I think we can get you something to drink," she said in a soft Dublin accent, a wooden crucifix hanging around her neck like a medieval relic. She returned a few minutes later with a pitcher and some cups for eager hands to grasp. Callum could feel his cracked lips sting as the cold water began to quench his dire thirst, bringing him slowly out of his delirium. He managed to sit up, looking around for the first time at the chaos of the deck and the mutilation of others whom were far worse than him.

"When'll we get into port?" he asked, in a rasping voice.

"Maybe another twenty minutes or so," said the nurse, still filling up cups and passing them around the more able men, who in turn helped those too far gone to help themselves.

"Is there any food? I haven't eaten for days," asked one soldier, whose face was badly disfigured.

"I'm sorry, soldier, but there are no supplies on the boat. They should have fed you before they put you on. There'll be food for you all when we get to Folkestone, God willing," she said, instinctively touching her crucifix, the fear of German torpedoes never far from her mind.

"What God?" said one man, with contempt in his blood-shot eyes.

The rain finally stopped as the hospital ship came into dock at the busy quayside. Callum was helped down the gang plank by two orderlies. He was still weak for the want of food, but glad to be moving onto dry land. His arm was now completely numb and the sea sickness had thankfully left him. The harbour was chaotic, with hideously wounded men lying around in their hundreds, waiting for the scores of ambulances to take them to surrounding hospitals. An orderly gave Callum a cigarette and found him some bread and cheese to eat, while he waited for his turn to be assessed by one of the doctors. The bread and cheese were stale and he struggled to swallow the food in his dry mouth. His feet were raw and his skin felt like it was attached to the inside of his boots. He wanted to take them off to ease the pain, but resisted the temptation, knowing fine well that he would never get them back on again. There was a cold wind blowing, adding to his misery as he shivered in his wet clothes. He could still hear the constant rat-tat-tat of the machine guns in his head, and he nervously looked up at the grey clouds, expecting German shells to come crashing down. He had left the war behind but the war had not left him.

In time, he found himself standing in a line of walking wounded inside a large hall, which had walls shrouded with large Union flags and colourful war posters. After an hour or so he shuffled up to a desk where an army doctor examined his arm and listed his injuries as minor. Minor to him, thought Callum, as he lifted a bundle of dry clothes from the next table. He felt weak again and the sound of another German barrage exploded in his head as an impatient sergeant major bellowed out an order for him to move along. Suddenly, the lights seemed to go as he felt himself falling into the

363

darkness beneath his feet.

Callum woke up the following morning in a hospital bed and, for a fleeting moment, he thought he saw Caitriona walking down the ward towards him. He quickly sat up only for the rat-tat-tat of machine guns to echo in his head again. He was afraid he was losing his mind and called out in anguish.

Duncan poured himself another whisky and paced around the room. Unnerved by the chimes of the clock, he stopped the pendulum. Afraid to go back into her bedroom, he walked back to the window and stared out over the loch. Many of the ancient trees around Loch Fay and on the surrounding hills had been felled to support the war effort and although he was paid well for the timber, it left the glen open to the cold easterly winds. He felt a shiver as he listened to the thunder rumbling above the clouds.

Dr Wilson shook his head again as he touched her cold, white skin. Her lips once pink with life were now purple with the poison she had sipped in her despair. He gently covered her face with the thin white sheet and went into the parlour.

"Who found her like this?"

"What?" Duncan muttered, still staring blankly out the window.

"Who was it that found her?"

"Mmm, the parlour maid, what's her name? Morag...something or other."

"Morag MacDonald."

"Aye...why?"

"Well, I take it that you'll no' want your sister's suicide to be common knowledge. Do you think she noticed the bottle in her hand?"

"Good God! How do I know what the stupid girl saw? She was

hysterical. I don't know; she may have seen it."

"Well, there's not much we can do about that now. If she saw the bottle, I'm sure the whole household would have heard about it by now and drawn their own conclusions. At least there is no way anyone could have suspected she was pregnant."

"Pregnant! What the hell are you talking about?"

"I'm sorry, Duncan. I thought you knew. She gave me the impression you did."

"Gave you the impression?"

"Yes, she came to see me last week about it. She was very depressed... are you all right?"

Duncan dropped the whisky glass onto the floor and staggered through the house and upstairs to his sister's room. He stood at the door and looked at her body shrouded in the white sheet.

"Oh, my God! If only I had known!" He said, sobbing as he fell to his knees at her bedside. "Forgive me. Please forgive me."

After Caitriona's funeral, Duncan, wretched with guilt, returned to France and his task of ensuring the lines of communication were maintained in his sector as the British army moved into the trenches now abandoned by the retreating Germans. He was called back to Headquarters at Albert one morning to be briefed. There he received fresh orders and ordinance maps on the areas of strategic importance now within Allied control. Colonel Henderson had noticed a change in the major and was concerned with his overall appearance.

"Now, Duncan, these signal lines must be laid at Cambrai before the offensive begins in earnest, but there's no need for you to risk yourself. Captain Stein is more than capable of leading the sapper unit," said the colonel as he studied the map of northern France and Belgium.

"I would like to go with my men. I feel it's my duty to take the same risks as they're taking, sir."

"Quite so, Major, but men are easily replaced. I've lost too many officers, and they're now sending me boys...No, no you'll be better organising the operation from the trenches at Guise, where you can keep me informed of developments. We all have to do our duty... I would love to be in the front line with the men, but who would be left to organise things if we all went off looking for glory?"

Callum was solemn as he sat on the veranda of the hospital with other recovering men. The spring sunshine was warm and he closed his eyes to try and remember how he got there. His only physical injury was the broken bones in his arm and wrist and they were taking care of themselves under the plaster cast. Although worn out with both physical and mental exhaustion, he was in no pain. While the other men played cards, one of the nurses handed Callum a copy of the morning newspaper. "Good news for a change," she said as Callum took the paper and read the headlines.

"Ludendorff's Spring Offensive Halted...*Thousands surrendering en masse as the bulk of the German army is pushed back towards the Hindenburg line. An Allied victory now seems assured."*

Callum then turned to the pages of the dead and missing, and looked at the columns of names until he could look no more. How can they even think to use the word victory with so many dead? Tiredness overwhelmed him and he dropped the paper and fell into a deep sleep.

From his field dug-out at Guise, Duncan watched as a dozen British tanks crushed through the barbed-wire defences to engage four German tanks on a strategically important, defensive ridge. At first the shells from both sides fell well short of the mark as the tanks screeched and roared, churning up the mud under their grinding tracks. A cheer went up in the British trenches when one of the German tanks took a direct hit, bursting into an infernal of flames and black smoke. The men inside could not get out in time and their screams were harrowing for those near enough to hear them. The other three German tanks made a hasty retreat.

"Major, the colonel is on the line."

Duncan passed his periscope to Captain Stein and followed the corporal into the dug-out, taking the telephone from the operator. "Yes, sir, we haven't seen any Bosch infantry for days, just a few tanks…Yes, colonel. Yes, sir," repeated Duncan before handing the phone back to the corporal. "Fetch Captain Stein!"

Duncan looked at the map of the sector, criss-crossed with the cables that were still to be rolled out by his men. Colonel Hanley was sure that the Germans had abandoned the trenches during the night as they had done in most of their positions in the area around Cambrai, leaving only pockets of men and a few tanks to protect their retreat. Duncan went back into the trench and climbed the first few steps of the observation post to scan the German trenches for any sign of life. The cratered ground between the lines looked no different from any other morning, but he could see no activity in the German trenches. He was still looking through his periscope when Captain Stein tapped him on the shoulder.

"You were looking for me, Major."

"Yes, George, have ye seen any life in the *Bosche* trenches this morning?"

"No, Major, it's been all quiet. I think they may be having a long lie in. I didn't want to disturb them."

"Here, give me that rifle," said Duncan, putting his helmet onto the butt and lifting it above the parapet. Nothing! Not even the sound of a sniper's bullet pinging of the metal helmet, never mind the spray of lead from a machine-gun.

"I think Colonel Henley may be right and they've pulled out

during the night."

A reconnaissance squad returned to confirm that the Germans had abandoned their trenches along the ridge. Duncan ordered the sappers to clear a way through the barbed-wire defences, before he led his men across 'no man's land' to survey the deserted German trenches. He stopped to look up at a solitary tree, burned black and leafless, but alive with the squawking cries of carrion crows. Wedged in the branches was the torso of a German soldier. The crows pecked furiously at the decaying flesh. The sight disgusted Duncan and he removed his revolver from his hip-holster and fired into air, scattering the crows in every direction. He ordered two of his men to bring down what was left of the body. "Bury it."

Duncan climbed to a nearby ridge with Captain Stein and observed through his field glasses the tail end of the retreating German forces in the distance.

All day the Allies continued their relentless march towards the Belgium border. The muddy, cratered roads were littered with abandoned German equipment. The skeletal remains of freshly slaughtered horses lay around, with the steam of decay rising from the warm guts. The starving German soldiers did not leave much for the packs of feral dogs now fighting over the gruesome remains.

North of the Cambrai sector, Duncan led his company of sappers through the ruins of a small Belgium town which had recently been liberated. The putrid bodies of dead German soldiers were left decaying in the road, their boots removed by those in more need of them. The only building still standing was the spire of what was once a beautiful medieval church now plundered and surrounded by its own rubble. Two British bi-planes flew overhead and the men cheered them on their way to bomb the German rear-guard. A company of Australians marched a line of utterly desolated-looking German prisoners through the town; their uniforms now filthy rags and their bearded faces gaunt and dirty. Their desperate condition convinced Duncan that the war was now coming to an end and the *Bosche* had nothing more to give. To the bemusement of the Australian guards, he ordered his men to salute the Germans as they passed. An officer at the front of the prisoners returned the salute. Duncan noticed he was wearing what remained of a Staff General's uniform.

After recovering from a protracted bout of pneumonia, Callum was discharged from the Royal Kent hospital, where he had spent most of the summer months. In time he was given an honourable discharge from the army when the doctors confirmed that the bones in his right wrist were so badly damaged that he would never be able to exert enough pressure to fire a rifle again.

When he finally received his back pay, he took a train to London to see if he could find some work, arriving at Charing Cross station in the late afternoon. In the city, the newspaper stands were proclaiming the imminent defeat of the *Hun*. He hesitated for a moment and looked at the bold headlines, before walking on. He had seen enough of the war and the thought of reading the jingoistic ranting of warmongering journalists angered him.

He found a tearoom near to Trafalgar Square where he sat for a while and watched the throngs of people moving through the vast open area under Nelson's column. The roads around the square were congested with horse-drawn carts, carriages, cars, and tramcars. He remembered that while he was in France he had thought that there would be no one left in Britain at the end of the war, but he was wrong…just very few young men. The waitress brought him a pot of tea and a soda scone, a poor imitation of his mother's bannocks, he thought, acknowledging the girl with a smile. He felt an uncontrollable urge to read Caitriona's letters again, taking them from his inside pocket and removing them from the oilskin wallet he kept them in. They were in a sorry state and he carefully unfolded their water and blood-stained pages. The ink had run in places and some of the words were unreadable, but he had read the last letter so many times that he knew every word off by heart.

My Darling Callum,

I hope you are safe and that this letter finds you well. The weather has turned cold and the summer now seems so far away, instead of only a few short months. My transfer was cancelled for some reason and I am still working in the same hospital with Nancy, who sends her love. I received your letter this morning and I have been eager all day to get a chance to write back to you. I can't believe you will be in Paris next week. I think the twentieth is a Friday and I have already told the staff nurse that I am taking that week off for personal reasons. She wasn't happy but I reminded her that I was a volunteer and had every right to take a break. Nancy checked at the train station for me, when she was in town this morning, and there is a train to Paris in the afternoon. I will be able to meet you at 6pm at the latest. As you are staying near to the Champs du Mar, we could meet at the Eiffel Tower, that's if the Germans have not already blown it up. Write and let me know that you will be able to be there. I have also something very important to tell you, but I would rather tell you when I see you.I hope you still love me as much as I love you and I can't wait to see you again. Write soon!

With all my Love, Caitriona.

Callum folded the letter inside the others and put them back into his pocket. At times he wanted to tear them up and be done with the pain they gave him, but he could not bring himself to part with the only things he had that proved to him that the months they had spent together were real. He finished his tea and then made his way to Covent Garden to see if there was any work to be had. The manager of one of the larger importers did not need much persuading, able-bodied men were in short supply, and Callum was offered work, which he accepted without hesitation, as a porter.

London was a noisy, vibrant place and he liked the excitement of the market with its colourful characters. He spent the first morning wheeling trolleys of fruit and vegetables to the waiting lines of horse-drawn carts, which in turn carried the fresh produce to the shops and restaurants throughout the city. Because of the injury to his arm and wrist, he could not lift the heavier crates. At first he had to listen to the occasional muttered name calling, until the foreman put the men straight about how to treat a 'war hero'. The market began to wind down in the early afternoon and Callum spent the rest of the day walking around the capital, visiting the landmarks he had heard so much about.

He stood on Westminster Bridge, and looked across the Thames, amazed at the spectacular sight of the Houses of Parliament. "There's the Prime Minister!" shouted someone from across the road as a stream of black cars passed by. Callum watched the smiling face of Lloyd George, who was in the back of one of the cars, his grey hair blowing untidy in the breeze as he waved his hat to the cheering crowds. News from the Front must be good, thought Callum as he turned to walk on.

On a cold November morning Callum bought a newspaper on his way to work. The headlines were a relief to him. The Kaiser had abdicated and fled into exile. The paper was scathing and urged the Government to have him extradited from the Netherlands and executed for the nefarious war he had started with his Prussian arrogance. According to the editorial, the abdication made the way clear for the long awaited Armistice. Callum looked at the list of thousands of men who had died in the last few weeks, and wondered about the young men in his battalion. How many, if any, had survived in one piece to go home to their families. Not many, he thought, as he scanned the columns of names again.

On the morning the Armistice was to come into effect, Callum was given the day off work. He was up early and walked through the congested streets, towards the massive crowds congregating outside Buckingham Palace. He hurried along the Mall, its bunting and Union flags blowing proudly in the November winds, to try and get a view of the Royal family who were expected to appear on the balcony.

As the crowds gathered in Paris and London to welcome the Armistice, in Belgium, a company of Canadian soldiers crossed the Canal du Centre into Ville-sur-Haine. They entered the town expecting little resistance, but came under sniper fire from the ruined houses. A few minutes before the church bells began to ring out the end of the war, Private George Lawrence Price was shot dead. He was the last soldier to die from enemy fire in the four years of unimaginable slaughter, during which man had reached a new low in his desire to annihilate his own species.

The cheers were deafening as the crowds erupted with euphoria and relief along the Mall and outside Buckingham Palace. The Royal family appeared on the balcony to wave to the rapturous crowds dancing in the streets below. The war was finally over and the church bells across the country rang out the news to an exhausted population. Callum walked from the exuberant celebrations and headed back towards Putney where he had a small room in a boarding house. *What was there to celebrate?* he thought as he walked through the streets with his hands in his pockets and his collar up. *What was it all for, nothing?*

When he got back to the boarding house, the landlady was beside herself with joy. Her son was still serving in France and she could not stop talking about how proud she was of him. She eagerly produced a copy of *The Times* and insisted on reading out the Armistice message of congratulations from King George V to the

Empire and the troops:

"I desire to send a message of greeting and heartfelt gratitude to my overseas peoples, whose wonderful efforts and sacrifices have contributed so greatly to secure victory, which is now won," she read, panting for breath in her excitement.

"I think I will go upstairs to bed, Mrs Richards."

"Hold on… there's more!"

"They're only words," said Callum.

"But they're the King's words!" she insisted as she cleared her throat and carried on reading.

"I rejoice that in this achievement…British forces have now grown from a small beginning to the finest army in our history, and have borne so gallant and distinguished a part in Germany's defeat. Your faith has never faltered; your courage has never failed; your hearts have never known defeat. With your allied comrades you have won the day. I am proud to have served in the navy. Never in its history has the Royal Navy done greater things or better sustained its old glories and chivalry of the sea. Let us bear our triumph in the same spirit of fortitude we have borne our dangers."

"I see he doesn't mention his cousin, the Kaiser, who started the bloody war," said Callum, going upstairs before she found something else to read.

"I'll keep this for when Edwin gets home! He'll be so proud when he sees it," she called after Callum, who was already halfway up the stairs. He hoped that her son had not caught a German bullet since he last wrote to her. How proud would she be then?

The room was cold and he made a fire with the last of the dross from the coal-scuttle. He then lay on the bed holding Caitriona's letters, which still had a hint of her perfume on the stained and torn paper. He fell into a deep dreamless sleep. His war was finally over.

Chapter 27

Glasgow. January 1919

Escaping from the deadly influenza epidemic that Mrs. Richards's son had brought back from the trenches, Callum arrived in Glasgow on a cold winter's morning with a suitcase and fifteen pounds, ten shillings in his pocket. From a kiosk outside the Central Station he bought a copy of the Daily Record and circled a couple of addresses where he hoped to find board and lodgings. It was freezing cold and he found it hard to walk through the busy throngs of shoppers without occasionally banging into someone. When he got to the corner of Hope Street and St. Vincent Street, he stopped to watch a procession of men marching down the middle of the road in the direction of George Square. Some of the onlookers cheered and others jeered as they passed by. The men were grim-faced under their caps, following behind banners and red flags with the discipline of old soldiers.

"What's happening?" he asked another onlooker.

"It's the strikers; they're heading for the Square."

Looking down the street towards George's Square he saw that there were already thousands of men outside the City Chambers. With nothing else to do, he walked to the Square to watch the demonstration. There was a group of men outside the City Chambers addressing the strikers. The square continued to fill up with more and more demonstrators and they began to spill over into the side streets around the municipal buildings. Callum took only a passing interest until he saw someone he recognised addressing the crowd. There, with his fist punching the air shouting himself hoarse, was Ronnie Walker with his military medal pinned to his chest.

"Comrades! The time has come when those in power in this

country must listen to the workers. The men, who build their ships, mine their coal and plough their fields. The same men, who for four long years, fought and beat the Germans in a war created by capitalist greed. We must stand together until the Government gives us what we demand. A forty-hour week is what we want and what we will get!"

A cheer of approval went up, spreading through the massive crowd until the next speaker appealed to be heard. Callum slowly pushed his way nearer to the front, hoping to get a chance to speak to Ronnie. If anyone could get him a job it looked like him. He only got so far before the crowd in front of him began to push back. They were angry and there was a massive surge forward. Before he knew what was happening, hundreds of police officers, who had been keeping the strikers hemmed in, began to charge those at the front. On the steps of the City Chambers, the representatives of law and order stood above the disturbance, as Sheriff Mackenzie read the Riot Act flanked by the Lord Provost and the Chief Constable. A bottle from the angry crowd suddenly hit the Sheriff. Stones and other missiles began to fly in all directions as the men retaliated against the unprovoked onslaught by the police. The panicked crowd began to scatter and Callum quickly found himself dodging baton blows from police officers on horseback. He tried to get away from the melee but, as he fought his way back through the crowd, he was suddenly hit on the back of the head with a police truncheon and he fell to the ground. The blow dazed him and his clothes were soon covered in blood. Some of the men pulled the policeman responsible from his horse and kicked him unconscious. The back of Callum's head was split open and he was only half conscious as two of the strikers carried him into the safety of the Post Office at the side of the square. There were appeals for calm from the strike leaders. The police finally backed off.

"You'll need tae go tae hospital wi' that, son," said one of the two men as he held a handkerchief to the back of Callum's head.

375

"Which union are ye wi', son?"

" I'm no' wi' any union. I'm just back from London. I was in the army."

"Yer no' even working then?"

"No' yet. I'm looking for work, but I don't think there's much point if everyone's on strike."

"No, yer no' back on the best day to be looking for work. Whit did ye dae before the war?"

"I worked on my feyther's croft."

"Are ye no' going back there?"

"No."

"What is yer name?"

"Callum, Callum Macnair!" At that moment a half brick came smashing through one of the post office windows, scattering broken glass everywhere and causing screams and panic from those sheltering inside.

"You'll have to get these people out of here," complained the postmaster.

"Why don't you just fuck off?" shouted the man tending to Callum's head. The postmaster went back behind his counter.

"Well, Callum, my name's Roy Clark and I'm a shop steward at Govan shipyards. Come up and see me there next Monday. I'm sure I can get ye a start doing something. That's if we're no' still on strike."

"Thanks, Mr. Clark. Where's Govan?"

"The name's Roy. Just get yerself on a number twenty six tram from the Square. The conductor will let ye know when tae get aff. Here," he said, handing Callum the blood-stained handkerchief, "just keep that tae the back of yer head and get yerself along tae the Royal

Infirmary and have it stitched up." He glanced over at the postmaster who was speaking frantically on the telephone and said, "I think we had better get out of here before the police come."

"Aye, and thanks again for yer help."

"Don't think twice about it."

Glasgow's general strike lasted only a couple of weeks, failing to achieve its objective of a forty-hour week. Roy Clark was as good as his word and Callum was employed as a general labourer at the massive Fairfield shipyard in Govan. He also managed to find digs in a tenement flat in Crown Street, in the Gorbals area of Glasgow, taking the underground each morning to work. The past held nothing but pain for him and he found that concentrating on the future was the only way to put the war and everything else behind him. To even think of his father would mean that he would also have to think of Glenfay and then he would be troubled with the memories of Angus, Hamish and Gavin. But it was the intense, troubled dreams he had about Caitriona that he feared most. They had a hold on him that he found almost impossible to shake. At first he had no resolve and would let his mind torment him day and night, overcome by waves of anguish and self pity. To live again, he had to push these thoughts from his mind or be lost to them. As the months passed, the nightmares of the war became less frequent and he even found it difficult to remember much of what had happened to him during those killing years. Only his memory of Caitriona never faded.

On November 7th, 1920, four corpses were exhumed from four different mass graves, and laid on stretchers draped with the Union Flag in the chapel of Ste Pol near the French town of Arras. Brigadier General L.J Wyatt went into the chapel to pick one of these decaying remains as a symbol of the sacrifice made by all those killed in the Great War. The general was blindfolded and taken forward to where the remains lay. He was silent for a moment as he considered the responsibility of his task before he placed his hand on one of the bodies. When the remains selected were lifted into a coffin, the dead soldier's mud-covered sporran fell to the floor. One of the officers picked it up and opened its brittle leather pouch where he found an oil-skinned wallet. It contained a photograph of three smiling soldiers, all wearing the uniform of the Argylls. The officer was about to call the general back when he heard the chapel door close with a dull bang. The general had already gone. The Major put the photograph back into the mud-caked sporran. The coffin was then sealed.

A company from the French 8th infantry regiment stood vigil over the coffin until the next morning when it was placed in a casket of oak timbers and banded with iron. A medieval crusader's sword and shield were affixed to the top of the casket bearing the inscription:

A British Warrior who fell in the Great War 1914-1918 for King and Country.

The casket was then placed onto a French military wagon which was drawn by six black horses. The church bells of Boulogne tolled, while the trumpets of French cavalry and bugles of French infantry played *Aux Champs*. Then, the mile-long procession, with a division of French troops forming the guard of honour, made its way down to the harbour. At the quayside, Marshal Foch saluted the casket before it was carried up the gangway of the destroyer, *HMS Verdun*, and piped aboard with an admiral's call. The *Verdun* slipped anchor just before noon and was joined by an escort of six battleships. As the flotilla carrying the *Unknown Soldier* sailed into Dover, it received a 19-gun field marshal's salute.

On the morning of November 11th, 1920 the casket was loaded onto a gun carriage of the Royal Horse Artillery and drawn by six horses through enormous, silent crowds. As the cortege set off, a further field marshal's salute was fired in Hyde Park. The cortège

was then followed by the King, the Royal Family and ministers of
state to Westminster Abbey, where the casket was borne into the
West Nave of the Abbey flanked by a guard of honour of one
hundred recipients of the Victoria Cross. The guests of honour were
a group of about one hundred women, chosen because they had each
lost their husband and all their sons in the war. The coffin was then
interred in the far western end of the nave, only a few feet from the
entrance, with soil from each of the main battlefields and covered
with a silk pall. The armed services then stood as an honour guard as
tens of thousands of mourners filed past. The following year the
grave was capped with a black Belgium marble stone featuring an
inscription, engraved with brass from melted down wartime
ammunition:

BENEATH THIS STONE RESTS THE BODY

OF A BRITISH WARRIOR

UNKNOWN BY NAME OR RANK

BROUGHT FROM FRANCE TO LIE AMONG

THE MOST ILLUSTRIOUS OF THE LAND

AND BURIED HERE ON ARMISTICE DAY

11 NOV: 1920, IN THE PRESENCE OF

HIS MAJESTY KING GEORGE V

HIS MINISTERS OF STATE

THE CHIEFS OF HIS FORCES

AND A VAST CONCOURSE OF THE NATION

THUS ARE COMMEMORATED THE MANY

MULTITUDES WHO DURING THE GREAT

WAR OF 1914 - 1918 GAVE THE MOST THAT

MAN CAN GIVE, LIFE ITSELF

FOR GOD

FOR KING AND COUNTRY

FOR LOVED ONES HOME AND EMPIRE

FOR THE SACRED CAUSE OF JUSTICE AND

THE FREEDOM OF THE WORLD

THEY BURIED HIM AMONG THE KINGS BECAUSE HE

HAD DONE GOOD TOWARD GOD AND TOWARD

HIS HOUSE.

The telegram from Mhairi was short and to the point. '*Your father's very ill. He has been asking for you. Please come home.*' This summons was a shock to Callum. Although he had sent money home whenever he could, he had not thought of his father for some time and the feeling of guilt engulfed him. In the last few years he had made a reputation for himself in the Trade Union movement at the shipyards and had little time to think of the past. That was the way he wanted it. In the war against his past, his father's memory had become an innocent casualty. He only hoped that he had time to make amends. He quickly packed a suitcase.

The journey from Glasgow took nearly two hours. At least now the line went through Marnock and all the way to a new station at Glenfay. As the train rattled through the familiar countryside, Caitriona was never far from his mind and he felt excited that he might see her again. He turned away, annoyed by his own weakness for her, catching his reflection in the opposite window. His hair was slightly grey and he looked old for his years. The war had not made a man of him; it had stolen his youth. He tried to think of his father but he could only see him in short bursts; in images of him playing his fiddle, or sitting by the fire smoking his pipe. He thought of Caitriona again.

He walked with some hesitation along the loch road from the station until he stopped near the crossroads to look over the water towards Leaburn castle. He walked on and passed the two storey house where Angus and Mhairi once lived; now boarded up and neglected as it had been once before. His heart felt heavy as he neared his father's croft when he noticed that there was no sign of smoke from the chimney as the wind blew the rowan trees in every direction. The cottage looked small and lonely on the side of the hillside, and he wondered how he had ever managed to live there for so long and not feel the isolation that overwhelmed him now. The sky around the high mountains was a mass of thick clouds, carried quickly by the cold winds that battered the shutters of the cottage. He walked along the short path to the front door, feeling a sharp pain in his chest when a young man wearing the dark clothes of a minister opened the door. It was not the Rev. Knox, but the young, kinder face of his successor. The minister forced a smile but his eyes betrayed his true feeling.

In spite of his haste, Callum had arrived too late. His father had died some two hours earlier, probably when Callum was changing trains in Lochgilphead. Mhairi was sitting by the fire waiting for him. They embraced. She wiped the tears from her eyes and left him alone with his grief. Callum stood over the bed. It all seemed so strange, so unreal. He did not cry for the frail, old man he saw lying there; the faint smile on his grey lips told him all he had to know. At the foot of the bed he saw Tess pining.

The funeral was a quiet affair. Most of the crofters had been forced out years ago by the high rent increases designed for that purpose. Jamie Macnair had managed to struggle on with the help of the few pounds Callum sent now and again.

After the funeral, Mhairi helped by making tea for the few friends that came. She stayed behind to clear away when the last mourner left. Tess had been whimpering all day and would not leave the foot of Jamie's bed. Callum went for the vet.

"Ah she's blind in one eye and too sick for anything," said the vet, who had replaced Donald Kirkland.

"Is she in pain, do you think?"

"It's hard tae say. But she looks pretty miserable to me. If she were my dog, I'd have her put down right away. She'll no' get any better."

"Ye mean shoot her? I can't do that!"

"No, I can give her a wee jag and she'll no' feel a thing. It's the best thing for her."

Callum looked into the dog's sad, glazed eyes. There seemed a hint of recognition for a moment and she tried to raise her paw, but didn't seem to have the strength. "Aye, ah guess yer right," he agreed, lifting Tess from the cold floor. "God, she's as light as a feather."

"Just put her on the table and it will be over before she knows anything about it."

Tess seemed to know what was happening but offered no resistance. Callum had to look away; he knew it was the best for her. Within a few minutes what little life she had left was gone. He buried her out at the back of the house. The tears streamed down his face as he remembered the day he had brought her home as a pup. There was now nothing for him but graves in Glenfay. As he threw the spade into the byre, his thoughts turned to the castle over the loch; he looked at it for a long painful moment. "To hell with her!" he spat, going back into the house to see if he could find anything to drink. There was a half bottle of whisky on the dresser. As he grabbed it, he accidentally knocked a biscuit tin onto the floor. In it he found some old photographs of his family and there was also a photograph taken at Angus's wedding; it was already turning brown at the edges. He looked at it with an overwhelming sense of sadness; Angus had a beaming smile, while Gavin and Hamish were looking the worse for wear; they were full drunk by the time the photographs were taken. He put the pictures back in the tin and sat down to get good and drunk himself.

There was a rare fire burning in the hearth and the whisky made him feel warm inside as the flames flickered wildly on the burning peat. It seemed strange to be sitting there in the same chair he had often watched his own father sit during cold winter nights, smoking his pipe and telling stories about the old days. The whisky caught his throat and made his eyes water as he looked over at the bed where he had watched his brother die. He wondered what Ewan would be like now as a man. He missed the feeling of being someone's brother and someone's son. He felt utterly alone. He wiped his eyes and took another drink. The door suddenly opened. "That's that done," said Mhairi as she came back into the cottage.

"Mhairi, God. I'm sorry. I should have given ye a hand," he said, staggering to his feet, surprised that she had not gone home with the other mourners.

"Don't be silly. It was only a few cups and saucers."

"I thought ye'd be away up the road by now."

"Ar' ye in a hurry tae be rid of me?" she said with mock scorn in her voice.

"Good God, no! I'd be glad of yer company. Do ye want a wee dram?"

"Ye sound as though you've had a few already."

"Here, have a wee dram wi' me," he insisted, taking a small glass from the sideboard. "It will heat ye up."

"Aye, well just a wee one then."

They sat and talked about the good times they had growing up in the glen. They laughed about things that they had all but forgotten about. The winter's night soon closed in on the cottage and a blustering wind began to blow against the shutters. They pulled their chairs in closer to the fire and had some more whisky to keep them warm. The hours passed.

"I had better get going," she said finally.

"Aye, ah guess ye will have the wee one tae get back tae."

"No, I asked Angus's mum to look after her. She'll just stay the night there."

"Aye, well I'll walk ye over the road then."

"No, don't bother. I'll be home in no time," she said, getting up to put her coat on. "Are ye going tae be all right?"

"Aye, I'll be fine."

"I've made the bed up in the back for ye."

"Here let me," he said, helping her to put on her coat.

She turned to say goodnight. Their lips met slowly. They kissed and she was first to move away. She smiled at him. "I haven't kissed a man for a long time. I had better get going."

"Mhairi," he said softly, looking into her sad green eyes. "Why don't ye stay?" he said, taking her hand. They stared at each other for a long time before she kissed him again.

The following morning Callum was awakened by the constant splatter of hailstones on the windows. The stone floor was freezing cold. He dressed quickly and packed his suitcase. He would get something to eat on the way to the station. He wanted to get back to Glasgow before it got late. He then thought of what happened the night before, his head was thumping and the smell of whisky made him feel a little sick. Mhairi had left some time during the night. He

384

wanted to leave before he had to face her again; he felt that he had taken advantage. A gust of wind splattered more hailstones against the window and brought him out of his guilty thoughts. He waited for a while until the worse of the hail was over, and then locked the cottage door behind him. As he walked to the gate at the bottom of the hill, he saw Mhairi coming up the brae. She was with a young girl, whose long red hair was blowing wildly in the wind.

"You're not away without saying goodbye?" she called.

"I was going over to see ye on my way tae the station," he lied. "This must be Fiona," he said, lifting her up in his arms. "Yer a big girl now." Fiona smiled at him shyly, but said nothing. She was happy to run to her mother's hand when he put her back down.

"Here," said Callum, taking the corn doll from his bag.

"What's that?" she asked, taking the doll.

"It's a corn doll. It protected me in the war. It will look after ye now. Keep it."

They walked down towards the brae. There was a silence for a while before Mhairi spoke. "Don't be feeling guilty about last night. I knew what I was doing. I wanted to take some of the pain from yer eyes... but I think I failed," she said as she caught Callum looking towards the castle. "Angus told me she was the only girl you ever looked at twice."

"Well, she's a married woman. She's gone back to her husband, there's no' much I can do about it."

"Gone back to her husband? Don't ye know?" she said.

"Know what?"

"Fiona, go and play over there for a minute."

"But why, mammy?"

"Just do it. Now hurry up," she said sternly, before turning back to Callum. "I thought you knew… she's dead... she died a few years back," Mhairi explained, saddened at the distress her words seemed to cause him. "Are ye all right?"

"Aye… aye, I'm all right," he said, turning away to look at the castle. "What happened to her? How did she die?"

"She killed herself. There was gossip for a while that she was pregnant..."

"My God."

"Callum! Where are ye going?"

"I have tae go, Mhairi. I'll get another train," he shouted as he leaped over a stone dyke and ran across the wet fields towards Leaburn. "I'll call in and see you before I go."

The huge oak door opened and Callum, expecting to see Roberts, was surprised to be addressed abruptly by a stout, little woman in a nurse's uniform. "His Lordship doesn't want to see anyone today," she snapped. The door slammed in his face before he had time to react. He knocked again until he bruised his knuckles but no one answered. Walking back along the gravel path, he stared up at the large bay windows above the door. For the first time he realised how rundown the place looked; the gardens were overgrown and neglected, the windows were dirty and there seemed to be no one working around the grounds. Suddenly, he noticed one of the curtains move to one side. It flicked back as soon as he looked at it. He did not see anyone, but a cold shiver went down his spine. What had happened here? He rushed back up to the door but as he raised his fist to knock, the door creaked opened.

"His Lordship will see you in his room. Follow me."

He followed the nurse into the hall and up the stairs. She stopped at a door halfway along the narrow corridor and opened the door without knocking.

"You can go in," she said, standing aside to let him pass. The room was in semi-darkness and the draught from the door scattered millions of dust particles from the furniture and cobweb-covered paintings. He saw the dark shape of Duncan Dunbar sitting by the window. The curtains were drawn but there was a little sunlight seeping through which was reflected in his staring eyes.

"Have a seat, Macnair. I was sorry to hear about your father. You have my condolences."

Callum was surprised that Duncan recognised him.

"I guess you're wondering why I've come to see you."

"No, I think I know why you are here," he said. His words were followed by a fit of coughing.

The nurse, who had been standing at the other side of the door, rushed in and poured Duncan a teaspoon of thick brown medicine. She forced him to swallow it. "I think you had better go," she said to Callum.

"No, no. I want to speak to him!" spluttered Duncan. "Get out! I want you to take the rest of the day off. Now get out!"

"What's happened to you, Dunbar?"

"I'm afraid I was caught in our own bombardment during the last real offensive before the Armistice." He coughed again.

"But why are you sitting in the dark?"

Duncan fumbled with the curtain and slowly pulled it aside. Callum stared in shock at Duncan's face; the side of which was grotesquely disfigured. The curtain fell closed again. "You see the light hurts my eyes and my face. Well, it's not so ugly in the dark."

"My God!"

"It was not the shrapnel that left me like this, but an infection that I picked up in the bloody field hospital. A virus of some sort; it eats away at your skin. They told me that they cut down to the bone to stop it spreading. If they hadn't I would have died. God, I wish they had just left me to die. I'm now the monster in the castle to the local children. They come here, daring each other as to how close they can get before they all take fright and run like rabbits." He forced a laugh, followed by a further spat of painful coughing. "You see," he finally resumed, "I wasn't thinking straight when I volunteered for front-line action. All I know is that I was sure I wanted to be killed and still wish I had been. I never expected to end up like this." He flicked back the heavy curtain and stared out at the still waters of the loch. "I once shot an osprey, you know. Just over there by the far shore. Beautiful bird... it still had a live trout in its talons when it crashed on to the bank. Beautiful bird it was. Every day I've watched, but I've never seen another one. Not one... I wish I hadn't shot it now..."

"Why did Caitriona kill herself?" Callum demanded.

"I've never been able to decide if it was love or shame that drove her to take her life."

"The shame of carrying the child of a common tenant, is that the shame you're taking about?"

"So you knew? I thought she hadn't told you."

"She hadn't. I just found out this morning. For God's sake, why did she kill herself? Why did she kill herself and the bairn?"

"Like I have said, maybe it was love! She thought you were killed during the war. That's why she never met you in Paris. She thought you were dead."

"What?"

"She was informed that you were killed in action."

"Jesus..." Callum sighed, still trying to gather his confused thoughts. "What about her husband? I thought he had been found."

"Yes, he was. He's in a mental home," Dunbar began coughing

violently as the nurse rushed in to tend to him. "He'll die in it."

"I think you should leave now!" the nurse insisted, pointing at the door.

"Shut up, you idiot, and get out!" shouted Duncan, pushing her away. "Get out and don't come back in. I told you to take the rest of the day off."

The nurse threw down her apron in a temper. "That's the last time you'll speak to me like that! I don't care if yer a bloody Laird. Ye can get someone else tae look after ye, if ye can!" she added, slamming the door behind her.

"Good riddance!" Duncan laughed, turning back to Callum. "She loved you. You may not have thought it all this time but she did. I could see it in her eyes. That's why I couldn't stand it. You see everything has its place and everything should be kept in its place or you'll have chaos, disorder. She didn't seem to see that. Anyway, I had to put a stop to it before she caused a scandal. Remember she was still a married woman. I had the letter sent to put an end to your affair."

"What letter?"

"I had the letter sent, informing her that you were killed. You see, she had to go back with her husband, even if he was a lunatic. Of course, I didn't know she was pregnant." He began coughing violently again.

"You sent a letter telling her that I'd been killed? Ye bastard!"

"I had to. Well, I thought I had to. Wish now I hadn't."

"Chaos? Disorder? Look at ye now! You killed her with yer bloody snobbery and yer lies," shouted Callum before turning to leave. "I'd kill ye, if ye were worth killing. But you're not. You can sit there and rot 'til kingdom come! You've only got what ye deserved."

"Macnair, does anyone deserve this?" Duncan shouted, pulling the curtains from their broken hangers. Banished from the castle for so long, the daylight streamed in through the dirty stained windows and conquered the darkness.

Callum turned away from the grotesque figure of Duncan, whose flesh seemed alive with decay, and rushed from the room. He could hear the shouts of anguish that echoed through the corridors as he ran from the castle into the derelict gardens. A sheet of grey rain came in across the loch as the wind blew into his face. He wandered around the overgrown borders until he eventually found the grave. He thought of all the times he had cursed her for abandoning him, and here she lay with their unborn, unknown child. The rain was running down his neck and a faint rumble of thunder broke the silence. He had no flowers or any prayers to say that would give him comfort. He looked up at the rumblings skies and cursed the heavens.

Mhairi was waiting with Fiona when he walked back down to the crossroads. They did not say much on the way to the station. It had stopped raining, and the wind had died down a little, but the loch was still violently splashing onto the quayside. They walked on the far side of the road to avoid the danger. Gulls braved the waves to catch small fish thrown up onto the cobble stones.

"Are you going back tae Glasgow?"

"Aye, for a while anyway. I think I'll eventually go back to London."

"London!"

"Aye, there's work there. The Clyde's finished. They don't need ships the way they did now that the war is over. They've been laying off men in their hundreds as the orders dry up. I'm expecting to get paid off when I go back. A land fit for heroes, what a bloody laugh.

Callum was relieved when the train finally pulled alongside the platform. He had to keep moving, the less time he had to think about things the better. He kissed Fiona, who quickly pulled away. He gave her a sixpence; she smiled at him and showed it proudly to her mother. As the guard blew his whistle he kissed and embraced Mhairi.

"Be careful,' she said.

"Aye and you take care of yerself. Goodbye," he replied, as he lifted his suitcase and boarded the train. Suddenly, there was a shout from the train driver, who was excited about something. The stationmaster walked briskly up to the locomotive with his red flag tucked under his arm.

"What's the matter, Robbie?"

"Look for yerself! The bloody castle is on fire."

Callum looked over the fields and the rows of stone dykes towards Leaburn, now engulfed in flames and thick black smoke.

"There's nothing you can do about that, Robbie, ye better get this train moving," shouted the stationmaster as he waved his red flag and blew his whistle.

The train slowly moved off. Callum watched the funnels of black smoke form a thick cloud above the blazing castle. The train took no notice and rattled on. He put his hand into his jacket pocket and found Angus's watch wrapped in a piece of paper. He read the note. "I would like you to have it, to remember us by. God bless and good luck, Mhairi."

The wind and the rain lashed against the window as he looked over the dark waters of Loch Fay towards Leaburn. At that moment he knew he would never see Glenfay again. The train rattled on.

Some other books from Ringwood Publishing

All titles are available from the Ringwood website (including first edition signed copies) and from usual outlets.

Also available in Kindle, Kobo and Nook.

www.ringwoodpublishing.com

Ringwood Publishing, 7 Kirklee Quadrant, Glasgow, G12 0TS

mail@ringwoodpublishing.com

0141 357-6872

Silent Thunder

Archie MacPherson

Archie MacPherson is well known and loved throughout Scotland as a premier sports commentator.

Silent Thunder is set in Glasgow and Fife and follows the progress of two young Glaswegians as they stand up for what they believe in.

They find themselves thrust headlong into a fast moving and highly dangerous adventure involving a Scots radio broadcaster, Latvian gangsters, a computer genius and secret service agencies.

"An excellent tale told with pace and wit"

Hugh Macdonald -The Herald

ISBN: 978-1-901514-11-7   £9.99

Black Rigg

Mary Easson

Black Rigg is set in a Scottish mining village in the year 1910 in a period of social and economic change. Working men and women began to challenge the status quo but landowners, the church and the justice system resisted. Issues such as class, power, injustice, poverty and community are raised by the narrative in powerful and dramatic style.

ISBN: 978-1-901514-15-5   £9.99

The Gori's Daughter

Shazia Hobbs

The Gori's Daughter is the story of Aisha, a young mixed race woman, daughter of a Kashmiri father and a Glasgow mother. Her life is a struggle against rejection and hostility in Glasgow's white and Asian communities.

The book documents her fight to give her own daughter a culture and tradition that she can accept with pride. The tale is often harrowing but is ultimately a victory for decency over bigotry and discrimination.

"The Gori's Daughter is quite possibly the most compelling novel based on a true story that you will ever read" - **Dr Wanette Tuinstra - Golden Room**

ISBN: 978-1-901514-12-4   £9.99

Torn Edges

Brian McHugh

Torn Edges is a mystery story linking modern day Glasgow with 1920's Ireland and takes a family back to the tumultuous days of the Irish Civil War. They soon learn that many more Irishman were killed, murdered or assassinated during the very short Civil War than in the War of Independence and that gruesome atrocities were committed by both sides. The evidence begins to suggest that their own relatives might have been involved

ISBN: 978-1-901514-05-6
£9.99

Calling Cards

Gordon Johnston

Calling Cards is a psychological crime thriller set in Glasgow about stress, trauma, addiction, recovery, denial and corruption.

Following an anonymous email Journalist Frank Gallen and DI Adam Ralston unravel a web of corruption within the City Council with links to campaign against a new housing development in Kelvingrove Park and the frenzied attacks of a serial killer. They then engage in a desperate chase to identify a serial killer from the clues he is sending them.

ISBN: 978-1-901514-09-4   £9.99

Good Deed
Steve Christie

Good Deed introduces a new Scottish detective hero, DI Ronnie Buchanan.
It was described by one reviewer as *"Christopher Brookmyre on speed, with more thrills and less farce"*.
The events take Buchanan on a frantic journey around Scotland as his increasingly deadly pursuit of a mysterious criminal master mind known only as Vince comes to a climax back in Aberdeen.

ISBN: 978-1-901514-06-3   £9.99

A Subtle Sadness
Sandy Jamieson

A Subtle Sadness follows the life of Frank Hunter and is an exploration of Scottish Identity and the impact on it of politics, football, religion, sex and alcohol.

It covers a century of Scottish social, cultural and political highlights culminating in Glasgow's emergence in 1990 as European City of Culture. It is not a political polemic but it puts the current social, cultural and political debates in a recent historical context.

ISBN: 978-1-901514-04-9   £9.99